Acclaim for

DARK MATTER: READING THE BONES

"Serves to remind us that fantastic literature . . . has barely begun to open its doors to alternative vision and sensibilities."
—*Locus*

"A powerful affirmation of the bold and adventurous writing that continues in the literary world of the diaspora."
—*Seattle Skanner*

. . . and for DARK MATTER

"A rich repository of fine black writers and African characters, stories, and sensibilities."
—*New York Times*

"Compelling . . . perfect . . . a fascinating collection that will provoke debate and delight well into this millennium."
—*Vibe*

"An important book, and nobody interested in speculative fiction or black literature should pass it up."
—*Washington Post Book World*

"This singular collection stands out for its breadth . . . uncovers a rich—but unheralded—tradition that deserves attention."
—*Ebony*

more . . .

"This is the anthology of imaginative, groundbreaking fiction I've waited a lifetime to own. Rich in must-read selections . . . a one-of-a-kind book that no library of speculative fiction or black American literature can be complete without."
   —Charles Johnson, National Book Award–winning author of *Middle Passage*

"A rich anthology . . . *Dark Matter* zooms in on black sci-fi writing."
   —*Milwaukee Journal Sentinel*

"Brilliantly diverse selections [that] manifest a powerful effect."
   —*Publishers Weekly* (starred review)

"A seminal work in black American literature and science fiction."
   —scifi.com

"Groundbreaking."

   —*Essence*

"*Dark Matter* is a celebration, and will for many readers be a revelation, and it may well be a watershed in the long overdue but rapidly accelerating diversification of sf as a whole."
   —*Locus*

"Chilling . . . *Dark Matter* boldly goes where no anthology has gone before."
   —*New York Daily News*

"Intriguing . . . expands the frontiers of speculative fiction into a new dimension . . . Charts a rich alternative strain of speculation on the human condition which will engage readers and writers for years to come."
   —*Black Issues Book Review*

"A profoundly important book."
   —BlackPlanet.com

"Outstanding works . . . should appeal to short-story fans of every persuasion."
—*Science Fiction Chronicle*

"Enchanting . . . entertaining, enlightening. Most of the stories are excellent and have a satirical bite to them . . . Fans of science fiction and fantasy will be delighted with this new anthology."
—*Midwest Book Review*

"A well-rounded anthology which can be read for sheer entertainment or for educational value . . . The year's best science fiction . . . proves that science fiction's golden age is not in the past."
—*BookPage*

"A stout anthology . . . well-crafted . . . sensual."
—*Booklist*

"Highly recommended . . . showcases a wealth of talent that spans over one hundred years."
—*Library Journal* (starred review)

"Some very good stories here . . . well worth reading."
—*San Diego Union-Tribune*

"Intriguing . . . groundbreaking . . . Editor Sheree Thomas's unique vision has transformed a bleak reality into a bright future where dozens of new voices are meeting critical acclaim."
—*Honey*

"Fascinating . . . Read. Enjoy. Ponder."
—*Kirkus Reviews* (starred review)

"A rich, absorbing collection . . . a great read."
—*Metropolitan*

The **Dark Matter** Series

*Dark Matter: A Century of Speculative
Fiction from the African Diaspora*

Dark Matter: Reading the Bones

DARK MATTER

READING THE BONES

EDITED BY SHEREE R. THOMAS

ASPECT®

NEW YORK   BOSTON

Copyright © 2004 by Sheree R. Thomas
All rights reserved.

Aspect® name and logo are registered trademarks of Warner Books, Inc.

Aspect
Warner Books

Time Warner Book Group
1271 Avenue of the Americas
New York, NY 10020
Visit our Web site at www.twbookmark.com

Printed in the United States of America

Originally published in hardcover by Warner Books
First Trade Edition: February 2005

The Library of Congress has cataloged the hardcover edition as follows:
    Dark matter : reading the bones / edited by Sheree R. Thomas.
        p. cm.
    Sequel to: Dark matter: a century of speculative fiction from the African diaspora.

    1. Science fiction, American. 2. Fantasy fiction, American. 3. American fiction—African American authors. I. Thomas, Sheree R.

PS648.S3D376 2004
813'.08762—dc21   2003048579

ISBN: 978-0-446-69377-6   ISBN: 0-446-69377-4

Cover design by Don Puckey
Cover illustration by Daniel Minter

This volume is dedicated to
a Conjureman and a Saint:

the late

David Earl Jackson

and

Fred Hudson
of the Frederick Douglass Creative Arts Center

With many thanks and praisesongs to:

My agent and Guardian Angel,
Marie Dutton Brown

Betsy Mitchell
for her vision

and

Jaime Levine
for her dedication

Contents

Essays

INTRODUCTION

Since ancient times, oracles and diviners have combined their collected wisdom with close observation of the world. Occupying a unique position in society and often living in the margins, these diviners attempted to gain insight into their personal circumstances and improve the lives of their communities. Whether they chose to cast bones and shells, palm nuts gathered in gourd and calabash, read footprints in the dust, or rely upon a complex system of calculations rooted in sacred works such as the *Path of Odu* or the *I Ching*, they drew upon cultural traditions handed down through generations. And these seemingly disparate practices of ancient cultures that spanned throughout Africa, Greece, Etruria, China, Tibet, and India shared one thing in common: the desire to change and impact the future.

This desire to alter one's path, to understand how things have come to pass, is one of our most basic human impulses, and over the centuries it has inspired and informed much of our creative art forms, including our literature. Speculative fiction writers share this in common with diviners, attempting to gain insight by examining the unique circumstances of our world and questioning it in ways that challenge and critique our fundamental beliefs, social conventions, and assumptions. Their work shares an affinity with these ancient traditions of divination in their desire to gaze into the future in order to anticipate developments, whether social, environmental, or technological in nature, to caution or offer counsel and direction, to identify and expose injustice, to heal, to protect. These various impulses are embodied and expressed in stories that often cut to the quick, through our assumptions to reveal deeper truths, borne in blood and carved in bone.

Dark Matter: Reading the Bones presents works of speculative fiction and nonfiction by twenty-eight writers of the African diaspora. In compiling this collection, I chose not to force the work into a preconceived political, social, or moral framework. Rather, I was interested in providing a more open structure to allow for the juxtaposition of unique and individual voices, ideas, styles, themes, and aesthetics from new and emerging black writers as well as acclaimed writers whose work offers bold and fresh insights for readers. Like the diverse communities and personal histories from which they hail, black writers are not a monolithic community. Their interests are manifold, their expressions and personal rhythms as wide and varied as the land in which their ancestors first gave voice. Their work reflects a vision that is two-headed in view and intent, looking forward as much as looking back, like the diviners of old—and those still among us—to cast a reading, a new vision that illuminates as it engages. I hope that this work acts as a catalyst for discussion and inspires others to explore black contributions to speculative fiction.

The oral tradition is central to Afrodiasporic writing and storytelling, and so I chose to begin with ihsan bracy's retelling of an old African-American folktale, "ibo landing," a work that is as much a testimony of the courage and sacrifice of a people as it is a praisesong to those who did not "fly away" and walk back across the waters to the land of their ancestors. This work, like Charles R. Saunders's "Yahimba's Choice," is an original exploration of the complexity of challenging and questioning ancient traditions such as the practice of female "modification"; it is also historically linked to a legacy of conscious resistance and the African tradition of call-and-response. The new voices of this collection, notably emerging speculative fiction writers such as Cherene Sherrard, Nnedi Okorafor-Mbachu, and Ibi Aanu Zoboi, as well as the acclaimed author Nalo Hopkinson, draw upon African and Afro-Caribbean legend and lore to craft tales that are as instructive as they are evocative, even as they deliver powerful critiques, but the tall tales of Douglas Kearney and Tyehimba Jess, that evoke the folkloric trickster Kwaku Anansi, "the Keeper of the Stories," Peter Parker, and a legendary soothsayer from ChiTown called Voodoo Vincent, remind us that the ability to laugh, to "signify," is an ancient skill, a vital strategy for black survival.

Black writers are now, as ever, it seems, struggling as all artists between the political and personal landscapes in their work, and this individual, creative struggle is a strong and recurring theme throughout *Dark Matter: Reading the Bones*. Three stories, "Whispers in the Dark" by Walter Mosley, "Whipping Boy" by Pam Noles, and "Aftermoon" by Tananarive Due, are strong, literal interpretations of this contemporary and historic struggle, both questioning how individuals—indeed, black communities, whether rural or urban—can hold on to self and their intellectual integrity in a world that is often intensely judgmental, hostile, and threatening, while W. E. B. Du Bois's "Jesus Christ in Texas" and Henry Dumas's "Will the Circle Be Unbroken?" offer a dark and haunting meditation on the spiritual and social implications for American society in particular. Historically, "new world" Afrodiasporic writing generally has been overtly political, with little reference to the erotic. Kiini Ibura Salaam's "Desire" and David Findlay's "Recovery from a Fall" draw the African aesthetic through an experimental fabric, creating a new veil of lust and lore and longing, while Kevin Brockenbrough's "Cause Harlem Needs Heroes" and John Cooley's "The Binary" offer tough, hard-edged characters who give as much as they get from the world.

In Jill Robinson's "BLACKout" reparations move from contested theory to a complex reality as Charles Johnson's "Sweet Dreams" and Wanda Coleman's "Buying Primo Time" cast us into a future where even our dreams have become commodities and the cost of living is a price few can afford to pay, while Nisi Shawl's "Maggies" and Samuel R. Delany's "Corona" are two compelling works that reveal that navigating childhood can be a difficult journey, no matter where in the universe the young traveler calls home. Andrea Hairston's "Mindscape" contemplates a future where a spiritual outcast and an "ethnic throwback" must help rechart a world thrown off its course, while Kalamu ya Salaam brings us full circle in his exploration of how a group of black scientists and revolutionaries might use time travel in his story, "Trance."

In addition to these stories, Jewelle Gomez offers a transcript of a historic meeting of some of our most influential black speculative fiction writers, and Carol Cooper and Nnedi Okorafor-Mbachu discuss the works of Andre Norton and the late Virginia Hamilton, who made significant contributions to speculative fiction and young adult literature, respectively, in the course of their careers.

In *Dark Matter: Reading the Bones*, these innovative writers present speculative fiction that reaches deep into Afrodiasporic traditions and push through to new forms. Their words and stories explore the languages of love and lore, oppression and abuse, identity and community, revelations and new frontiers. By bringing together this shared history and the rich diversity of these writers and their visions, I hope *Reading the Bones* captures your imagination and offers a memorable window into a vital period in the evolution of speculative fiction.

Sheree Renée Thomas
New York City, 2003

DARK MATTER

READING THE BONES

IBO LANDING

ihsan bracy

(1998)

they would not remove themselves from his mind.

he dreamt of them, of her, every night. they all did.

the mass of human flesh lay beached upon the shore. in the pale early dawn they were indistinguishable.

they were poured upon the sands, fished out of nets like pounds of shrimp.

as his eyes adjusted to the light, he could make out land. he wondered, as he watched the ghosts move about, to what special hell he had been brought.

he would never forget the sound of teeth gnashing as she gave herself to the sea.

*

she gave herself to the sea. there was no struggle. she sensed him behind her. she reached back as his hand found hers. she squeezed it tight. she had only time to grab him before being engulfed by water.

*

razzberry heard the unloading all night. as the sun began to rise he could make out the mound of brown human flesh on the shore and the shadow of the ship beyond.

*

he could feel people all around him. he had grown used to this communal form. he had lost the parameters of his own body, just as he had given up the designs of his soul. it took all his effort to open his eyes. for so long it had seemed so useless, confined to the shadows and darkness as he had been.

*

ghosts moved about freely, unconcerned for their cargo. there was the sense of exhilaration and completion that came at the end of each journey. satisfaction, having delivered over half of their cargo safely. they waited for the auction and the payment of their money.

*

as the sun rose, the mound began to move. warmed as they were by the sun, they no longer clung to each other. as the thaw of the journey and last night's unloading set in, the cold subsided. they each began to take back their limbs.

*

they all remembered kiobe's screams, among those of the other women the ghost had chosen.

*

kiobe had been taken for the longest, passed around as she was. no one had seen her for two risings of the moon. they had begun to think of her as lost when she returned bloody, taken, wet with the pollution of many ghosts. she cried until she fell asleep, then she screamed until she woke herself to cry.

*

atiba saw from her one corner of the vessel. she saw him. he saw it in the look in her eyes. she knew it in his. by the time he reached the railing she had already leaped. he focused on where the waters had withdrawn her. he eluded the hands of many ghosts reaching. he jumped after.

sharks that followed the ship of death continued in the process of their evolution, cleaning the waste and filth, drawn as they were by the blood of her taking and the remains of the communal blood in which they had lain.

they all remembered. it would not escape their dreams.

*

slowly they returned to life. scared. scarred by the passage. they had crossed. they were the bridge. generations would cross through their collective womb.

each in their own way understood the distance. they would never again be home.

there were many tongues, many peoples among them. most were still chained. slowly they were released into a pen, washed, clothed, then given some gruel to eat, passed by ladle, by ghosts, from one communal pail.

as they were released they drifted together in the communal pen. it was here that for the first time many of them were able to find the sister tongues they had heard in the darkness.

*

that darkness. lying one upon the other. barely breathing. constant endless shifting, in the struggle for room. all would not survive. it had seemed an eternity before the one voice called out for silence. those of his tongue indicated this to each who was near. in this way slowly the silence had been achieved.

calling the name of a people, those of that tongue would cry out
searching for information: a sound, a name, a place, anything familiar, any vestige of their ever distancing home.

it was on that day, when a young warrior son urged the people to
learn the sounds of the one in bondage beside them, that resistance
was born. resistance which gave birth to survival.

so many died. so many gave themselves to the sea.

*

amazingly the eyes adapted to the darkness, to whatever little light
surrendered itself through the virtually non-existent openings in the
belly of the wooden ship.

next had come the arduous task of moving. each day at least one
shift. as the voyage continued there had been more room.

there had been death, left to rot amongst them. they had lost so
many. fluids everywhere, from every opening of the living, the dying
and the dead. this was the constant in which they survived.

one quarter of the cargo was brought above each day. drenched in the
waters of the sea, made to move, dance, then returned to the constant, the methodology developed by the success of the many cross-
ings.

*

among them were a people who did not speak.

the people of the silence could hear the thoughts of one another.
they alone knew the fate in each cargo's hold.

atiba had known each of kiobe's thoughts, through every scream.
they all had.

*

they waited until the washing was complete. the morning moon watched. silently they turned and began walking back toward the water.

*

movement was undetected for several minutes. their guard was down. they had passed the night. the cargo had been washed, fed, clothed and penned. auction was set for high sun.

the pens were guarded heaviest on the sides near the woods, near where the auction would take place. the slavers held the hill over-looking their prized cargo. it was a while before they noticed the silent band of thirty or more moving without hesitation toward the waters.

*

as they reached the limits of the pen they jumped it as one. they turned not a head, even as the sounds of agitation grew behind them. they quickly crossed the distance of the natural harbor.

*

the slavers were stunned. cautious, they sprang into action. quickly they realized they could cut off every path except the one which led to the water. they reached for their guns, but were confused, fearful to injure even a single piece of cargo if it could be helped. suddenly angry, they contemplated their loss.

as if breaking out of a dream state, the slavers suddenly broke into a panicked run, each cursing non-stop, blaspheming their god and their luck. then they suddenly stopped, silenced by what they saw but could not comprehend.

razzberry watched from the hill. it was through him the story was re-membered and the truth told.

as they reached the place of waves, each one would grab the hand of
the one before.

stepping over wave after wave, they strode confidently, unhurriedly,
past the ship lying in the sunrise.

*

nearly everyone in the vicinity of ibo landing that day came to see,
before the silent band was lost from sight.

THE QUALITY OF SAND

Cherene Sherrard

(2004)

Del adjusted her spyglass, focusing on the crimson and royal of the Union Jack as it was hoisted up the mast of the *Queen Anne*. She panned the ship from bow to stern, noting the position of the first mate as he barked orders to three underlings on deck. The deck, she noted, was scrupulously clean. Now that the ship was on its way to port, the crew sought to erase all traces of their cargo until it could be quietly disposed of in a private auction. In the early morning light, the *Queen Anne*'s captain was as yet unaware of the smaller vessel bearing down their starboard side. She inhaled the stinging air, astringent with salt; the wind licked her shoulders as it ballooned their opening sails. It was almost peaceful.

Jamal was suddenly beside her. He gestured to the left side of the *Queen Anne*'s bow—his eyes sharper without a lens—to where a deckhand had removed a plank with the ship's name, replacing it with a new plank that read *Sea Dog*.

"No matter." She lowered her glass. "She was the *Queen Anne* at Goree, and she will be the *Queen Anne* when she is docked at the bottom of the sea."

Arsemma wept that morning. She had not cried in many uncountable days. The sweetness of salt was now foreign to her lips. She had not seen the sun since the day her father died and their chief claimed, then sold, her and her sisters. Forfeit for the tribute her father had refused to make. She did not know if any of her sisters were still alive, nor did she feel the empty tightness of her stomach, swollen as a cassava. *I must finally be dying,* she thought, relieved as the planks above came apart, spilling in white darkness.

After the last of the Africans had been safely transported from the hull of the *Queen Anne* to the *Meridian*, Del wiped her machete clean with a torn scrap of sail. They had affixed the ship's captain to the mast while the first and second mates were hog-tied on deck. The mulatto interpreter had already slit his own throat, saving Del and her crew the unsavory task of soiling their blades on his traitorous flesh.

Ali tore bites from a peach impaled on his knife. He uncovered a coffer brought from the captain's quarters and set it at her feet; the metal casket was full with gold coin.

"Portuguese spoils," he said, grinning, pulp glistening between his teeth.

Del directed him and the others to return quickly to the *Meridian*. Once safely aboard, she gave the orders to fire the decrepit vessel as they had sunk so many other slave ships. Delphine felt the tightness in her groin release as she watched the fire eat the ship's hull, leaving the masthead bobbing once, twice before disappearing with its load beneath the waves. The torn sails fell, a curtain of red-gold sparks to ash, racing toward the Union Jack, which crumpled into the sea in a streak of black, its authority desecrated. Yoyotte cleared her throat, interrupting Del's pleasure. For expediency's sake, they would have to forgo the ocean's final gurgle as it swallowed the remains. They had already fired several cannons in sight of land, not many leagues from the port of San Salvador, where the governor would soon send reconnaissance to investigate. Del nodded to Yoyotte; by the time the navy arrived, only charred rubble would remain. The sharks, drawn to dinner by the flailing of the few survivors, would finish off the rest of the English.

The *Meridian* dropped anchor in a small cove several miles north of the port. With the aid of the crew left on land, and the people of a nearby quilombo, they transported the three hundred freed Africans ashore.

Yoyotte, Del's first mate and friend since her days at the maroon colony on Haiti, read from the captain's log as they paddled the last of the rowboats to shore.

"As we suspected, three hundred remain out of an original transport of close to seven hundred."

Del shook her head at the loss. "If only we had been able to attack sooner."

"Do you think the quilombo will accept all of them?"

"They will when they see the guns and gold we liberated along with the cargo."

Yoyotte yawned. After sixty-seven days at sea, with little to eat and no time to sleep lest they lose sight of their quarry, they were all exhausted.

"We'll rest here for a few days. And then sail home. I miss Ville-Fleur."

Yoyotte smiled. "I miss my husband."

Arsemma made her way quietly up the winding trail to the cave where her saviors rested. She had been fed pounded fruit with a rich meat-flavored broth. The food was unfamiliar, but there was as much of it as she wanted. And it did not cause her stomach to heave as before. An aged woman with many markings on her face, dressed in blue and white cloth, had given her a strong tea she called "mate" to ease the cramping in her stomach. It had been good to rest and breathe air unclogged by the stench of feces, maggots, and dying. But she had not taken part in the shouts and greetings and dancing. Her sisters were not among those clasping hands and reuniting with loved ones or those who spoke the same tongue. There was not a one who could understand her among these Yoruba, Fon, Igbo, and Asante. But she had seen the man in the dark gold cloak watching her. He was tall like her, taller than many of the others. He had the look of her people, the desert people. She had seen around his neck the iron crescent—maybe he would know the way back to the desert.

* * *

Del awoke to the soft gray-green light of morning on her face. Her pallet was empty, but the tonal chanting of Jamal's prayers soon soothed her. In the valley below the cave where they set up camp, the people of the quilombo were stirring. They had taken the Africans along the river and deep into the jungle heights. Peeking outside of the tent, she saw that someone had already left a basket stuffed with a morning meal of starfruit, pomegranates, and corn.

The sun filtered through the ancient towering trees, casting a jade glow on Jamal's back and chest. She closed her eyes again and listened to his prayers. By now, she recognized many of the words and inflections, although she did not speak his first language. As the intonations softened to a whisper, she crept behind him, circling her arms around his waist and resting her palms on his chest, over the heart. She let the mud cloth, which she had draped over them while they slept, fall to her waist. Pressing her breasts against his back, she slid her nipples along the ridges and valleys of his deep scars. Only in their most intimate moments did he bare his tortured flesh to her. At all other times, he wore long, billowy robes and a turban so that only his eyes, jet and opaque, set in a face of carved bronze, were visible. The crew, who knew them to be inseparable, called him her second sword.

She licked at the three moles at the nape of his neck. She marveled at how innocuous they were, like small freckles arranged in a triangle. It only took a moment before they released the blood as he continued to chant in a tone only notes above a whisper. She mouthed the words with him, ignorant of their origin, secure in their meaning:

> I am the flame and the sound of vengeance
> I am the prayer and the scent of grace
> I am the knife and the stroke of hope
> I am the goldweight and the measure of truth
> I am the blood and breath of life.

He turned so they faced chest to palm, her mouth and lips oily, ready to receive the blessing.

Afterward, while they lay again in each other's arms, impervious to the stirring about the camp, Jamal spoke. "Did you notice the very tall girl among the survivors? The one with the long, pulling eyes and skin like red clay?"

Del shook her head. "They all seemed the same to me."

"She is . . . familiar."

"I am beginning to feel jealous. You rarely mention another woman more than once," she said. Dismissing the pensive look in his eyes, she climbed astride him, drawing his attention back to her. "I miss home."

"We will be back in Haiti soon enough."

She nodded. "As soon as we can repair the damage sustained during our last engagement and get out of the lagoon without drawing too much attention."

"Many of the Africans have requested to be returned to the continent."

"Impossible."

She swung her legs together, stood up and reached for her garments. Jamal watched as she dressed. Her crimson tunic, woven of fine but sturdy Eastern silk, was high necked but slit almost to the waist on each side to allow her freedom of movement. Del always took long strides, her arms swinging out in front as she walked, ever clearing obstacles from her path. Underneath the long tunic, she wore heavy sailor's trousers and leather whaler's boots. She fastened a thick leather belt around her waist. It was a new addition, ornamented with cowries and ivory. She had found it among the bartered goods of the last ship they'd liberated too late, a Dutch vessel off the coast of Curaçao. She wore it for remembrance.

Someone had propped a large piece of reflective steel in the corner. She patted her hair, not that it needed much attention. Her burnished black and copper locks were twisted into tight, shiny knots all over her head, drawing attention away from her pointed ears—her one flaw, she complained, the right from which hung several gold rings and the left, a single teardrop emerald worth as much as her ship, called "Cleopatra's Tear."

It was her first gift from him.

She pulled her knife from under the bedclothes and affixed it to her belt. Feeling around her neck, she grasped the plain iron crucifix and smoothed the worn leather string upon which it hung to her collarbone. Feeling Jamal's question still lingering in the air, she replied, "It's a better life here. Free. Not on a plantation."

Delphine Toutsuite was the only member of her crew who had never known slavery's harness, but she still bore its scars. Her mother had been born a slave. She escaped from a plantation just outside Port-au-Prince, leaving her days-old daughter with the nuns of Saint Sebastien. She willed her daughter freedom and a name, Delphine, which she had embroidered in red on a soiled linen napkin tucked under her swaddling. The sisters of Saint Sebastien ran a small church and orphanage just outside Port Royal. The church faced the sea and Del knew the tides as well as the church bells marking every hour of her day. The sisters taught her to read, to sew, and to be a devout Catholic until the revolt launched. Del was ten when French loyalists torched the convent and raped the nuns for bringing food to the rebels camped in the nearby mountains. She fled into those same mountains and joined the maroons. Among them and their wild proud ways she learned to fight, to hate, and found purpose.

At fifteen she still possessed the thin, bony frame of a boy brought up hard on fish stew, coconut rice, and christophine. Whatever one could catch and kill. She began to accompany the fisherfolk on their daily runs. A trick of fate found her impressed into service off the coast of Jamaica. She sailed back and forth across the Atlantic, studying navigation from the kitchen of a man-o'-war, learning everything about sea battles, strategy, and men. When Moorish pirates attacked off the coast of Spain, their captain, Jamal Al-Din, recognized her for the woman she had become in spite of six years at sea. United by oath and their shared hatred of slavery, funded by Jamal's merchant vessels, they turned the *Meridian* into the scourge of the triangle trade.

From the outside, their two-story maison seemed suspended only by a dogged determination to see the next spring, but inside, the rooms were filled with treasures: books, carpets, salon paintings, ivory, woven baskets filled with salt and black pearls. Del had grown accustomed to spartan living; Jamal introduced her to the pleasures of fine paper, incense, and brocade.

Jamal watched her face soften. "You are thinking of Ville-Fleur?"

Their refuge was named for the stubborn, resilient flora and fauna that bloomed no matter the season.

"I am." She began to gather their things. "The sooner we leave the better. I do not sleep easy so close to Portuguese dogs."

She flung back the curtains of their tent and smacked into Arsemma, who flopped to the ground like a sack of flour.

Cursing, Del recognized her as the girl Jamal seemed fascinated with. "What do you want?" she asked first in Yoruba, then in Igbo.

"She doesn't understand you."

Arsemma looked through Del as if she were made of mist and rose to her knees, cupped her left hand over her right fist. Jamal raised her up and spoke quietly in a language Del knew was his native tongue.

"Arsemma," she heard the child say as she opened her fist. Three dusty braids of hair coiled into knots fell at Jamal's feet.

Del grew impatient.

"We have to alert the others. I want an early lunch."

"Go on without me." Jamal helped Arsemma into the draped cavern.

I keep dreaming of saffron; that fragrant spice whose precious threads are the color of molten gold. My veils were saffron colored, dyed with the vats of spice stored in a secret cave in the desert. So rich in it, we could afford to waste it as dye for our clothes. The trade routes of my people connected the east and west coasts of the continent now called Africa. For my sisters and I, it was simply the land, the earth, the place where men walked. I am the youngest of four daughters in my father's house. Many men had put aside wives who gave birth to two daughters in a row, much less four. But my father would not part from my mother. Amongst his friends he was ridiculed and called Vas Put Ry, he who has no line. He did not care. We were rich. He would choose for us wise husbands, and the business would flourish under his sons-in-law's care. We were sought after. Chants were composed and sung throughout the Bedouin lands and beyond of the daughters of Ahmad Kabril. They sang of our dark hair, the color of a star-

less midnight sky, and our skin as gold as the saffron itself. We giggled and laughed to hear our beauty so proclaimed, for no man outside our father's house had ever glimpsed our black hair or golden limbs. Never did we walk the streets except in long black veils.

But there were whispers on the caravan, where propriety was often trumped by the sun's heat. Farah, Aisha, Yasamin, and I would steal to an oasis. In the dim light of sunset, steadfastly guarded by our father's men, who kept their backs turned, we would wash with the other women. It was a hedonistic luxury, to splash and rub our scented soaps against each other, loosing the sand from our skin and braids. The sighs of the guards and young, unmarried men in the caravan were palpable as the winds carried our musk to their nostrils. We knew we were safe. It was forbidden to gaze even one moment on the daughters, sisters, and wives of the merchant chiefs. Their eyes would be poked from their sockets and replaced with sand. They would be abandoned to the desert, to forever haunt the sloping plains, beset by an eternal thirst.

Rumors circulating about the wreckage of the *Sea Dog* reached the quilombo through traveling peddlers. It was not long before the connection would be made, the ship would be missed, and the Portuguese navy would begin to scour the coast for the ship that had sunk her. Claude, the ship's navigator, had plotted their course, a winding way through the most dangerous and, as such, rarely traveled currents of the Eastern Caribbean. Not the most direct route but the best for avoiding the British, who were always on the lookout for pirates and would likely sink a ship manned with blacks and Indians without questioning why they flew French colors. As they lingered, trading for supplies and sounding the *Meridian*, Arsemma never left Jamal's side. To Del's annoyance, they spent hours conversing in the tented cave.

After thanking the chief of the quilombo and making an offering to the iyalorixá, the resident priestess of Iansá and Iemanjá, in exchange for blessing their journey home, Del discovered Arsemma crouched beside their sleeping mat. After a few weeks of constant food, fresh air, and freedom, the girl resembled the woman she was. Del watched the incessant twitching of her eyelashes as if she were caught in a desperate dream. Del almost sympathized. She allowed that the girl was beautiful, with her coppery skin like burnished pottery with flecks of sandstone and her slick soft hair. Jamal had told her the braids she carried belonged to her sisters, woven of hair never cut before the ships. She rarely spoke, but when she did it was always to Jamal; her eyes never left him, the look in them almost devout.

"You are like a god to her."

Jamal laughed, startling her because his laughter, terse and hoarse, was a rare thing.

"We are both of the desert people, the Khartoum, but to her I am a much more ancient thing. I am a familiar terror. Fearful but nevertheless something she can cling to in this new world."

"She wants to go home? Like the others?"

"No. She simply wants to find her sisters."

"We are not about to spend the next weeks searching . . ."

"Have we ever turned away any seeking solace through justice?"

He had repeated the founding words of the *Meridian*'s crew. They would hunt, but only those who benefited from the evils of human trade. They would kill, but not those who were innocent victims. For seven years, since Jamal and Del had christened the newly liberated *Maria Christina*, the *Meridian* sailed the Atlantic. From the Sargasso, as far as the Cape, they always had the luck of the winds in any waters and could overtake many more stately vessels.

"*Jinn*," Del replied, denying the question. "She used that word as if it was your name."

Jamal continued to sharpen his scimitar, an ancient thing of iron in these days of gunpowder. He never fought with it.

Del persisted. "What does it mean?"

"Spirit. Where she comes from it is the breath that causes the sands to whip. A being of air and fire. Fickle, amoral, but who can be temporarily held to do the bidding of one powerful enough to control it."

"Is that what she thinks you are?" *Is that what you are?*

Jamal went still. He held the wicked curved edge away from him as he sharpened.

"It is what I was."

Del looked at him, the sword held before him like a cross, and tried to see him, to know this man who had pulled her from the sea to her destiny.

"It is your decision. You are the captain." He seemed preoccupied, detached.

She shrugged. "It makes little difference to me. We can always use another hand in the kitchen."

Arsemma chewed the last bit of her dried meat slowly, sipping water as she swallowed to draw out the flavor. They had warned her to ration it throughout the trip, but the salted savory taste was addicting and she enjoyed the pull of it against her teeth. Devon, the ship's cook, merely tolerated her in the kitchen. She did not like to go on deck and see the empty miles of indigo with patches of azurine. Devon's round yellow face and laughing eyes put her most at ease. He was teaching her to speak their language, French, by showing her the names of food.

Of her sisters, Arsemma knew best how to season and salt the meat, how to pound and roll the dough to make their flat bread, and how long to let the grains boil before adding the vegetables to the stew. When she looked at Jamal, she remembered her sisters in the days before her father died. Farah, the mischievous one who could do no wrong in her father's eyes. Next was Yasamin, with eyes like a snake and a tongue just as sharp. Aisha, the eldest, responsible, quiet, promised already to the son of their father's partner. He had turned his back when Arsemma's mother, prostrate with grief and desperate, appealed to him to honor his son's promise to Aisha, or return the bride price. Instead, he took their mother as his fourth wife and turned her children over to a slave trader from the West.

The sisters were kept together until they reached the castle of stone. Before boarding the ships, they each cut off one of their braids and gave it to the other. Although they all had the waving black hair of their mother, Arsemma knew even now which braid belonged to which sister. She loved them all, and the sounds of their voices had carried her above the tumultuous violence of the bodies and the blood.

Taking one of the hard, sour fruits from Devon's basket, Arsemma crept up the steps of the galley to the deck, tiptoeing past the captain's quarters so as not to disturb Del. She was a little afraid of Del, who always glowered at her as if she was a half-grown fish that should have been thrown back into the sea. Arsemma wondered: What kind of woman wore a knife like a man and killed with the alacrity of a leopard? She recalled the blurred image of Del on the deck of the *Queen Anne*, swift as an *ifritah*, her hunger for blood transforming her into a stinging wind. That red garment of hers had been re-dyed many times with the blood of slavers. The crew, however, loved her—she could see it in the way they followed Del into battle; they moved like one mind. It was Jamal they kept their distance from.

She did not know what to make of him. He was not a man. She had learned as a child from her grandmother how to spot a *jinni*, a man or woman enthralled by the *jinn*. He glowed with the touch of the other world. Among the camps, they called it the *zaar* sickness— the spirit had to be sated with ritual, offerings, and ceremony in order to be expelled. In her village, the ritual had been a women's mystery; the spirits, she had thought, did not care for the flesh of men. She had never seen the *jinn* moving in the human world, outside of a host. Jamal was an aberration. But she knew he was not evil. He looked upon her with hunger, but was not lustful. She knew he did not need her for that. They shared a desire for sand untouched by salt water, bounded by trees and mountains, endless, enduring.

She smelled the stain of the other world on Del as well, but she was still human, though perhaps a little mad.

There were only a handful of crewmembers on deck as it was a calm, clear day. She could see the mountainous islands rising from the water in the distance and wondered who inhabited them. Most of the crew came from an island called Haiti; they had been slaves there at one point or another until the day they reverently referred to as the glorious revolution. There were two or three that called themselves Carib. Like Yoyotte, the only ones next to Jamal to gainsay Del's commands. Leaning against the ship's railing, she gazed into the water, so clear at times she felt she could see straight to the bottom. After a few moments, she felt the dried meat swerve inside her belly. Fearing another bout of seasickness, which had plagued her those first days after they cast off from the mainland, she retreated to the stable dark of her cabin.

By that night, she was spinning with fever. Her damp curls, finally beginning to grow long, stuck to her sweating forehead. She thrashed underneath the blankets and called for cold. Was she back aboard the *Queen Anne*? Where were her sisters? She dreamed of a man with a face like a hyena cackling above her, holding a molded pinch of bread in his hand. He wanted her to take it between her teeth like a dog. She moaned against the pillow and could not rest.

Ali swabbed her forehead with a cool towel. "It's the fever. Malaria. Squatting inside her like a loa. Pauvre petite fille won't last the night."

Yoyotte shook her head sadly. "To travel all this way only to die when we are so close to home."

"It was not her home," Del commented.

Yoyotte look up to see Del leaning against the door frame, arms crossed, stoically watching as they attempted to force-feed Arsemma. It saddened her that Del seemed so contrary where Arsemma was concerned. Yo liked her quiet ways and rare smiles.

Jamal called to Del from the hall. She left Arsemma under Yoyotte and Ali's care and accompanied him to her quarters. She sat down at her table and smoothed the edge of the map that lay there, admiring the dry, smooth feel of it. They were almost within sight of the signal fire. With some strange luck, they had made it to familiar waters without a hint of pursuit.

"There is a way to save her," Jamal began.

Claude had traced their route in red triangles, weaving through the rocky seas of the Grenadines, then straight past Jamaica. She would not meet his eyes.

"You don't mean to do it to her, then? Make her like us? She has no thirst for our work."

"She seeks her sisters. Isn't that purpose? To wish for life instead of death?"

Her eyes whipped to his face. "That is what you think of me, that I seek death?"

"Delphine, mercy is a foreign thing to you."

"Mercy," she screamed. She did not care who heard. "Mercy for devils, for slave traders?"

She felt the iron of her cross hot against her collar. She yanked it off and threw it onto the map; it landed on the American colonies. Reflected in the iron were the eyes of the nuns as they pleaded for the lives of the orphans. Their habits glowed in the light of the flames engulfing the church while they watched, pinioned beneath the makeshift soldiers who promised freedom. Delphine ran away, never looking back. It was years before the scent of ash no longer clung to her skin.

"What way?" she asked.

"I am old, Del. This body is no longer able to sustain me."

"What do you mean?" Frightened now, she put up a hand to stop him.

"I can make her impervious to disease, to death, for a long time. And I can stay with you."

"No. I don't want her. Find another body."

"Another will not do. It must be one from the land of my birth, one who shares my memories. Inscribed in her bones and impressed upon her flesh is the numberless remembrance of centuries. More than that, she has a reason to cherish life. I no longer desire this existence."

"And what of us?"

"You are becoming dangerous to yourself. You use violence as a balm."

Del pulled away from him, and pushed past him out of her cabin to the open air. It was a moon-dark night. The seas were black and endless and Haiti seemed as far away as Africa.

While she searched the sea for the answers that still eluded her, Jamal sat alone with Arsemma. He was thinking of the ritual—did he have what was needed? Would he remember the chants and the dance and the words?

Arsemma was sleeping. He had prepared a tincture of lemongrass to numb and calm her while he prepared her body to receive him. He watched as her breathing slowed, the tea taking effect, until she took only one deep breath every thirty to forty seconds. He wanted her mind as far from her body as possible. Opening his pouch, he withdrew a small, sharp penknife and black ink. He tattooed her forearms with the warding glyphs; they would keep the *jinn* from absorbing her conscious mind, her self in this life. She shuddered, but he knew she was released from pain. He murmured a few words of comfort; the tranquilizing effect of the infusion induced a deep trance. She would sleep until he was done.

Arsemma heard someone calling her name. At first she thought it was her father, and she wanted him to wait. She was not ready to go to the bleeding tent with the others. She wanted one more year before she was a woman. Then she saw it was not her father; it was Jamal. The room was filled with light. She blinked to adjust her vision, but still could only see him.

"Hot," she told him. "I'm so hot."

"Arsemma, I need to ask you something. . . ."

He told her what sort of being he was. A spirit of flame and sand and wind with a will strong enough to force himself into the material world and take up residence in the body of an ancient prince. Never fear, the soul and mind of the prince was still present; his body carried the stamp of his history. They had shared many things, the spirit explained, but the prince was tired, he wanted to go home and rejoin his ancestors. But the *jinn* was not ready, the centuries the *jinn* had maintained the prince's form were but an eyeblink in time. The *jinn* wanted. Once more the *jinn* did not want to leave Del. The prince's simple mortal love for her was magnified in the abundance of the *jinn* and honed to a sharp point. He would not leave her.

He wants me instead, Arsemma wondered. I am dying and he is offering a way of life forever if I want it. But why not share this with Delphine? And the answer was there. He *had* shared part of himself with Del; it was his blood, which made her strong, which created the blood lust in her when she fought. But she had not the other means by which to temper the spirit's power. The knowledge, the memories. Arsemma could feel the *jinn*'s presence. He was hot like her fever. He was not a he. When Del looked at him she saw only the prince. Arsemma felt herself rising. Here was a spirit from home offering to save and strengthen her so that she might find her sisters, to seek knowledge forbidden to her as a woman in Khartoum. But she must stay with Del, the *jinn* warned of that; she must never leave Del.

Yes. Arsemma answered and reached for Jamal. Only then did she see the glyphs on her arms and shoulders begin to glow. Her affirmation vibrated throughout the room and soon she was glowing with his fire. Drink, the *jinn* instructed. Arsemma reached for his neck, but he stopped her.

No, from here.

He took the tip of his scimitar and nicked his chest. Arsemma lapped up the blood that beaded there and was strengthened by it. Jamal felt desire spread through his thighs and groin as she siphoned from his heart. The *jinn*-light rippled around the room, creating a warm wind, which dried the sweat on Arsemma's forehead. The fever broke, but she was still hot. She pulled away from Jamal to breathe, the blood tingled her lips; it was sweet and intoxicating, a rich paste. As she licked it from her lips, Jamal caught her tongue between his lips and kissed her. His hands pressed against her gown and she took the weight of him.

"I need your blood to complete the ritual." His voice was thick, toneless. In the dark irises she saw the *jinn* dancing.

She knew what blood he meant. The blood of a virgin. She held her head in shame. "I am unclean."

She had not yet been circumcised when the men came and took her. It was to be done after the rains, when there would be less chance of disease. A huge feast had been planned. She knew Jamal would be disgusted. She was unfit for marriage. And she knew it was a marriage he offered her now.

But Jamal was smiling. "So much the better." He did not believe now as he once did that an uncircumcised woman was unclean—he wanted to feel her pleasure. Arsemma felt a joy in his acceptance. Together they succumbed to the wind. To Arsemma it was a simoon—the hot desert breeze that stirred sands into an avalanche.

She was laughing high above the tents, watching the caravan plod through the well-worn paths like so many beetles, steady in their pace. She could harness the winds; she could drown an army in a waterfall of sand, preserving their awestruck faces for eternity.

Then, soft as it began, it was over. She was sitting up on the edge of the bed. Jamal used his thumb to trace a crescent upon her forehead with her own blood. He slumped forward. It took all his strength to stand and hold out a shaking palm to her.

"Let us finish this."

He handed her a gown made of a shimmering gilded fabric. She pulled it over her head. Her thighs ached with the weight and heat of their joining. But she felt strong, animated. She stood and straightened her gown in the small mirror. She was thirsty. She climbed the stairs to the deck and was surprised to find the entire crew assembled. The sails were still; the ship was moored. A few of the men held drums between their legs and the others were dancing. The steps were familiar. It was a wedding dance. Arsemma could feel the hot breath of the *jinn* all around her. There, she was no longer on the ship, but lying on her back in a vast blinding plain of sand. Columns of stinging white rained like glass against her skin. She could make out three robed figures: one red, one white, one black.

"You who have come here." Had the black-robed one spoken? She wasn't sure. "What is your will?"

She knew the words. "I am the flame and the sound of vengeance."

The second hooded figure, the red, spoke. "You who have come here. What is your bond?"

She replied, "I am the prayer and the scent of grace."

The last, white-robed, figure screeched, "You who have come here, what is your offering?"

"I am the knife and the stroke of hope."

The figures sounded their acceptance in unison and she could feel the glyphs burning like the brand on her upper shoulder blade that had stamped and sizzled pain through to her bones.

Arsemma crumpled to the ground and the crew stopped the drumming. Jamal had vanished. All that remained was his hooded cloak and a pile of sand where he had stood. Del fingered the cloth of his robe, empty of him. Arsemma placed her hand on Del's shoulders, her eyes kindled with a new light. In halting French, still foreign to her tongue, she spoke: "I am the goldweight and the measure of truth. I am the blood and breath of life."

Her eyes were a familiar blackness. Del felt she could see Jamal, or what was once Jamal, peering out at her. Then, suddenly that flicker was gone, and the others were laughing and Devon was swinging Arsemma's slight form in the air and she was no longer fragile. Del felt cold as she watched Arsemma's golden robes flutter in the air; the glyphs were dark and outlined with crusted blood. She seemed unaware of pain.

Del sifted the fine pile of sand through her fingers. The wind was blowing most of it into the waves. Yoyotte grabbed her other hand, her gray eyes bright, as if there had been no casualties on this voyage.

"We are home." She gestured ahead at the harbor of Port-au-Prince, rising closer with the sun. She was thinking, Del knew, of her husband and child.

Arsemma leaned down, pressing her lips against Del's ear.

"Yes," she repeated. "We are home."

And together the three of them swept the last traces of sand into the sea.

YAHIMBA'S CHOICE

Charles R. Saunders
(2004)

1

Yahimba was fighting a losing battle to control her fear. The battle had begun three months ago, with her first moon-bleeding. It was then that her initiation into womanhood had begun: a transition that consisted of weeks of fasting, purification, and learning that would culminate in the ritual Yahimba was to undergo this night.

She stood fifth in a line of seven *mwatas*—candidates—who had begun their moon-bleeding at the same time she had. The *mwatas* stood motionless in a grove in the bush outside the village of Guromem. The ground in the grove had been carefully cleared of vegetation, and the fires that burned there cast crimson reflections on the kaolin-whitened bodies of the *mwatas*, each of whom held a small iron bell in her hands.

With the candidates were three older women who would be the *mwatas*' initiators. The seven girls wore only white kaolin clay that coated them from head to toe, while their initiators were clad in raffia skirts that hid the lower half of their bodies. Above the waist, they were naked save for beaded bracelets and raffia headpieces. Their ebony skin contrasted with the kaolin that covered the *mwatas*. The initiators' pendulous breasts swayed as they danced in a slow circle around their charges.

Neither singing nor music accompanied the initiators' dance. The only sounds to be heard in the grove were the shuffle of the initiators' feet and the crackle of the flames from the ceremonial fires. Yahimba imagined that the others could hear the rapid drumming of her heart. . . .

She focused her attention on Morihinze, the eldest of the initiators. In one hand, Morihinze carried a long, wooden rod. In the other, she held a small knife with a notched tip. With that knife, Morihinze would perform the final step in the transformation of Guromem girls into women: *akpema*, the cutting of the *dipa* . . . the "dart" of flesh inside each woman.

The initiators' dance stopped. Yahimba's fears burgeoned. Her hands closed tightly on her bell, which she was holding against her kaolin-whitened stomach.

Morihinze pointed to the first *mwata* in the line. The girl stepped forward, then lay flat on her back. She placed her bell on her chest, then laced her fingers behind her neck. She was ready for *akpema*.

The other two initiators bent down and held the *mwata's* legs apart. Morihinze performed the cutting swiftly, expertly. The *mwata* remained silent, as did her bell. If she had cried out, or if the bell had sounded, Morihinze would have beaten her with the rod that lay by her side.

When the *akpema* was done, the other initiators helped the girl—now a woman—to her feet. As they gave her a clump of grass to stem the flow of blood between her legs, Morihinze took the *dipa* she had excised and hurled it into the nearest fire. The burning of the dart would placate the Tarusi, the *futa* or spirits that held sway over the forest in which the people of Guromem dwelt.

One by one, the other *mwatas* submitted to *akpema*. Their blood seeped into the soil. None of them cried out. No sound came from any of the bells.

Yahimba silently commended the courage of her age-mates. And she begged her ancestors to bestow similar bravery upon her. For the closer she came to her turn for *akpema*, the greater her terror grew. It had begun to feed upon itself, like a fire with an endless supply of fuel.

In Guromem, girls were prepared almost from birth for *akpema*.

Yahimba's mother and older sisters had taught her much about the rite. She knew how it was done, and why it was done. But no one had told her about the quiet voice that whispered fear into her heart. And there was no one she could speak to about that voice. . . .

The girl ahead of Yahimba was next. She was Iverem, born on the same day as Yahimba and thus her sister-in-spirit, closer to her than her sisters-in-family. Yahimba had talked about *akpema* with Iverem after their moon-bleeding had begun. But she had not told her friend about the voice inside her. Iverem was brave. She would have laughed at Yahimba's fears.

"It will be nothing," Iverem had told her the day before. "You will feel no more than you would if you cut your hand while digging yams. One slice, and it's over."

Iverem had been confident then. Now, she was almost unrecognizable beneath her covering of white clay. She lay down, and placed the bell on her chest. The initiators grasped her ankles and parted her legs. Morihinze lifted her knife, then began to lower it.

Then the bell made a small, tinkling sound.

And a choking sob came from Iverem's throat.

Morihinze's hand halted. Flickering firelight illuminated the scowl of disgust that crossed her dark, weathered face. She picked up her rod and raised it to strike Iverem, who was now weeping uncontrollably.

Iverem is afraid! Yahimba thought wildly. *Iverem is afraid! If Iverem is afraid, how can I be brave?*

And the voice of her own fear became so loud and insistent that she could hear nothing else in her mind.

"No!" she cried, her voice cutting into Iverem's sobs.

Flinging her bell aside, Yahimba broke and ran from the initiators and the other *mwatas*. For a moment, the firelight captured her kaolin-white, wraith-like form. Then she was gone, crashing heedlessly into the bush.

2

Dossouye rested her head against the saddle of Gbo, her war-bull. A small fire burned in the clearing she had chosen for her campsite. She did not need the fire to discourage predators, for the presence of Gbo provided more than sufficient deterrent. Instead, the fire provided companionship of a sort, beyond the rapport she shared with Gbo.

At times, she believed the war-bull understood more than just the commands she had trained him to obey since the time when he was little more than a newly weaned calf. And Dossouye had learned the significance of many of the sounds and movements Gbo made. The war-bull had saved her life more than once, and he had carried her through dangerous country she might not have survived without him. Still, Gbo was only an animal, and the quality of his companionship was limited.

Dossouye looked at the war-bull. In the circle of firelight at which he stood guard, Gbo was a silhouette darker than the night. The scythe-like sweep of his horns marked his kinship to the wild buffalo that roamed the forest and plains, a beast so formidable that even lions fled before it.

Turning her attention to the dancing flames of her fire, Dossouye reflected on the vast distance she had traveled from her homeland of Abomey, which was located far to the west, where the land met the sea. There, she had been an *ahosi*, a woman soldier in the army of the Leopard King. From that life, she retained only Gbo, her sword, and the leather loin-protector that was her only remaining garment. Her cuirass and helmet had long since been lost in the battles she had been forced to wage to survive in the wilderness.

She had saved Abomey from an invasion by the kingdom's enemies, the Abanti, only to be forced into exile at the hands of an enemy of her own. Now, she was wandering in the lands far to the east of Abomey and its neighboring kingdoms. In this rain-forest country, human habitations were few and widely scattered. Only rarely did Dossouye visit any of those villages, whose inhabitants were wary of strangers.

The few people with whom she had talked had told her there were kingdoms that lay to the east, where the rain forest ended—places that seemed more mythical than real. By following the sun and the stars, Dossouye could make her way to more civilized lands, if she so desired. But she avoided the direction in which the sun and stars would have led her. Having left her homeland behind, she had convinced herself that she needed solitude. Lately, however, her thinking in that matter had begun to change. . . .

A *whuff* from Gbo jolted Dossouye out of her reverie. She knew what that sound meant. It was a warning signal. The war-bull had sensed the approach of an animal—or person. Whoever—or whatever—the intruder was, Gbo's *whuff* indicated that he did not consider the intruder to be dangerous. If he had, his reaction would have been much more emphatic.

Dossouye rose in a single, fluid motion. Her tall, slender frame was sheathed in lean muscle. Her small head and long limbs were reminiscent of those of the cheetah, the swift hunter of the savanna. Her hair, once cropped close to her scalp to accommodate a helmet she no longer possessed, grew in wooly, uneven locks, lending her even more of a feral aspect. Her indigo-black skin merged with the darkness as she went to the war-bull's side.

"Who is coming to visit us, Gbo?" she murmured. "It must be a person. An animal would not be drawn to our fire."

Gbo *whuffed* again, as if in agreement.

Although the cities of Abomey were her heritage, Dossouye had, from necessity, acquired sufficient woodcraft to understand that the sounds that now reached her ears were being made by someone who was running from something.

"What pursues this one?" the *ahosi* wondered aloud. "A leopard? Bandits? Spirits?"

Without thinking about it, Dossouye had picked up her sword when she rose. She held the hilt lightly, easily, as though the weapon was an extension of her arm. Her grip tightened when she saw a pale, ghost-like figure push its way through a barrier of bush.

Catching sight of the fire, the figure redoubled its efforts, breaking through the foliage and running directly toward Dossouye. Gbo's hoof pawed the ground, but the war-bull did not react further.

Lowering her sword, Dossouye allowed a frightened and exhausted Yahimba to stumble into her arms.

3

At first, Dossouye thought she was holding an *eusi*, a person born without pigmentation. But the texture of the kaolin beneath her hands quickly belied that impression. Gently but firmly, she disengaged herself from the trembling girl's grasp. Then she held Yahimba at arm's length.

Yahimba attempted to speak, but she could not. Her mouth hung open as she gasped for breath, and her legs could hardly hold her upright. Slowly, her eyes drifted upward, exposing bloodshot corneas.

Dossouye realized then that the white clay covering the girl's skin was slowly suffocating her. Before she could take action, however, Gbo suddenly emitted a sound that was half snort and half bellow. Someone else was approaching—and this time, the war-bull sensed danger.

Yahimba cast a fearful glance over her shoulder. Then she pressed closer to Dossouye. The *ahosi* looked beyond the girl, scanning the stretch of darkness outside the reach of the firelight. Gbo moved forward to stand beside Dossouye.

Seeing the war-bull for the first time, Yahimba let out a small gasp of terror. She pushed harder against Dossouye, smearing kaolin on the skin of the *ahosi*. Dossouye paid scant heed to the girl. Her attention was claimed by the person who quietly emerged from the darkness.

There was no white clay on the ebony skin of the raffia-skirted woman who now confronted Dossouye. The *ahosi* noted the signs of the woman's advanced age: wizened face, gnarled hands, drooping, uncovered breasts. One of the woman's hands held a knife with a notch at its tip. Dossouye frowned at the sight of fresh blood embedded in the notch.

Morihinze gazed fearlessly at Dossouye and Gbo, strange though the warrior-woman and the war-bull must have appeared to her. Dossouye could sense the depth of the spiritual power within this woman. Sheer good fortune was the only reason the girl had been able to survive her blind rush through the forest. Dossouye sensed that the woman had no need for luck.

"Give the girl to me," Morihinze said quietly.

Dossouye did not fully understand the Guromem dialect. During her wandering, however, she had picked up elements of many of the languages spoken by the forest-dwellers. But she did not need fluency in the Guromem tongue to grasp Morihinze's meaning. The command in the woman's tone was unmistakable.

"No," Dossouye said in a tone that was equally unmistakable.

She spoke in the language of the last village she had visited, not far from this place. There, she had traded some game she had killed for cooked yams and plantains, foods she sorely missed during her travels. The words of those people seemed similar to the ones the elder spoke.

To make certain she would not be misunderstood, Dossouye decided to allow her actions to speak more eloquently than her words. She pushed Yahimba behind her. Then she lifted her sword. Beside her, Gbo lowered his head in a menacing manner.

Morihinze eyed Dossouye's sword and Gbo's horns. She knew her *akpema*-knife had never been intended for use as a weapon. Lowering the blade, she stared hard at Yahimba. Although the girl cringed beneath the elder's scrutiny, she did not look away.

"Yahimba. Come with me," Morihinze ordered. "Finish *akpema*. You know what will happen if you do not."

Yahimba shuddered and buried her face against Dossouye's shoulder.

"You can see that she does not want to go with you," Dossouye said. "So leave us. Now."

Morihinze looked at the *ahosi*.

"Why do you interfere, stranger?" she asked. "Of what concern is this to you?"

Dossouye was not sure what answer she could give. She surmised that the kaolin on Yahimba's skin signified a ritual. From the girl's apparent age, she gathered that it was some sort of coming-of-age ceremony. Dossouye's people in Abomey also had rites that marked the passage from childhood to adulthood.

However, Dossouye was certain she knew the significance of the notch in Morihinze's knife. And the practice that notch bespoke had long since been eschewed in Abomey as an unnecessary act of cruelty. It was thought to continue in places outside the reach of Abomey and its neighboring kingdoms, but the practice was continued clandestinely, if at all.

Dossouye had never before imagined that such a thing could still be done openly. But since she had departed from Abomey, she had seen many things that she had never before imagined. . . .

"This girl will not be mutilated because of ignorant superstitions," Dossouye finally said.

Morihinze's eyes hardened.

"You, stranger, are the ignorant one," she said.

"Go," Dossouye said, gesturing with her sword.

"Yahimba?" Morihinze said, ignoring the *ahosi*.

Entreaty, not command, was now the message in the elder's eyes. Yahimba would not look at her. Sadly, knowing she had no chance to wrest Yahimba from the grasp of the warrior-woman, Morihinze turned to go back into the bush.

"Will you send warriors to get this girl?" Dossouye demanded.

Morihinze turned her head and spoke over a bare, bent shoulder. Pity glimmered in her eyes.

"There will be no warriors," she said. "There will be *others*. I will not send them. You will have brought them on yourself."

Then Morihinze disappeared into the darkness of the bush.

Dossouye turned to Yahimba.

"Come," she said. "We must wash that clay from your skin before it kills you."

The *ahosi*'s words were intelligible enough for Yahimba to nod her acquiescence. She had made her choice. Its consequences were now beyond her control.

4

Firelight splashed Dossouye and Yahimba as they bathed in a woodland pool. The *ahosi* had taken a brand from the fire at her campsite and used it to start a new one by the pool's shore. She had come upon the small body of water earlier, and she and Gbo had drunk from it. Now, the war-bull stood guard while Dossouye scrubbed the kaolin from Yahimba's skin. Yahimba submitted mutely. The white film on the surface of the water might have been her soul, separated from her body by Dossouye's tireless hands.

The girl who slowly emerged from the coating of kaolin had seen the passing of no more than twelve rains. Her breasts were just beginning to bud. Her skin was a deep jet in hue. Her head was shaved; indeed, there was no hair anywhere on her body, other than her eyelashes.

Part of the ritual, Dossouye assumed. She also guessed that Yahimba's people would have washed the clay from her body at the end of the cutting-ceremony, had the girl not fled.

It had been easy enough for Dossouye to eliminate the smears Yahimba's kaolin had left on her own skin. But much more effort had been needed to cleanse the girl. Now, the task was done. Dossouye removed her hands from Yahimba's body and stepped away from her.

Only a few faint streaks of white remained on Yahimba. The girl stood quietly, waiting for the next action from this strange, harsh woman to whom she was certain her ancestors had directed her.

"We will dry ourselves by the fire," Dossouye said.

Taking Yahimba by the hand, the *ahosi* led her out of the pool. Then they reclined by the fire, letting its heat evaporate the beads of water that covered them. Behind them, Gbo stood watch silently.

"What am I to do with you, girl?" Dossouye mused.

But then what am I doing with myself? she wondered silently. What was she doing, other than wandering without any purpose or destination, without companionship?

Yahimba remained silent.

"I heard the old woman call you 'Yahimba,'" Dossouye said. "Would you not like to know my name?"

Yahimba said nothing. She could barely think, hardly function. Through her own actions, the scope of her life had been reduced to the confines of the space lit by this stranger's fire.

Fear had motivated her flight from the *akpema* ceremony. Now, she was even more fearful than before, and she did not know what to do next. And so she sat in a cocoon of silence.

Dossouye reached out, took Yahimba's chin in her hand, and forced the girl to look at her.

"Can you understand my words?" she asked, speaking slowly.

Yahimba nodded. The *ahosi* removed her hand from the girl's face.

"My name is Dossouye," she said.

Yahimba did not respond.

"This is Gbo," Dossouye continued, gesturing toward the war-bull. "He will not harm you. Neither will I."

Yahimba gazed straight ahead, without speaking.

"Why did the old woman want to cut you with that knife?" Dossouye demanded abruptly.

A spark of life returned to Yahimba's eyes then.

"To remove my *dipa* . . . my dart," she said in reply.

Those were the first words Yahimba had said to Dossouye since she blundered into the *ahosi*'s campsite. Despite the sudden focus in her eyes, the Guromem girl's tone was flat, as though she was reciting words that had been said to her repeatedly throughout her childhood.

"Your 'dart,'" Dossouye echoed. She was certain she knew what that word symbolized. "Why do your people remove women's 'darts'?" Dossouye asked.

"If a man is stabbed by the *dipa*, he will die."

Yahimba was about to say more, but the expression that suddenly set into the warrior-woman's features forestalled her.

"Men command; women obey—even to the point of doing harm to themselves," she said in a voice that sounded like the growl of a leopard. "*How* do the men die, girl?" she demanded, staring intently at Yahimba. "Do they bleed to death?"

"The Tarusi kill them," Yahimba replied almost inaudibly.

"What are the Tarusi?"

Despite the heat of the rain-forest night and the warmth of the fire, Yahimba shivered.

"They are *futa*," she whispered.

"Ghosts?" Dossouye asked, not certain of the word's meaning.

"No," Yahimba said. "*Futa* . . . spirits. The Tarusi kill men who are stabbed by the *dipa*, and they kill women whose *dipas* have not been removed by *akpema*."

Yahimba's words reverberated in Dossouye's mind.

Should I tell her? the *ahosi* asked herself. *Should I? Yes* . . .

She laid her hand on Yahimba's shoulder and searched carefully among the limited number of words she knew in the languages of the forest people.

"Listen to me, Yahimba," she said. "I am a woman, and I still have my 'dart.' I still have it, and no 'Tarusi' has ever come to kill me."

Yahimba's eyes widened into white circles of terror as she absorbed the full import of what Dossouye had said. She tried to pull away, but the *ahosi*'s grasp was as unyielding as iron.

"In my homeland," Dossouye continued relentlessly, "women do not have their 'darts' cut out. No Tarusi kill them. And no man in my country dies when the 'dart' stabs him."

Yahimba shook her head in denial and covered her ears to shut out the warrior-woman's words. Dossouye forced the girl's arms back to her sides.

"I have been to many places where this cutting is not done," the *ahosi* said. "And in none of those places have I seen any Tarusi. In none of those places do people die because their women keep their 'darts.'"

Yahimba shut her eyes tightly. At that moment, she would have preferred the pain of *akpema*; she would have welcomed it rather than continue to listen to the mad words of this strange woman who carried a sword and tamed a buffalo to do her bidding.

"Please," Yahimba begged. "Say nothing more. . . ."

Dossouye seized the girl by both shoulders and gave her a shake, forcing her to open her eyes.

"You fled your ceremony," the *ahosi* said harshly. "What will you do now?"

"Die," Yahimba replied bleakly.

Dossouye lowered her head and shook it sadly. She wanted to help Yahimba, but she didn't know how to do so. What could she offer this girl, other than a rootless life, a shared exile? Yet her repugnance for the cutting-ritual stood as a barrier against any notion of returning her to her people.

Dossouye's hands remained on Yahimba's shoulders, and she could feel the girl trembling beneath her touch.

"What to do?" the *ahosi* murmured in her native language, which she had not spoken aloud for a long time. She caught herself, then returned to words Yahimba could understand.

"If you had not stumbled into my camp, the cutting-woman would have caught you and taken you back to the ceremony you fled. Now . . ."

She grimaced at the fear that was plain in Yahimba's eyes.

"Maybe I should have allowed the cutting-woman to take you," she said. "But if you do not want to be cut, *why should it be allowed to happen?*"

Dossouye had raised her voice when she asked that question. Before she could say anything else, Gbo suddenly bellowed, startling both Yahimba and Dossouye. The *ahosi* was on her feet in an instant, sword in hand. She knew that such a sound from the war-bull signaled imminent danger.

Gbo's attention was focused on the pool. The war-bull's head was lowered, and his eyes rolled, showing flashes of white. Dossouye realized then that Gbo was afraid of whatever it was his senses had detected. Never before had she seen Gbo show fear. . . .

Her own fear rising, Dossouye stared intently at the pool and the cloak of darkness beyond it. But she saw nothing . . . heard nothing. Then she looked more closely at the pool . . . and saw a ripple moving across the white film the kaolin had left on the water's surface. No wind was present to account for that ripple.

Glancing back toward Yahimba, Dossouye saw the girl huddled beside the fire, her eyes peering fearfully over her bent knees. Then the girl's eyes widened even farther, and she tried to make herself as small as possible.

Gbo bellowed again. And Dossouye felt a feathery touch on her shoulder. Slight though that contact was, its force was still sufficient to send her sprawling to the ground. And the single word Yahimba screamed echoed inside her skull:

"*Tarusi!*"

5

Despite the force of the unexpected blow she had received, the battle-training Dossouye had undergone in Abomey had honed her reflexes to catlike quickness. The moment she hit the ground, she rolled once and sprang to her feet, sword in hand. What she then saw in the wavering firelight rooted her to the ground and caused her mouth to fall open in astonishment, and her eyes to dilate with fear.

The Tarusi had come . . . for the impossibly tall, spectral shapes that surrounded her could be nothing other than the spirits of which Yahimba had spoken.

In daylight, they might have been only men who were perched on stilts and wearing elaborate costumes for some festival or celebration. With darkness blurring their outlines, they appeared much more sinister. Their heads, bodies, and arms were of normal proportions, but their legs were far longer than Dossouye was tall. Pale garments that looked as though they were made of mist rather than cloth covered their elongated legs and hung loosely from their gaunt torsos.

Their faces were their least-human aspect: eyes like circular pits of demon-fire; gaping mouths filled with square, grinding teeth; scores of tusk-like projections sprouting from their heads in place of hair. The projections moved independently, like tentacles.

Their eyes blazed. Their teeth gnashed. And all of the towering shapes stared mercilessly at Dossouye.

"Tarusi," the *ahosi* whispered, echoing Yahimba's outcry.

Half a dozen of the *futa* had come to the clearing. They loomed over Dossouye like trees. Next to them, the *ahosi* appeared as diminished as a child among adults. The sword in her hand seemed pitiably ineffective, even though the Tarusi were not armed.

Fear coursed through Dossouye like the current of a flooding stream. But there was anger within her as well—anger at the very existence of beings like the Tarusi, and anger at what that existence had meant for the women of Yahimba's village.

Yahimba!

In the corner of her eye, Dossouye detected movement. She turned, and saw yet another Tarusi. This one was moving toward a transfixed Yahimba, its legs carrying it in an awkward, high-stepping gait. The others continued to ring the *ahosi*.

Then she heard the sound of Gbo's hoofs churning the soil of the clearing. Despite his own terror, the war-bull was charging toward Dossouye's side. The *ahosi*'s rush of gratitude was immediately superseded by another imperative: *Yahimba must be saved.*

"Gbo! Stop!" Dossouye shouted, even as the other Tarusi began to close in on her.

The war-bull halted. Dropping her sword, Dossouye leaped through the narrowing space between two of the Tarusi. Then she raced toward Yahimba, who had still not moved from her place beside the fire. On the way, Dossouye snatched Gbo's dangling reins and pulled him toward the girl. Before Yahimba could react, Dossouye hauled her to her feet, pushed her onto the war-bull's back, and looped the reins around one of the girl's wrists.

"Run, Gbo!" Dossouye cried even as she heard movement behind her.

The war-bull hesitated only a moment before plowing into the bush, bearing his dazed rider away from the Tarusi. Then something struck Dossouye heavily across her back. Ignoring the sharp pain the impact caused, Dossouye whirled and scrambled through a mobile forest of sticklike legs. The Tarusi lashed at her, their legs as flexible as whips, but she managed to avoid their blows. Supernatural though they were, the Tarusi could not match the quickness of the *ahosi*.

Dossouye reached the spot at which her sword had fallen. When her hand found the weapon's hilt, she scrambled to her feet and faced her foes. The Tarusi had tested her. Now, she would test them.

She swung her blade at the nearest Tarusi, aiming at its legs. The blow struck . . . but instead of chopping through the leg and felling the Tarusi, the steel sliced harmlessly through a substance that was heavier than air, but less dense than water.

Dossouye had expected her blade to meet much greater resistance than it had. Overbalanced, she fell. Like a thick, heavy whip, the leg of a Tarusi lashed into her side, bruising her ribs and jolting her breath from her lungs. Another Tarusi's leg—blunt-ended, lacking a foot—slammed against her wrist, forcing her to drop her sword.

The *ahosi* twisted away from the next blow. Then she leaped back to her feet, and saw that two Tarusi stood between her and her weapon.

My sword is useless anyway, she thought bleakly. *They can touch me, but I cannot touch them. . . .*

Not with your steel and not with your dart, woman.

Dossouye went instinctively into a defensive crouch when she heard the chorus of deep, low voices both outside and inside her head. The Tarusi could easily have slain her at that moment, had they chosen to do so. They did not.

Why do you seek to take from us what is ours? the Tarusi's voices demanded.

The question enraged, then emboldened, Dossouye.

"Why do you take from women what belongs to them?" she shouted in response.

The men must not die.

Outrage seared its way through the fear that had enveloped Dossouye since she had first seen the Tarusi, and understood that these *futa* truly existed, and were not just tales handed down from one generation to the next in justification of *akpema.*

"That is a lie," Dossouye cried. "A *lie!* Women in other places keep their 'darts.' And men do not die because of it. Why do you hold the people here hostage to a lie?"

If this is what the men want, then it cannot be a lie. If the men did not believe it to be true, then we would not be here.

Dossouye fell silent then, stunned into speechlessness by what the Tarusi had said. *Men's fears . . .* was that the true source from which these *futa* had come, not the forest? *Men's fears . . .* and those of women as well?

The Tarusi crowded closer to Dossouye.

Call back your mount, they commanded. **Return the girl to us.**

We are the ones who will claim her, not you. Do so, and we will allow you to leave this place with your life.

Dossouye backed away from the slowly advancing Tarusi. She was naked, weaponless. Fingers of despair clutched at her heart. She could not call upon the deities of Abomey to aid her, for she had left them behind when she departed her homeland.

The Tarusi were herding her as though she were a calf. They were forcing her toward the fire. In a moment, its flames would begin to burn her skin.

She could give the Tarusi what they wanted, and live—or she could die a fiery death. *Fire!*

Suddenly, the *ahosi* realized she was not weaponless after all. She turned and reached into the flames. Unmindful of the pain that seared her hands, Dossouye seized two brands from the blaze and whirled them high over her head. Crimson streaks pained the darkness as she advanced on the Tarusi. The nightmarish shapes hesitated as Dossouye moved toward them.

Sparks from Dossouye's improvised weapons flew toward the Tarusi and touched their wavering substance. Flares of light and hissing sounds rose from the places the sparks hit, and the Tarusi's teeth gnashed in pain.

Embellished by the firelight, the *ahosi*'s lean body appeared to grow in stature as she advanced. Fury blazed in her dark eyes, and her countenance was reminiscent of that of the first humans to have mastered fire, the scourge of beasts and demons alike. . . .

The Tarusi retreated. They could still touch Dossouye . . . but now she could touch them, as well.

We cannot harm you, the Tarusi said. No longer did their chorus sound so commanding. **You can only harm yourself.**

"And *you* will not harm Yahimba!" Dossouye shouted.

We will not, the Tarusi agreed. **We will not harm her. But think well on what you have done, woman. Think well. . . .**

Before Dossouye could respond, the Tarusi withdrew. As they drifted over the white-tinged pool, their bodies lost substance. Before they reached the other side, they vanished from sight, leaving behind only a ripple to mark their passage.

6

Dossouye's summoning-call echoed through the forest. No other sounds competed with it—the coming of the Tarusi had silenced the wildlife within the environs of the pool.

Gbo responded to the call more quickly than Dossouye had anticipated. He had not gone far. He would never stray any great distance from Dossouye's side, no matter what she commanded him to do. The war-bull trotted quietly into the clearing. Yahimba was still clinging to his back.

Dossouye went to Gbo and spoke softly into the war-bull's ear.

"You did not run far enough, Gbo," she chided.

Gbo *whuffed* as if to say: *I never will.*

Shaking her head in a combination of gratitude and resignation, Dossouye reached up to unwrap Gbo's reins from Yahimba's wrist. She looked into the girl's eyes . . . and was startled by what she saw there. Where before there had been only fear and incomprehension, Dossouye now saw a glint of determination in the girl's gaze.

"You know that the Tarusi will not harm you?" Dossouye asked.

"Yes," Yahimba replied. "I heard them . . . in my head."

Dossouye helped the girl down from Gbo's back. A moment after Yahimba's feet touched the ground, the brush rustled. For a single, awful moment, Dossouye thought the Tarusi had returned. She had re-donned her loin-protector and her sword was sheathed at her side.

However, it was Morihinze, not the Tarusi, who stepped into the open.

Gbo did not react to the elder's presence. Dossouye did. She immediately stepped in front of Yahimba, placing herself between the girl and Morihinze. Morihinze still held the notched *akpema*-knife in her hand. She looked directly at Dossouye, as though she were truly seeing the *ahosi* . . . and other things . . . for the first time.

"The Tarusi spoke to me, too," she said.

"Then you know there is no need for *that*," she said, gesturing toward the *akpema*-knife.

Morihinze shook her head.

"The Tarusi said they would spare Yahimba," she said. "But they did not say she would be safe in Guromem. And what of all the others? Who will protect them, and the rest of us, after you ride away from here?"

"You don't need me to protect you!" Dossouye said, her voice rising in exasperation. "Do you not understand how to protect yourself? Use fire! Ring your village with flames, if you need to. Fire will protect you from the Tarusi. You no longer have to sacrifice part of yourself to keep them from harming you."

Morihinze's eyes did not waver from Dossouye's. The two women held each other's gaze for a long moment. Then Morihinze shook her head again.

"Fire can protect us from the Tarusi, warrior-woman," she said. "But fire cannot protect us from the men. If men's fears give life to the Tarusi, they can give life to other things that may be even worse. Can you protect us from that?"

Dossouye remained silent, for she had no answer to Morihinze's question.

Then she felt a stirring at her side as Yahimba moved away from her and took a step toward Morihinze.

"I still have my *dipa*, and I am still alive," she said, unintentionally echoing Dossouye's earlier words. "When the men see that the Tarusi have not killed me, they will see that there is no more need for *akpema*."

For the first time that night, Morihinze smiled.

"You are a brave child, Yahimba," she said. "But I am afraid that the men would kill you before they had the chance to learn whether or not you were speaking the truth."

Yahimba bowed her head in acknowledgment of Morihinze's words.

"What can I do, then?" the girl asked, her voice barely audible.

"Much time will have to pass for us to teach the men that they have no reason to fear the Tarusi or the *dipa*," Morihinze said. "That will not happen in my lifetime. But it can in yours, Yahimba. You can be the one to end *akpema* . . . but you must undergo it yourself nonetheless; for if you do not, you will have no place in Guromem, and no one will listen to you."

"And if she chooses not to submit to this cutting?" Dossouye asked in a harsh tone.

"Then she can go with you, warrior-woman," Morihinze said. "The choice is hers."

Yahimba looked at Morihinze, then at Dossouye. Her indecision showed clearly on her face as she continued to shift her gaze from one woman to the other. She had a question for Dossouye:

"Will you take me with you, if that is what I decide?"

Dossouye did not reply immediately, for part of her was elsewhere, in a different forest . . . a forest in her native Abomey. . . .

The forest was a *fedi*-grove: orderly rows of tall trees, beneath which were buried the umbilical cords of generations of Abomeans. All Abomeans were born with three souls: their personal soul, and two others that linked them to their ancestors and the deities. The latter two souls were imbued in the umbilical cords that the trees protected. If a *fedi*-tree died, so did the souls it guarded; and so did the person to whom the souls belonged.

Dossouye saw herself standing in front of the *fedi*-tree that guarded her souls. She saw it lying on the ground, cut down by an enemy even as she had wielded the magical sword of one of her ancestors to save Abomey from an invasion by a rival kingdom, the Abanti. She should have been as dead as her tree; as dead as two of her three souls . . . as dead as the enemy who had felled the tree. But she wasn't.

She had rescued her kingdom . . . but she was also an anomaly, a person whose very existence now stood in contradiction to the age-old beliefs of her people. She believed she no longer had a place in Abomey . . . not when she should not even have been alive. She had departed before anyone else could see what had happened to her *fedi*-tree, or see that she continued to live with only a single soul.

Yet in all her subsequent roving, Dossouye had always wondered whether she should have remained in Abomey. Having saved the kingdom from the Abanti, could she not also have changed its beliefs? Or would she have been such an anomaly that the priests and wizards of her nation would have had no choice other than to slay her? She would never know, but there were still times when she regretted her decision to exile herself from her homeland. . . .

"Dossouye?"

Yahimba's voice brought the *ahosi* back from Abomey.

The *ahosi* looked down at the girl, who was wide-eyed with anxiety over Dossouye's prolonged silence. Dossouye could see something of herself in Yahimba. And when she answered, she was speaking as much to herself as she was to the Guromem girl.

"I will take you with me if you wish to leave," Dossouye said. "But your place is here."

Yahimba's eyes delved deeply into Dossouye's, and what she saw there was the truth. Then the girl turned to face Morihinze. The elder gave Dossouye a slight nod before turning her attention to Yahimba.

"If you wish to stay, then you know what you must do," Morihinze said.

Yahimba was silent a moment longer. Then she said: "I am ready for *akpema*."

She turned once again to Dossouye. The fear that had dominated Yahimba since she first heard the tinkle of Iverem's bell had subsided. The beginning of a lifelong determination was replacing the fear. The child who had blundered blindly into Dossouye's campsite was gone now. Dossouye could see that the young woman standing before her now was capable of one day freeing her people from *akpema*, and the Tarusi. She could do for Guromem what Dossouye had done for Abomey . . . and she would not have to leave her homeland afterward.

"Will you hold my legs, Dossouye?" Yahimba asked.

Dossouye looked toward the fire, for she did not want Yahimba to see the anger in her eyes. She did not want Yahimba to think that the anger was directed toward her. Dossouye was angry with herself. Had she not fought the Tarusi to prevent the very act in which she was now being asked to participate?

She could teach Yahimba how to survive in the wilderness. She could instruct her in the way of the warrior; the girl had shown that she had the courage to overcome her fears. But Dossouye did not know whether Yahimba could master in a short time the skills she herself had learned only after many rains of teaching.

Dossouye could be a mentor . . . a mother . . . to Yahimba. But to what purpose? In Guromem, at least, Yahimba had a destiny to fulfill. That was more—much more—than Dossouye could offer her.

Dossouye looked at Yahimba then, and nodded her assent.

7

As Yahimba lay on her back, Dossouye gripped the girl's ankles firmly, as Morihinze had instructed. Gbo was standing nearby, and Dossouye's carefully tended fire cast fitful light on the ceremony.

From somewhere inside the raffia skirt she wore, Morihinze pulled out Yahimba's *akpema*-bell, which she placed in the middle of Yahimba's chest. The bell remained silent during the cutting, which Morihinze performed even more swiftly than usual. Yahimba neither moved nor cried out. She did not look at either Morihinze or Dossouye. Instead, she stared into the night sky, as if the stars could tell her whether or not she had made the right decision.

As Yahimba sat up and made a conscious effort to conceal the pain she felt, Morihinze pressed a handful of grass between the girl's legs to stanch the bleeding. Then the elder held her closed hand in front of Yahimba. Both Yahimba and Dossouye gazed intently at that hand, knowing what it concealed. Yahimba knew what would happen next: Morihinze would throw her newly removed *dipa* into the fire, and *akpema* would be over.

Slowly, Morihinze opened her hand, revealing . . . nothing. Her hand was empty. No *dipa* was there.

Both of the younger women stared at Morihinze.

"Where is my *dipa*?" Yahimba asked. I felt the pain when you cut it. . . ."

"But you didn't," Dossouye said, looking closely at Morihinze.

"I cut only enough to draw blood," the elder said. "The *dipa* remains. The blood will be enough; the men will ask no questions. And the Tarusi will taste fire if they come to claim our lives over the *dipa*."

"You needed to see if she would be strong enough to keep the secret, until the time was right to reveal it," Dossouye said, looking at Morihinze with a respect she had not felt for her before.

Morihinze merely nodded. Together, she and Dossouye helped Yahimba to her feet. The girl stood unsteadily, both hands holding the clump of grass that reddened between her legs. Gently, but deliberately, Morihinze eased Yahimba away from Dossouye.

"We must return to Guromem," Morihinze told Yahimba.

Dossouye nodded. She understood why Morihinze did not ask her to accompany them to the village. She might have been welcome among the people of Guromem, but she would have been forever a stranger—a stranger with a secret.

"You have our gratitude, warrior-woman," Morihinze said.

Yahimba pulled away from Morihinze then, and embraced the *ahosi*.

"I will never forget you, Dossouye," she said.

Then she returned to Morihinze's side. Without further conversation, the two Guromem women departed from the clearing. Yahimba looked back once before the brush swallowed them. For a long time afterward, Dossouye gazed at the place where she had last seen them.

Then she cinched Gbo's saddle into place. She was bone-weary, and needed sleep. But she also needed to be gone from this place when the sun rose.

Slowly, she climbed into the saddle. Before urging Gbo forward, she stared across the pool, now only a dim smear in the guttering firelight. She could neither see nor hear the Tarusi. But she guessed that they had not truly disappeared; they may have been lingering somewhere near—powerless, yet vengeful.

Dossouye wondered if Morihinze and Yahimba would succeed in freeing the women of Guromem from *akpema*. She wondered what would have happened if Yahimba had chosen to remain with her. She wondered whether she should have stayed in Abomey, regardless of the death of two of her souls. She wondered who was truly more courageous—her, or Yahimba?

"Maybe one day we will go back to Abomey," she said to Gbo. "But not yet. Not yet . . ."

As she rode away, Dossouye heard a soft, whispery sound amid the trees. She thought it was the wind. But it was the Tarusi, mourning the future they foresaw for themselves . . . a future in which an adult, raffia-clad Yahimba would hurl the *akpema*-knife into the very pool Dossouye passed, and even the sham of the ceremony Morihinze had devised would be abolished by the women and men of Guromem.

The wind was the sound of the Tarusi, weeping.

THE GLASS BOTTLE TRICK

Nalo Hopkinson
(2000)

The air was full of storms, but they refused to break.

In the wicker rocking chair on the front verandah, Beatrice flexed her bare feet against the wooden slat floor, rocking slowly back and forth. Another sweltering rainy season afternoon. The arid heat felt as though all the oxygen had boiled out of the parched air to hang as looming rainclouds, waiting.

Oh, but she loved it like this. The hotter the day, the slower she would move, basking. She stretched her arms and legs out to better feel the luxuriant warmth, then guiltily sat up straight again. Samuel would scold if he ever saw her slouching like that. Stuffy Sammy. She smiled fondly, admiring the lacy patterns the sunlight threw on the floor as it filtered through the white gingerbread fretwork that trimmed the roof of their house.

"Anything more today, Mistress Powell? I finish doing the dishes." Gloria had come out of the house and was standing in front of her, wiping her chapped hands on her apron.

Beatrice felt the shyness come over her as it always did when she thought of giving the older woman orders. Gloria was older than Beatrice's mother. "Ah . . . no, I think that's everything, Gloria. . . ."

Gloria quirked an eyebrow, crinkling her face as if running a fork through molasses. "Then I go take the rest of the afternoon off. You and Mister Samuel should be alone tonight. Is time you tell him."

Beatrice gave an abortive, shamefaced "huh" of a laugh. Gloria had known from the start, she'd had so many babies of her own. She'd been mad to run to Samuel with the news from since. But yesterday, Beatrice had already decided to tell Samuel. Well, almost decided. She felt irritated, like a child whose tricks have been found out. She swallowed the feeling. "I think you right, Gloria," she said, fighting for some dignity before the older woman. "Maybe . . . maybe I cook him a special meal, feed him up nice, then tell him."

"Well, I say is time and past time you make him know. A pickney is a blessing to a family."

"For true," Beatrice agreed, making her voice sound as certain as she could.

"Later, then, Mistress Powell." Giving herself the afternoon off, not even a by-your-leave, Gloria headed off to the maid's room at the back of the house to change into her street clothes. A few minutes later, she let herself out the garden gate.

"That seems like a tough book for a young lady of such tender years."

"Excuse me?" Beatrice threw a defensive, cutting glare at the older man. He'd caught her off guard, though she'd seen his eyes following her ever since she entered the bookstore. "You have something to say to me?" She curled the Gray's Anatomy possessively into the crook of her arm, price sticker hidden against her body. Two more months of saving before she could afford it.

He looked shyly at her. "Sorry if I offended, Miss," he said. "My name is Samuel."

Would be handsome, if he'd chill out a bit. Beatrice's wariness thawed a little. Middle of the sun-hot day, and he wearing black wool jacket and pants. His crisp white cotton shirt was buttoned right up, held in place by a tasteful, unimaginative tie. So proper, Jesus. He wasn't that much older than she.

"Is just . . . you're so pretty, and it's the only thing I could think of to say to get you to speak to me."

Beatrice softened more at that, smiled for him and played with the collar of her blouse. He didn't seem too bad, if you could look beyond the stocious, starchy behaviour.

*　　*　　*

Beatrice doubtfully patted the slight swelling of her belly. Four months. She was shy to give Samuel her news, but she was starting to show. Silly to put it off, yes? Today she was going to make her husband very happy; break that thin shell of mourning that still insulated him from her. He never said so, but Beatrice knew that he still thought of the wife he'd lost, and tragically, the one before that. She wished she could make him warm up to life again.

Sunlight was flickering through the leaves of the guava tree in the front yard. Beatrice inhaled the sweet smell of the sun-warmed fruit. The tree's branches hung heavy with the pale yellow globes, smooth and round as eggs. The sun reflected off the two blue bottles suspended in the tree, sending cobalt light dancing through the leaves.

When Beatrice first came to Sammy's house, she'd been puzzled by the two bottles that were jammed onto branches of the guava tree.

"Is just my superstitiousness, darling," he'd told her. "You never heard the old people say that if someone dies, you must put a bottle in a tree to hold their spirit, otherwise it will come back as a duppy and haunt you? A blue bottle. To keep the duppy cool, so it won't come at you in hot anger for being dead."

Beatrice had heard something of the sort, but it was strange to think of her Sammy as a superstitious man. He was too controlled and logical for that. *Well, grief makes somebody act in strange ways.* Maybe the bottles gave him some comfort, made him feel that he'd kept some essence of his poor wives near him.

"That Samuel is nice. Respectable, hard-working. Not like all them other ragamuffins you always going out with." Mummy picked up the butcher knife and began expertly slicing the goat meat into cubes for the curry.

Beatrice watched the red lumps of flesh part under the knife. Crimson liquid leaked onto the cutting board. She sighed. "But, Mummy, Samuel so boring! Michael and Clifton know how to have fun. All Samuel want to do is go for country drives. Always taking me away from other people."

"You should be studying your books, not having fun," her mother replied crossly.

Beatrice pleaded. "You well know I could do both, Mummy." Her mother just grunted.

Is only truth Beatrice was talking. Plenty men were always courting her; they flocked to her like birds, eager to take her dancing or out for a drink. But somehow she kept her marks up, even though it often meant studying right through the night, her head pounding and belly queasy from hangover while some man snored in the bed beside her. Mummy would kill her if she didn't get straight A's for medical school. "You going have to look after yourself, Beatrice. Man not going do it for you. Them get their little piece of sweetness and then them bruk away."

"Two patty and a King Cola, please." The guy who'd given the order had a broad chest that tapered to a slim waist. Good face to look at, too. Beatrice smiled sweetly at him, made shift to gently brush his palm with her fingertips as she handed him the change.

A bird screeched from the guava tree, a tiny kiskedee, crying angrily, "*Dit, dit, qu'est-ce qu'il dit!*" A small snake was coiled around one of the upper branches, just withdrawing its head from the bird's nest. Its jaws were distended with the egg it had stolen. It swallowed the egg whole, throat bulging hugely with its meal. The bird hovered around the snake's head, giving its pitiful wail of, "Say, say, what's he saying!"

"Get away!" Beatrice shouted at the snake. It looked in the direction of the sound, but didn't back off. The gulping motion of its body as it forced the egg farther down its own throat made Beatrice shudder. Then, oblivious to the fluttering of the parent bird, it arched its head over the nest again. Beatrice pushed herself to her feet and ran into the yard. "Hsst! Shoo! Come away from there!" But the snake took a second egg.

Sammy kept a long pole with a hook at one end leaned against the guava tree for pulling down the fruit. Beatrice grabbed up the pole, started jooking it at the branches as close to the bird and nest as she dared. "Leave them, you brute! Leave!" The pole connected with some of the boughs. The two bottles in the tree fell to the ground and shattered with a crash. A hot breeze sprang up. The snake slithered away quickly, two eggs bulging in its throat. The bird flew off, sobbing to itself.

Nothing she could do now. When Samuel came home, he would

hunt the nasty snake down for her and kill it. She leaned the pole back against the tree.

The light breeze should have brought some coolness, but really it only made the day warmer. Two little dust devils danced briefly around Beatrice. They swirled across the yard, swung up into the air, and dashed themselves to powder against the shuttered window of the third bedroom.

Beatrice got her sandals from the verandah. Sammy wouldn't like it if she stepped on broken glass. She picked up the broom that was leaned against the house and began to sweep up the shards of bottle. She hoped Samuel wouldn't be too angry with her. He wasn't a man to cross, could be as stern as a father if he had a mind to.

That was mostly what she remembered about Daddy, his temper— quick to show and just as quick to go. So was he; had left his family before Beatrice turned five. The one cherished memory she had of him was of being swung back and forth through the air, her two small hands clasped in one big hand of his, her feet held tight in another. Safe. And as he swung her through the air her daddy had been chanting words from an old-time story:

> *Yung-Kyung-Pyung, what a pretty basket!*
> *Margaret Powell Alone, what a pretty basket!*
> *Eggie-law, what a pretty basket!*

Then he had held her tight to his chest, forcing the air from her lungs in a breathless giggle. The dressing-down Mummy had given him for that game! "You want to drop the child and crack her head open on the hard ground? Ee? Why you can't be more responsible?"

"Responsible?" he'd snapped. "Is who working like dog sunup to sundown to put food in oonuh belly?" He'd set Beatrice down, her feet hitting the ground with a jar. She'd started to cry, but he'd just pushed her toward her mother and stormed out of the room. One more volley in the constant battle between them. After he'd left them Mummy had opened the little food shop in town to make ends meet. In the evenings, Beatrice would rub lotion into her mother's chapped, work-wrinkled hands. "See how that man make us come down in the world?" Mummy would grumble. "Look at what I come to."

Privately, Beatrice thought maybe all Daddy had needed was a little patience. Mummy was too harsh, much as Beatrice loved her. To please her, Beatrice had studied hard all through high school: physics, chemistry, biology, describing the results of her lab experiments in her copy book in her cramped, resigned handwriting. Her mother greeted every A with a non-committal grunt and anything less with a lecture. Beatrice would smile airily, seal the hurt away, pretend the approval meant nothing to her. She still worked hard, but she kept some time for play of her own. Rounders, netball, and later, boys. All those boys, wanting a chance for a little sweetness with a light-skin browning like her. Beatrice had discovered her appeal quickly.

"Leggo beast . . ." Loose woman. The hissed words came from a knot of girls that slouched past Beatrice as she sat on the library steps, waiting for Clifton to come and pick her up. She willed her ears shut, smothered the sting of the words. But she knew some of those girls. Marguerita, Deborah. They used to be friends of hers. Though she sat up proudly, she found her fingers tugging self-consciously at the hem of her short white skirt. She put the big physics textbook in her lap, where it gave her thighs a little more coverage.

The farting vroom of Clifton's motorcyle interrupted her thoughts. Grinning, he slewed the bike to a dramatic halt in front of her. "Study time done now, darling. Time to play."

He looked good this evening, as he always did. Tight white shirt, jeans that showed off the bulges of his thighs. The crinkle of the thin gold chain at his neck set off his dark brown skin. Beatrice stood, tucked the physics text under her arm, smoothed the skirt over her hips. Clifton's eyes followed the movement of her hands. See, it didn't take much to make people treat you nice. She smiled at him.

Samuel would still show up hopefully every so often to ask her to accompany him on a drive through the country. He was so much older than all her other suitors. And dry? Country drives, Lord! She went out with him a few times; he was so persistent and she couldn't figure out how to tell him no. He didn't seem to get her hints that really she should be studying. Truth to tell, though, she started to find his quiet, undemanding presence soothing. His eggshell-white BMW took the graveled country roads so quietly that she could hear the kiskedee birds in the mango trees, chanting their query: *"Dit, dit, qu'est-ce qu'il dit?"*

One day Samuel brought her a gift.

"These are for you and your family," he said shyly, handing her a wrinkled paper bag. "I know your mother likes them." Inside were three plump eggplants from his kitchen garden, raised by his own hands. Beatrice took the humble gift out of the bag. The skins of the eggplants had a taut, blue sheen to them. Later she would realize that that was when she'd begun to love Samuel. He was stable, solid, responsible. He would make Mummy and her happy.

Beatrice gave in more to Samuel's diffident wooing. He was cultured and well spoken. He had been abroad, talked of exotic sports: ice hockey, downhill skiing. He took her to fancy restaurants she'd only heard of, that her other, young, unestablished boyfriends would never have been able to afford, and would probably only have embarrassed her if they had taken her. Samuel had polish. But he was humble, too, like the way he grew his own vegetables, or the self-deprecating tone in which he spoke of himself. He was always punctual, always courteous to her and her mother. Beatrice could count on him for little things, like picking her up after class, or driving her mother to the hairdresser's. With the other men, she always had to be on guard: pouting until they took her somewhere else for dinner, not another free meal in her mother's restaurant, wheedling them into using the condoms. She always had to hold something of herself shut away. With Samuel, Beatrice relaxed into trust.

"Beatrice, come! Come quick, nuh!"

Beatrice ran in from the backyard at the sound of her mother's voice. Had something happened to Mummy?

Her mother was sitting at the kitchen table, knife still poised to crack an egg into the bowl for the pound cake she was making to take to the shop.

She was staring in open-mouthed delight at Samuel, who was fretfully twisting the long stems on a bouquet of blood-red roses. "Lord, Beatrice; Samuel say he want to marry you!"

Beatrice looked to Sammy for verification. "Samuel," she asked unbelievingly, "what you saying? Is true?"

He nodded yes. "True, Beatrice."

Something gave way in Beatrice's chest, gently as a long-held breath. Her heart had been trapped in glass, and he'd freed it.

They'd been married two months later. Mummy was retired now; Samuel had bought her a little house in the suburbs, and he paid for the maid to come in three times a week. In the excitement of planning for the wedding, Beatrice had let her studying slip. To her dismay she finished her final year of university with barely a C average.

"Never mind, sweetness," Samuel told her. "I didn't like the idea of you studying, anyway. Is for children. You're a big woman now." Mummy had agreed with him too, said she didn't need all that now. She tried to argue with them, but Samuel was very clear about his wishes, and she'd stopped, not wanting anything to cause friction between them just yet. Despite his genteel manner, Samuel had just a bit of a temper. No point in crossing, it took so little to make him happy, and he was her love, the one man she'd found in whom she could have faith.

Besides, she was learning how to be the lady of the house, trying to use the right mix of authority and jocularity with Gloria, the maid, and Cleitis, the yardboy who came twice a month to do the mowing and the weeding. Odd to be giving orders to people when she was used to being the one taking orders, in Mummy's shop. It made her feel uncomfortable to tell people to do her work for her. Mummy said she should get used to it, it was her right now.

The sky rumbled with thunder. Still no rain. The warmth of the day was nice, but you could have too much of a good thing. Beatrice opened her mouth, gasping a little, trying to pull more air into her lungs. She was a little short of breath nowadays as the baby pressed on her diaphragm. She knew she could go inside for relief from the heat, but Samuel kept the air-conditioning on high, so cold that they could keep the butter in its dish on the kitchen counter. It never went rancid. Even insects refused to come inside. Sometimes Beatrice felt as though the house were really somewhere else, not the tropics. She had been used to waging constant war against ants and cockroaches, but not in Samuel's house. The cold in it made Beatrice shiver, dried her eyes out until they felt like boiled eggs sitting in their sockets. She went outside as often as possible, even though Samuel didn't like her to spend too much time in the sun. He said he feared that cancer would mar her soft skin, that he didn't want to lose another wife. But Beatrice knew he just didn't want her to get too brown. When the sun touched her, it brought out the sepia and cinnamon in her blood, overpowered the milk and honey, and he could no longer pretend she was white. He loved her skin pale. "Look how you gleam in the moonlight," he'd say to her when he made gentle, almost supplicating love to her at night in the four-poster bed. His hand would slide over her flesh, cup her breasts with an air of reverence. The look in his eyes was so close to worship that it sometimes frightened her. To be loved so much! He would whisper to her, "Beauty. Pale Beauty to my Beast," then blow a cool breath over the delicate membranes of her ear, making her shiver in delight. For her part, she loved to look at him, his molasses-dark skin, his broad chest, the way the planes of flat muscle slid across it. She imagined tectonic plates shifting in the earth. She loved the bluish-black cast the moonlight lent him. Once, gazing up at him as he loomed above her, body working against and in hers, she had seen the moonlight playing glints of deepest blue in his trim beard.

"Black Beauty," she had joked softly, reaching to pull his face closer for a kiss. At the words, he had lurched up off her to sit on the edge of the bed, pulling a sheet over him to hide his nakedness. Beatrice watched him, confused, feeling their blended sweat cooling along her body.

"Never call me that, please, Beatrice," he said softly. "You don't have to draw attention to my colour. I'm not a handsome man, and I know it. Black and ugly as my mother made me."

"But, Samuel . . . !"

"No."

Shadows lay between them on the bed. He wouldn't touch her again that night.

Beatrice sometimes wondered why Samuel hadn't married a white woman. She thought she knew the reason, though. She had seen the way that Samuel behaved around white people. He smiled too broadly, he simpered, he made silly jokes. It pained her to see it, and she could tell from the desperate look in his eyes that it hurt him too. For all his love of creamy white skin, Samuel probably couldn't have brought himself to approach a white woman the way he'd courted her.

The broken glass was in a neat pile under the guava tree. Time to make Samuel's dinner now. She went up the verandah stairs to the front door, stopping to wipe her sandals on the coir mat just outside the door. Samuel hated dust. As she opened the door, she felt another gust of warm wind at her back, blowing past her into the cool house. Quickly, she stepped inside and closed the door, so that the interior would stay as cool as Sammy liked it. The insulated door shut behind her with a hollow sound. It was air-tight. None of the windows in the house could be opened. She had asked Samuel, "Why you want to live in a box like this, sweetheart? The fresh air good for you."

"I don't like the heat, Beatrice. I don't like baking like meat in the sun. The sealed windows keep the conditioned air in." She hadn't argued.

She walked through the elegant, formal living room to the kitchen. She found the heavy imported furnishings cold and stuffy, but Samuel liked them.

In the kitchen she set water to boil and hunted a bit—where did Gloria keep it?—until she found the Dutch pot. She put it on the burner to toast the fragrant coriander seeds that would flavour the curry. She put on water to boil, stood staring at the steam rising from the pots. Dinner was going to be special tonight. Curried eggs, Samuel's favourite. The eggs in their cardboard case put Beatrice in mind of a trick she'd learned in physics class, for getting an egg unbroken into a narrow-mouthed bottle. You had to boil the egg hard and peel it, then stand a lit candle in the bottle. If you put the narrow end of the egg into the mouth of the bottle, it made a seal, and when the candle had burnt up all the air in the bottle, the vacuum it created would suck the egg in, whole. Beatrice had been the only one in her class patient enough to make the trick work. Patience was all her husband needed. Poor, mysterious Samuel had lost two wives in this isolated country home. He'd been rattling about in the airless house like the egg in the bottle. He kept to himself. The closest neighbours were miles away, and he didn't even know their names.

She was going to change all that, though. Invite her mother to stay for a while, maybe have a dinner party for the distant neighbours. Before her pregnancy made her too lethargic to do much.

A baby would complete their family. Samuel *would* be pleased, he would. She remembered him joking that no woman should have to give birth to his ugly black babies, but she would show him how beautiful their children would be, little brown bodies new as the earth after the rain. She would show him how to love himself in them.

It was hot in the kitchen. Perhaps the heat from the stove? Beatrice went out into the living room, wandered through the guest bedroom, the master bedroom, both bathrooms. The whole house was warmer than she'd ever felt it. Then she realized she could hear sounds coming from the outside, the cicadas singing loudly for rain. There was no whisper of cool air through the vents in the house. The air conditioner wasn't running.

Beatrice began to feel worried. Samuel liked it cold. She had planned tonight to be a special night for the two of them, but he wouldn't react well if everything wasn't to his liking. He'd raised his voice at her a few times. Once or twice he had stopped in the middle of an argument, one hand pulled back as if to strike, to take deep breaths, battling for self-control. His dark face would flush almost blue-black as he fought his rage down. Those times she'd stayed out of his way until he was calm again.

What could be wrong with the air conditioner? Maybe it had just come unplugged? Beatrice wasn't even sure where the controls were. Gloria and Samuel took care of everything around the house. She made another circuit through her home, looking for the main controls. Nothing. Puzzled, she went back into the living room. It was becoming thick and close as a womb inside their closed-up home.

There was only one room left to search. The locked third bedroom. Samuel had told her that both his wives had died in there, first one, then the other. He had given her the keys to every room in the house, but requested that she never open that particular door.

"I feel like it's bad luck, love. I know I'm just being superstitious, but I hope I can trust you to honour my wishes in this." She had, not wanting to cause him any anguish. But where else could the control panel be? It was getting so hot!

As she reached into her pocket for the keys she always carried with her, she realized she was still holding a raw egg in her hand. She'd forgotten to put it into the pot when the heat in the house had made her curious. She managed a little smile. The hormones flushing her body were making her so absent-minded: Samuel would tease her, until she told him why. Everything would be all right.

Beatrice put the egg into her other hand, got the keys out of her pocket, opened the door.

A wall of icy, dead air hit her body. It was freezing cold in the room. Her exhaled breath floated away from her in a long, misty curl. Frowning, she took a step inside and her eyes saw before her brain could understand, and when it did, the egg fell from her hands to smash open on the floor at her feet. Two women's mouths gaped open; frozen, gutted bellies, too. A fine sheen of ice crystals glazed their skin, which like hers were barely brown, but laved in gelid, rime-covered blood that had solidified ruby red. Beatrice whimpered.

"But Miss," Beatrice asked her teacher, "how the egg going to come back out the bottle again?"

"How do you think, Beatrice? There's only one way; you have to break the bottle."

This was how Samuel punished the ones who had tried to bring his babies into the world, his beautiful black babies. For each woman had had the muscled sac of her womb removed and placed on her belly, hacked open to reveal the purplish mass of her placenta. Beatrice knew that if she were to dissect the thawing tissue, she'd find a tiny foetus in each one. The dead women had been pregnant too.

A movement at her feet caught her eyes. She tore her gaze away from the bodies long enough to glance down. Writhing in the fast congealing yolk was a pin-feathered embryo. A rooster must have been at Mister Herbert's hens. She put her hand on her belly to still the sympathetic twitching of her womb. Her eyes were drawn back to the horror on the beds. Another whimper escaped her lips.

A sound like a sigh whispered in through the door she'd left open. A current of hot air seared past her cheek, making a plume of fog as it entered the room. The fog split into two, settled over the heads of each woman, began to take on definition. Each misty column had a face, contorted in rage. The faces were those of the bodies on the bed. One of the duppy women leaned over her own corpse. She lapped like a cat at the blood thawing on its breast. She became a little more solid for having drunk of her own life blood. The other duppy stooped to do the same. The two duppy women each had a belly slightly swollen with the pregnancies for which Samuel had killed them. Beatrice had broken the bottles that had confined the duppy wives, their bodies held in stasis because their spirits were trapped. She'd freed them. She'd let them into the house. Now there was nothing to cool their fury. The heat of it was warming the room up quickly.

The duppy wives held their bellies and glared at her, anger flaring hot behind their eyes. Beatrice backed away from the beds. "I didn't know," she said to the wives. "Don't vex with me. I didn't know what it is Samuel do to you."

Was that understanding on their faces, or were they beyond compassion?

"I making baby for him too. Have mercy on the baby, at least?"

Beatrice heard the *snik* of the front door opening. Samuel was home. He would have seen the broken bottles, would feel the warmth of the house. Beatrice felt that initial calm of the prey that realizes it has no choice but to turn and face the beast that is pursuing it. She wondered if Samuel would be able to read the truth hidden in her body, like the egg in the bottle.

"Is not me you should be vex with," she pleaded with the duppy wives. She took a deep breath and spoke the words that broke her heart. "Is . . . is Samuel who do this."

She could hear Samuel moving around in the house, the angry rumbling of his voice like the thunder before the storm. The words were muffled, but she could hear the anger in his tone. She called out, "What you saying, Samuel?"

She stepped out of the meat locker and quietly pulled the door in, but left it open slightly so the duppy wives could come out when they were ready. Then with a welcoming smile, she went to greet her husband. She would stall him as long as she could from entering the third bedroom. Most of the blood in the wives' bodies would be clotted, but maybe it was only important that it be *warm*. She hoped that enough of it would thaw soon for the duppies to drink until they were fully real.

When they had fed, would they come and save her, or would they take revenge on her, their usurper, as well as on Samuel?

Eggie-Law, what a pretty basket.

DESIRE

Kiini Ibura Salaam

(2004)

Sené. Pregnant Sené. Sené of the tired skin. She whose face held a million wrinkles, each one etched deeply as if carved over the course of forty years. Sené whose blood was only twenty-four years young.

[Faru, Faru running through the bush.]

The shining eyes of her boys made her smile, but not much else touched her. Not a full-throated bird's song, not the sun peeking pink at dawn, not her husband's fleeting caresses.

[Faru leaped right, darted left, his hoof
slipped and his hind legs buckled.
Faru stamped his front hoof,
shook himself off and leaped up again.]

Sené had hardworking hands: dry and cracked and bloated. With them she beat the dirt out of her family's cloths, scaled fish, pounded root vegetables, carried crops to her husband's mother, and avoided touching herself.

[Thin branches whipped against Faru's face as he ran.
Faru, the flawless. Faru, the godly. Faru reeking of thick sensuality.

His huge yellow goat eyes darted back and forth.
His lips—lips that forced one to think of sucking—lay open in a
forced pant. His nose—a nose that appeared to be full of the scent
of everything—quivered. His god's heart beat a fearful rhythm in
his chest. Desire—his and his sister Quashe's own special force—
throbbed through his skinny goat legs.
Desire. That which made Faru who he was.
Faru, Faru running through the bush.]

Sené's hands were always busy. Just now, they were sweeping out the
corners of the cliff dwelling she, her husband Na, and the two boys
called home. Now her hands were rolling up the sleeping mats and
tucking them away. Now they were building a fire.

[Faru heard the thump, thump of Laloro
thundering behind him. Laloro, great god of disease.
Faru did not look back. He reached the edge
of the bush and teetered on the edge of the cliff.]

Sené pulled down a bundle of lemongrass from the hanging basket.
She squatted, one hard hand holding her bulging belly. She threw
the fragrant herb into the pot and watched as the bits danced and
dove with the boiling water.

[Faru glanced over his shoulder. Laloro—huge and angry,
a godly elephant covered in hideous warts—charged at him.
Faru jumped. His hooves found footholds on the slenderest
of rock surfaces. He bounded from rock to rock until he landed
on a large outcropping. Faru skidded to a stop.]

Rocks tumbled across the entrance to Sené's home. She put her
hands to her knees and strained to rise. Her joints throbbed as she
shuffled to the entrance of her dwelling.

Faru jumped down from Sené's roof and landed on all fours. Sené
opened her cracked lips to scream, but the sound died in her throat.

Faru rose on his hind legs and stretched, exposing the expanse of his human torso to Sené's gaze. The thrumming of thousands of dragonfly wings beat in her chest. Without closing her open mouth, she bent down to one knee.

Faru preened as he always did when admiring eyes drank in the vision of him. He was a god, yes, but he was vain. He twisted his body this way and that. Light languished across his fur in shimmering waves. He brushed his hooves from wrist to shoulder, from ankle to hip. He smoothed the flat gray circle of fur collaring his throat. Sené was powerless to look away.

Faru fixed his luminous eyes in Sené's direction. He licked his lips. A muscle in his jaw flexed as his nose twitched. Sené held herself stiff until the tea hissed and spilled over. Wet tumbled into the fire.

Sené leapt to her bare feet. "Faru, honorable one, would you like some lemongrass?"

"No, no time," Faru said. "Come."

Sené's skin pulsed as she neared the god. She stood, shaking before him, waiting. With a grunt Faru grabbed Sené by the neck. His hooves scratched her skin. Godly lips pressed against common ones. A godly tongue coaxed Sené's mouth open. She gagged, almost choking as an intangible force flowed down her throat.

[A large shadow swooped across the opening of Sené's home.]

Faru broke away from Sené. Her muscles twitched; her brow lay crumpled, bewildered.

"Don't leave here," Faru said, "I'll return."

With that, he turned and bounded away.

[Laloro swooped by the cliffs.
Laloro flying by on chicken's wings.
The tiny appendages didn't seem enough

to hold his elephant heft. He delighted in this,
the most surprising of his godly powers,
but he wanted more.]

Sené. Sené full of dancing light. Laughter long buried came twisting
up into her throat. She stared at the empty space where Faru had
held her, and clapped her hand over her mouth. Giggles seeped from
between her fingers.

The lemongrass hissed again. Sené looked over at the fire. Even the
water, boiling over, seemed something to delight in. She bent down
over the water, dreamily drumming her fingers on her cheek. Her lips
would not lie flat. They twisted up and open, surprising Sené with ir-
repressible mirth.

[The moment Faru reached the top of the cliffs,
Laloro wrapped his trunk around Faru's body
and flew into the thick of the bush.]

Sené tipped the tea over, dousing the fire. Her nostrils flared as the
scent of lemongrass filled the dwelling. Inexplicably, she began to rub
the back of her hand over her face. Her fingers wound into her hair,
curling the rough strands into knots, then setting them loose. She
smoothed her eyebrows, massaged her neck. Those hard ugly hands
found delight in the curves of her body. Her breasts, sagging and full,
were a wonder to touch. So was the tight swell of her belly.

[Laloro did not care that his trunk made breathing hard for Faru.
In fact, he coiled his trunk tighter. Faru laughed.
"What's so funny, doomed one?" Laloro asked.
"I have nothing for you. It's gone," Faru said.
Laloro's tiny eyes rolled in their sockets.
"I want the bewitching power and I want it now,"
Laloro said. Faru laughed again.
"My sister will not fall for such tricks," Faru said. "Quashe
will not be seduced by an ugly hulk of flesh covered in warts."

"Shut up Faru," Laloro roared.
"Give me the power or I will crush you."]

Sené's hardworking hands parted the front of her cloth. Her finger-tips alighted on the curly tangle of hair between her thighs. Lust un-curled and snaked in dizzying circles inside her loins. Her feet, bare and flat, backed her body to the wall. She trembled and pushed her spine against the rock. It was with pleasure that her hand swiveled and writhed, her hips rotating in delight.

["Where is it?" Laloro asked.
"I've lost it," Faru said. "Nobody's perfect;
even gods have their days off."
Laloro stared deeply into Faru's eyes.
Faru looked back, unblinking. Laloro knew, from the calm
in Faru's face, that he was telling the truth.
Laloro unfurled his trunk and dropped Faru to the ground.
"I'll get it one day," Laloro said. "Even if I have to
make up a disease to kill you. Desire will be mine."]

Sené's fingers were knuckle-deep inside herself. She was reaching for the mirth that Faru had trickled down her throat. Reaching to stroke the sudden burst of joy filling all the tired and flat parts of her. When she was trembling, pleasure shooting from the pressure of her fingers, all of her skin sighed. She withdrew her wet fingers and used her own juices to draw patterns on the wall. Each mark was a re-minder of this sensation; a sign to her self, a message to her husband Na, that everything had changed.

Sené. Slow Sené. Sené of the new urges climbed down the cliff. She crossed the dangerous ledges and narrow passes carefully. As she stepped down onto flat ground, she glanced up at the peak of the cliff. She saw two forms running there. The wind carried their laugh-ter to her. They were, unmistakably, her boys. "Na," she yelled, ex-pecting to see her husband's form just behind them. Instead, she saw the large frame of Na's mother lumbering in the distance. Just as she was wondering where Na could be, a hummingbird hovered near her ear. Her heart leaped and she felt Faru's power pulsating inside her.

Sené swayed through the meadow, her thoughts suddenly preoccupied by a flock of yellow butterflies. She was sensitive to all sensations: the wind on her cheeks, the sun on her shoulder, the tall grass brushing against her hips. From the other side of the meadow, she could smell the sweet, sharp scent of ripe berries. In seconds, she was squashing berry juice across her lips, tucking little buds of fruit under her tongue.

[Faru, Faru running to the cliffs.]

When her belly was full, Sené's skin ached for coolness. She headed straight for the river, Quashe's river. As she neared the riverbank, before her toes met the moist river earth, before she could submerge her fingers into the cool dark waters, Sené heard the deep bouncing of her husband Na's laughter.

[Faru leaped down from Sené's roof and landed on all fours. He snorted. The sight of her empty dwelling tore through him. Faru, Faru. Without the power of desire, his breath did not call forth horny submission. His presence did not attract an aroused audience of winged and slithering and walking things. He was invisible. No one desired him, and the horror of it pained him.]

Na? Laughing? Sené crept along the bank toward the unfamiliar sound. She hid behind a tree and peered around the trunk. Na was sitting, legs spread, feet dipped in the water, the seductive crocodile head of Quashe—goddess of desire—leaning against his bare chest. Quashe's back formed one gleaming stretch of reptile skin. Her torso, neck, and arms were honey amber, human-soft skin moist with river dew. Na's fingers were sticky with her. His palms full of tight god breasts, his grasp cupping the curve of fertile god belly. Quashe's thick tail swished back and forth as she dripped water into Na's mouth from her crocodile snout.

[Faru, Faru needing the power of desire
just as Sené needed breath.]

A flash of anger interrupted Sené's joy. How could Na be sharing sweetness with this . . . this . . . crocodile god? Without a thought, she opened her mouth and sang a cracked and imperfect love song:

"Lover the length of you
Your weight between my thighs
Lover the scent of you
An oasis of sighs"

Both Quashe and Na turned to face the sound of Sené's singing. Sené. Sené who had so long been a dry discarded thing, stepped toward her husband. Unwavering, she pointed her big belly right at him and sang him to his feet.

Na was, for a few seconds, stilled, his body trapped between godly pleasures and the pull of his wife. Not his wife, a juicy apparition of Sené as a goddess; Sené as a queen, a swarm of butterflies hovering over her holy head.

[Laloro found Faru, bereft, lying flat on his back outside
of Sené's dwelling. Laloro laughed aloud.
"You really have lost it?" he sneered,
hovering close to Faru's face.
"Shower me with some horrible disease,"
Faru said, reaching for Laloro's trunk.
"Give me some fatal sickness or leave me alone."]

To Na's ears, Sené's song was nothing less than enchanting. In the thrall of her voice, he forgot about Quashe. He forgot the honeyed skin that coaxed him through a labyrinth of pleasure. Quashe—who gifted him with fish and seduction—slipped from his mind.

Sené opened her arms to her husband and he stepped into them.
Neither of them heard Quashe snarl. Their hands too busy groping
each other, fingers remembering a dance from old forgotten times.

[Laloro took pity on Faru. "Climb onto my back,"
Laloro said. "And I'll fly you to the Old One."
Faru climbed on without
complaining about Laloro's warts.
"You are weak," Laloro teased.
"Worse than a mortal. The great vain Faru
begging ugly Laloro to disease him?"
Laloro raised his trunk and pointed it at Faru as he flew.
"Shall I do it? Shall I put you out of your misery?"
Faru's lips didn't move in response.]

Quashe lifted her snout and shrieked a series of clicks and trills.
Teeth bared, she belched. With every belch, a ripple disturbed the
surface of the river. As Sené and Na's tongues found each other's
throats, tasted each other's salt and dirt, Quashe kept belching.

The river waters swirled, and finally folded in on themselves. From
the folds, a humongous crocodile surfaced, its back covered with
algae. It lumbered onto shore, barreling between Sené and Na at the
point of Quashe's finger. Sené screamed as the creature, paying no
heed to her belly, knocked her onto her back.

[Laloro dumped Faru at the entrance to the
Old One's cave. With his trunk, he tipped
the bell to announce their presence.
The Old One's voice drifted out in irritation.
"Who is it calling so loudly?" he demanded.
"Oh, honored elder, it is Laloro.
I am dropping Faru here at his request."
"How rude," muttered the Old One.
He approached the mouth of his cave slowly.
His old gnarled hands clutched two ancient wooden canes.

His long white cloths trailed behind him in the dirt as he approached at a snail's pace. Each of his steps was executed with an enormous amount of concentration and energy.

"Have you no knowledge of protocol?" the Old One said when he finally came face to face with Laloro.

Laloro dropped to one knee and rubbed the pads of his feet together.

"Great one, without whom we'd have no accordance, great settler of confusing matters, we are blessed to be in your presence."

"Yes, child," said the Old One, rubbing his groin. "How can I be of service?"]

Still Na had no eyes for Quashe. He leaped onto the crocodile's back and twisted his arms around its neck. The crocodile shook its massive head and Na went flying into a tree. His head thudded against bark. He lost consciousness and Quashe laughed.

Quashe sprang onto the crocodile's back and looked down on Sené. As the god searched Sené's face, river snakes slithered up the riverbank. The snakes slid over the crocodile's back and settled in coils around Quashe's arms and waist. Quashe stared without a blink of her reptilian eyes. She stared until the secret to Sené's power was revealed to her. When she recognized it—the force Sené used to attract Na—Quashe threw her head back and laughed.

[The Old One sniffed and wiggled his nose toward the gourd bowl that rested on the floor near the cave entrance. Faru didn't move. Laloro sighed and dropped a few coins into the bowl. The Old One sniffed and looked at Laloro disdainfully. Laloro dropped a few more coins into the bowl.

"So Faru has given away his powers, and now he's sick and wants my help," said the Old One.

"That is correct," said Laloro, gazing longingly in the direction of Quashe's river.

"Why would such a vain god do such a thing?" asked the Old One. Laloro blushed. He scratched a patch of dry skin on his back. His skin flaked and fell to the grass. The grass turned brown and wilted.]

"Faru," Quashe said, recognizing the mark of her brother. She leaned forward and opened her huge crocodile mouth over Sené's face. A forked tongue flipped from the flat of her mouth and flicked over Sené's lips. Sené turned her head away. Quashe's snakes writhed. "Open," she demanded. Sené clamped her mouth shut. Quashe released a snake. It slid around Sené's neck into a tighter and tighter yoke until Sené's mouth burst open in panic.

Quashe's tongue wrestled Sené's. Sené choked and tried to scream. It was useless. Quashe speared the power Faru had banked in Sené's body and swallowed it. Power sparked through her divine thighs as she leaned back, satisfied.

["It appears you are somehow involved in this matter. Speak, Laloro," said the Old One. Laloro dug into the earth with one huge foot. "I threatened him," Laloro said. "What's that?" asked the Old One. "I told him I would kill him if he didn't deliver his power of desire," said Laloro. "Rather than give it to me, he hid it somewhere; now he can't find it." "Ahh," said the Old One, rubbing his nipples thoughtfully, "you have created discord among the gods. I believe you should throw more coins into my gourd."]

"Now, let us see who Na finds more desirable," said Quashe, stretching languidly across the crocodile's back. She sent her snakes slithering over to Na. Each snake curled around a different limb. Together, they pumped blood through his body, forcefully, consistently, until Na's eyes fluttered and he returned to consciousness.

Na's heart constricted at the sight of Sené trapped beneath reptilian heft. Then Quashe called to him. His gaze leaped from Sené to

Quashe, who lay on top of the Sené-crocodile-Quashe pile. Quashe's voice yanked all of him into stiff hardness. Quashe shook with clicking laughter and leaned over to confront Sené. "You cannot hold the desire of gods, ugly one. I should let my crocodile eat you for trying."

A brief flash of emotion sparked in Na's eyes, but he remained silent. Every inch of him strained toward Quashe, but, entranced or not, he knew the rules: not without Quashe's permission. "Stay there," Quashe barked at him and commanded her crocodile to back off Sené. "You have refused me. I must find something sweet to clean myself of this bitterness. Stay standing until I return."

> [Faru's powers surged in Quashe's body. She sat stiffly, eyes trained forward, as she nudged her crocodile in the direction of the cliffs. Na's betrayal pulsed in her memory over and over, goading her to seek a few men to ravish.]

Night fell and Sené did not want to move. She heard Na crying and gasping as he stood immobilized, waiting for Quashe's return. Sené put her hands over her ears. The contact of hand to skin ran through her body like lightning. Her fingers fluttered. She thought this day's delight was due to Faru's gift, but here she was, still shocking herself with sweetness.

Sené ran a finger from her forehead to her chin. Her skin shivered. She held her hands before her face. They looked just as they had always looked: dry, cracked, swollen. Yet today, they had done different things. She had fed herself berries, lured her husband away from a goddess, and painted the walls of her dwelling with the juices from her own coming.

> [A flapping sound echoed in Quashe's ears. As she crossed the meadow, fruit bats attracted by the double sweetness vibrating under her skin hovered close. The first bite happened quickly. A dark figure swooped by and nipped the soft of Quashe's throat. Her hand leaped to her neck. She lay flat and hugged her crocodile,

hoping to protect the human parts of her body by keeping her tough crocodile scales facing the sky. Another dark winged figure swooped by and broke the skin at her elbow. Quashe yelled at the top of her lungs. "Aaaaaaiiiiiiieeeeeeee."]

Sené rolled onto her side and paused, waiting for the prickly pain in her limbs to subside. She climbed up onto her hands and knees. With each movement, an ache rippled through her muscles, reminding her of the terrible weight of the crocodile. As she crawled over to Na, she felt her blood circulating fiercely through her body. When she reached him, she pressed her cheek against his shins. A bout of dizziness swept over her. She settled herself against the earth and lay curled around Na's feet.

["Quashe!" Laloro yelled upon hearing Quashe's scream. "Old One, I must go," said Laloro. "Quashe needs me." "Yes," said the Old One. "Go help Quashe and bring her back here, I believe she can help with Faru's problem."]

Sené touched her charged hands to Na's ankles. Her fingers massaged their way up his calves and shins. She pressed her thumbs into the indentations behind his knees. Tears crept down her face. Her fingers shook. But she kept touching him.

Sené rose to her knees and kneaded Na's thighs and his buttocks. Her hardworking hands drifted up his spine, pushing energy through immobilized muscles. She spread her fingers over his back and raked her fingernails across his skin. She did not think of pain or pleasure; she wanted only to bring Na back to life.

[Laloro flapped his tiny chicken wings and flew in the direction of Quashe's screaming. When he reached the meadow, all he could make out was Quashe's huge crocodile and a Quashe-sized lump covered in bats. Even before landing, Laloro pointed his trunk at the bats and covered them with a spray of bat plague.

The furry black wings began quivering. Bat skin bubbled, bat bodies burst into flame. Laloro took a deep breath and blew all the burning creatures from Quashe's back. Quashe raised her beautiful crocodile head and looked at Laloro, eyes glittering in gratitude.]

Sené stood, her belly brushing against Na's back. If she closed her eyes, she could feel him shivering, ever so slightly. Her arms tightened around his torso and she massaged his chest and belly. Her teeth found his neck. She pinched his skin with little bites. Still Na did not move.

When Sené faced Na, he didn't blink. It was almost as if he couldn't see her. She stroked his forehead with thoughtful fingers. Her hard, raw hands danced gracefully over the contours of his face. "Come back, husband," she whispered, "please. Quashe doesn't care about you." She rubbed his ears. "Na," she whispered, "please, return to me."

[Quashe touched Laloro's warted skin and he almost burst from pleasure. She looked at him with new eyes, seeing for the first time how useful he could be. "I hope . . ." she said in a wavering voice, "I hope I can call on you again." Laloro bowed, "I'm at your service always."]

Sené pressed her lips against her husband's. She no longer had Faru's desire coursing though her body, but she was resolved to bring Na back. Her tongue darted out and licked Na's lips. She barely felt a tremor through his body. Her tongue darted out again, this time parting Na's lips, moistening his dry mouth with her saliva.

Sené pried Na's mouth open with her fingers. It had worked for Faru and Quashe. Why shouldn't it work for her? Her tongue fought past the barrier of Na's teeth. It danced along his gums, tapping a few times against the roof of his mouth. Sené rubbed her tongue against her husband's, trying, through sheer will, to rouse him from Quashe's spell.

Sené took a deep breath and blew all she had down Na's throat. She blew the remembered delight of lying together in the grass, her strong fingers on his bare hip, their lips all over each other way before marriage and children. She blew the memories of Na rushing home from the river to hold their new son and ask gentle whispered questions of all the new things the baby had done that day. She blew everything that had been aroused in her today. Finally he began to blink. His tears sprinkled Sené's face. "Sené," he said, "forgive me. I'm so sorry." He took her callused hand in his and pressed his lips against her knuckles.

"Shhhhhh," Sené said. "Please husband, let's go home."

[Deep in the Old One's cave, old fingers dribbled honey in intricate swirling patterns on the floor. Faru lay inert at one end of the design. When Laloro delivered Quashe to the other end of the design, the Old One sprinkled brother and sister with cinnamon. "Laloro," the Old One said, "I am calling on my brothers to help. Please stay in the corner until they have safely gone again. You would not want to pay the price if you should accidentally crush one of them." Laloro backed away and agreed not to move. The Old One rested one of his canes against his hip and pulled a tiny snail's shell from the folds of his cloth. He blew a thin high-pitched shrill from it, and a parade of snails slowly crawled into the room. The Old One took the lead, and his brothers followed, treading a circle around Quashe and Faru. The pace was slow, but the Old One's powers were potent. With each shuffle of the Old One's feet, each undulation of his snail brothers' bodies, Quashe's wounds healed. Once the Old One and his brothers completed a full revolution, once Quashe's skin was once again made whole, Faru's powers slipped from Quashe's body and returned to his.]

*   *   *

Sené and Na supported each other all the way home. Na stroked Sené's arms. Sené squeezed Na's hip. As they climbed, Na pulled Sené up the cliff when her belly became an intrusion. At the top of the cliffs, Sené turned away from home, walking in the direction of Na's mother's dwelling. "Sené, sweet wife," said Na. "Where are you going?" "To get the children, Na. Did you not leave them with your mother?" Na shuddered at Sené's unspoken words. Her intonation reminded him that just that morning he had abandoned Sené and his children in favor of Quashe's delights. He took Sené's hand. "They are safe with Mother. Let us go home and be new with each other."

The cave was spilling over with the scent of Sené's juices. It was an intoxicating thing, but Sené was no longer enchanted. There were things that needed to be done. She reached into the hanging basket and grabbed an armful of twigs. She dumped them onto the fire pile and kneeled to light a fire. Na stopped her. With the scent of her vibrating in his chest, he lifted her to her feet. Trembling, as if this were indeed new, he pulled her to the mats. With his free hand, he tipped two mats to the floor and unrolled them with his foot.

[The Old One lay curled in the corner, snoring. The floor was clear of his snail brothers and Quashe was stirring. Laloro lifted Quashe in his trunk and carried her outside. Both she and her crocodile mounted his great diseased back and he flew them home. Quashe sent her crocodile down into the river as Laloro paced the riverbank. She stepped into the waters. Laloro watched as the river swirled around her. Quashe began to sink home, then paused. "Will you be waiting there for me?" she asked. "Perhaps we can feed together when I rise." Laloro could not speak. Quashe lifted her tail and slapped it hard against the water's surface. Drops of water splashed Laloro's face. He lifted his trunk and trumpeted a loud "yes."]

Na kneeled before Sené, parted her cloth, and rubbed her bare belly. He rubbed his chin between her thighs and kissed her moistness. Sené looked into her husband's eyes as if questioning the reality of the moment. Na lay back on the mats and opened his arms to Sené.

She lowered to her knees and settled herself in her husband's embrace.

[Faru, Faru bounding up the cliff.]

[Rocks flew away from Faru's angry hooves as he rushed toward Sené and Na's cave. Despite his joy at his powers being returned to him, Faru was not satisfied. Sené had disobeyed him. He could see the scar he intended to rip across her face. He would not kill her, he would do worse; he would kill anything desirable about her. Faru's goat eyes flashed at the end of Sené and Na's home. He reared up on his hind legs, ready to attack. But they did not see him. They saw only each other's stretches of skin. Faru's anger turned to wonder as he watched their hands squeezing love into each other's bodies. How could they be touching each other in that way? Sené was an old used-up woman. How could she be calling up such desire from Na? Faru dropped down to all four hooves and backed away. He suddenly felt as weak as Laloro accused him of being. He hesitated at the mouth of the cave. Was there some powerful entity such as himself conjuring up the magic on Sené and Na's behalf? He listened to the power of desire pounding in his blood. He would not allow himself to recall what it had been like without it. Sené felt its power, yet she had not died without it. She was moving, breathing, calling forth the power of passion without Faru's magic.]

[Faru, Faru pausing for the truth.]

[A moth brushed against Faru's ear. Behind him a pack of flying night creatures swarmed. He turned away from Sené and Na. The flying things brushed against his skin, thrumming with desire. Faru laughed and went bounding up the hill toward the bush. He leaped and twisted with his throng of admirers. Sené and Na were forgotten forms, coupling mysteriously on the periphery of his memory. He sprang to the top of the cliff, reveling in his power to

make all living things horny. As he leaped into the bush, ecstasy exploded inside him. He heard the hoarse groans of animals bellowing in heat.
It seemed as if the entire night was singing a love song to him.
Faru parted his godly lips and let out a triumphant yell.]

[Faru, Faru running through the bush.]

RECOVERY FROM A FALL

David Findlay

(2004)

Sometimes I feel like a motherless child ... a long way from home.

—African-American spiritual

Junior sat in the sun at the junction of two back roads miles from nowhere, spitting crabapple juice on the steaming tarmac. He was tired, stoned, and uncomfortably overdressed in leather trousers. An old injury in his side ached as if it were new. The pipe they'd been smoking was hot and cracked and the filter had fallen out.

Ants and sow bugs rolled and crept around his feet, doves and eagles flew above him across the expanse of sky. In the range between heaven and earth, a whining buzz resolved into a large mosquito, which landed on his cheek. Junior felt the caress of tiny feet, light as Lily's dreadlocks had touched when she'd bent to kiss him.

Years ago, Lily had stalked off cursing into the garden, her belly full with child. There were lots of rumors, but no one knew where she'd got to. Not much had worked out since she took off. In her place, Zoe had appeared while he was passed out, drifting in and out of his life to fight, fuck, get pregnant, and leave again. He and she had figured out how to do that much on their own, unguided and without example. The consequences were more complex. Junior was the first of his line, and parenting felt like an alien chore.

He couldn't guess what compelled Zoe to return, but two quarrelsome sons and many years later, she seemed to be back. It must be her. Junior watched her erratic, twitchy pacing from the corner of his eye. Looked like she'd been smoking rock for a while this time. She was still pretty, though. Round, big-eyed face, glasses, alluring hint of a double chin. Her bra strap had slipped down over one freckled, muscular shoulder.

The mosquito rammed its slender mouth through Junior's skin, tasted his blood, and dropped to the gravel motionless.

Zoe returned from her pacing and stood over the strange, familiar man. She laughed and grabbed his matches as he fiddled with the pipe.

Junior took a long time to look up at her face.

This pipe was a problem. Its tiny, bent, and thickly encrusted screen wouldn't wedge back properly in the bowl. This woman (Zoe? Was she still calling herself Zoe?) was a problem. She was going through his supply like it came for free. Now she held the matches in a sweaty hand, dangling them at her waist, fingering the cardboard and grinning like she knew shit about anything. Squatting at her feet, Junior calculated the reach to grab her ankle and yank, pictured that dazed, dreamy smile changing to shock as her world shifted a rapid ninety degrees. Bet she'd scream good and loud. Her features were pointier and paler than Lily's, her build less curvaceous but almost as solid. There were things he needed to remember about her. Important things, probably. For the moment, it was hard enough remembering her name. This wasn't Lily.

Zoe shifted her hips, stretched, and nearly fell over. Wobbly-legged, she got her footing, snorted self-consciously, readied for ridicule. He hadn't noticed, engrossed again in getting the screen to fit. She imagined the rasp of sun-warmed concrete against her nipples. Added a layer to the imagining: upthrust points of gravel digging into her belly and thighs, his cock and fingers filling her from above.

Zoe snorted again and hiked her shorts up a little higher, wondering how much of her crotch he could see from down there. If he would look. Maybe he'd turned gay or something. Usually men were ready to give her anything. This one, the original one, acted as if the drug were gold. Usually men (and women, too, sometimes) read her body language before she even knew she was flirting. They started the dance instantaneously, jockeyed for position around her, got jealous and territorial the second she looked at anyone else.

This one had just nodded when she first woke him. Not a word. Each time she came back was a struggle to make him acknowledge her presence. Damned dysfunctional bastard never learned to communicate. Eventually, this time, he had pulled the pipe from his waistband, loading it with irregular dull gray crystals while she paced before him, her boots crushing crabapples against asphalt.

She thought about walking away again. Still no contact here, no admission of what they were to each other, to the world. She stretched and considered, stared at his body one more time. The hard ridges of his shoulders and abdomen shaped shadow by gradations from dusty red through deep chocolate earth tones. His contours were accentuated by thin lines of scars, some crisp and sharp-edged, others faded to smudged blue suggestions. Maybe he'd spent more time in jail—some of the new ones looked pretty rough. Zoe absently, casually pulled her vest up a little farther so he could see the top of her own new snake tattoo where it arched across her belly.

Junior had first produced the pack of matches from his pocket, lit one over the pipe bowl, and inhaled until the crystals glowed and blackened at the edges. He'd sat, smoked, said nothing.

Fine. She wasn't looking for pillow talk anyway. Reaching for the pipe was as easy as any act of surrender.

Junior was sizzling. He sucked a long, deep lungful of blue smoke before passing the pipe. He could almost hear the popping and frying of nerves that marked the drug's passage through his body. Miles away above him, he saw her hand close around the stem, draw it to her mouth. She choked, sputtered, and tried again.

Woman. Other person. For a frightening second, Junior could envision her as a being like himself. Another fearful island of awareness looking out at impossible choices through flesh that felt and chafed and wanted like his. He exhaled, and the nightmare vision passed.

She still had a hurt-me vibe a mile wide. Her little thin-lipped mouth worked and pouted as if she was about to form words. She wore her bleached hair short and spiky, now. Just long enough to get a good handful, hold her head in place while he rubbed his cock across her face, across her lips, shoved it deep in her mouth.

Her eyes would water and look up at him and he'd push back into her throat. Junior's hard-on jumped against the sweaty leather. She'd been gone a long time. He'd have to start from scratch with her, work up to it slowly. Maybe talk romance and stuff.

You wanna go up behind the tracks and fuck? Zoe rehearsed the question and discarded it unsaid. Damned if she was gonna be the one to ask. In contrast to his silence, anything she said would come out whiny or loud like Lily. Screw that. What, was she supposed to do everything?

She could get dick anywhere she wanted. Anywhere. White guys, black guys, cops, bouncers . . . hell, this creep wasn't anything special. He just happened to have some rock when she wanted it. And a look like he was made outta hard-packed earth. Well made, this man, her first and only family. Zoe watched his long, strong hands as he loaded the pipe with a sprinkling of crystals, shaking them even in the bowl with a perfect concentration like he was tuning an instrument. Cicadas and the passing train were singing harmony. Frogs peeped rhythmic counterpoint.

No one else in sight. The way these strips of road curved up behind the station, she'd hear anyone coming before they were visible. He was nearly naked already. His bare feet were the brown of old beer-bottle glass on top, lined with gray creases and fading to bright pink on the edges. His soles, from what she could see, were asphalt-black. Toes thick around as—

Zoe kicked off her boots. Junior reached out his hand, shell-pink palm upturned.

Huh?

He looked up slow again. Wide, ageless brown face hung on high cheekbones. Spooky eyes, with glossy black pupils shrunk to pinpoints. Like you could tell anything from someone's eyes. What was he reaching for? Zoe stood her ground, stared back. Fucking creep.

Unless . . . maybe he wanted the matches. Where'd they go? She squirmed her hand into the near-useless ornamental front pockets of her faded suede shorts.

Not there. Searched in her back pockets, lingering a moment to let him see how the shorts tightened around her pussy with the added pressure. Not there.

Maybe he was just too stoned to react. Hands to her hips, beneath her waistband. Sweeping around her waist to undo the button. Junior held his hand out steadily. She drew the shorts down slowly, slowly. She looked down over the curve of her own bone-white belly and tried to see herself as he would. He had to be watching the dark horizontal line of sweat-soaked suede inching down to reveal her pubes: orange whorls on near-translucent skin. She paused, feeling the shorts like a second skin stretched tight over the widest point of her hips. A wiggle to dislodge them, then she was stepping free to feel the breeze and sunshine warm on her butt. This was what it must feel like being a kid, except this was sweeter, faster, nastier.

With the rock pumping in her system, it took a moment to figure out her next move. Half turning, she stuck out her chest and crept her fingers up under the vest. Was he still watching? He must be.

Zoe unbuttoned the vest and pulled her bra over her breasts, left it sitting around her shoulders. Guys like it when you're not quite naked. Still no one else in sight. Just him and her, and the station way over there shimmery with heat past the cedar, acacia, and scraggly crabapple trees. The cicadas changed key. Rising buzz from one tree, sliding down through the scale as another one answered from across the way.

How'd she get so goddamned wet? Fingers on the rings in her nipples, Zoe pulled and twisted harder than she'd like if anyone but her were doing it. She would not look over at him. Let him see how full and pointy they got. Let him see. . . .

Junior felt the sunshine like a rain of hammers. His breathing, her breathing, the train and cicadas and distant traffic all crashed and tumbled around him. This was good shit. He had more and it was ready—where'd she put the blessed matches!

Sun outlined her body in orange and silver. Zoe looked like she'd been dipped in fire.

The concrete was painfully hot beneath her hands. Maybe she'd fallen? No, that would have hurt more. Whatever the process was that got her to the ground, it must have been even easier and more natural than falling. Behind her, the man shifted. She heard change jingle in his pocket and the slow intake of his breath. They liked to watch her ass. They all did.

She was too high to balance on one hand. There it was, the road surface against her chest. Shit, that was hot! Her breasts stung, screamed where they touched the blazing tar. Zoe balanced her weight on knees and shoulders, laid her face on the discarded shorts, and wondered what the man was waiting for. Inches from her nose, the matchbook lay open on the pavement. One match left. She fingered her clit and spat out chunks of sour crabapple.

She was distracting. Lord knows he could use some distraction, some escape. Twice, he'd tried to inhale from the pipe before remembering it wasn't lit. Now it sat in the dust at his side. The woman in front of him looked sweet as ripe fruit. Her thighs flexed and quivered enticingly. Again, he was tempted.

You think those little white bitches you're chasing respect you? You think they see anything but a cock driving a wallet? Go ahead, run away. See where it gets you. Lily's voice was no quieter in his memory than it had been in person. She made everything so damned complicated, Lily did. Wonder what she was doing now?

The motion of Zoe's hand was steady between her puffy lower lips. Familiar rhythm, familiar image. Familiar pressure in his cock. Salt-sweet, the tang of her scent merged with the sharp fragrance of crabapple juice. Junior breathed deep and craned his head back. The sky was blue and flat and coming down to crush him. While he waited for it to fall, Junior watched the snake tattoo that curved around her waist to end against the plumpness of her ass. Its head was startlingly realistic, grinning in a splash of red and orange on her skin. As her muscles bunched, the snake's long, twisted tongue seemed to retract and advance toward her anus.

Zoe wiggled, stroked, eased two glistening fingers into her bright pink slit.

The snake tattoo said, "What you gonna do about it, crackhead?"

Junior and Zoe jumped. The voice was deep, raspy, and assured. This time it sounded like snooty Boston schooling filtered through millennia of smoke and whiskey.

Junior reflexively shifted his leg to cover the pipe, misjudged distance, and knocked it into gravel by the roadside.

"Smooth," said the snake.

Zoe was perfectly still.

"Sweeties," said the snake. "Relax a bit, we're going to try for a different vibe. Let's just forget the last few times ever happened. Now . . . Junior, just be yourself. If it helps, pretend she's me. Umm . . . the pants have gotta go."

Over her shoulder, Zoe squinted through fogged glasses as Junior stripped in relaxed obedience to the ageless voice. His pristine white undershorts were a shock. He *was* staring at her ass.

"I want you both to be perfectly natural. When I cue you, continue as you were, but fresh this time. Zoe, make some new choices about your motivation. Junior, lose the shorts already."

Zoe's return to rubbing her clit was instinctive and immensely comforting. Half closing her eyes made her spine the axis on which the planet spun dizzyingly.

She clutched at her wetness, clung to the earth, stroked farther and farther away into a heavy, tilted place that was all pumping blood and waiting for his touch. She pictured Lily scowling with sisterly concern, and deliberately overwrote the image with sensation spreading from her crotch and the memory of huge hands cradling her, delivering her whole.

Junior's eyes were also half closed. He focused his narrowed range of sight on the generous roundness of her rear and the toothy reptile guarding it.

"In five," said the snake. "And four, three, two . . . and ACTION."

Woodchucks and foxes gamboled among the trees. Earthworms and millipedes made space for each other in the warmth of Junior's discarded pants.

"Are you still my girl?" asked Junior, settling to his knees behind

Zoe. "We could do it another way. . . . It could be different." He clasped her hips in either hand, his fingers sinking deep.

"Bring it on, brother." Zoe's reply was quiet. "I am so ready. Let's make some magic." She drifted, felt his tongue competing with the snake's, his hands squeezing and spreading her wide. When he pulled away for breath, the breeze licked her moistened skin.

"So am I. Ready for a change." The tattoo squirmed beneath his hand and twisted free. Junior felt the dry, cool weight of the snake pouring around them. It shifted up his body, circling his torso and pushing his face back between Zoe's cheeks. He dripped sweat, saw bright shapes flickering across his drooping eyelids. Some large animal barked nearby.

"Deeper, daddy." Zoe giggled. "I know, I know. It just sounded right. Hell, you really are a daddy, now. How's it feel?"

Junior stretched his tongue past pain.

Zoe gasped. "Mmmm. Just like that."

There was a slithering constriction around his cock. The smooth-scaled pressure felt indescribably good. Where else was the snake squeezing? Was it lavishing as much attention on Zoe? Curious as he was, Junior would not, could not open his eyes any farther.

Zoe groaned. Her rectum tightened on his tongue.

"You're gorgeous, Junior," the snake whispered in his ear.

Junior sat up.

"Flattery will get you everywhere, Steve."

"Hope so," said the snake.

"Junior? Now? Please."

It was strange to hear her speak his name. Strange, too, not to reach for a rubber as he got into position behind her. There were red circles on her skin where his fingertips had pressed.

Steve unwrapped from his cock with a parting squeeze. Seemed like there was more of the snake every minute—longer and longer coils draped around both of them. Junior felt the forked tongue on his shaft, teeth gently nipping at his balls.

"This what you meant, girl?" Junior spread clear fluid on her fingers and outer lips with the head of his dick. "This what you were wanting?" Teased her open, drew back to paint wet strokes from perineum to clit, pressed in again just deep enough to feel her contracting around him.

Zoe thrashed in the snake's grip, struggling to envelop more of Junior's hardening dick. "I always wanted more than that. C'mon, honey. In me, all the way in me. Damn!" The flickering tongue danced between her fingers on her button, around and between them both.

Junior drew out all the way, pushed slowly in again, began a rhythm of slow, shallow strokes. Zoe roared and arched her back.

Steve hugged them both, bearing their weight and pressing them together, exploring Junior's asshole with his tail tip and hissing encouragement. His tongue was a whip, darting and teasing with impossible speed. In the trees, dim predatory shapes frolicked with small winged shadows, free and unnamed.

"Sis?" Junior pulled all the way out again, paused.

"Yeah?"

"Can you feel it?" he shifted closer, grabbing handfuls of her thighs and driving his full length into her. Hard. "It's happening. We're almost there. And you feel so fucking good! So sweet, you're wrapped around me tighter than I could—Hell, you're BOTH wrapped around me in the best way."

She ground back against him, crowed and growled her pleasure. A chorus of animal voices responded. Junior pumped deep and steady, eased his thumb into her ass and held on tight.

"Fabulous!" said the snake.

Zoe felt a loop close between imagination and actuality. She bit down on Steve's sinuous bulk where it slid before her face as the snake writhed around her. Junior's cock and thumb were the fiercest, slickest friction, filling her with alternating waves of heat and light. She remembered to breathe, tightening around the pleasure that flew up her backbone and reverberated through her body. The reverberations kindled deeper quakes, shaking up tears and memory and voices in her head.

"You can't go back," said the voices. Zoe went back to her orgasm.

Junior shrugged his shoulders loose from Steve's embrace. He got down on the road beside Zoe, laid his old friend's long body across her back. Between them they held her tight. Birdsong rang from the trees.

Zoe's glasses were cracked. Junior slid the bent frames from her head and tossed them away. Her vest came off easily, but the bra was a complex tangle around her neck and arms.

"What's with you? Lay off before you strangle me, man!" Zoe was laughing again, her face streaked with tear-soaked dust.

"Perhaps it's a gendered genetic problem," offered Steve. "The statistical incidence of men having traumatic or complex relationships to women's undergarments is proportionately—"

"Horseshit, you snake-who's-not-a-snake. If you had a buttcrack to get panties stuck in, you'd know better. Talk about traumatic! Gimme a fig leaf any day."

Junior was prudently silent. He lay on his back, watching the sky through slitted eyes and thinking about simplicity. A dark mass of angry storm was gathering in the sky to the east, headed toward them.

"I won't miss underwear," said Zoe, throwing the sodden bra into the bushes. "Or traffic, or nine-to-five, or superabsorbent tampons, or misguided missiles, or global warming." She leaned heavily on Junior's ribs, cupped his balls in one hand and massaged her cramped calves with the other.

"Or zoos, or fast food, or the World Bank, or always being the bad guy." Steve twined between their legs. Thunder muttered nearby.

"Or cops, or factory farming, or custody battles," Junior added. He chewed on Zoe's neck and angled his arm to stroke the snake.

"Stop that! It tickles." Zoe squeezed his balls warningly, felt him rub erect against her breasts, squeezed harder. "Won't miss televangelists, or driving tests, or banks."

"Or landlords, or harvesting combines, or walking upright."

"Easy for you to say," said Steve. "I've been crawling on my belly all the days of my life. Personally, I'm looking forward to limbs like you would not believe. Mind you, there are some advantages to this form." Steve licked at their sweaty crotches, flowing around Zoe's waist as she sat up and pulled Junior's cock into her.

"Sometimes I feel like I'm almost gone. . . ." Junior sang.

"Don't we all, brother? I guess the old guy's gonna be pissed at how much we're undoing, huh?" Zoe patted the asphalt beneath them until she found Junior's hands. The snake watched their fingers intertwine, relished the view from below and behind as Zoe rode the first man. The point of his tail found puckered sanctuary under Junior's testes and slid deep inside.

"Ah, mammals," Steve sighed. "Hold tight, kids. We are gathered here, far from prying eyes, to join this woman, man, and . . . snake, as they were once—No. Umm . . . As they have never been joined before. Simpler. Harder. Faster. Deeper . . ."

The snake's last words were bubbly and muffled as he pressed his slender head into Zoe's flesh. He paused, pushed, waited.

"I do," said Zoe. She felt the shifting inside, breathed openness and welcome and leaned down to kiss the first face she'd ever seen.

Junior returned her kiss and wondered what Lily would make of it all.

"I do," said Junior. "We do. What was the question?"

Steve pressed again, smooth as a ring on a finger into the fragrant warmth and darkness, drew the thickening bulk of his body after.

Zoe, Steve, and Junior bucked and humped, cried out to the darkening sky and flowed into each other. The threefold beast they had become stretched and righted itself, looked around to see the tail sticking out its backside, and howled joy. Where there had been eight limbs there were now four. Where there had been bare skin there was soft-furred hide. The nameless creature sniffed the matchbook in the dust and bounded away into the trees.

A first splatter of rain fell on new growth where roads had been. Lily tasted the rain blended with her tears, and it was good.

The downpour that followed washed eons of pain and promise to rest beneath the oceans. Lily watched the storm from the mountaintop, saw rainbows crest the fresh-grown forests as sun spat slivers of day from behind retreating clouds. She reached down to pet the hairy quadruped that gamboled without care around her bare feet. This time, it was going to be different.

ANANSI MEETS PETER PARKER
AT THE TACO BELL ON LEXINGTON

Douglas Kearney

(2000)

So i'm at the taco bell on lexington across the street from pizza hut & panda express. you know the one? i'm tryin to eat my sixty nine cent (times is hard) bean burrito when this cardigan wearin m.i.t. lookin muthafuckin shutterbug grubbin chilitos like a deep throatin flick chick clicks a pic of me.

now, crazy ain't my way, figure fool on some ansel adams kick, could be snappin shots of fast food spots & other americana ka-ka for the *ny post* the *daily planet* or the *times*. so i ig him, rip the plastic packet of semi-salsa, spread red on the skid marked tortilla taco bell call bean burrito (times is hard) when *click:* mr. shutterbug has another private kind of kodak minute with me in it. i say "do i look like tyra banks? best slow your roll or i'll crop your shot but good!" he reach in his pocket & pass me a business card. hmmph. "*peter parker* with the *daily bugle*? never heard of you." six inch thick glasses mask his face but i know he a white boy when he say he doin "research on quaint & obscure local characters" all national geographical & shit. i wave eight arms say, "i look obscure to you muthafucka?" he do a no offense crawfish, say "i mean, i've never seen anyone with your style.

Anansi is the major trickster figure of the Ashanti and Akan. He alternatively takes the form of a man or spider. Peter Parker is the secret identity of the American superhero, Spiderman.

i'll pay you if you let me take some more pictures" figure mr. pentax
pack stacks of dinero & bean burritos (times is hard) ain't been tasty
for awhile. & cash for a couple of shots—why not get over? so we step
outside. i profile against the wall like the baller i was back in the day.
tell him how i used to be a playa swingin hut to hut, chick to chick,
friendliest daddy-long-stroke in the hood. he smile like it's all good,
quit clickin pics, slip me two benjis, shake all my hands & he down
the street before you could say *chalupa*.

two weeks later benji lookin more like abe & i'm back at the border
orderin bean burritos (times is hard) when out the window i see some
jackass in red & blue spandex swingin down lexington with some
half-ass spider moves. next day the same clown get front page of
the—*daily bugle*? hmmph *spiderman*. got his own book, tv show,
movie & everythang. ain't that a bitch. but i ain't bitter. ain't nothin
new. i mean you saw what happened to that nigga b'rer rabbit after
that bugs bunny shit. hmmph. couldn't be me cause see, it's like i told
you: crazy ain't my way.

The Magical Negro

Nnedi Okorafor-Mbachu

(2004)

Thor the Brave stood on the edge of the cliff panicking, his long blond hair blowing in the breeze. Behind him, they were coming fast through the lush grassy field. All Thor could do was stare, his cheeks flushed. Once upon him, they would suck the life from his soul, like lions sucking meat from the bones of a fresh kill. He held his long sword high. The sword's silver handle was encrusted with heavy blue jewels and it felt so right in his hand.

In that moment, he felt a deep love for his sword that had helped him bring justice to the world so many times. He'd fight to the end. His life for his country. If only he knew how the amulet around his neck worked. The ruby-red jewel bounced heavily against his chest as if to taunt him more with its difficult riddle. He was never very good at riddles. He took a deep breath, a tear falling down his rosy cheek.

"My life for my country," he whispered. "If it must come to this."

But it could have been better. It could have been more.

Any moment now. It wouldn't be quick and it would be very painful. The shadows were savage beasts. The horrible black things were known to skin a man alive, tear off his fingernails one by one, boil a man's flesh till it fell apart, dirty his very soul; all this would be done very slowly so that he wouldn't lose consciousness or go into shock. The shadows came from the heart of darkness in the forbidden zone.

I never should have gone there, he thought.

The shadows were almost upon him, devouring the light of the grassy field, leaving only rotten filthy blackness behind. Thor closed his eyes in a silent prayer for his beautiful fair wife and lovely daughter, Chastity, back at the castle. When Thor opened his eyes, he almost fell over the cliff. *What* is *that?* he thought.

Standing before the approaching shadows was an equally dark figure. The African man floated a few inches in the air, his large crown of puffy hair radiating from his head like a black explosion. His skin, a dirty brown, almost blended in with the shaded evil behind him. He held up a dark black hand and brought it to his thick lips.

"Shhh, no time," he said in a low smoky voice. He wore no shirt or shoes and carried no weapons. He'll be killed, Thor thought sadly. He didn't like the idea of someone else dying on the cliff with him. This moment was about his martyrdom only. Thor shook his head, his long blond hair shaking.

"Please, you must—"

"Look there's no time, so just listen," the African said. "The amulet responds to your heart."

The shadows were only meters away. Who is this man? Thor thought. Where did he come from? How can he levitate?

"Look deep within yourself. You have the power—you just haven't tapped into it. . . ."

The black man's eyes suddenly bulged and a dark red spot ate its way into the middle of his chest. He'd been pierced with an evil blackness deeper than his own. He fell to his knees, coughing up blood. The shadows paused behind him, as if to savor the death of the black man. Thor watched him with a sad frown. The man had only moments to live.

Then the African man looked up at him. Thor would have jumped back, but even in his fear he knew that to do so would send him prematurely plummeting to his death. The African man looked angry. Angry as hell.

"Yo, what the *fuck* is this bullshit!" He quickly stood up and looked at the red hole in his chest that was oozing blood and other fluids. "Oh *hell* no! It ain't goin' down like this. Damn, *how* many *times*? *Always* the same shit!"

He turned to the shadows and held up a black finger.

"Y'all should know better. They made you stupid or some shit?"

The looming shadows retreated. Thor was shocked. Could this man possibly be commanding the shadows? The shadows were pure evil power. How can he control them? The black man turned to Thor and pointed a finger.

"Look . . . *fuck you*." Then he looked up at the blue sky and said, "My ass comes here to save his ass and after I tell him what *he* needs to do, I get sixed? Whatchu think I am? Some fuckin' shuckin', jivin', happy Negro still dying for the massa 'cause my life ain't worth shit?"

He cocked his head and looked back at Thor.

"I'm the mutherfuckin' Magical Negro—what makes you think I'm gonna tell you how to use that damn amulet you been carrying around for two months because you too stupid to figure how to use it and then fuckin' die afterward? What world is you livin' in? Some kinda typical fantasy world from some typical fantasy book? Like I ain't got no family of my own to risk my life fo' and shit!"

The Magical Negro reached into the pocket of his black pants and brought out a fat cigar and a lighter. He lit it and took two puffs. He blew several rings and, with a wave of his hand, linked them into a chain that settled around his long neck. Then he laughed as the chain dissolved.

"I . . . I . . . in my heart?" Thor asked. He was terribly confused. He could barely understand the dark man. What a strange dialect he was speaking. Controlling evil darkness? Could it be because he had internalized the evil of the shadows? Could that be what turned his skin that horrible color? Blew out his lips? Gave him such a huge de-formed nose? Corrupted his hair? Thor frowned. Why am I thinking of such things in my last moments? He stepped forward, holding up his sword again, trying to look brave.

The Magical Negro shook his head.

"Had enough of this," the Magical Negro said. With a wave of his hand, Thor plunged over the cliff to his death. The Magical Negro listened for the thump of Thor's body on the rocks below. Then he smiled. He took a puff from his cigar. He picked up his black jacket that sat in the grass and shrugged it around his narrow shoulders. Then he picked up his black top hat and placed it on his head and laughed a wheezy laugh.

"Sheeeit," he drawled, looking directly at you, the reader. "All this bullshit you readin' is 'bout to change. The Magical Negro ain't gettin' his ass kicked 'round here no more."

The Magical Negro rested his red cane on his shoulder and leisurely strolled into the forest to see if he could find him some Hobbits, castles, Rastas, dragons, juke joints, princesses, and shit.

Jesus Christ in Texas

W. E. B. Du Bois

(1920)

It was in Waco, Texas.

The convict guard laughed. "I don't know," he said, "I hadn't thought of that." He hesitated and looked at the stranger curiously. In the solemn twilight he got an impression of unusual height and soft, dark eyes. "Curious sort of acquaintance for the colonel," he thought; then he continued aloud: "But that nigger there is bad, a born thief, and ought to be sent up for life; got ten years last time—"

Here the voice of the promoter, talking within, broke in; he was bending over his figures, sitting by the colonel. He was slight, with a sharp nose.

"The convicts," he said, "would cost us $96 a year and board. Well, we can squeeze this so that it won't be over $125 apiece. Now if these fellows are driven, they can build this line within twelve months. It will be running by next April. Freights will fall fifty per cent. Why, man, you'll be a millionaire in less than ten years."

The colonel started. He was a thick, short man, with a clean-shaven face and a certain air of breeding about the lines of his countenance; the word millionaire sounded well to his ears. He thought—he thought a great deal; he almost heard the puff of the fearfully costly automobile that was coming up the road, and he said:

"I suppose we might as well hire them."

"Of course," answered the promoter.

The voice of the tall stranger in the corner broke in here:

"It will be a good thing for them?" he said, half in question.

The colonel moved. "The guard makes strange friends," he thought to himself. "What's this man doing here, anyway?" He looked at him, or rather looked at his eyes, and then somehow he felt a warming toward him. He said:

"Well, at least, it can't harm them; they're beyond that."

"It will do them good, then," said the stranger again.

The promoter shrugged his shoulders. "It will do us good," he said.

But the colonel shook his head impatiently. He felt a desire to justify himself before those eyes, and he answered: "Yes, it will do them good; or at any rate it won't make them any worse than they are." Then he started to say something else, but here sure enough the sound of the automobile breathing at the gate stopped him and they all arose.

"It is settled, then," said the promoter.

"Yes," said the colonel, turning toward the stranger again. "Are you going into town?" he asked with the Southern courtesy of white men to white men in a country town. The stranger said he was. "Then come along in my machine. I want to talk with you about this."

They went out to the car. The stranger as he went turned again to look back at the convict. He was a tall, powerfully built black fellow. His face was sullen, with a low forehead, thick, hanging lips, and bitter eyes. There was revolt written about his mouth despite the hangdog expression. He stood bending over his pile of stones, pounding listlessly. Beside him stood a boy of twelve—yellow, with a hunted, crafty look. The convict raised his eyes and they met the eyes of the stranger. The hammer fell from his hands.

The stranger turned slowly toward the automobile and the colonel introduced him. He had not exactly caught his name, but he mumbled something as he presented him to his wife and little girl, who were waiting.

As they whirled away the colonel started to talk, but the stranger had taken the little girl into his lap and together they conversed in low tones all the way home.

In some way they did not exactly know how, they got the impres-

sion that the man was a teacher and, of course, he must be a for-
eigner. The long, cloak-like coat told this. They rode in the twilight
through the lighted town and at last drew up before the colonel's
mansion, with its ghost-like pillars.

The lady in the back seat was thinking of the guests she had invited to dinner and was wondering if she ought not to ask this man
to stay. He seemed cultured and she supposed he was some acquaintance of the colonel's. It would be rather interesting to have him
there, with the judge's wife and daughter and the rector. She spoke
almost before she thought:

"You will enter and rest awhile?"

The colonel and the little girl insisted. For a moment the stranger
seemed about to refuse. He said he had some business for his father,
about town. Then for the child's sake he consented.

Up the steps they went and into the dark parlor where they sat
and talked a long time. It was a curious conversation. Afterwards
they did not remember exactly what was said and yet they all remembered a certain strange satisfaction in that long, low talk.

Finally the nurse came for the reluctant child and the hostess
bethought herself:

"We will have a cup of tea; you will be dry and tired."

She rang and switched on a blaze of light. With one accord they
all looked at the stranger, for they had hardly seen him well in the
glooming twilight. The woman started in amazement and the
colonel half rose in anger. Why, the man was a mulatto, surely; even
if he did not own the Negro blood, their practiced eyes knew it. He
was tall and straight and the coat looked like a Jewish gabardine. His
hair hung in close curls far down the sides of his face and his face was
olive, even yellow.

A peremptory order rose to the colonel's lips and froze there as he
caught the stranger's eyes. Those eyes—where had he seen those eyes
before? He remembered them long years ago. The soft, tear-filled eyes
of a brown girl. He remembered many things, and his face grew
drawn and white. Those eyes kept burning into him, even when they
were turned half away toward the staircase, where the white figure of
the child hovered with her nurse and waved good-night. The lady

sank into her chair and thought: "What will the judge's wife say? How did the colonel come to invite this man here? How shall we be rid of him?" She looked at the colonel in reproachful consternation.

Just then the door opened and the old butler came in. He was an ancient black man, with tufted white hair, and he held before him a large, silver tray filled with a china service. The stranger rose slowly and stretched forth his hands as if to bless the viands. The old man paused in bewilderment, tottered, and then with sudden gladness in his eyes dropped to his knees, and the tray crashed to the floor.

"My Lord and my God!" he whispered; but the woman screamed: "Mother's china!"

The doorbell rang.

"Heavens! Here is the dinner party!" exclaimed the lady. She turned toward the door, but there in the hall, clad in her night clothes, was the little girl. She had stolen down the stairs to see the stranger again, and the nurse above was calling in vain. The woman felt hysterical and scolded at the nurse, but the stranger had stretched out his arms and with a glad cry the child nestled in them. They caught some words about the "Kingdom of Heaven" as he slowly mounted the stairs with the little, white burden.

The mother was glad of anything to get rid of the interloper, even for a moment. The bell rang again and she hastened toward the door, which the loitering black maid was just opening. She did not notice the shadow of the stranger as he came slowly down the stairs and paused by the newel post, dark and silent.

The judge's wife came in. She was an old woman, frilled and pow-dered into a semblance of youth, and gorgeously gowned. She came forward, smiling with extended hands, but when she was opposite the stranger, somewhere a chill seemed to strike her and she shuddered and cried:

"What a draft!" as she drew a silken shawl about her and shook hands cordially; she forgot to ask who the stranger was. The judge strode in unseeing, thinking of a puzzling case of theft.

"Eh? What? Oh—er—yes,—good evening," he said, "good evening." Behind him came a young woman in the glory of youth, and daintily silked, beautiful in face and form, with diamonds around her fair neck. She came in lightly, but stopped with a little gasp; then she laughed gaily and said:

"Why I beg your pardon. Was it not curious? I thought I saw there behind your man"—she hesitated, but he must be a servant, she argued—"the shadow of great, white wings. It was but the light on the drapery. What a turn it gave me." And she smiled again. With her came a tall, handsome, young naval officer. Hearing his lady refer to the servant, he hardly looked at him, but held his gilded cap carelessly toward him, and the stranger placed it carefully on the rack.

Last came the rector, a man of forty, and well-clothed. He started to pass the stranger, stopped, and looked at him inquiringly.

"I beg your pardon," he said. "I beg your pardon,—I think I have met you?"

The stranger made no answer, and the hostess nervously hurried the guests on. But the rector lingered and looked perplexed.

"Surely, I know you. I have met you somewhere," he said, putting his hand vaguely to his head. "You—you remember me, do you not?"

The stranger quietly swept his cloak aside, and to the hostess's unspeakable relief passed out of the door.

"I never knew you," he said in low tones as he went.

The lady murmured some vain excuse about intruders, but the rector stood with annoyance written on his face.

"I beg a thousand pardons," he said to the hostess absently. "It is a great pleasure to be here—somehow I thought I knew that man. I am sure I knew him once."

The stranger had passed down the steps, and as he passed, the nurse, lingering at the top of the staircase, flew down after him, caught his cloak, trembled, hesitated, and then kneeled in the dust.

He touched her lightly with his hand and said: "Go, and sin no more!"

With a glad cry the maid left the house, with its open door, and turned north, running. The stranger turned eastward into the night. As they parted a long, low howl rose tremulously and reverberated through the night. The colonel's wife within shuddered.

"The bloodhounds!" she said.

The rector answered carelessly:

"Another one of those convicts escaped, I suppose. Really, they need severer measures." Then he stopped. He was trying to remember that stranger's name.

The judge's wife looked about for the draft and arranged her shawl. The girl glanced at the white drapery in the hall, but the young officer was bending over her and the fires of life burned in her veins.

Howl after howl rose in the night, swelled, and died away. The stranger strode rapidly along the highway and out into the deep forest. There he paused and stood waiting, tall and still.

A mile up the road behind, a man was running, tall and powerful and black with crime-stained face and convicts' stripes upon him, and shackles on his legs. He ran and jumped in little, short steps, and his chains rang. He fell and rose again, while the howl of the hounds rang louder behind him.

Into the forest he leapt and crept and jumped and ran, streaming with sweat; seeing the tall form rise before him, he stopped suddenly, dropped his hands in sullen impotence, and sank panting to the earth. A greyhound shot out of the woods behind him, howled, whined, and fawned before the stranger's feet. Hound after hound bayed, leapt, and lay there; then silently, one by one, and with bowed heads, they crept backward toward the town.

The stranger made a cup of his hands and gave the man water to drink, bathed his hot head, and gently took the chains and irons from his feet. By and by the convict stood up. Day was dawning above the treetops. He looked into the stranger's face, and for a moment a gladness swept over the stains of his face.

"Why, you are a nigger, too," he said.

Then the convict seemed anxious to justify himself.

"I never had no chance," he said furtively.

"Thou shalt not steal," said the stranger.

The man bridled.

"But how about them? Can they steal? Didn't they steal a whole year's work, and then when I stole to keep from starving—" He glanced at the stranger.

"No, I didn't steal just to keep from starving. I stole to be stealing.

I can't seem to keep from stealing. Seems like when I see things, I just must—but, yes, I'll try!"

The convict looked down at his striped clothes, but the stranger had taken off his long coat; he had put it around him and the stripes disappeared.

In the opening morning the black man started toward the low, log farmhouse in the distance, while the stranger stood watching him. There was a new glory in the day. The black man's face cleared up, and the farmer was glad to get him. All day the black man worked as he had never worked before. The farmer gave him some cold food.

"You can sleep in the barn," he said, and turned away.

"How much do I git a day?" asked the black man.

The farmer scowled.

"Now see here," said he. "If you'll sign a contract for the season, I'll give you ten dollars a month."

"I won't sign no contract," said the black man doggedly.

"Yes, you will," said the farmer, threateningly, "or I'll call the convict guard." And he grinned.

The convict shrank and slouched to the barn. As night fell he looked out and saw the farmer leave the place. Slowly he crept out and sneaked toward the house. He looked through the kitchen door. No one was there, but the supper was spread as if the mistress had laid it and gone out. He ate ravenously. Then he looked into the front room and listened. He could hear low voices on the porch. On the table lay a gold watch. He gazed at it, and in a moment he was beside it,—his hands were on it! Quickly he slipped out of the house and slouched toward the field. He saw his employer coming along the highway. He fled back in terror and around to the front of the house, when suddenly he stopped. He felt the great, dark eyes of the stranger and saw the same dark, cloak-like coat where the stranger sat on the doorstep talking with the mistress of the house. Slowly, guiltily, he turned back, entered the kitchen, and laid the watch stealthily where he found it; then he rushed wildly back toward the stranger, with arms outstretched.

The woman had laid supper for her husband, and going down from the house had walked out toward a neighbor's. She was gone but

a little while, and when she came back she started to see a dark figure on the doorsteps under the tall, red oak. She thought it was the
new Negro until he said in a soft voice:

"Will you give me bread?"

Reassured at the voice of a white man, she answered quickly in
her soft, Southern tone.

"Why, certainly."

She was a little woman, and once had been pretty; but now her
face was drawn with work and care. She was nervous and always
thinking, wishing, wanting for something. She went in and got him
some cornbread and a glass of cool, rich buttermilk; then she came
out and sat down beside him. She began, quite unconsciously, to tell
him about herself,—the things she had done and had not done and
the things she had wished for. She told him of her husband and this
new farm they were trying to buy. She said it was hard to get niggers
to work. She said they ought all to be in the chain-gang and made to
work. Even then some ran away. Only yesterday one had escaped,
and another the day before.

At last she gossiped of her neighbors, how good they were and
how bad.

"And do you like them all?" asked the stranger.

She hesitated.

"Most of them," she said; and then, looking up into his face and
putting her hand into his, as though he were her father, she said:

"There are none I hate; no, none at all."

He looked away, holding her hand in his, and said dreamily:

"You love your neighbor as yourself?"

She hesitated.

"I try—" she began, and then looked the way he was looking;
down under the hill where lay a little, half-ruined cabin.

"They are niggers," she said briefly.

He looked at her. Suddenly a confusion came over her and she insisted, she knew not why.

"But they are niggers!"

With a sudden impulse she arose and hurriedly lighted the lamp
that stood just within the door, and held it above her head. She saw

his dark face and curly hair. She shrieked in angry terror and rushed down the path, and just as she rushed down, the black convict came running up with hands outstretched. They met in mid-path, and before he could stop he had run against her and she fell heavily to earth and lay white and still. Her husband came rushing around the house with a cry and an oath.

"I knew it," he said. "It's that runaway nigger." He held the black man struggling to the earth and raised his voice to a yell. Down the highway came the convict guard, with hound and mob and gun. They paused across the fields. The farmer motioned to them.

"He—attacked—my wife," he gasped.

The mob snarled and worked silently. Right to the limb of the red oak they hoisted the struggling, writhing black man, while others lifted the dazed woman. Right and left, as she tottered to the house, she searched for the stranger with a yearning, but the stranger was gone. And she told none of her guests.

"No—no, I want nothing," she insisted, until they left her, as they thought, asleep. For a time she lay still, listening to the departure of the mob. Then she rose. She shuddered as she heard the creaking of the limb where the body hung. But resolutely she crawled to the window and peered out into the moonlight; she saw the dead man writhe. He stretched his arms out like a cross, looking upward. She gasped and clung to the window sill. Behind the swaying body, and down where the little, half-ruined cabin lay, a single flame flashed up amid the far-off shout and cry of the mob. A fierce joy sobbed up through the terror in her soul and then sank abashed as she watched the flame rise. Suddenly whirling into one great crimson column, it shot to the top of the sky and threw great arms athwart the gloom until above the world and behind the roped and swaying form below hung quivering and burning, a great crimson cross.

She hid her dizzy, aching head in an agony of tears, and dared not look, for she knew. Her dry lips moved:

"Despised and rejected of men."

She knew, and the very horror of it lifted her dull and shrinking eyelids. There, heaven-tall, earth-wide, hung the stranger on the crimson cross, riven and blood-stained, with thorn-crowned head and pierced hands. She stretched her arms and shrieked.

He did not hear. He did not see. His calm dark eyes, all sorrowful, were fastened on the writhing, twisting body of the thief, and a voice came out of the winds of the night, saying:

"This day thou shalt be with me in Paradise!"

WILL THE CIRCLE BE UNBROKEN?

Henry Dumas

(1974)

At the edge of the spiral of musicians Probe sat crosslegged on a blue cloth, his soprano sax resting against his inner knee, his afrohorn linking his ankles like a bridge. The afro-horn was the newest axe to cut the deadwood of the world. But Probe, since his return from exile, had chosen only special times to reveal the new sound. There were more rumors about it than there were ears and souls that had heard the horn speak. Probe's dark full head tilted toward the vibrations of the music as if the ring of sound from the six wailing pieces was tightening, creating a spiraling circle.

The black audience, unaware at first of its collectiveness, had begun to move in a soundless rhythm as if it were the tiny twitchings of an embryo. The waiters in the club fell against the wall, shadows, dark pillars holding up the building and letting the free air purify the mind of the club.

The drums took an oblique. Magwa's hands, like the forked tongue of a dark snake, probed the skins, probed the whole belly of the coming circle. Beginning to close the circle, Haig's alto arc, rapid piano incisions, Billy's thin green flute arcs and tangents, Stace's examinations of his own trumpet discoveries, all fell separately, yet together, into a blanket which Mojohn had begun weaving on bass when the set began. The audience breathed, and Probe moved into the inner ranges of the sax.

Outside the Sound Barrier Club three white people were opening the door. Jan, a tenor sax case in his hand, had his game all planned. He had blown with Probe six years ago on the West Coast. He did not believe that there was anything to this new philosophy the musicians were talking about. He would talk to Probe personally. He had known many Negro musicians and theirs was no different from any other artist's struggles to be himself, including his own.

Things were happening so fast that there was no one who knew all directions at once. He did not mind Ron and Tasha coming along. They were two of the hippest ofays in town, and if anybody could break the circle of the Sound Club, it would be friends and old friends of friends.

Ron was bearded and scholarly. Thickset, shabbily dressed, but clean. He had tried to visit the Club before. But all of his attempts had been futile. He almost carried the result of one attempt to court. He could not understand why the cats would want to bury themselves in Harlem and close the doors to the outside world. Ron's articles and reviews had helped many black musicians, but of all of them, Probe Adams had benefited the most. Since his graduation from Yale, Ron had knocked around the music world; once he thought he wanted to sing blues. He had tried, but that was in college. The best compliment he ever got was from Mississippi John or Muddy Waters, one of the two, during a civil rights rally in Alabama. He had spontaneously leaped up during the rally and played from his soul. Muddy was in the audience, and later told Ron: "Boy, you keep that up, you gwine put me back on the plantation."

Ron was not fully satisfied that he had found the depth of the black man's psyche. In his book he had said this. Yet he knew that if he believed strongly enough, some of the old cats would break down. His sincerity was written all over his face. Holding Tasha's hand, he saw the door opening. . . .

Tasha was a shapely blonde who had dyed her hair black. It now matched her eyes. She was a Vassar girl and had once begun a biography of Oliver Fullerton. Excerpts had been published in *Down Beat* and she became noted as a critic and authority on the Fullerton movement. Fullerton's development as an important jazz trombonist had been interrupted soon after Tasha's article. No one knew why.

Sometimes Tasha was afraid to think about it. If they had married, she knew that Oliver would have been able to continue making it. But he had gotten strung out on H. Sometimes she believed her friends who said Oliver was psychopathic. At least when he stopped beating her, she forgave him. And she did not believe it when he was really hooked. She still loved him. It was her own love, protected deep inside her, encased, her Oliver had died trying to enter. IT would be only a matter of time. She would translate love into an honest appraisal of black music.

"I am sorry," the tall brown doorman said. "Sessions for Brothers and Sisters only."

"What's the matter, baby?" Jan leaned his head in and looked around as if wondering what the man was talking about.

"I said—"

"Man, if you can't recognize a Brother, you better let me have your job." He held up his case. "We're friends of Probe."

The man called for assistance. Quickly two men stepped out of the shadows. "What's the trouble, Brother?"

"These people say they're friends of the Probe."

"What people?" asked one of the men. He was neatly dressed, a clean shaven head, with large darting eyes. He looked past the three newcomers. There was a silence.

Finally, as if it were some supreme effort, he looked at the three. "I'm sorry, but for your own safety we cannot allow you."

"Man, what you talkin bout?" asked Jan, smiling quizzically. "Are you blockin Brothers now? I told him I am blood. We friends of the Probe."

The three men at the door went into a huddle. Carl, the doorman, was skeptical, but he had seen some bloods that were pretty light. He looked at this cat again, and as Kent and Rafael were debating whether or not to go get Probe's wife in the audience, he decided against the whole thing. He left the huddle and returned with a sign which said: "We cannot allow non-Brothers because of the danger involved with extensions."

Jan looked at the sign, and a smile crept across his face. In the street a cop was passing and leaned in. Carl motioned the cop in. He wanted a witness to this. He knew what might happen but he had never seen it.

Jan shook his head at the sign, turning to Ron and Tasha. He was about to explain that he had seen the same sign on the West Coast. It was incredible that all the spades believed this thing about the lethal vibrations from the new sound.

Carl was shoving the sign in their faces as the cop, a big, pimpled Irishman, moved through the group. "All right, break it up, break it up. You got people outside want to come in . . ."

Kent and Rafael, seeing Carl's decision and the potential belligerence of the whites, folded their hands, buddha-like. Carl stood with his back to the door now.

"Listen, officer, if these people go in, the responsibility is yours."

The Irish cop, not knowing whether he should get angry over what he figured was reverse discrimination, smirked and made a path for the three. He would not go far inside because he didn't think the sounds were worth listening to. If it wasn't Harlem he could see why these people would want to go in, but he had never seen anything worthwhile from niggers in Harlem.

"Don't worry. You got a license, don't you?"

"Let them go through," said Rafael suddenly. A peace seemed to gather over the faces of the three club members now. They folded their arms and went into the dark cavern which led to the music. In front of them walked the invaders. "See," said Jan, "if you press these cats, they'll cop out." They moved toward the music in an alien silence.

Probe was deep into a rear-action sax monologue. The whole circle now, like a bracelet of many colored lights, gyrated under Probe's wisdom. Probe was a thoughtful, full-headed black man with narrow eyes and a large nose. His lips swelled over the reed and each note fell into the circle like an acrobat on a tight rope stretched radially across the center of the universe.

He heard the whistle of the wind. Three ghosts, like chaff blown from a wasteland, clung to the wall. . . . He tightened the circle. Movement began from within it, shaking without breaking balance. He had to prepare the womb for the afro-horn. Its vibrations were beyond his mental frequencies unless he got deeper into motives. He sent out his call for motives. . . .

The blanket of the bass rippled and the fierce wind in all their minds blew the blanket back, and there sat the city of Samson. The white pillars imposing . . . but how easy it is to tear the building down with motives. Here they come. Probe, healed of his blindness, born anew of spirit, sealed his reed with pure air. *He moved to the edge of the circle, rested his sax, and lifted his axe.* . . .

There are only three afro-horns in the world. They were forged from a rare metal found only in Africa and South America. No one knows who forged the horns, but the general opinion among musicologists is that it was the Egyptians. One European museum guards an afro-horn. The other is supposed to be somewhere on the west coast of Mexico, among a tribe of Indians. Probe grew into his from a black peddler who claimed to have traveled a thousand miles just to give it to his son. From that day on, Probe's sax handled like a child, a child waiting for itself to grow out of itself.

Inside the center of the gyration is an atom stripped of time, black. The gathering of the hunters, deeper. Coming, laced in the energy of the sun. He is blowing. Magwa's hands. Reverence of skin. Under the single voices is the child of woman, black. They are building back the wall, crumbling under the disturbance.

In the rear of the room, Jan did not hear the volt, nor did he see the mystery behind Probe's first statement on the afro-horn. He had closed his eyes, trying to capture or elude the panthers of the music, but he had no eyes. He did not feel Ron slump against him. Strands of Tasha's hair were matted on a button of Ron's jacket, but she did not move when he slumped. Something was hitting them like waves, like shock waves. . . .

Before his mind went black, Jan recalled the feeling when his father had beat him for playing "with a nigger!" and later he allowed the feeling to merge with his dislike of white people. When he fell, his case hit the floor and opened, revealing a shiny tenor saxophone that gleamed and vibrated in the freedom of freedom.

Ron's sleep had been quick, like the rush of post-hypnotic suggestions. He dropped her hand, slumped, felt the wall give (no, it was the air), and he fell face forward across a table, his heart silent in respect for truer vibrations.

The musicians stood. The horn and Probe drew up the shadows now from the audience. A child climbed upon the chords of sounds, growing out of the circle of the womb, searching with fingers and then with motive, and as the volume of the music increased—penetrating the thick callousness of the Irishman twirling his stick outside of black flesh—the musicians walked off, one by one, linked to Probe's respectful nod at each and his quiet pronouncement of their names. He mopped his face with a blue cloth.

"What's the matter here?"

"Step aside, folks!"

"These people are unconscious!"

"Look at their faces!"

"They're dead."

"Dead?"

"What happened?"

"Dead?"

"It's true then. It's true. . . ."

'Cause Harlem Needs Heroes

Kevin Brockenbrough

(2004)

If you could add some years to your life by killing someone else, would you do it? I know at least one person who decided to go for it. Know how I know? Because I'm the other guy: the one left holding the short end of the stick. The one left watching the clock. Rather than just getting it over with nice and quick, I get to die a piece at a time: an arm here, a leg there. Born Black and a clone; died bone by bone.

Until twenty-four hours ago, New York City had a law forbidding the capture of clones by the original cell donor for the forced removal of body parts. The mayor's spin doctor had even developed a politically correct term for it: "harvesting."

Of course, it had been going on for years "on the sly," but the repeal of the law had every money-hungry thug in the city looking to cash in by returning "missing property."

I figured killers were like most folk: It takes one to know one. So I asked my man Trane to meet me here for a drink. His job was to kill. And he was damn good at it.

Heaven was the hottest jazz club in Harlem. It was early evening and both the band and the crowd were just arriving.

Trane waved me over to his table, tucked off to the side, next to the bar's wall-high fish tank. The back of the tank had pictures of famous jazz musicians pasted to it at odd angles so it always looked as if something was swimming out of Satchmo's horn. Every time I came here, the game was the same: The sisters loved looking at the fish, while all the brothers would stare at the TV monitors hanging over the bar, trying to catch the latest scores.

The angle of our table allowed us to check out both the game and the pretty women looking at the fish—or using the fish as an excuse to look at us. On any other night, a little flirting would have been fun. But tonight sex was the last thing on my mind, although my new synthetic body parts probably worked as well as their human originals.

"I miss playing ball," Trane said, his eyes on a computer simulation of a battle between the 2001 LA Lakers and the 2050 Knicks. At six foot seven, Trane once dreamed of playing for the Knicks. Born in 2040, he was old enough to have seen a few flesh-and-blood games prior to the first vampire sightings in 2053.

The bloodred dreadlocks grazing his shoulders marked him as a Harlem Ranger, a special unit within the police force whose job was to protect our neighborhoods from the Undead. The *Times* estimated that in Harlem alone there were approximately 1,000 vampires to every Ranger. But everybody knew that number was way too low. And once word got out that the mayor himself had decided Harlem was expendable, even fewer people signed up. Trane used to joke that the Rangers always needed "new blood." Against his father's wishes, Trane joined the Rangers at the age of seventeen, a year after he got his driver's license. Ten years later, even the most conservative estimates had him killing more vampires than anyone ever to wear the badge. He was the most feared man in Harlem.

He was also my best friend.

"What took you so long?" he said, eyes still on the game.

"I got delayed."

"That ain't what I heard," Trane said. "I heard you got jumped."

"Who told you that?"

"I just know what I heard," he said. "Is it true?"

And that was the hard part: dealing with the reality. What they had done to me and what they *would* do to me. And to make matters worse, some of the faces in the crowd looked a lot like the men who had tortured me.

As if he was reading my mind, Trane said, "Chill. In here, I can help you. You hit the streets; you're on your own."

He gave me what was left of his drink, but my hand was shaking so badly I ended up with more of the rum on my shirt than in my mouth.

"You starting to embarrass me, bro," he said as he handed me a napkin. "Get a grip."

"You don't know what it's like. Being chased. Hunted."

"You'd be surprised what I know," he said, waving to get our waitress's attention. "Tell me about your new legs."

Despite hiding the plastic-covered metal under my best pinstripe suit, my interview suit, Trane's ears must have picked up the buzz of the cybernetic motors. But with the crowd noise and the TV that couldn't be happening. Unless . . .

"You know who did this, don't you?" I said.

"Yeah," he said. "And so do you."

Which meant I was definitely running out of time.

"I don't understand you, Joe," Trane said. "You're just gonna let them take you apart piece by piece? Hell, if I was you—"

"But that's just it: I'm not you," I cut in. "You're the law. Me, well, I'm just spare parts. I don't have a choice."

"That's where you're wrong," Trane said. "You got a choice. When it comes to how we live or die, everybody's got a choice. But don't worry. You roll with me, nobody'll do anything stupid."

I couldn't argue with that. Those words, and a few more drinks, actually got me to relax a little. Heaven actually had a reputation of being the safest spot in Harlem. The security system was state of the art, supplementing the burly bouncers and their Tasers with a central air-conditioning system that delivered high-grade tear gas when things got really wild.

"Let's talk about something else," he said. "You still want to do that interview?"

A week ago, we had discussed my doing a feature story on the Harlem Rangers. I was already making a nice living doing freelance pieces for both magazines and TV, but stories involving the Rangers were so rare that this one-on-one was guaranteed to make me a very rich man. I just had to live long enough to cash the check.

I tapped the right arm of my eyeglasses, turning on the nano-optic routers that would allow interested cable viewers both to see and hear the story live.

"I'm ready. You want to talk about the charges?" I said.

"I got nothing to hide," Trane replied. "Like I said, I didn't kill him."

Both fellow officers and the press were talking about the "presumed" death of the first Harlem Ranger, Thelonious "Monk" Smith. "Presumed" because they couldn't find the body, despite the huge amounts of blood at the scene. The police report said that Monk's blood had been found all over Trane's shirt, but Trane had refused to reveal what had happened to his fellow officer.

One more thing you should know: Monk was Trane's father.

"If you didn't do it, then who did?" I asked.

"Ask Monk," Trane said.

"So you're saying Monk is still alive?" I asked.

"I didn't say that. You said that," Trane said. "I just said I ain't kill him."

I placed my copy of the police report on the table.

"Then how do you explain the blood?" I asked.

"That's the wrong question," he said. "What you should be asking is this: Who had a reason to see my father dead?"

"All right, I'll bite. If you didn't do it, then who did?"

"To quote the DA, 'No body, no motive, no case.' Can you believe that?" Trane said. "He didn't even try to solve the case. Know why? Because to solve the case would shed light on things City Hall would prefer to keep quiet, that's why."

He lit a cigarette but his words lingered in the air much longer than the smoke.

"You know the DA never did like Pops," he said. "People on the street saw Pops as a hero. But the district attorney? The chief of police? That whole City Hall clique? Never. None of them ever gave Pops his due. The most dangerous job in the city and not a single commendation. But I'm gonna tell you something: The streets know a hero when they see one. And Harlem needs heroes."

Trane's eyes circled the room, then settled on the fish tank. A larger fish chased a small fish. Just missed.

"I hear what you're saying—and this might seem cold—but you had the man's blood all over you. You have to know who did it," I said. "Why aren't you doing something about it?"

"I am doing something about it," he said. "I'm recruiting."

"What you need is somebody who could pull some strings," I said. "Like the mayor. He's known Monk for years."

"No. He's the worst one," Trane said. "Read between the lines, kid. Nobody really wants to know what happened."

"I do," I said.

And that was true. I worshiped Monk. He was the closest thing to a father I ever had.

Maybe I'd see him on the other side.

"Somebody was happy to see him go," Trane said. "Everyone was given strict orders not to ask any questions."

"Okay. But that's never stopped you before," I said.

"True," he said. "All right. What if I told you that what happened to Pops is tied up with the folks who stole your legs?"

But before I could answer, the band began to play.

Which meant I'd have to ask him about the case later.

Heaven had strict rules prohibiting all electronic transmissions once the performance started. The world outside might be chaos, but here, jazz ruled.

"You still play?" I asked.

Trane nodded, as much to the music as to the question.

"Once a Jazz Boy, always a Jazz Boy," he said.

The Jazz Boys were Trane, or as his birth certificate says, John Coltrane Smith; his father, Thelonious Monk Smith; and me, Joe Jones Smith (Monk wanted to go with Philly Joe Jones, but thought better of it). Monk's father had loved jazz and named his only son after his favorite artist. Not to be outdone, Monk then named his two boys after his two favorite musicians. It didn't matter that Monk had adopted me. If he knew then what I was, he never mentioned it. He treated me just like Trane. He even had me pick up an instrument: the drums.

The waitress brought over some buffalo wings and more booze. At this point the liquor was really starting to kick in and I was starting to drift, but Trane looked none the worse for wear. He held up his glass for a toast.

"To life. And family," he said.

He actually smiled at me when he said that. I damn near dropped my drink, 'cause Trane never smiles.

Once we downed our drinks, he leaned back in his chair and turned his attention to the crowd. Several women seemed eager to get his attention, but he blew them off. Searching for what?

"Are there any vampires in here?" I asked.

"Plenty. But you're safe. The clubs are neutral territory," he said just as he made eye contact with a very pale Billie Holiday wanna-be walking to the stage. "In here, they can't hurt you and I can't hurt them. It's the law. But don't let me catch her outside. . . ."

Anyone else would have just run, get as far away from New York—from Harlem—as they possibly can. But you don't have a city as media-friendly as New York get overrun by vampires without someone noticing it. After an isolated vampire sighting as far south as Princeton, the feds dropped a laser net that went from Westchester down to Trenton. Whether you were human or vampire, the result was the same: One touch, and you were ashes.

The only thing separating us from death were the Rangers.

The Rangers were the bloodshot eye in the center of the storm, forgotten soldiers who worked the darkest streets—and lived to talk about it. Whenever I sat down with Trane and Monk, my status as a reporter meant that I was sure to get an earful.

"Folks need to know what we're up against," Trane would say. "What's happening up here ain't no different than Vietnam, or Kuwait, or South Mars. Harlem got mommas crying and babies dying, just like all them other places. Why aren't we on the evening news every night? What, since it's only Harlem, you can't send in the army, the marines, the Green Berets—all those folks that get paid good money to kill—and put an end to this nonsense? The rest of Manhattan—naw, skip that, the rest of the world—needs to learn what the vampires already know: Black folks bleed too."

Of course, smack dab in the middle of all that righteous indignation, Monk would pop another garlic-coated bullet into his clip and spit the truth:

"Son, I hear ya. But it all comes down to this: Somebody's gotta die. You know it won't be the rich folks. So guess who's left?"

Of course one of the questions I asked was "Where'd the vampires come from in the first place?"

An FBI buddy of Monk's, a brother who still had a grandmother living up on Striver's Row, had e-mailed Monk some documents that said an experiment to find a cure for AIDS ended up spreading something far worse.

The study tested the vaccine among both adults and teenagers. All the adults died. And stayed dead.

It was the teenagers that became the problem.

They weren't like those creatures you'd see in the old movie tapes: They couldn't turn into bats, and once they bit you, you didn't return from the grave. But they did have fangs, unnatural strength, and speed.

And they also had something Hollywood hadn't thought of: the ability to breed.

The drug seemed to supercharge their metabolisms: Overnight, boys grew into men, and girls grew into women. And vampire sex produced baby vampires. Reports claimed that the baby vamps reached adulthood in about a year's time. Pretty soon, vampires were as common in New York as roaches: They were everywhere. And hungry; always hungry.

Monk said, "The laser net was what changed the game. Whether you was human or a vamp, you could see the writing on the wall. Nobody was getting out and no help was coming in. Them was some dark days."

Rumor has it that the mayor knew he had until sundown to come up with a plan. Over the next three hours, police rounded up every psychic, witch, and any other practitioner of anything even remotely supernatural, and when darkness came he succeeded in working out favorable terms for Manhattan.

Everybody else—Brooklyn, the Bronx, Harlem, Washington Heights, Queens, Long Island and Westchester, and northern New Jersey—was on their own.

Only one survived: Harlem.

You see, Harlem had something the other neighborhoods didn't: a talisman developed especially to kill vampires. Many people have heard of it, but only one person knows where it is.

Monk. He called it "soulfire."

Trane nodded over toward the bar. "You know that guy?" he asked.

At first I didn't know who he was talking about. Then I noticed that one of the patrons was looking at us a little too hard. He whispered to a friend. Both looked like some guys I had seen at a Giants game.

Playing linebacker.

I clicked my recording equipment back on.

The hell with the rules.

"I wanted to be a Ranger from day one," Trane said.

He had seen me click on the equipment and probably thought I wanted to continue the interview.

But that wasn't it. I wanted to catch a killer—my own.

"Some things are just in the blood, you know what I'm saying? Yo, I was so hyped I killed my first vamp before I even got my first injection."

"Injection? What injection? I don't remember reading about—" I said.

"And you never will," he said. "I'm telling you stuff that's pure Tuskegee 626. Magic came up with a problem and Science came up with an answer. Straight up. They called it Molecular Enhancement Therapy, but we used to call it Bounce, because that's what it would do to you: have you bouncing off the walls."

"So it was just you?" I asked. "No partner?"

"Just me, dawg. I guess the other Rangers wanted to see if Monk's kid was coasting on his daddy's rep or if I was the real deal. But I was holding my own. . . . Then I found a little present stashed beside a dumpster: a HOTTY."

Even in our high-tech age, the rules for killing vampires were the same: sunlight, wooden stake, decapitation, or fire. The HOTTY was a flame-thrower someone had developed that was the size of a .22. Who ever thought it up probably made a fortune. They weren't legal, but plenty of folks had one.

I could have used one this afternoon.

Then it hit me where I had seen those two thugs who were staring at me.

"Yo, Earth to Joe," Trane said. "This is some deep shit I'm getting ready to share up in here. I need you to focus."

Some part of me must have heard him. But I could still feel myself gripping the edge of the table extra hard.

They just took my legs. Could they really be back for more already?

"You remember how the mayor used to come over the house when you and me was little?" Trane asked.

"Yeah. Seemed like he and Monk would spend all day and all night arguing," I said.

To this day, I don't know why Monk adopted me, but he always made time for us, even on nights when he "played the dozens," his term for days when he pulled twelve-hour shifts back to back. He always put family first, no matter what the consequences. Then there was the mayor, who was just the opposite. Even back when he was just an assistant DA, there were two things he always had plenty of: cheap suits and big dreams.

The mayor was easily the most hated man in Harlem, especially after word hit the street that he had struck a deal with the vampires to protect Manhattan—but only Manhattan below Ninety-sixth Street. That meant you were fair game if you lived in Harlem, or Washington Heights, or even Morningside Heights, home of Columbia University and so many rich white folks they didn't even call that part of the city Harlem anymore.

It was he who installed the twenty-four-hour-a-day border patrols; every guard armed to the teeth. But it wasn't the vampires they were trying to keep out. Once word of the mayor's "arrangement" hit the streets, everybody suddenly had a "cousin" downtown they had to "visit." And just as quickly, if you couldn't produce proof of residence, you were shot on sight. It got ugly fast. Real fast.

"The mayor's been asking about you," Trane said.

"What does he want?"

But I knew. Probably knew the first time I met him.

The mayor and Monk would argue late into the night. I never knew what they said, but I always knew who they were talking about. I could tell by the way that the mayor kept looking at me.

Like he owned me.

"He's got your legs," Trane said.

"What? Who told you that?"

"You work the streets, you hear things," he said. "Question is: What are we gonna do about it?"

Perhaps I was too stunned by his words to hear the hiss of the jets as the room filled with gas. It was the panic that ensued that caught my eye, the logjam at the door, tables and chairs being kicked over. I remember hearing several shots being fired (that would be Trane). And feeling water hit my arm (bye-bye, fish tank). Then the quick pinch of a needle. The rest was darkness.

I woke up in a bedroom full of uncomfortable furniture and no mirrors. It had that old-man smell. That's how I knew where I was before anyone even entered the room. But I was still surprised that the white man facing me was wearing my watch.

And my arms.

My black arms.

"Do you want the watch back?" the mayor said.

"You know what I want back," I said.

He made a point of crossing his legs as he sat. His pants legs rose above his nylon socks just enough to reveal what used to be my Black legs.

"Sorry, son. I rather like these legs. In fact, I like them so much I had my friends bring you back so I could get the arms as well. "

"But Boss," one of his vampire thugs asked, "what's with the back and forth? You got him right here; why not just take it all?"

I was wondering the same thing myself.

"That would be out of the question," the mayor said. "Both the donor and the recipient need at least two hours to heal per attachment. Even though he is my property, I wouldn't want to damage the merchandise," the mayor said.

"How about his face?" the thug asked. "You need that?"

"Oh, I'd never use that," the mayor said.

As if on cue, the thug smacked me so hard I thought it was the Fourth of July.

I woke up to the smell of marijuana and coconut incense. I was back in my own apartment, back in my own bed. I must have spent a good five minutes staring at my new synthetic arms before it clicked that I wasn't alone.

"Yo, Joe—you okay?" Trane asked. He was smoking a blunt, a cigar-sized marijuana joint. You could still get good drugs uptown. Just not at night.

"Yo, you want some of this?" he asked.

Before I could answer, I felt another pair of hands helping me up. The same hands that had held me as a child.

Monk.

"Give the boy a minute," he said.

As my eyes adjusted to the light—a soft glow, like the first rays of sunrise—I finally noticed the body of the vampire thug that had hit me earlier. At least that was who I thought it was. It was a little hard to tell since the body had no head.

"We'll clean that up later," Trane said, again holding out the blunt for me to take a hit. But I didn't need it.

"I'm just, I mean, I can't believe this," I said. "Tee, I knew that you was still out there. I just felt it. But Monk . . . Pop," I said reaching out to give both a hug. A thousand pinpricks ran up my new arms, but I didn't care one bit.

"I thought you was . . ."

"Dead?" Monk smiled.

"Well, yeah."

"I am," he said.

This time when Trane offered the blunt, I took it.

* * *

"Welcome home," Monk said.

We were standing outside what looked like a record store on Malcolm X Boulevard. Once upon a time, this street was home to the jazz-kissed nightlife that gave Harlem its luster. The gravity-defying swing and sway of dancers at the Savoy Ballroom. The clink-clink of champagne glasses in the Cotton Club, home to both the Mob and High Society.

Now it was home to a black-market trade in Black body parts. The record store was only one of many "body shops" lining the street.

"I was tracking two vampires when I stumbled across my first body shop—and you," Monk said. "I found out later that it was run by two well-known geneticists who got trapped in Manhattan when the feds dropped the net."

"What's that got to do with the mayor?" I asked.

"Gimme a minute, and I'll tell ya," Monk said. He motioned for Trane to set the timing device on a bomb attached to the door of the record store. Trane made sure to grab a few jazz CDs first.

"Everybody knew that once the net was in place, there was no place to run. And it didn't take a rocket scientist to figure out that it wouldn't take long for the vamps to run out of food. The scientists saw a business opportunity," Monk said as we stepped across the street and crouched behind what was left of a Harlem Hospital ambulance.

"They saw human cloning as a way to serve two markets: rich folks who wanted to live forever and the vampires who could never get enough to eat. Only problem was, most of the rich clients had too much ego to stand seeing someone who looked exactly like them get cut up for spare parts. It struck too close to home. So they asked the doctors to toss some Black pepper into the genetic stew. Catch my drift?"

Which explained why I had the mayor's eyes and some unknown sister's nose and lips.

"The resulting package was genetically similar enough to allow for harvesting: the replacement of failing 'original equipment' with younger—and darker—'spares.' Throw in a little—what do they call it now?—'pigmentation engineering'—which ain't nothing but high-tech makeup and skin-bleaching—and the White original could live out his days with significantly younger body parts. They'd let the poor Black clone keep just enough of his human body parts to be sold as food to the vamps."

"And the mayor knew all about it?" I said.

"Yeah," Monk said. "That was part of the deal he cut with the vampires. He offered to set them up with a steady source of grub."

"I'm not ready to be somebody's chicken nugget," I said.

"No, son," Monk said. "The mayor and I had a deal too: He'd leave you alone and I'd leave him alone. But that was then. This is now."

As if to dramatize Monk's point, the bomb exploded, sending glass and brick in every direction. The alarm system on the ambulance honked in response, until Trane blew that up too.

"Who else knew?" I asked.

"Your brother," Monk said, as Trane helped me to my feet. "I figured the mayor would come after all of us one day," Monk said. "One thing about politicians: They never keep a promise."

"So what happens now?" I asked.

"You got a choice to make, son," Monk said as he inspected the damage. "This ain't the only lab out here."

"Yeah, I figured that," I said.

"Then you know we can't be spending all day watching your back," Trane said. "You know we love you—far as I'm concerned, you're blood—but Harlem needs us too."

"So while you're off playing superhero, I'm left here to die?" I said.

"That's not what I'm saying," Trane said. "I'm saying if you want to live, you gotta be ready to die. You can't just walk into the light, kid. You gotta *be* the light."

"You lost me. What do you mean?"

Monk broke it down.

"When they started the Rangers, the idea was to go the vampires one better," Monk said. "So we all went through Molecular Enhancement Therapy, thinking the drugs would make us faster, stronger, and harder to kill."

"The Bounce," I said.

"That's right. But what we didn't know was that by accelerating everything, your body breaks down faster," Trane said.

"So where we started off with Science fighting Magic, eventually we realized we had to fight fire with fire," Monk said.

"Soulfire?"

"Right. Ever since the vamps first hit, I've been reading everything I could get my hands on about them," Monk said. "Not just the Eastern European stuff, but the vampire legends out of India, Malaysia, and even Africa."

"They had vampires in Africa?" I asked.

"The Ashanti spoke about witches called obayifo, that drink the blood of children. Not only would they kill your kids, they would also kill your crops," Monk said. "There was only one way to stop them: A dying warrior must have his blood shed at sunrise. His soul would then capture the first rays of the sun and keep them as his own."

That explains why Trane's shirt had Monk's blood on it.

"Now Pops is like a living HOTTY," Trane said. "He can fire both heat and light."

"The Ashanti called us Children of the Sun. I kinda like that," Monk said.

"And the magic object you're supposed to have that kills vampires?" I asked. "The Soulfire?"

"A bluff," Monk said. "Something to give the vamps—and the mayor—something to think about until we could come up with the real thing."

"How would the Bounce work . . . on me?" I said. As if on cue, both my arms and my legs began to twitch.

"My guess is you'd have to detach the ones you got, since the Bounce'll cause you to grow back real ones," Monk said.

"But I'd be able to defend myself, right?" I asked.

"You won't be playing defense," Trane said. "After we show you everything we know, no one will mess with you. Believe it."

"Maybe," Monk said. "Problem is, to my knowledge, they've never tested the Bounce on a clone. This might sound harsh, but since you're a copy and not the original . . ."

"I could break down even faster," I said.

"Afraid so," Monk said.

Damn. Why can't anything in this life ever be easy?

"Yeah, but the way I see it, this move still beats the alternative," Trane said. "It's your choice, but I know what I'd do."

Sunrise on 125th Street.

It took several very stiff drinks for me to get up the nerve to take Trane's life. He was—and still is—my best friend. But as the blood poured out of him, golden beams of morning sun flowed into him. Seeing Trane rise up and stand before me—smiling—was both unsettling and uplifting. Steadying me was Monk's hand upon my shoulder.

"Thanks, D," Trane said, grinning.

"What's it like?"

"I can't tell you," Trane said. "But I can show you."

Trane had talked a few Rangers into helping him set up our instruments on the street in front of the Apollo Theater. As I sat down at my drum set, one of the Rangers injected me with the Bounce.

I felt an immediate rush, but I'll never know how much of it was from the drug and how much of it was from hearing Trane and Monk hit their first few notes.

This afternoon I would begin battle training with the Rangers. I had decided to pay the mayor a visit on Father's Day, which was next week. I had even picked out his gift: a trip to Manhattan. Above Ninety-sixth Street. After dark.

Soon. Not now, but soon. I had time.

Tomorrow belonged to Harlem, but this morning was all about the music. All about the Jazz Boys. As if they had read my mind, the music hit the break where I was given the chance to solo. I tore it up. But my real moment to shine was still to come.

WHIPPING BOY

Pam Noles

(2004)

Aunt June told Dexter to take his cousin to the top floor of the tower and stuff him into a closet.

The tower was the tallest building in Citrus Groves. Its nine floors were the last Section 8 in the city to be sent up to the sky that year before a quirky electorate swept new thinking into the administration. The Groves were renewed then, blossoming around the tower in clusters of concrete and stucco, with a patch of green next to each stoop and walls glazed lightly with peach or cerulean, to match the sunset. But the tower and the city's promises were slowly abandoned over the years as residents were shifted from above to below the city's priority list with big promises made for something special to come when its walls were finally brought down.

Instead, the tower hulked and crumbled for decades, its crisp gray walls wearing away with the fading sunset stain of the village surrounding it, its lower windows marked with plywood and wire. The city planned to demolish the building soon and turn it into a parking lot, but when mention was made now and again of the promised park, the concern was noted and an apologia delivered. Attention moved on, as it must, to the next agenda item.

Dexter waited until the substation closed and the cops had left for the night. He saw only four people as he made his way to the tower with his burden. All of them crossed to the opposite sidewalk when he drew near. He was prepared for trouble as he entered the tower through a boarded window, but when the pipeheads saw him pulling the bag in behind him, they fled. He heard them scurrying on all sides as he tripped and stumbled his way to the stairwell.

Inside, Dexter was stopped only once by someone sitting on the stairwell between the second and third floors. The man reeked of curdled milk and stale grape MadDog, laced with the acrid bite of urine. The drunk spoke with a rough wheeze.

"Hey boy." He grabbed Dexter's ankle as he tried to climb past. "The voodoo man dead, huh," he said, clutching with a thin, shaking hand.

"You never know. Better lemme go 'fore he come out the bag." Dexter breathed through his mouth as he squinted down at the drunk, but he couldn't see anything, save a dark blob against black.

"He ain't comin' out. I know." The drunk coughed hard, squeezing Dexter's ankle with each hack. He spat. "I seen others make this trip. I seen him make this trip, long time ago. Now I'm seein' you make this trip."

"Lemme go, man."

The drunk loosened his grip and Dexter pulled away. "Next time you make this trip it be you in the bag," the drunk said as Dexter continued up the stairs. "I prob'ly won't see that, though. I prob'ly be dead myself by then."

Dexter failed to tune the drunk out, but he managed to hold it in check for a few steps. He broke down when he reached the third floor, sobbed all the way to the ninth. Nineteen years old and bawling like a baby.

By the time Dexter reached the top floor, he had dropped the bag three times because he was so tired and had fallen twice because it was dark. His thick leather work gloves protected him from the broken crack pipes and needles that littered the stairway, but he couldn't use the gloves, covered with filth and slick with the blood leaking from the bag, to wipe his eyes.

God, how he needed to wipe his eyes.

He didn't want to be anybody's whipping boy.

Dexter had to force the stairwell door open once he reached the top of the tower. Hauling the bag down the silent hallway, he listened to his steps echo and bounce back from the empty apartments. He picked one, entered, and used the dim streetlight filtering through tattered window shades to find a closet. He stuffed the bag inside and left quickly.

Aunt June had told him that he would leave no prints in the dust, but he had forgotten to bring a flashlight to check. He headed back down the stairs. The drunk was still sitting in the same spot, but he said nothing as Dexter passed.

Dexter got home at around 2 A.M. and spent an hour in the bathroom scrubbing his face and standing motionless beneath the hot, weak streams of the shower. Then he rubbed cajeput and caraway oils on his arms and shoulders to soothe the deep ache in his muscles. When he climbed into bed, he fell immediately into a fitful sleep.

He dreamed he stood at the intersection of two wide and dusty roads yelling at an old, old man. Dexter was hungry and very hot. He couldn't make the man understand that he wanted a burger and a cola, not the water and hog maws the man offered. And he wanted rain to cool his skin and thin the thick and humid air. But the heavy, black clouds above refused to burst.

Dexter awoke just before dawn, surprised to feel tears still streaking down his face.

One month later, during a final sweep of the tower to clear it of transients, the substation cops found the body. Neither of them was pleased.

"Overtime," Don Terry, balding and loud, said to his partner. "I want overtime and I want several aspirin. And I want somebody to do something about that smell up there because I am not going back up there until that smell is gone."

Dexter, standing among the crowd of several dozen residents gathered to watch the action, saw Terry's white partner, Philip Cade, continue his conversation into a cellular telephone.

"And I want all of you people to go home," Terry said, glaring at the crowd milling behind the lines of yellow-and-black CRIME SCENE DO NOT ENTER tape. Dexter did not duck when Terry's gaze swept past him. "Unless, of course, one of you happened to see something. Then by all means do step forward."

The residents ignored him, chatting among themselves as they watched the teams of crime scene technicians, clad in black jumpsuits and thin rubber gloves, move in and out of the tower with their tape measures and camera equipment. Terry gave a snort and turned his attention back to the clipboard he carried, placing his broad, flat nose inches from the legal pad.

It was a late afternoon in March and the sun, though bright in the sky, did little to warm the air. Dexter pulled his thin jacket tighter around his body and, with a shiver that had nothing to do with the weather, began shouldering his way through the crowd, heading home. A sharp laugh from Cade made him pause.

"What?" Dexter heard Terry ask his partner.

Cade pulled the mouthpiece of the phone down below his chin. "He said he loves it when people bury bodies in garbage bags. All the pieces are still there and the body decomposes at a significantly reduced rate. He said he can't wait to get his hands on it."

"Tell him about the gooey shit all over it. That's not even blood. I don't know what it is," Terry said. "Tell him about it all looking like mummy bits."

"I did," Cade said. "He said 'Hummmm . . . eeen-ter-est-ing.'"

"When they finally get me, Cade, promise you won't let that medical examiner within ten feet of my weary, dead bones."

Dexter slipped through the familiar hues of blackness around him and headed toward home. He moved briskly at first, but then a scent running deep and mellow through the cold air caught him, and he slowed so she could catch up.

He had lost his mind the first time that smell brought her to his attention, that night at the strip mall. Tamika had set herself aside from everyone else. Balanced by butt heels on a rusted engine block, she hunched over her arms and hugged her knees, a blunt burning down to her knuckles. Dexter couldn't figure out exactly who she was talking to. Her eyes were half closed and looked to be rolled up in her head, showing a damp slit of eyeball turned pale orange by the streetlight, shot through with tiny red lines. He slid a little closer to catch snatches of her mumbled stream, but all he could get was the whiff from her skin rumbling beneath the sweet tang of her smoke. For no reason he could tell, she abruptly stood, flicked her spliff at his feet, and walked off without a wobble or a missed step. He followed.

And every night after, he followed. He'd sometimes try to catch the edge of her eye, but she'd keep about her business, often with Peek, that weird girlfriend of hers, as if he were just another fool. His crowd was beginning to talk and, as he had no defense, he'd shuck and smile it off and keep on staring her way. He pulled his shifts at the five-and-dime, but his mind was everywhere but on the deals that rolled up, one after the other, with windows rolled down just low enough for the money and product to pass through. But that day Tamika's mother walked up to his spot bold as day, in the middle of everything, having decided it was time to negotiate a wholesale rate considering her longtime customer loyalty and all, Dexter knew he was lost. He didn't even ask her to put in a good word after surviving her intense haggling, which she at least had the decency to do away from the corner.

His cousin would have known what to do. Just talking to him about it, talk and nothing else, would have helped Dexter cut through this fog of woman. But he just couldn't bring himself to pull back the beads and hear them click click click behind him as he entered the dark room, telegraphing confusion and sending out his pain. Instead, he tossed Tamika in his head every waking moment, looking for a way out. So he wasn't paying attention that night he was trailed and circled.

A cough ahead startled him. She stood in a waning pool of yellow streetlight, its haze shading all but her shape and the glint of gold at her ear and throat.

"How you end up wit' that Poindexter name, anyway?"

"You gonna be a mouse, or you gonna say what you want?" Dexter did not turn toward her.

She moved beside him, the light, sweet scent of hair oil mingled with too much perfume masking what she wanted. Thick gold bangles on her wrist tinkled as she reached to take his hand, but when she suddenly folded her arms across her chest instead, the bangles clanged.

"Hard to tell when you want to be alone," Tamika said.

"Maybe I do," Dexter said.

"You probably don't," she said.

Old routine. It took some of the edge off Dexter's hostility. They strolled through the complex, past the rows of one-story buildings laid out like barracks in a concentration camp. They stepped on shredded diapers and chunks of brown malt liquor bottles. They passed green Dumpsters and junked cars in the asphalt parking lot. They ignored it all. Each had been born and raised in Citrus Groves and they knew the rules. There were four apartments to a building and you lived in one. You were allotted a tiny, grassless patch of yard and one crumbling concrete stoop. And when a trainee social worker stopped by and "tisked" at how you could live surrounded by such a state of decay, you looked at her. Because she was white and from the southside—they were always white and from the southside—she didn't understand that loathing a life was no excuse not to live it. And when she said so sorry, but the state was cutting back the welfare check because you got a part-time job in a burger joint, you looked at her with a brown-eyed, blank stare. And when she left, she always wrinkled her nose.

"You headed home?" Tamika said.

"Yeah. Cold out here," Dexter answered.

They walked on, kicking crushed aluminum cans back and forth between strides. The game stopped when one can dislodged a scrap of steel wool from its scorched top, sending the curled metal on a tipsy tumble out of their path. Homemade crack pipes could be found everywhere if you knew what to look for. But Dexter was surprised by the surge of guilt he felt. When his cousin had been here, most of the druggies—the ones who used him anyway—confined their activities to their homes or the tower.

But the whipping boy had been dead for a month, and no one had stepped in to take his place. Now the things that were always there, held in check by the force of one man's will, were clawing back out into the open.

Dexter glanced at Tamika, but she was staring over at the police substation in apartment 118 as they passed it, making no sign that she sensed his shame.

"What are all them cops doing here?" she said. "There's as many in there as there is in the tower."

"Can't say," Dexter said, not looking. "I went over there this morning to do my hours, but Cade said to come back later."

"Is that a fact. How many hours you got left?"

"Four."

"Twenty hours of picking up trash for stealing one car, huh?"

"One car they know about."

"You feel reformed? They call that paying your debt to society."

"Society can go to hell."

Tamika laughed, but it wasn't real. She stepped closer to Dexter and took his arm. She slipped her hand down into his jacket pocket to hold his. She looked over her shoulder at the substation again. "I kinda feel sorry for them. Cade and Terry, I mean."

"Community-oriented policing can go to hell too."

"It's just that they think all this is their fault. They been trying so hard this past year. Working out here and all. Moving some of the crime and drugs and all somewhere else so we can have a chance, y'know. So we can have some breathing room and try to come together and take this place back."

"Back to where?"

"You know what I mean."

"Sounds to me like somebody's ma joined their little neighborhood watch program. Sounds like a southside thing to me. Don't sound like a downtown thing."

"At least it's *something*."

"Also sounds like you blamin' me." Dexter pulled his hand away from Tamika's, nudging her away with his elbow. "You blamin' me too, Tamika?" He stopped walking and stared at her.

"I ain't say that. I ain't sayin' it was your fault. I'm just sayin' Cade and Terry don't under*stand*."

Dexter loved it when Tamika got real mad. She dropped all that enunciation.

"Oh. But *you* do?" he said. "You know what it's like to be next in line to end up stuffed in a bag and sittin' on a pile of rat shit in a closet."

"I ain't sayin' that *either*, Dex." Tamika stomped one foot then paced in a tight circle. She tapped one of her gold hoop earrings with a sharp fingernail. "I'm just sayin' that Cade and Terry don't understand why all this shit coming down again just when it looked like things was gonna work out."

"Lemme know when you try to explain it to them. I wanna be there to hear it," he said.

"I'm not gonna tell them nothin', Dex. Ain't nobody gonna tell 'em a thang."

She walked on. After a moment, Dexter followed.

"Everybody's actin' like this is my fault, Tamika. I don't want all this shit on my back."

"Dex, I know for a fact that nobody's come out and told you we were doing the wrong thing."

Dexter shrugged. Unspoken blame was blame nonetheless and, as he had come to find out, could be expressed in many ways.

They came to his apartment. "Bye," Tamika said and stopped on the sidewalk. "No way I'm going in there. That aunt of yours hates me." She gave Dexter a quick hug and turned away.

"Wait," Dexter said. He held her arm and pulled her back. He grabbed her chin as she tried to jerk away and held it still while he examined her face. Tamika had light skin—his aunt called her "high yella"—and though she had obviously tried, her makeup could not hide the fading bruise that spread from her right cheekbone down to her neck. "How's your ma doin', Tamika?"

"She's doing quite well, Dexter, thank you for asking."

"You're lying, Tamika."

"Prove it." She tossed her head back and broke his grip. "You don't want to be bothered with other people's problems anyway, remember?"

"You're not other people, Tamika." Dexter struck a pose, puffing out his chest and placing his balled fists on his hips. He lowered his voice two octaves and rumbled, "You my woman." He smiled. The joke did not ease the tension.

"I'm still other people, Dex. Bye." She turned and walked away.

"I'll call you at home," he said.

"I sure as hell won't be there," she answered, turning to pace backwards while she spoke. "Ma's got a new supplier. You shouldn't a stopped selling to her, Dex. Now the coke she gets is clean."

She took her time walking away from him, each deliberate step swaying her hips a little too far to the right, rolling her teardrop bubble of a butt along, then a little too far to the left. He could watch that gait all day long, he once told Marcus, that day toward the end when his cousin was still lucid and needed to share a secret.

I can't stand them, Marcus had whispered. He hated all those who knelt on his floor and threw their hurt into him. When they lifted their snot-slicked faces up to his, their eyes blinded with tears, he wondered what they saw. Not his grimace. Not his teeth grit so tight that sometimes, if his lip was caught between, it tore and bled. These people, many who knew him when he was still in the world, had forgotten him when he was taken away.

Did Aunt June tell you that, Marcus asked, pushing his hand along the cushion to press against Dexter's thigh, 'cause that is the hardest thing at the start. Harder than the sucking in, harder even than keeping it back once it's gone through you to the holding place. As soon as I am all used up, and it's your time, it will happen to you, boy. You will fall out of the head of every person you know. Each thing that you were to them, every memory held of you, will be gone.

Yeah, she told me, Dexter said.

See, that's why you'll hate them, Marcus said, his voice catching thick in his throat. But hate will make you weak, and this is not a job for a weak man.

With effort, Marcus slid his torso across the wall at his back, until he leaned against Dexter's shoulder, his weight surprisingly heavy despite his emaciated frame. He turned his head so his lips were inches from Dexter's ear, his breath hot and damp. Here's what you do, he said. Don't tell Aunt June.

You can send yourself through the roil of the holding place, through the between of this world and the eternal one. And you can find that one person who was the last to forget you, because in that soul you were truly loved. But when you do it, you got to put aside what it felt like when she forgot. That, what that will feel like, I can't describe to you.

When I get to be all hate, I go to where mine is, to feel her breathe, Marcus said. It's the way she does it, rolling deep from her stomach up languid to the top of her throat, where she'd hold it for barely a second before letting it loose and doing it again. And when I breathe with her a little while, I almost don't hate anybody anymore.

Marcus fell quiet and still for a few minutes, save for the occasional tremor through his legs and torso, which he could not control. Dexter thought he had fallen asleep. But then he asked, what does your girl do.

She walks, Dexter said.

Tamika once used that walk on a boy her friend Peek thought was a man and was stupid for, because it needed to be done. She had warned Dexter what was about to happen, in case it got back to him the wrong way, but she didn't tell Peek. The girl was all head and no sense, Tamika said. None of those books she buried herself in contained the fact that sometimes attention from a male came because, if there was one thing they could pick up on, it was easy desperation. Peek thought he hung the moon, but since Tamika only ever called him "that fuck," Dexter never found out who the boy was, or where he came from.

Tamika waited for a day hot and moist, the kind that drove people in the Groves outside before the sun on the walls turned their apartments into ovens. She settled herself against the chain-link fence surrounding the tower, and watched Peek's door. Eventually, the girl came out onto the stoop, pen in her teeth, spiral notebook in hand. Instead of her usual uniform of baggy T-shirt and shapeless jeans, she was actually wearing a dress. It was brown with huge splotches of pink roses, and its hem swept the tops of her tennis shoes, but still. Tamika had to squint, but she was pretty sure Peek had actually tried to do something with her hair. Several thin twists snaked back from her forehead to just past the tips of her ears, where little butterfly clips held them neatly against her skull, leaving the rest to puff at the back of her head. Peek sat on the top stair, opened her notebook on her knees, and ignored it, staring down the sidewalk.

It wasn't long before that fuck showed up. Tamika winced as she watched Peek stand and wave, then sit back down, then wave again, in case he didn't know she was there, waiting. He didn't even sit down next to the girl, just stood with one foot propped up on the step, the other in the dirt, his body turned half away from her as he scanned the area around them, as if looking for someone more interesting. Peek beamed and patted at her hair and touched at his knee as she leaned back too far, her laugh a too-loud squeal.

Tamika watched this for as long as she could stand, and the next time that fuck's eyes turned toward the fence, she started walking. Slow. Not going anywhere in particular, except past Peek's stoop, nodding at folks along the way. She said hey to Peek as she strolled past, barely glancing at that fuck, who had put both feet on the ground and had turned to watch her come. One hip out just a little too far, then the other. That fuck turned to watch her go, her butt rolling with each step. Then he remembered something he had to do, and that was all he said to Peek as he left her there on her stoop in her new dress and her fresh hairdo, watching him jog down the sidewalk to catch up with Tamika.

When Dexter heard about it, carried to him a good five minutes later by somebody who told somebody that he needed to be told, he laughed.

Peek still ain't talked to her, Tamika had said, digging her nails into Dexter's ribs to let him know again this is *not* funny. Ouch, he had said and pulled her closer, resting his chin on top of her head, which lay against his chest. I gave her his cell, which she didn't have, and his home, which she didn't have either even after all this time, and figured she would get the point, Tamika said. All she did was get mad. At me.

Then maybe you should have just let that weird-ass girl go on and learn something, Dexter said. You not the one should be all tore up like this. I cain't see why you ain't just let her get used and get left, like everybody else.

Because she's the only other one, Dex, Tamika said. I let that happen, she know enough that I could have tried to say something, and didn't, and then she leaves me. This way, maybe when she stops bein' hurt, she still know I'm her real friend, and she still there with me. I got to think about the future, when you're gone. I don't want to have nobody there for me.

Dexter almost told her don't cry. Instead he said, I'm still here, and squeezed. For now, she said, wiping her nose against his shirt. Sorry, she said, and squeezed back.

Marcus was quiet when Dexter finished. He sighed and slowly pushed himself upright, using the wall as a brace. When you go back to walk with her, Marcus finally said, just remember you can't do it for very long, because your will is needed here.

As Tamika paced away from him, still moving backwards through the cool air, Dexter couldn't imagine her ever forgetting him, let alone see himself ghosting back from someplace he still couldn't imagine, to move by her side.

"You better turn around," he shouted, "'fore you fall over something."

Tamika smiled, and took a few more backwards steps before she flipped him off, spun on one foot, and headed down the sidewalk. He watched her until she was a speck, until she was gone, before turning toward apartment 33, home, and went inside.

His cousin had been gone for a month, but his heavy, musky odor, not quite unpleasant, still oozed from every crack in each wall. Dexter took shallow breaths as he tried to slip down the short hallway to his room.

"Come here, boy," his aunt called from the kitchen. "It's time we talk."

Dexter went. Aunt June sat at a tiny Formica table. Cigar smoke and steam from a cup of tea fused to form a shifting veil before her lean face. She waved him to the chair opposite her.

"I saw you talking to that skinny girl of yours out there," she said, after taking a long pull on her slim black cigar. Her lipstick left a blackberry-colored stain on its gold tip. "She was by here earlier looking for you. She tell you what happened?"

"Not really." Dexter laced his fingers on the table and stared down at his knuckles.

"Told me somebody snatched her chains this morning. I figure she was lying."

"Oh."

"I figure it was that two-bit mother of hers."

"She ain't said."

"She didn't look hurt too bad. Just a little beat up in the face."

"No. She didn't look too bad." Dexter shifted under his aunt's unblinking gaze. "I'm sorry."

Aunt June crushed her cigar in a small clay bowl. "She didn't blame you. She wouldn't, not in so many words."

But Aunt June would, Dexter thought, as she quickly ran through the incidents from the past four weeks, starting with the latest.

He'd heard a little bit about the baby already from snatches of conversation in the crowd around the tower. A chunky little boy born last month to the woman over in 217, who tried real hard to make her man see himself in the child's deep brown eyes, in the way he wrinkled his nose just the same, in the size of those feet. He would smile, and hold the baby, and nod and hold the baby, and last night when he held the baby the light hit it wrong, and he knew.

"She said he did it so quiet, all she heard was a little sound, a tiny sound," Aunt June said. "Said she thought it was gas. She was sitting right next to him, watching the TV, and until she took the boy to feed him, she didn't even know."

"Mmn," Dexter said.

"Mmn," Aunt June repeated. "That's what you say. She didn't know her boy was dead until she had him at her tit, and felt his head was not holding right, and saw the blood bubbling on his lips."

From the corner of his eye, he saw Aunt June stir the butt of her smoldering cigar in the ash piled nearly to the brim of the bowl. "And you say, 'Mmn.'" She sat back. He did not look up.

"Should I bother with the rest, then? Because that was my trump. Maybe I played it too early. Maybe I should have started with that fight broke out last week over the mailman putting a birthday card in the wrong box, and that girl thought it got stolen. Or how somebody been stomping down Old Miss Johnson's little bit of gardenias. Chin, you heard about Chin, didn't you? Took that baton upside that boy's head six, seven times? Because he didn't stop fast enough."

"Cops do that," Dexter said, fast and almost loud.

"Not Chin," she said. "That's why they transferred him in here."

She continued, and Dexter half listened to her stories of neglect and theft and violence. These things happened every day in the Groves. So what if it all had escalated in the last month. So what if she thought he had something to do with it.

He sat silent when she finished. "Sorry for those, too." Though a question, Aunt June's tone was flat. She pushed herself up from the table and went to the stove to remove a boiling pot of water. She fixed Dexter a cup of tea. Still silent, she set a jar of honey in front of him, along with a spoon. Finally she sat again and lit another cigar. "It has to be you, boy, there's nobody else. Your mamma only had you, and I can't have any more," she said, exhaling pale blue smoke. "You've never seen what happens when we don't have a whipping boy to go to. But I know you understand."

Yes, Dexter thought, picking up his spoon and dragging it through the thick honey. He understood.

Marcus was the most beautiful man Dexter had ever seen. Dexter remembered how, as a toddler, he would sit on the porch and watch his cousin move through the complex, greeting people and sometimes disappearing in their apartments for hours. Dexter would sit and wait.

Dexter wanted to be just like him.

By the time Dexter was ten, Marcus didn't go out anymore. He stayed in the dimness behind the curtain of wooden beads that separated his area from the rest of the apartment and received his visitors there.

Dexter knew he was never to bother Marcus when he "had company," as Aunt June put it, but once, drawn by the constant weeping and groans he heard back there, he crept beneath the curtain and huddled in the corner, watching.

Marcus was slumped against the back wall, arms and legs splayed across the pile of pillows and blankets on which he sat. Normally his head would be just about even with the blacked-out window above him, even though he sat on the floor. But that day his head lolled to the right as if his neck were broken. A string of drool, glistening in the candlelight, hung from his mouth.

Aunt June sat beside Marcus. She dipped a rag into a clay bowl filled with water, squeezed out the excess, and wiped his face. Water and sweat sheened on his skin.

A sobbing woman knelt before both of them, her back and shoulders heaving. Something was coming out of her and eating his cousin's eyes.

Dexter tried to stifle a gasp and hold his water at the same time. He finally swallowed a gulp of air and quietly wet his pants.

The blue-black mass seeped from the woman's skin and writhed in a cloud around her. Gashes appeared within it and sealed themselves with red tinged puckers as they vanished. A thick tendril of the mass, which Dexter instantly labeled a "blue meanie," stretched out from the woman's chest and snaked toward Marcus. It forked at the end nearest his cousin, wavered, then entered the man's eyes. Smaller tendrils probed across Marcus's body, sometimes sinking beneath his skin, sometimes moving on.

Dexter suddenly thought about his latest English lesson in school. He had gotten a C on the exam because he had messed up most of the word definitions. He had written "to hurt a lot" in the space beside the word "agony." His teacher gave him only half credit for the answer.

Now he knew what the word meant.

Marcus had a lean body, and even toward the end, people could still see the hint of muscles worked to the point of peak performance beneath his skin. That day, they all stood out in stark outline as he strained on the cushions, turning his body into a landscape of hills and valleys covered with writhing blood vessels.

The effect was truly weird at his neck, where, even in the dim light, Dexter could see his cousin's pulse bulge and relax the skin with a steady, slow rhythm.

But through all the body of his pain, his cousin's face was calm.

Dexter thought that was a pretty cool trick.

"And you know I'm right, don't you, boy."

Aunt June's silence brought Dexter back to the kitchen. He had heard nothing she said. "Yes, ma'am."

"That's right," she said with a short nod. "They call us the white man's burden, but if we let them carry it all they'd snap their lily-white backs."

Dexter's teacup had changed from warm to clammy, and he stared down at the liquid. The tea shone with the same oily flatness of all the goldfish he had plucked stiff from their bowls throughout his life. He had been ten when the first one died. At last count, he had flushed five more down the toilet.

"That's real fucked-up if you think I'm gonna die for the white man."

"Wipe those words on the mat when you walk into my house, boy." Aunt June swirled her fingernail around in her cup. "This is not about helping the white man. I'm talking about survival of our spirit. Our people come to us, boy, to your kind, when they just can't *take* it anymore and they have to let it out. You have to be there to trap it and feed it and give the people a chance to heal."

"I say if the people can't take life in the war zone then they need to get out."

"You find me a place on this earth that wants black people and I'll have everybody's bags packed by morning."

"It's not my problem, Aunt June."

"Yes, it *is*." She slammed her fist on the table, making everything on it bounce once. Her ashtray skittered to the side, and Dexter's tea sloshed over his hands. "More yours than anybody. I know how you got the money for those pumped-up shoes and I know how you keep that skinny girl of yours looking so fine in all that gold. I am not blind."

"So you know how I keep the lights on here and a little extra food in the fridge. If you standin' on a moral high ground all of a sudden, I could just leave."

"Don't you *dare* talk to me about morality." She closed her eyes, sighed, then opened them again. "I don't want you to go, boy, I want you to *redeem*. Don't you know that white people will continue to be a danger to us until we learn to live with them? God doesn't give all of us the strength we need to live in their world. That's why some of us turn to you for your drugs. That's why some of us sit and rot and die."

"Pipeheads wouldn't come if they didn't want to, Aunt June. Nothin's stoppin' 'em from walkin' right on by."

Aunt June took a deep breath, curling her hands into tight fists, which she squeezed before relaxing. She calmed her voice. "Get back to my point, boy. You and Marcus and all the ones before you, all the ones all over the world, were put here to help them find that strength. You'll understand when you take what Marcus left for you."

The way she talked, it was a gift wrapped tight with a shiny bow, sitting on the counter. But the memory of his aunt's thick arms straining as she slammed her cousin's skull with a hammer, until it finally popped, made him flinch. Her words were as clipped as her movements precise that night, and with the first scoop, her fingers were glossy. That's all Dexter saw before he turned and pressed his palms against his eyes, leaned forward, and dropped his forehead onto the table top. He did not look up again.

Jesus cast the Legion into pork, she had said. He heard the dull splat of meat tossed into the mason jar by her elbow on the counter.

And the pork was made unclean. He heard the scritch of her nails against hollow, wet bone.

But the pork was all we had. He heard a clatter, then the quick, dull thunks of metal on wood. A light sting of peppers wafted past his nose.

So in that pork is put the spice of man, the insanity of man, she said. The spice of his insanity and his woe.

He heard the sizzle of the pot of salt-laced water boiling over on the stove, heard it scrape when she snatched it from the burner, heard the liquid pour into the jar.

For the one who is cursed by God to work for God, this spice will be the key to his awakening; it is the wisdom and the joy of the ages, and it will see us through. He heard a lid fumble lightly onto the mouth of the jar, heard it thread three times.

And his sons will serve down through the generations, she said. The refrigerator door opened with a sticky suck. Glass tinged gently against a shelf inside. The door closed too quietly for him to hear.

Until God's claim is satisfied, she said.

Dexter remembered how Aunt June said nothing after that; all he heard was the sound of her cleaning. A scouring pad, that sounded like a sponge. The trash bag at his feet crinkled when she placed the skull fragments inside. She stood still when she finished, and sighed. When she left the kitchen, she turned out the light.

"That shit is whacked," Dexter said.

She flinched at the profanity. "What are you going to do, boy, run from your blood? Pretty soon now it will come to you, and you need to be ready."

"I see it pretty clear right now, and it looks like all these little problems you keep pointing out ain't got shit to do with me. It's just *life*. Things *happen*."

"That they do, and God put your kind here to do something about it. Not everything. Just enough. When you refuse to step up, you leave a void, and that angers Him. Every day you rebuke Him, that lurking rage grows. It will feed on us as it searches for you."

"I don't care!"

Aunt June stared at Dexter for a long time. "Then get out. And don't come back. I gave you too much, boy." She gazed at him with her deep golden eyes. "Too much of all the wrong things."

And so he left.

Dexter went first to a stash house two blocks away from Citrus Groves. He cleaned a few guns. He kept an eye on the wannabes, making sure their count was up and matched what they carried. He fixed the spokes on three of their bikes and replaced the batteries of one of their headsets. When Cook ran out of baking soda and cookie sheets, Dexter went to the store and got some, then helped Cook cut the coke with the soda, mix in water, and then they spread the paste on the sheets. Cook put the sheets in the oven and watched them bake, while Dexter rolled melted candles into small pebbles for sale to the stupid and the desperate users.

They sat side by side: Dexter with his knees beneath the metal table and his back to the oven as he worked the wax, Cook leaning his back against the table as he watched the oven. Dexter just wanted to work. Cook wanted to talk.

"How it hang?" Cook said.

"Low."

Laugh. "Don't it always."

"Twenty-four, seven, three sixty-five."

Pause. "Shit man, I got a problem wi' my woman."

"I got my own. Of both."

Silence. Cook got up from his chair, and Dexter heard the scrape of the oven door opening, then felt a short blast of heat against his back. He heard the thump of the door closing again. Cook came back. The cookie sheet sizzled with heat and scraped on the metal table as Cook pushed it toward him. The heat was right by his arm. "Break dis up," Cook said. "Don't be makin' 'em boulders, either."

They all wanted to talk. They had never heard of *Danbhala-Wedo*, the father of all *loas*. They didn't know a shaman from a shank of pork. But still they came, drawn to his blood like flies to cola made thick and syrupy in the sun. After a night and a day Dexter fled to the streets, delivering the rocks, picking up the money, making the rounds and keeping the connections tight.

In the mix. With players black and white and tan. Some with balls and some with slits. Word all over in tit joints and white bars and hoe street. Raw goods moving up from the south next week. Bout time the shit came in. Runnin low. Shit been movin hot all month. Hey Dex, gotta minute? Dex. What up wit him? Vice gonna take down a den on fifth street. Don't know which one they got shit on so clear em all out fo a coupla weeks. Gotta find out who da fuck dimed out. How yo Aunt, Dex? Hey man you hear me? Yo Dex, you hear Wampole got chilled? Yeah it gon stick this time. Uh huh I wuz thinkin the same thang. Wanna take out his second or buy him? Either way we get his shit and turf. Gotta move tho cuz we ain't the only ones thinkin. Lemme know. Naw, man, I don got da cash. Shit, man you ain't gotta be like dat. I git it. Tomorrow. Day after. Wait Dex, I gotta ask you sumtin. Naw it just take a minute. Hey Dex, you hear Old Lady Bowie got kicked out? She over on Patterson. Say we work outta der fo a week maybe two. Maybe three. Depends on five oh. Bet we pull down four, five thou and be out. Dex I gotta talk to you. Dex. Man, ain't you listnin?

In the mix. And out.

Dexter knew the streets, but cocooned within his cousin's thick walls, fortified by the rough realism of his Aunt June, he had never been forced to truly live them. At first, he tried to re-create that stability around himself. He rented an efficiency at a downtown flop. He called Tamika and asked her to join him, and called again after she hung up crying, and kept calling until the time she screamed from so far away I'm *supposed* to forget and I *don't* know why I'm *not* and I can't *do* this *please* stop. But the desperate followed him to the flop and he eventually abandoned it and lived nowhere. By the end of his fourth week on the streets, Dexter had lost himself in the life.

Days passed in a numbing blur of sun and streetlight. He kept on the move by day, jumped the joints and jams by night. He tried to make the world whip by, but the faces of the desperate, all the time, with their moving lips and dripping pain, freeze-framed.

He came across a strawberry pumping down her sidewalk late one night or black one morning. He couldn't tell.

"Jus gimme a dime man, a lil bit." Her hips flowed smooth left to right as she matched his pace. She kept bumping her thigh against his for no reason, like the sidewalk wasn't big enough. "My boy bein so hard on me. Look at what he done." She tilted her head back and pulled the neck of her T-shirt down just until the edge of the dark pink ring of her right tit showed. He glanced over at the scar ripped through her skin, but glanced away when he saw a glimmer of blue ooozing out. "Said I was holdin back. I ain't even do nuthin like that. He jus bein mean."

"No cash, no flash." He continued walking and looked straight ahead.

"Jus a small one, Dex, come on. I trade you." She turned to the side and pressed her belly hard against his thigh, trying not to trip as she did it. "I pay if I could, but I gotta think about my baby girl. She so hungry and I'm so tired." She started to cry.

At the edge of his vision, Dexter saw blue-violet stream from her mouth between gasps.

"I ain't the state, baby. Nothin' for free."

Another night a different street. A wannabe making like he was a man threw all of his twelve-year-old weight behind a bat in a full swing arched tight and low at the knees of another who screamed high and sharp like a woman. From inside the storm raging around them, flecked with bright hot flashes of red and blue-white, came the thud of wood on meat; the pop of a knee losing its anchors to bone. They saw him pass and paused in the heat of it to stare as he walked by. The boy with the bat looked like he would charge and the bleeding boy crawl at him if he so much as skipped a step.

More even, some at night and some during day. Just like Aunt June had warned. The blue meanie felt him and reached for him, even when those it was inside didn't cast it out.

It hurt so much. Dexter tried to block it. But heroin warped and loosened his brain and let so much more in. Powder coke was too smooth, its rock form an all-too-brief shock. He settled for ice, letting the crystal meth sizzle and click his synapses one by one until they shut and fused and left him safe inside an opaque glacial case. The blue meanies turned pastel against the shield and couldn't get through.

Tamika found him in a joint off an alley of a long, dark street.

"Dexter," she said, distant. "Damn, man. You look like shit."

"Clarencecarterclarencecarterclarencecarter. I be strokin. Uh."

"Dexter. Listen to me. Look at me, Dex. Right here, Dex. Look at me."

Tamika tapped two fingers on the scratched bar top. Her nails clicked rapidly against it until Dexter cut his eyes away from the jukebox and focused on her.

"I stroke it to the woman that I love the best. Uh."

"That aunt of yours said it was time. I been all over looking for you. Come home, Dexter."

"You carryin'? You got any money? I only need a little bit. I pay you back."

"You got to come home, Dexter, or you got to leave and die someplace else. It's all out there looking for you with no place to go. So you *got* to come with me. I'll put you on a bus, or I'll take you home."

Tamika leaned closer, dripping violet and blue and black.

"You know what?" Dexter said.

"*Listen* to me, Dexter. It's all gonna bust open. Even I can feel it and I'm not . . . like you. That aunt of yours said if you go, we get back to normal, eventually. God help whoever happens to be around you wherever you end up, though. She say it's gonna get really nasty before it kills you. And it's gonna kill you, Dex. You know that, right? She said because you won't become awake, you won't be able to survive."

"But you know what?"

"Damn you. *Choose.* Wake up and let it in. Or get up and let it follow you away."

"People who fuck with other people ain't got no moral high ground."

Tamika sat very still on the bar stool, staring at him and slowly blinking her eyes.

"You hungry, Dex?"

"Um humn."

"Then let's go. That aunt of yours been stinking up the place all night."

Tamika took him back to the Groves and sat on the stoop outside his apartment while Aunt June led him inside. It was hot in there and Dexter felt the heat pulsing from the walls and the kitchen and the warm concrete floor. He inhaled deep through his nose and held the mingled scents of musk and simmering chitlins inside his lungs. He let it out with a hard whoosh. Aunt June took him to the back of the apartment, holding the curtain of beads aside so he could pass. They clicked when she let them fall back into place.

"I'll get you cleaned up later, boy," she said, stripping off his shirt before pushing him to sit on a pile of cushions. "You need something to eat first."

She lit a candle and left. Dexter leaned against the stucco wall with his back, letting its heat seep through his skull. Aunt June returned with a bowl of steaming chitlins, a spoon, a white dishrag, and a mason jar filled with a substance thick and cloudy.

"I like a lot of peppers in my chitlins," Dexter said. "They got to be hot."

"I know how to cook them, boy."

Aunt June knelt beside him, placing the food to her right and the jar to her left. She lifted the lid of the jar and it opened with a hiss.

"If chitlins ain't got enough peppers, the meat's all rubbery."

"I know that, boy."

Aunt June dipped the spoon in the jar, scooping out gelatinous chunks of gray white meat, which she put into the chitlins. When the jar was empty, she stirred the chitlins until the two were well mixed and handed him the bowl and spoon.

"Eat it fast, before it cools," she said.

Dexter wolfed the food down, hardly tasting the spicy blend of red pepper and onion and celery and potatoes boiled soft. He swallowed rather than chewed; partly out of a need to consume real food after such a very long time, but mostly because he didn't want to feel the soft mash of flesh between his teeth and have to wonder if the meat came from the guts of a pig or the head of a man. He made a mess, which Aunt June wiped away from his face before sticking the dishrag into his mouth and holding it there firm. She pressed his head against the hot wall and held his shoulder firm against it with her other hand.

"Now. Wait."

Too much food in a shrunken stomach, Dexter thought at first when his muscles began to clench and buck, trying to vomit. But then his heart dropped and his head pounded and the ice there shattered. And the voices came. First Marcus. Then his uncle. Then others from farther back: baritones and tenors sing-scatting of marches and nooses and clunking chains and cotton and survival. Beneath it all the rumbling bass of old Pappa Legba, laughing and storming and strict. Dexter felt them and listened to them and learned. They taught him how to draw the blue meanies, and they laughed at his name for it. They told him how to hold it in his blood until it boiled thick through all the layers and grew weak and trapped in his muscles. The lesson took forever and a day.

"The first is always the hardest because you have to leave the one you love most," Marcus told him, because he was closest. "Bringing in what's built up is hard too. I remember. But you'll manage. And you'll learn."

Cool wet against his cheek brought Dexter back to the small, square room. Aunt June wiped the rag across his forehead, then down and across his eyes. He opened them and looked at her.

"You can come on in now, girl," she said, staring back at him.

The curtain clicked, and Tamika walked in slowly. She knelt before both of them and stared at the floor. She glanced up at him once, winced, dropped her eyes again, and began to cry.

Dexter watched the swirls rise out — blue from her arms and legs, red from her head, black and violet from her heart.

"You remember what I told you," Marcus said, closer still, as if he pressed tight against Dexter with his lips at his ear. "You can still walk with her. Sometimes."

Dexter reached out and drew her in. She crawled across his flesh and bit and clawed as he sucked her roil into his skin. It felt like spit, her anger at his choosing to abandon her, even though she knew the truth of his helplessness. It felt like brine, her fearful grief of being alone because he left, falling against him in wave after unrelenting wave.

Good-bye, Dexter. I loved you. Not fair. What about me?

And when he felt the last bits of him flow from every part of her, the shocking sense of peace she felt with him forgotten, it made him scream.

That's when, from everywhere, it came. All the rage.

OLD FLESH SONG

Ibi Aanu Zoboi

(2004)

> *mati pa a wélé—*
> *mati pa a wélé wélé.*
> *wélé wélé kojo polo polo*
> *wélé kojo pa a polo—*
> *kojo pa a polo.*

She did not sing for money. Nor did anyone want to get close enough to drop a coin in her basket. She reeked of death—the odor of the underworld, the nether life, where the aroma of things sustaining growth and change is halted. Her life cycle was stagnant, circulating in its own juice—like cells forming blood clots. She lived in death and emanated its essence—stale, old flesh. Nothing sweet and joyous would come from this. So she sang a melancholy song, with no audience and no requests for charity.

Of all the sidewalks, subways, and street corners in the callous city, she decided to settle in front of the Willoughby & Company Toy and Gift Shop on Seventy-seventh and Lexington. There were no others of her kind around. She was an isolated sore oozing bitterness onto the lively, cosmopolitan Upper East Side of Manhattan. She sat there on the cold concrete wrapped in African mud cloth, the tapestry of her native home. It was neither dirty nor clean; mud cloth has the semblance of filth even in its purest state—like her face, blueblack, hard, old, yet innocent. Her hair was matted into seven coils extending from her head with lives of their own like serpents. Around her sat three bags: one of the same mud cloth, a woven backpack basket embroidered with cowry shells, and a pastel-colored baby bag. All three filled with life, contrary to the odor, stuffed with odd things she's picked up from here and there and claimed as her own.

They've held her and fed her to this point—kept her grounded and connected to this material world—treasured things of no value. She carried the three bags with her, never let them out of her sight, and held on to them, just as they held her, for dear death.

She would sing her sad song whenever a stroller passed her, usually being pushed through the sliding doors of Willoughby & Company. Always in a stroller, never in a slingy or carried in enveloping arms. And only certain babies—babies that were not pushed by their own relatives, but by temporary, rented parents. She would see the baby nestled in blankets cooing and waving pinkish hands and feet at her. They never winced or turned up *their* tiny noses at her. She would watch the guardians send a quick cold glance—their faces contrasting the pale, transparent hue of the fresh young blood— some blue-black like hers and others in various shades of brown.

Baby's parents are gone for the day. So Ms. Nanny will take care of precious Baby. Keep Baby in a stroller so there's no confusion. Here's a list. Ms. Nanny can take Baby for a walk over to Willoughby & Company for some toys. And here's a little extra for Ms. Nanny if she wants to get herself something nice. Watch out for Lady Bag, though. She likes babies.

Old Flesh was hungry. Not for food. Nothing grown or processed in this decaying world would sustain her. She yearned for something fresh and abundant with life. It would keep her here in this sprawling city, watching everything else decay around her, and she remaining on the brink of death itself, never entering its gateway.

It was mid-May, and nannies were to take the babies out of their luxuriant condos for some spring air. Always with the list for Willoughby & Company. *Not that they don't trust Ms. Nanny's taste, but they know just what Baby needs. A ceramic oriental-painted rattle for Baby. Stay away from Lady Bag. They understand that those people need a little help . . . well, some more than others. Ms. Nanny may want to help, but she shouldn't get too close with the baby and all.*

Old Flesh had noticed them crossing the busy intersection. A three-wheeled carriage, something she's been seeing more of lately. Maybe not called a stroller, but a jogger, since she'd watched parents pushing the baby along while they went for early morning or late afternoon jogs through Central Park. Of course Ms. Nanny wouldn't be the one jogging. But this one was pushing the jogger toward the corner nonetheless. Young Blood had no socks; plump legs and tiny feet were exposed. Old Flesh licked her lips. And sang her invocation:

> *"mati pa a wélé—*
> *mati pa a wélé wélé.*
> *wélé wélé kojo polo polo*
> *wélé kojo pa a polo—*
> *kojo pa a polo."*

Her focus shifted toward this Ms. Nanny. She was young, her skin a smooth caramel brown, high cheekbones, thick lips, and broad nose—raw features from native soil. Starting out too early. Lured to leave home with the promise of food, shelter, and if lucky education, to be at the beck and call of nice folks—good families that take care of you, if you take care of them.

Put you out your misery, girl, Old Flesh thought. She grunted, wiped her salivating mouth with the back of her hand, and continued her commanding chant.

Young Blood noticed her immediately. They always did. Bright blue eyes glared at her from the shadow of the hood. Ms. Nanny swerved the jogger toward the edge of the sidewalk away from Old Flesh, nearly bumping a pedestrian. Old Flesh wrapped the mud cloth around her shoulders and large bosom and began to move from her comfortable spot. She pushed the basket aside and pushed herself up to her feet. Ms. Nanny and Young Blood were making their way into Willoughby's, of course. Old Flesh sang louder—sound vibrations luring them back to her. Her muscles ached as she moved closer to the sliding-door entrance. She did not walk placing one foot in front of the other, but wobbled—her rotund hips moving from side to side, adding an invisible drumbeat rhythm to her chant. Her stench followed her like a ghost, deterring pedestrians from her presumed path. She waited. They would soon come out. Young Blood first, then Ms. Nanny pushing behind. Old Flesh's song came to a stop. Its spell had reached.

The doors slid open; the first wheel was visible. White bottom of Young Blood's feet greeted her. Ms. Nanny was looking around as if searching. Old Flesh nodded to herself in approval of the traveling words of her song. Young Blood had heard and obeyed. So had Ms. Nanny, but not in the same way. Old Flesh knew she would recognize the broken cadence—not as a pleasant spell, but as a bold command. Old Flesh watched Ms. Nanny search for the spell caster. Their eyes met. Ms. Nanny's face twisted in confusion. The grating sound resonated from Old Flesh, but her lips merely drizzled saliva like a feasting predator. Ms. Nanny looked elsewhere. Her attention was diverted, the stench was concealed from her, and she focused on her mission to search for the lips sending incantations into the noisy city wind.

Then and there Old Flesh seized her opportunity to quench her hunger. Quick as the tongue, a fatty charcoal hand pulls the pink/white tiny feet, its body came with it, wiggling, squirming, but not resisting. A mere fifteen pounds, feather-light to Old Flesh. It was routine for her, scooping babies with one large hand. A Ms. Nanny's skill—baby in one hand, and dusting, cooking, or perhaps twin in the other. This Ms. Nanny was too young and unseasoned. *Keep one eye on Baby and the other on everyone else.* Old Flesh pulled Young Blood toward her and underneath her mud-cloth wrap—like stealing a porcelain baby doll from Willoughby's.

Young Blood didn't cry, of course, lulled by the remnants of the command/spell. Old Flesh didn't move just yet. She saw Ms. Nanny's face disappointed, looking every which way for the witch's lips. The incantation withered into an echo, far into the distance, away from its victim's ear. Ms. Nanny was now conscious of the odor. She took a quick glance at Old Flesh. Old Flesh returned a toothless grin. A perfectly still Young Blood bulged from beneath the mud-cloth wrap. Ms. Nanny was oblivious; she turned the empty stroller toward the other direction, away from Lady Bag. Old Flesh watched her. She wouldn't look into the stroller for a while, still mesmerized by the chant now only echoing in her memory.

Old Flesh smiled, then giggled, then laughed—deep and hard, throwing her head back in amusement at herself and the stupidity of herself. She remembered being just as oblivious at one point in her life/death. She had succeeded. First of the three Young Bloods she needed to feed on to keep her alive in death. These Young Bloods would be different since they were not in her immediate possession like the ones before. Two more attempts like this and she was done.

Young Blood began to squirm. Its instinct told it to search for food just the same. Old Flesh felt its head move around her right breast. Of course she had no milk. But it was the sensation she longed for—the quenching of her thirst/hunger. She went back to her spot, and eased down onto the concrete with Young Blood wrapped in the mud cloth and her thick arms. She leaned against the brick wall and sighed to herself, smiling in pleasure. She pulled the three bags securely around her and Young Blood: protection. Old Flesh uncovered Young Blood's face. White with the semblance of purity, cheeks pink for love needed, eyes blue reflecting Old Flesh's matron Yemaya, goddess of deep ocean waters—motherhood. She pulled out a sagging left breast and placed a shriveled black nipple in Young Blood's mouth. Young Blood was eager, deprived of its natural joy, since probably weaned at a too-young age. *They know what's best for baby. But a baby need milk like mother breast need sucking. But IT AIN'T YOURS! IT AIN'T. . . . But it mine if I care for it. It mine if I feed it with my own.*

Old Flesh gasped at the sensation of Young Blood's tiny, warm mouth wrapped around her nipple. Young Blood sucked and pulled, making snapping sounds at the back of its throat. It began to writhe in frustration. No milk. Young Blood was not the one hungry, Old Flesh was. But she fed it emptiness/death nonetheless—feeding herself in the process. Young Blood pulled, Old Flesh pulled harder—her desiccated breast suctioned for life, for blood. Young Blood's plump cheeks stiffened in the pull, Old Flesh's breast inflated. Not giving milk, but receiving fresh young blood for her old flesh. She leaned her head back, ecstatic from the sensation. *Ms. Nanny, Baby hungry now. Can't eat until Baby is fed. Can't go home until Baby sleep.*

wélé kojo pa a polo, Old Flesh whispered to herself.

Young Blood lay limp in her arms. Skin pale, no more pink cheeks, frozen eyes a deathly gray. Old Flesh, her soul now one-third vitalized, bent her head to place a chapped-lip kiss on its forehead. Not a young blood anymore, but a lifeless thing—flesh, not old but young, useless just the same. She pulled its mouth away from her now perky nipple. She looked up to watch passersby afraid to look in her direction wondering what she was up to, diverting from her shielding stink. Old flesh discreetly took young flesh from the warmth of the mud cloth, opened the pastel-colored baby bag, and gently placed the body inside. There was room for two more.

Old Flesh zipped the baby bag, and gently tapped the young flesh inside. She readjusted the mud cloth around her and caressed her left breast. She felt the blood travel from what was once the food source for young bloods, penetrate warrior cells, travel through her veins and into her pumping heart. Decayed body ached for more if only to slow its putrefying process. Old Flesh breathed in, gathering all else that was consumed from Young Blood in her lungs: its soul. No use for it in her body—blood and flesh was sufficient. She held her breath, grabbed the mud cloth bag, opened it, and released Young Blood's life force into it, along with the others. The distant cries of young blood souls emerged—like smoke from a burning inferno. She quickly closed the bag so no one else heard.

Rest. Only two more.

Old Flesh was awoken by another young blood's cry penetrating the afternoon city noise. She wiped her eyes, licked her lips, and smiled. The sound came from the fruit stand in the middle of the block. The carriage faced her. A large one, enough for two. Twins. Old Flesh kissed her fingertips and raised them up to the sky, thanking her matron Yemaya. With the same hand, knocked on the concrete beneath her three times for the nameless gods/ancestors of the underworld. She took another look at the twin young bloods—plump hands and feet moving in unison. She licked her lips, cleared her throat, and pulled the magic sound vibration from her soulless body:

"mati pa a wélé . . ."

The song traveled past irrelevant bystanders to reach its subjects. She craned her neck to see the Twin Young Bloods. One, just as pale as she liked, wispy blond hair with blue baby suit. The other a contrast to its sibling with lush dark hair, large fisted hands, and pink baby suit. Blond Twin Young Blood moved about in its section of the carriage. It had reached. To Old Flesh's surprise, Fisted Young Blood began to whimper, defiant to the command/spell. Louder. *mati pa a wélé* . . . Old Flesh saw the back of a large woman turn in her direction. Thicker, stronger than her. She did not look around, but gazed right at her. This Ms. Nanny was old and conditioned. Old Flesh's challenge.

You been in this for a long time, woman. Put you out your misery too. Be easy if only you know you miserable, Old Flesh thought, while stirring the entrancing words into the city noise.

Ms. Nanny's high-yellow face twisted—not in confusion, but in resentment. She was beautiful. Long dark hair braided above her shoulders. Eyes deep and suspicious. *Keep one eye on baby and the other on everyone else.* She watched Old Flesh. Old Flesh continued her command/spell. Louder. *wélé wélé kojo polo polo* . . .

Ms. Nanny picked the crying Fisted Twin Young Blood from its section of the carriage. She held it against her bosom, rocking back and forth. Fisted Twin Young Blood continued to cry. Old Flesh could not stop until both young bloods obeyed. The echo of the command/spell was to be left for Ms. Nanny.

It did not reach. Old Flesh's eyes traveled down to Blond Twin Young Blood. His tiny head was moving from side to side as if annoyed by the grating sound. He was most vulnerable. Louder. *wélé kojo pa a polo* . . . If not the other, then definitely this one. But one of them had to be out of Ms. Nanny's protective glare. Ms. Nanny tried to hush Fisted Twin Young Blood, and began to push the stroller with her free hand—a Ms. Nanny's skill. *Shit! She ain't 'posed to come to me.* Ms. Nanny's jaws were clenched, eyes fierce, ready for confrontation. Old Flesh reduced the chant to a whisper, strengthening its power to her defiant subjects. She could hear Ms. Nanny as she approached.

"Shh, *mija. No tengas miedo.* Don't be scared, my daughter." She wrinkled her nose as she approached Old Flesh's stink shield.

Old Flesh merely stared up at her. Softly. *mati pa a wélé* . . .

"What are you doing, old lady?" Her Spanish accent was thick, her voice was commanding—typical of a seasoned Ms. Nanny.

Old Flesh could not stop the command/spell. They were too close. She was still hungry. Two more to go. She had at least one young blood within her reach. She could not let it slip. She whispered one last strong verse to herself, watching Blond Twin Young Blood, hoping its eyes would meet hers for confirmation:

> *"mati pa a wélé—*
> *mati pa a wélé wélé.*
> *wélé wélé kojo polo polo*
> *wélé kojo pa a polo—*
> *kojo pa a polo."*

(come to me young blood—/come to me fresh young blood/fresh young blood feeds stale old flesh/young blood feed my old flesh—/feed my old flesh.)

"No!" Ms. Nanny yelled, holding Fisted Twin Young Blood away from Lady Bag.

Old Flesh's whispered spell/command had not reached. Fisted Twin Young Blood's cry permeated its power. She glared at them, curious of their shield.

"*Qué haces?*" Ms. Nanny repeated. She heard the words. Merely words to her that she had deciphered.

"Exactly what I just said. You heard me, ain't you?" Old Flesh's voice raspy, strong, and commanding just the same.

"You can't have them!"

"I *can* if you give 'em to me," Old Flesh toyed with her. "I won't hurt you. Just need a little something to sustain me, that's all."

Ms. Nanny chuckled—a knowing, confident laugh. Old Flesh joined her. She had already been defeated with the spell/command song. Now she would charm her way to one of the young bloods.

"Come on. Won't you give 'em to me. They ain't yours."

"*Pendeja loca!* Crazy bitch! I know what you've been doing. *Chupasangre! Soucouyant!* Bloodsucker!" Ms. Nanny's eyes glowed red, ready to aim at Old Flesh. Fisted Twin Young Blood stared just the same.

Old Flesh smiled, giggled, then laughed. "You can see me? You know what I want? I know what you want. Let's make a deal." Old Flesh reached over to open the backpack basket in front of her, releasing more of the deathly aroma—her last resort.

Ms. Nanny watched her and quickly placed her hand over her mouth, releasing her firm clutch on the stroller.

Old Flesh saw her mistake from the corner of her locked stare. "Them babies ain't yours. Why care for them so? Give 'em to me and you can go back to your own children."

Ms. Nanny tightened her hold on Fisted Twin Young Blood and reached into her bag for . . .

Old Flesh seized her moment. Quick as the tongue, she grabbed the foot of Blond Twin Young Blood; its body came with it, wiggling, squirming, but not resisting. This one was heavier—one quick pull toward her bosom and beneath her mud-cloth wrap.

Ms. Nanny leaped forward. "*No, mijo! Dame mi hijo, chupasangre!*"

"Somebody call the cops! Police, over here. Emergency!" A faceless voice yelled from the now encircling crowd. Not too close; Old Flesh's stink shield kept them far enough away not to interfere.

Ms. Nanny froze when the baby in her arms began to cry again. "*Por favor, Señora.* Don't hurt my baby," she pleaded, choking on tears. "Is fresh blood you want? I can give to you, please."

"*My? My baby?* Now you know damn well they ain't your babies. I'm trying to help *you* out, Ms. Nanny. Get you back to your own children." Old Flesh's mouth watered, her heart raced. The young blood against her bosom increased her hunger.

Ms. Nanny straightened herself, hoisted the baby onto her hip, and sniffed back her tears. "My name no Ms. Nanny. You know who I am. *Dame lo.* Give me the baby, Lorraine." Her eyes glowed red again.

"Don't make a difference what your name is." Old Flesh caressed Blond Twin Young Blood's face. "It's all the same work. Other people's babies suck the life out of you. Ain't even have time to watch your own seed die. Just taking back what's owed to me, that's all." She slowly began to uncover her left breast. "And I ain't nobody's Lorraine, you hear. Lorraine is gone. Gone!"

"You no want to keep doing this, Lorraine," Ms. Nanny responded.

Old Flesh's stink shield began to take form as the crowd began to grow. It became a thin, pale green resistant wall of smoke surrounding her and her prey. The city noise was muffled. The cops had already surrounded it, punching and shooting unsuccessfully at the stink shield.

"Oh yes I do. Fed, cleaned, healed them little sickly things 'til my breasts fell flat. Never had enough for my own. My own . . ." Old Flesh looked down at Blond Twin Young Blood. Its drooling mouth was instinctively searching for food from her breast. She would fulfill its desire.

"mati pa a wélé . . ."

Old Flesh looked up. The command/spell did not come from her. Blond Twin Young Blood looked around in curiosity, its attention diverted from the breast.

Ms. Nanny sang the words. Sweet and tender. Deadly and entrancing, nonetheless.

"You not too smart, Lorraine. You no let them suck you dry like that. You come first. Feed you first."

"You *soucouyant* woman too, eh? Who you?"

"Celia. I clean up your mess, Lorraine. You eating all those babies. You put yourself out of work, you want to put us out of work, too? Have those good people going crazy looking for missing babies? No one wants to hire us. I serve Yemaya." She kissed her fingertips up to the sky. "This is my life's work. I will cook you in your own stolen blood before I let you take what's mine!" Celia hissed, eyes enflamed.

"How dare you blaspheme her name!" Old Flesh leaned toward Celia. "Yemaya don't take, she give. I mothered them babies like they my own. But they wasn't. Was supposed to be taking care of mine. Let them die instead. She cursed me. Can't go nowhere but here, in between. Can't live, can't die. I need young blood."

Celia laughs. Baby fully alert in her arms. "*Pobrecita.* You got it all wrong. That's why you here. Yemaya, the great mother, she no curse. She love and cares. You, *mija*, hurt yourself. You don't know there's enough love in those *tetás* to feed the whole world. Heh, Lady Bag?"

"Ain't enough love for me! Ain't enough love for me!" Old Flesh pounded her free hand on her chest, tapping into the vacant body. If a soul were there, she would've been crying by now.

"Yes, there is, *mija*." Celia placed out a warm hand. "You serve good, and you will get what you want."

Old Flesh, confused by the sudden warmth and kindness, didn't know if she should reach for Fisted Twin Young Blood or Celia.

"No! You can't fool me!"

"Give me the young blood, Lorraine," Celia's commanding voice returned. She stepped closer into the stink shield and knocked over the mud-cloth bag with her foot. Surprisingly light, it fell over and opened. Smoke from the burning inferno of young-blood souls escaped from the opening.

"No!" Old Flesh screamed, unable to grab the bag from her sitting position. Blond Twin Young Blood, startled by the sound, began to cry. A melody of baby cries joined with it. The weeping souls escaped from the bag, permeating the stink shield, lingering above Old Flesh in search of their blood and bodies.

"*mati pa a wélé*—" Celia began to sing the command/spell, sweetly, luring the weeping souls out of the bag. Both babies cried along with the weeping souls, moving their heads about as if watching the souls fly around.

"You can't have 'em." Old Flesh needed the souls; they sustained her just as well.

"*mati pa a wélé wélé*—" Celia continued, with a chorus of crying babies, adding harmony.

The weeping young-blood souls formed a halo of smoke above Old Flesh's head. Old Flesh was getting weaker. She needed young blood to continue. She could no longer hold Blond Twin Young Blood in her arm. She quickly grabbed the pastel-colored baby bag to place its squirming body into it.

Celia smiled at her mistake. The baby was no longer in her possession. "*wélé wélé kojo polo polo*," she continued, commanding the bodiless young bloods.

The halo of weeping souls encircled Old Flesh. Baby cries became shrieks, piercing Old Flesh's ears. She placed both hands over her ears and began her grating version: *"mati pa a wélé,"* contrasting Celia's melody, impenetrable to the screams.

Old Flesh's command/spell could not reach. She felt her body become weaker as the strength of the previous young blood began to diminish. The halo descended. Screaming. *Old Flesh feed my young blood. Feed my young blood.* The smoke of weeping souls surrounded her body. Her blue-black skin began to sag, and fade. The smoke of weeping souls spiraled her breast, pulling life, just as they were supposed to.

"No!" Old Flesh screamed, feeling her death pulled from the life source.

The smoke of weeping souls grew larger, high-pitched sounds muting the encompassing noise. Old Flesh's body became a deflated prune, slowly decaying, releasing her life/death into the stolen souls. The halo grew larger. Old Flesh dissipated into the sea of screams, becoming one with the halo. No more Old Flesh. Old soul merged with young blood. The baby screams diminished into the noise. A slight echo of the whispered broken command/spell trailed off into the wind: *wélé kojo pa a polo— kojo pa a polo."* (young blood feed my old flesh—feed my old flesh)

The twin babies stopped crying just as the halo of smoke disappeared.

"I put you out your misery, Lady Bag," Celia said. She looked at the three bags, then noticed the perplexed crowd around her. The frightened cops didn't know which way to point their guns. The stink shield dissipated with the spring breeze. She placed the dark-haired baby girl in her section of the stroller. She reached down into the pastel-colored baby bag and removed the blond baby boy and placed him next to his sister. She grabbed the body-filled bag and licked her lips.

There were enough bodies to feed on for a while.

She turned the stroller away from the stench and the other two bags and made her way through the crowd.

" 'Scuse me, *por favor."* She pushed the stroller over to Willoughby & Company and reached down into her pocket for her list.

WHISPERS IN THE DARK

Walter Mosley

(2001)

1

"Yeth he did too. Popo called me on the vid hithelf an' he wath on'y two year ole," Misty Bent said to her wide-eyed niece, Hazel Bernard. They were sitting out on the screened porch above the Tickle River. Misty's drooping left eyelid and gnarled, half-paralyzed hands did not mask her excitement.

"You kiddin'?" Hazel exclaimed.

"Tole me hith mama wath thick on the flo', that he called the hothpital but he wanted me to know too." Misty shook her head, remembering Melba's death. "I beat the ambulanth but Death got there quicker thtill. Doctor Maynard called it a acthidental overdoth tho we could put her in the ground with a prietht and thome prayer beadth, but you know Melba had had all thee could take. You know it hurt me tho bad that the blood vethel broke in my head."

"Her life wasn't no harder than what we all have to go through," Hazel Bernard said. She shifted her girth looking for a comfortable perch in the cheap plastic chair, but there was none.

"But you cain't compare her an' uth, or you'n me for that matter. Ith all diff'rent."

"What's that crazy talk s'posed to mean?" the big woman challenged. Hazel said she dropped by to see how Misty was coming along after the stroke but really she was there to see if Chill Bent, Misty's ex-convict son, had come back to live with her as she had heard.

"Ith juth what you thinkin'," Misty replied.

"What you know 'bout what I'm thinkin'?" Hazel asked. She was thirty years younger than Misty, but she was also the eldest of thirteen. Hazel had been the ruler of the roost since the age of nine, and no old woman's pretending was going to trick her.

"You thinkin' that the tht'oke done methed wit' my mind, that I'm feeble in the head 'cuth my left thide ith parali'ed. You think I cain't take care'a Popo but you wrong."

"I do not think any such thing."

"Oh yeth you do too," Misty said. "That'th why you heah. I know. And you wrong but you done anthered your own queth'ton in bein' wrong."

Hazel shifted again and grunted. This was a day taken away from her housework and her children.

She swallowed her anger and asked, "Are you tired, Auntie?"

Little Popo wandered onto the deck then. He was small for thirty months but his movements seemed more like those of an old man lost in memories than those of a child discovering the world.

"Hi, Popo," Hazel said. "Come here."

"Huth," Misty hissed. "He thinkin'. He'll talk when he want to."

"What? You don't call him to come sit on your lap?"

Popo went up to the edge of the deck and pressed his face against the loose screen.

"Don't fall, baby," Misty whispered.

The boy rocked back on his heels, his tiny black hands replacing his face upon the screen. He wore a white T-shirt and denim blue jeans with no shoes. His thick hair stood out long and wild but it wasn't matted.

"Rain's comin'," Popo said.

"That's right," Hazel said. "Weatherman said that a storm's gonna come outta the Gulf tonight. You're right, Aunt Misty. He is smart to hear that on ITV and remember it like that."

"No Internet in thith home," Misty proclaimed. "Not even no old TV or radio that work. Thill thay it would meth Popo up."

"Chill? No ITV?" Hazel didn't know which road to hell was worse. Both together tied her tongue.

"I smell it," Popo said, looking at the big visitor in the purple dress. "It smells like the knife an' fo'k when they wet."

The boy climbed up onto Hazel's big thigh and sat like a tiny Buddha staring into her eyes. Beyond him Misty wheezed and doddered, grinning madly.

"He been readin' though," Misty said. "Thometime he read in the paper an' then he try an' fool uth, actin' like he got the thight."

"No uh-uh Gramma no. Not Popo. I smelt it. I did."

Hazel was a little disconcerted by the steady stare of the toddler. She was used to children his age having wandering, slightly amazed eyes. She shifted him to the crook of her left arm and bent over to snag the edge of the newspaper from the dinner tray between her and Misty. Popo giggled at the sudden movement. When Hazel sat back he hugged her big breast.

"Read to me from this," she commanded, handing him the *Thaliaville Sparrow*.

Popo took the paper from his aunt and looked at it as if it were some sort of foreign document that he had to study before he could even tell which way it was meant to be read.

"Hm," Hazel grunted.

Misty grinned and drooled just a bit.

Popo shifted the paper around and finally held it sideways.

"'Jacksonville, Mississippi,'" he said, pronouncing each syllable as if it were its own word, "'was rewarded yesterday by one of its native sons, Lyle Crandal. Today that son of a carpenter performed a miracle by breaking the four zero second bar-I-er on the four zero zero met-er at the two zero two four Oil-Im-pics.'"

"No," Hazel said on an intake of air.

"Uh-huh," Popo squeaked indignantly.

"This is amazin'," Hazel said to Misty.

"You thee," Misty replied. "You cain't compare yo'thelf to Melba'th mind or mine or hith. I got a blood clot and Melba had the blueth tho bad that thee couldn't breathe right half the time. Popo got thometim' in hith head that thmell thunderthtormth an' read before he potty trained. Tho Melba could die if thee want to and that don't make her leth than you. Ith on'y God can make a judgment. On'y God can thave uth or no."

"On'y God," Popo said, staring deeply into Hazel's eyes.

"You got to get him tested," Hazel said over the child's head. "You got to get him registered and trained by the Elite Education Group in Houston or San Francisco."

"No." At the sound of the masculine voice Popo's head jerked around.

"Chilly!" the boy shouted excitedly.

Popo jumped out of Hazel's lap, tumbled down her shins and hit the floor. His tiny lips trembled near tears from the fall but his eyes stayed focused on the powerful man in the denim overalls.

"Hey, baby boy," Chill said. He bent over and scooped Popo off the floor with one hand. In his other arm he cradled a colorful box and a big red book. "You got to stay up off'a the flo'. It's dirty down there."

"Sorry," the boy said as he snatched the book from the crook in his uncle's arm.

"My first shimistree set," the boy read out loud.

"It's got all kinds'a experiments you could do with chemicals," Chill said. "They got ones for electricity and computers too."

Popo giggled and bounced on Chill's arm to indicate that he wanted to be put down. Chill leaned over again, allowing Popo to sit in an empty plastic chair. The clear-eyed child was already deep into the words of the book.

"What you mean no?" Hazel said.

"I mean we not sendin' Popo away to some white man's idea of what smart and good is. All they do is wanna turn him against hisself. He's my nephew an' he belongs with his family."

"But you can't help him, Chill," Hazel argued. "He needs computers and tests and teachers smart enough so he cain't fool 'em."

"He ain't gonna fool me," Chill said dismissively. The pale and jagged scar along his black jawline spoke of the violence and rage in the young man's life. "An' the books all say that he just needs to keep his mind busy learnin'. First books and things to keep his hands and mind busy, and then later he can be taught by teaching computers. That's what the experts say."

Chill put the bag down next to his nephew, who was already halfway through the children's chemistry primer.

"Look," Hazel said, pointing. "He almost finished with that book already."

"Naw. He just read the words. He have to go through it five or six times 'fore he be through with it. It'a be more than a week 'fore he gets through all those experiments."

"And you gonna buy him a chemistry set or whatever every week? Where you gonna get money like that? Do you even have a job?"

"I'm workin' for the catfish farms and doin' some work around here and there."

"That's gonna pay for a boy like Popo's education?"

"I got other plans."

"Like the plans put you on Angola Farm?"

"Prison," Popo said even as he turned a page.

Chill stared at Hazel. He clenched his fists hard enough to make his sinewy forearms tremble.

"Thtop!" Misty Bent commanded.

Popo sat up in his Buddha position and Hazel flinched.

Misty had pulled herself to her feet by holding on to her plastic walker.

"Aunt Misty, sit down," Hazel said.

"You go," the elder woman replied. "You go and don't meth with uth. Thilly want do right. Popo jutht lotht hith mama an' he never knew hith daddy. That Johnny Delight wath juth a hit'n run with hith mama. We ain't thendin' him nowhere."

2

"M Bill Bent?" the white man asked. He was standing at the front door, tam in hand.

Chill had been doing push-ups and wore only a pair of sweatpants. His muscular chest was heaving and sweat poured down his face.

"No," Chill said.

"Oh." The white man hesitated. "Then is M Misty Bent here?"

"She in the bed."

"Oh, I see," the small white man said. There was a hint of Mississippi in his voice but in spite of that he spoke like a Northerner. "Well, you see, I'm Andrew Russell from the state board of education. I've come to speak to someone about Ptolemy Bent."

In the background Chill could hear the radio receiver that Popo was experimenting with in his grandmother's room. The high-pitched wavering reminded Chill of the sound effects from the old science fiction movies that they showed on Saturdays at the juvenile delinquent detention center.

"What you want wit' Popo?"

"Popo. Is that what you call Ptolemy? We have been informed by various interested parties that the child is exceptional, bright. There's a state law that we must test exceptionally bright children to make sure that they're getting the proper education. You know IQ is our greatest resource." Andrew Russell smiled and nodded a little. He wore a tan blouse and a brown tam.

"State law is you can't touch 'im till he sixty-one mont's," Chill said.

"But with his guardian's approval we can test as early as twenty-foah," Russell said in what was probably his friendliest tone.

Chill closed the door slowly, controlling his rage. He knew that he couldn't lose his temper, not while Popo was his responsibility.

"Popo," Chill called.

"Wit' Gramma," the child shouted.

She was surrounded by colored lights that Ptolemy had wired around the room. Yellow and blue and green and pink paper shades that had been colored with food dyes, lit by forty-watt bulbs. Four-year-old Ptolemy sat at his grandmother's vanity working on six disemboweled antique radios that he had dismantled and revived. He turned the various knobs, roaming the electronic sighs, momentarily chancing upon talking or music now and then. Six bright green wires connected the radios to an archaic laptop computer on the floor. Waves of color crossed the old-fashioned backlit screen. Now and then an image would rise out of the haze of pixels.

His hair had never been cut but Popo brushed it out as well as he could every morning. In the afternoon Kai Lin would come over and comb out the tangles that Popo missed at the back of his neck.

Misty had cranked her Craftmatic bed to the full seated position. She smiled at her little mad scientist while he searched for something, a secret that he wanted to surprise her with.

"Popo," Chill said.

The boy glanced over at the screen and giggled.

". . . former Soviet Union today gave up its last vestige of sovereignty, much less socialism, when it entered into a partnership with MacroCode Management International in a joint venture to return order to Russian society . . ."

A long pure note wailed between the stations.

". . . born to be wi-i-i-ld . . ."

Static came after the song, but the volume rose.

"Popo!" Chill called again, but the static drowned out his words.

An almost imperceptible clicking blended in with the white noise. The volume dropped. The clicking became clearer. Popo brought his hands to the sides of his head and pulled both ears.

"Popo," Misty Bent said as loud as she could.

"Yea, Gramma?"

"Thill ith talkin' to you."

The boy turned around and stood on the white satin vanity chair. He was naked and smiling.

"Chilly."

"They wanna take you to get tested an' sen' you to Houston, Po," Chill said.

Ptolemy automatically put his hands in the air when the man came near. The child loved the feel of his skin against the muscular man's bare chest.

"No," Popo said. "I don't wanna go."

"I don't want you to go neither. But we got to figger sumpin' out."

"We could run," the boy suggested. "We could go in the swamps like them slave men you said about."

Almost every night Chill told Popo stories of runaway slaves on the Underground Railroad. He said that it was because he wanted

Popo to know African-American history, "like them white kids know their history. From stories at home." But escape was the real story he wanted to tell. He had been obsessed with escape ever since the day he was convicted of armed robbery. The only way he could fall asleep in his cell at night was by imagining himself a slave who had slipped his chains, pried open the bars, and outrun the dogs. Even after his release Chill needed this fantasy to drop off most nights.

For a moment he considered his nephew's innocent suggestion.

The desire for flight burned perpetually in his chest. He owned an illegal ember gun. With that he never needed a reload, one LX battery could last a year.

But then his eyes fell upon his mother, Misty. She only walked for exercise now—fifteen minutes in the morning and five at night. Ptolemy loved his grandmother more than anything.

"No, baby boy," Chill said. "No."

"Then, what?"

"If we had money we could prove to the state that we could afford to get you hooked up to the EEG's Prime Com Link. If they could give you tests and we could get you into that Jesse Jackson Gymnasium they got for city kids, then maybe you could stay."

"I could get money," Ptolemy said.

"It's gonna take more than your dollar allowance, honey."

"How much, then?"

"Just to pay for the computer link is a hundred fi'ty thousand a year. And then there's forty thousand for the JJ Gym, 'cause you not in the city limits. Three million prob'ly do it with costs goin' up like they do."

"I could get that," Ptolemy said.

"Where at?"

"On the computer."

"Naw, man," Chill said. "Computer's all linked up. They got identity cards along with your PBC on every computer."

"Nuh-uh," Ptolemy said, shaking his head and grinning. "My Personal Bar Code ain't on my computer."

"That thing? That's just a toy. It ain't connected up."

"I can wit' my radios. I can too."

"Show me."

The child jumped around in the chair and started turning dials. The computer's gaseous-looking screen went black. Letters and numbers appeared and reappeared in rapid succession on a line in the center of the screen.

Ptolemy hummed and sang while the computer spoke French and Chinese through the various radio speakers. Chill sat down on his mother's bed and watched.

"Don't let my boy get in trouble, Thill," Misty said.

"He was born in trouble, Mama. Born in trouble."

"But that don't make him no thief."

"If we cain't get in the money then the government gonna take him. I'ma just get 'im to show me, Mama. Ain't nobody gonna steal nuthin', but even if they do it's gonna be me. I'll push the button. But don't worry, I'm just lookin'."

As they spoke, words appeared and remained on the screen:

WORLD BANK INTERNATIONAL

B OF A, CITICORP, AMEX, HITO-SAN

WELCOME TO OUR ENTRY SCREEN

UNAUTHORIZED ACCESS IS PUNISHABLE

BY NATIONAL AND INTERNATIONAL LAW

Below the words were a series of codes and blank lines.

"See," Popo exclaimed. "They gots lotsa money."

"An' they don't know your bar code?" Chill asked.

"They get the bar code from your eyes," Ptolemy said. "When you buy your computer they make you give 'em a eyescan. But they didn't do that way back when they made these laptops. I just borrow somebody else's bar-c from one'a the Jacker DBs and then I put it back when I'm through."

While Ptolemy spoke the blanks were being filled in one at a time by an automatic code-breaking program that the boy had adapted from the illegal Jacker Database. After all of the blanks had been filled in, a flurry of screens passed in quick succession, ending finally on a screen whose header read

PROJECT MAINTENANCE FUNDS.

"This ain't nobody's money," the child said. "It's what they got for extra."

There were sixteen place numbers on each coded entry of the file. Chill's upper lip began to sweat.

"Turn it off, Popo."

"But—"

"Turn it off!"

3

"Ow!" Ptolemy Bent yelled.

"You'll need a haircut soon," Kai Lin told him as she dragged the large brush up from the back of the child's neck. "There's more hair than there is little boy."

Misty hissed her paralytic laugh and held a gnarled hand up to shoulder level. She was sitting straight, thanks to her mechanical bed, watching the squat Vietnamese woman torture the poor boy's head.

"He don't wan' it cut," Misty said.

"He'll look like a girl, then," Kai said, giving a hard tug.

"Ow! I don't care," Popo said. "I want my hair like the Jewish man who made relatively. Bushy and big."

"By the time you're his age all we'll be able to see will be your feet." Kai tickled Ptolemy's skinny ribs and the boy doubled over in her lap.

Misty rocked back and forth in sympathy with the boy's glee. Even Kai's impassive face broke into a smile.

Popo grabbed Kai's brush hand, trying to wrest away the implement of torture. But Kai laid him flat on her lap and bent over to blow a loud kiss against his belly.

"I give! I give! You can brush, you can brush." All of the air rushed out of the boy's lungs, making him too weak even to sit up.

"No," Kai said. "All done."

The boy cheered and jumped down, hurrying over to the radio corner, as Misty called it. By then he had deconstructed fifteen old radios, putting their parts together again on every available space. The wires and transistor chips resembled some new form of technologic life growing like fungus down the sides of the vanity onto the floor. There were three old-time laptop computers connected here and there. One of these cast indecipherable images of color and light. The forms sometimes seemed to have an alien sense about them, but mostly they were abstract events appearing for a nanosecond or an hour, changing almost imperceptibly or faster than the eye could follow. Another screen flashed strange characters at various intervals and in differing colors. These characters were being printed horizontally across paper, slowly unfurling from a two-hundred-foot roll on an antique dot matrix printer that Chill had brought home from a yard sale in Jackson, he said.

The final screen was connected to a HondaDrive AE storage system. The three-foot-high canister, encased in crystalline green plastic, was one of the two new pieces of equipment that Popo owned. The HondaDrive was a micro-level storage system that held trillions of bytes of information. It also had an I-crunch that could encode data, making it possible to exponentially expand its capacity. Three years ago a HondaDrive AE would have cost a million dollars. But within the past year, General Electric had stunned the scientific world—and the stock market—with the GE-AI-Drive and its virtually unlimited storage capacity. The GE-AI was big, the size of a refrigerator, but it answered the memory problems of even the most demanding user.

Now a HondaDrive AE cost only ten thousand dollars. No one wanted them, so security had dropped to the point where Chill had been able to steal one from a Radio Shack in Memphis. Along with the drive, Chill stole a LIBCHIP library box, a series of two hundred library chips containing over ten million volumes.

"Let's see you read your way outta that," Chill dared his nephew.

"I will," the boy replied.

The computer connected to the HondaDrive was taking information from the radio receivers, translating it to mathematical codes, and storing the equations. Ptolemy sat naked in lotus position between the screens, watching them and making adjustments to the radio dials now and then.

Kai sat behind the boy and pulled him into her lap. He didn't resist. She usually came to the Bents' house last on her rounds as visiting nurse for the state. She told her supervisor that it was because Misty needed to take her walk late in the day, but really it was to be able to spend more time with the child.

"What is all this?"

"Computers," the boy said. "Computers and radios and electricity and, and, that's all."

"But what are they doing?" Kai asked the same question every day. And every day Ptolemy said that it was a secret.

"It's readin' what the radio says and then it's puttin' it into numbers and then it's puttin' the numbers on the HondaDrive."

"But how do you know how to do all that?"

"I don't," Ptolemy said as he leaned over to turn a dial. The clicking from the speakers changed tempo, and the boy nodded his head as if he were listening to a piece of music.

"But how can you do something and not know how to do it?" Kai asked.

"You use words that you don't know what they mean sometimes. You drive a 'lectric car but you cain't make one." Ptolemy was talking but his attention was on the screens. The image screen showed an eerie landscape of pastel greens and metallic blacks interwoven and slipping away into a distant red maw. "I just count the numbers in the radio waves and then use a equation that I got from the math lib'ary on the Net. It makes up the numbers and then I look at 'em later."

"What are you looking for?" Kai asked almost timidly.

Ptolemy turned to the visiting nurse. His deep brown eyes were like polished stones.

"It's God, I think," he said. "It's God sangin' through radio waves."

"What do you mean? How could that be? I mean why hasn't anybody else heard it before?" An instant hysteria bloomed in Kai's chest.

"Maybe they did," Ptolemy said in a matter-of-fact tone. He had turned back to his screens. He wasn't really thinking about his nurse. "Maybe they did and then when they talked to him they lefted."

"Left where?"

"To God, I guess. Maybe not, though. Maybe they went to heaben."

"Isn't that where God is?"

"No," Ptolemy said, turning again to the squat, mask-faced woman. "Heaben is somewhere else."

"But, Popo," she said. "Why hasn't anybody else heard these messages?"

" 'Cause they don't play with the radio like I do. They all wanna make things but they don't listen too much, you know?"

"No, I don't know."

"When I listen to the radio waves I can hear little pieces of him talkin'. And then, when I turn the knob I hear a little more. His words comin' through in pieces all over. They think it's static. They made the digit-thingy to block it out. Nobody wanna hear it in they music, so they miss it."

"What does God say?" As Kai heard the words coming from her mouth she realized that she meant them.

"Hi," answered Ptolemy. "How are you and can you hear me."

"Could it be some alien race and not God at all?"

"I guess. But I don't think so."

"We should tell somebody about this," Kai said. Behind her Misty Bent had fallen asleep.

"I did."

"Who? Who did you tell?"

"Chilly."

4

"I have to talk wit' you, Kai," Chill Bent said three weeks after the social worker/nurse was forced to reconsider the existence of God.

It was a cool autumn day. The Tickle River was swollen with waters from recent rains, and fish could be seen darting around in schools numbering in the hundreds.

"Yes, Mr. Bent?"

"I'm gonna have to go away for a few weeks."

"Where?"

"Outta the country."

"Oh." The nurse frowned.

"I gotta get some money or they gonna take Popo away. My cousin Hazel been talkin' to child welfare and the EEG. They wanna take Popo to Houston but I won't let 'em."

"But maybe it would be better," Kai suggested hesitantly. "M-maybe if he was in Houston you could visit and he'd have all the best guidance and education."

"Boy needs a family and a home," Chill said. "I been in the state institution before. It ain't no good."

"But that was a detention center," the short nurse argued.

"No different. He gonna be detained in the school too. He cain't come home when he want to. You know his grandmama'll die a week after he's gone."

Kai Lin didn't argue that point. She watched the large man's dark face. He had aged in the two years since Kai had met him. Deep furrows had appeared in his cheeks, and something was wrong with his knees. He was still very handsome, though Kai would have never said so out loud.

"Where are you going?" she asked.

"I can't say. But I want you to take care'a Popo. I want you to make sure that Hazel or M Russell don't get him."

"They won't."

" 'Cause I know you love that chile," Chill said. "I seen how you are wit'im. How come you over on your days off. And you know I'm right too. He learnin' all he can right here, right here in this house."

Tears sprouted from the ex-con's eyes. They rolled down his face.

"I love the boy more than I love anything," he said. "I will not let them take him. I will not let them white people and them people wanna be white turn him into some cash cow or bomb builder or prison maker. He will find his own way an' make up his own mind, god dammit."

Kai reached out to touch Chill's arm. He pulled her close, holding her forearms in a powerful grip. Kai winced but didn't fight him.

"Maybe that's what they're afraid of," she said. "Maybe they don't want these children to make up their own minds. Maybe if they did that, the world would change."

"I know you know," Chill said. "They afraid Ptolemy would be their king if they didn't brainwash 'im."

"Maybe you're right," Kai said. "Sometimes I'm afraid when he talks. Sometimes I'm afraid of what he can see."

"When I come back you an' me gotta talk," Chill said.

Kai did not ask about what.

Chill was gone for six weeks. The first ten days he called every evening. Ptolemy traced the call on his illegal Internet connection and told Kai and Misty that he was in Panama City. After the third week, they received only one faxgram.

Dear Mama, Ptolemy, and Kai,
I'm out in the backcountry down here and so I can't call. I'm fine and I will be home as soon as I can. Just a little more work and I'll have enough money to pay for Ptolemy's home education and we don't have to worry about what anybody else wants to say. Take care of your grandmother and Kai, Ptolemy.
I'll be home soon.

Chill

"Thill din't write nuthin' like that," Misty Bent said after Kai had read it out loud to both her and Ptolemy.

"Sure didn't," Popo agreed. "Chilly never say no Ptolemy when he talkin' t' me."

"He must have had somebody write it for him. Maybe he dictated it over some kind of radio system," Kai said to allay the family's fears. She wasn't worried whether the faxgram came from Chill. What bothered her was how the ex-convict intended to make so much money in Panama.

The Vietnamese nurse had found a home in southern Mississippi. She loved the land and the people more than her native Hanoi, and more than Princeton, where she'd spent so many years going to school. The people reminded her of the stories that her grandmother told. The great jungles and the wild forests. By 2010 Vietnam was divided into twelve highly developed corporate micro-states that produced technical and biological hardware for various Euro-corps. Gone were the farms and rice paddies. The back roads, the thick drawl on the English words, and the life that sprang from every tree and rock and stream.

And then there was the child who listened to God. Kai had only lived in Hazel's house since Chill had been gone, sleeping on the Bents' couch, but she had felt that that house was her home since the day she'd crossed the threshold.

Six weeks after Chill had gone, a private ambulance drove up the Bents' dirt driveway. The attendants were from New Orleans, as was the van. The two white men rolled Chill into the house on the wheeled stretcher.

Chill was there under a thin sheet. His head was shaven and his eyes were covered with bandaged gauze. The form his legs made under the sheet was straight and motionless.

"Where should we bring 'im, ma'am?" one of the attendants asked Kai Lin.

"What's happened to him?"

"Uncle Chilly!" Ptolemy screamed in dismay.

"Don't know nuthin' 'bout that, ma'am," the second paramedic said. "We just picked him up from the airport with instructions to brang 'im here."

"Am I in the livin' room?" Chill asked.

"Yeah," the paramedic replied.

"Chilly!" Ptolemy yelled again. He hid behind Kai Lin's red silk dress, afraid of the white men, the chrome stretcher, and Chill's decimated form.

"Then leave me here. Kai?"

"Yes?"

"Give these men fifty dollars each. I'll pay you back later on."

The white men were surprised at the generosity of the black paraplegic. They both thanked him, gave their apologies to Kai Lin, and left.

"There's a clinic in the hills," Chill was saying. They had wheeled him into his mother's room and cranked his cot until he could sit up, too.

"What have they done to my baby?" Misty cried. But when Chill smiled in a way that Misty hadn't seen since he was a child, her tears subsided.

". . . up there they cain't be bothered and so they can operate with no problem. They wanted my eyes—"

"And you give 'em up?" Misty said, louder than she had spoken in years.

"That was one million seven hundred an' fi'ty thousand," Chill said. "My eyes were a perfect fit for a Swiss banker's son who lost his in a ski accident. But when I was there they had a emergency. It was a Russian general needed the nerve in the spine where he could use his legs. They offered two million for that. I figgered that if I cain't see then I really don't need to walk. One thing led to another and I got outta there wit' six million. They transferred the whole thing into my name 'fore I went under the knife."

"Why you do that, Uncle Chilly?" Ptolemy asked.

Chill put his hands up in front of him and found his nephew's face.

"I was worried that I couldn't keep on payin' for the house, baby boy. You know mama's social security an' disability been payin' for me, so now my disability be payin' for her."

"Thill, no," Misty cried.

"It's okay, Mama. You know I been lost outside'a the house any-way. Anytime I ain't here I just wanna come back an' hear you laughin' or Popo readin' an playin' his radio. Don't worry, Mama. Everything's fine now."

5

That night, when Misty and Ptolemy were asleep in their beds, Kai and Chill had their talk.

"I want you to marry me," Chill said, his empty eye sockets star-ing at the ceiling.

"What?"

"I cain't see. I cain't walk. I got the money to p'otect Popo but I cain't move to block a thing if they wanna come in here and take him away from us. But if you marry me, and move wit' us to Jackson, we could get a big house and a Prime Com Link for Popo's education. You could have boyfriends and free time, just look after Mama and Popo like you been doin'. Just do that an' we can share the money in style."

Chill could have told no more about what she was thinking even if he still had eyes. Kai's face was impassive, even hard.

She blinked once and fifteen seconds passed.

She blinked again.

"Okay," she whispered. "I accept."

"You do?"

"Of course. It's a trust. It's holy."

"There's one thing I gotta tell ya," Chill said.

"What's that?"

"I sold my manhood too. With no legs I knew I wouldn't be able to function no way. So you wouldn't be marryin' a man at all."

"Oh yes I will be," she said. She took his hand in hers and hummed a song she'd once heard on the radio and thought she'd for-gotten.

6

No one believed the lie about a fall at work that left Chill Bent paralyzed, blind, and rich from the insurance he got. They all knew that poor men and women often sold pieces of themselves to the rich in order to give their children a chance. Hazel Bernard tried to get the marriage between Chill and Kai annulled but failed. At the age of nine, in 2030, Ptolemy Bent joined the Jesse Jackson Gymnasium for Advanced Learners so he would have a social life among other children. But his education came from tutors and texts provided by the Prime Com Link. He worked hard on his radio receiver, which he never discussed outside of home, and one day he convinced Kai to buy him a $300,000 transmitter, the state of the art in amateur radio communications.

"Chilly, you awake?

"Is that you, Popo?" The ex-convict put out a hand to gently caress his nephew's face.

"Uh-huh."

"You got peach fuzz on your chin."

"You always say that. When you gonna call it a beard?"

"Peach fuzz," Chill said behind a chuckle.

"I made contact, Chilly."

"You did?"

"Uh-huh. An' I told 'im 'bout you."

"You think the big man'd have somethin' better t'do than worry 'bout a blind an' crippled thief."

"You the best man in the world, Uncle Chilly. He said he wanna meet you, you'n Gramma Misty."

"Really? He said that? Damn. Well I guess it won't be too much longer anyways. Kai said that the doctor said that my kidneys wouldn't get a nickel down in Panama."

"You don't have to die, Chilly," Ptolemy said, his voice wavering between high and low adolescent tones. "I'm'a just put some wires on your head. You and Gramma."

"You there, Mama?" Chill called out.

"Yeth, baby. Popo gonna make uth out a ethperiment. He thure look fine." Misty's ancient voice was weaker. Chill knew that time was short for both of them.

"I bet he do, Mama."

After what seemed like hours of preparation, Ptolemy said, "Ready?" Then came a white-hot flash at Chill's temples and then the feeling of electric fingers going up under his skull and into his brain.

Suddenly he could see again. Ptolemy was sitting there looking at another Chill lying on the bed. The boy, almost a man, wearing a lavender andro-suit with no shirt, had hair that made him look like the king of lions. He was still skinny, and darker than he had been. *From brown to black*, Chill thought, and then he was gone forever from the Earth. First his thoughts were elsewhere, and then slowly, electron by electron, the matter of his soul was transported. Somewhere there were bursts of stars and lines of reality that connected uncounted voices.

God, Chill thought. But there was no answer to his assertion. A halo of winking lights radiated next to him, mingled with him, and he knew in some new language that this was his mother. The word *freedom* occurred to Chill, but the meaning faded with the clarity of his light. So much he knew that he was unaware of. So much beyond him even then.

It's like I'm a breath, he wanted to say.

Yes, Misty's new form replied.

Ptolemy Bent was arrested and tried for the euthanasia killing of his uncle and grandmother. He was sentenced to twelve years to life in a private prison run by the Randac Corporation of Madagascar.

At the trial God was ruled an improbability.

"He is aware that he disintegrated their brain tissues," claimed Morton Tremble, the prosecution's expert psychiatrist, "by using feedback from a powerful radio transmitter. Maybe he thought, consciously, that he was sending their souls to God or whatever. But in truth, he only did this because both were so close to death already, as he himself has testified. He admitted that he knew their bodies, including their nervous systems, would die. This is a classic case of mercy killing. And Ptolemy Bent was completely aware that euthanasia is against the law."

Kai Lin, who was by Ptolemy's side every day of the trial, stored his radio equipment in her basement. She never visited her husband's grave.

AFTERMOON

Tananarive Due

(2004)

At six-thirty, the moon was already faintly visible in the waning daylight, patiently awaiting its turn to light up the streets in pale blue and gray. The Aftermoon, Kenya always called it. It wasn't the real Moon, the full moon; it only looked like it, except chewed smaller at the rims. The Aftermoon was startling and nearly as beautiful, but it ultimately held no more allure to Kenya than it would if she were any other city-dweller tossed suddenly into its sight.

Kenya ignored the moon as she walked from the Clark Street subway stop toward her building, vanishing inside the purposeful stream of twilight home-goers. She felt it watching her as she always did but she refused to look up. She'd decided a long time ago that just because the moon tried to talk to her didn't mean she had to listen. Her grandfather had felt differently about that; but, then again, he was different in a lot of ways. Kenya was especially proud that she didn't allow ghosts and memories to steer her life.

Kenya's stomach growled. At dinnertime, especially during the summer, Brooklyn Heights always smelled like the sidewalks had been basted with butter, pine nuts, and garlic. All the take-out places had their doors propped open, trying to tantalize people like Kenya who never planned their meals in advance.

But tonight she knew *exactly* what she wanted, because she'd withheld it from herself the night before, when she'd wanted it most: a barely seared, blood-red steak. The meat was waiting for her in her freezer at home, so she'd thaw it and cook it, maybe twenty seconds in the pan on each side. This was the only time of month Kenya knew exactly what she wanted to eat. Not a *need*, she reassured herself, just an appetite. Her grandfather might even be proud of her, if he'd still been living and could have shared a moonlight meal. (Except, she reminded herself, he would have been irritated with her for the ritual of cooking the flesh at all).

Kenya's mind was on food, so it was only an accident when she walked past a basement office she must have passed every day for nearly a year, dwarfed beneath the Indian/Chinese video store and a Northern Italian restaurant, Giovanni's, that all the people in her building raved about. Today, the glint of the buffed brass sign caught her eye because it so perfectly complemented the day's last light. The bold letters were embossed into the shiny plate in black: JACK REEVES, DERMATOLOGY. And beneath that, following Dr. Reeves' mumbo-jumbo of degrees and licenses, it said in script: *Lycanthropy*.

Kenya's first thought was to go in and give this quack a piece of her damned mind. She wasn't offended easily, but the sign set off sparks that made her teeth tighten. Maybe it was only because of the time of month, she tried to reason with herself, but the nerve of this guy, this so-called doctor, poking such callous fun in a sign posted on a public street!

She wasn't sure why she found herself descending the cracked concrete steps leading to the office door, because a doctor wouldn't keep hours this late, and what was she going to do if he did? Still, sparks didn't need reason; they improvised just fine. Maybe she'd slide a nasty note beneath his door. Maybe she'd write down his telephone number and lodge an anonymous complaint on his voicemail. Ignorant fool, she thought. She'd like to rip his face into shreds.

The light was on, illuminating a waiting room beyond the glass door. A small, handwritten list of office hours taped inside proclaimed that Dr. Jack Reeves, Dermatology, was open until 7 P.M. on all weekdays except Wednesdays. Which meant he was still there. Good, she thought, and flung the door open to a cacophony of jangling chimes. Inside the office, though, her mood softened, retreating from the places it had been trying to lure her.

By all appearances, there was nothing unusual about the doctor's office. The light inside was bright, welcoming, making the waiting room and the gaily colored magazines neatly fanned on the coffee table feel like part of a life-sized display case. Very familiar. And yet . . .

Thinking about it later, she wondered if maybe she had first been arrested by the smell. Burning incense was so thick in the air that her nostrils smarted for an instant before she relaxed and allowed herself to breathe in the luxurious scent. Part campfire, part lavender, part . . . cedar closet? Oh, it was something, that smell! It was a smell to bottle and steal whiffs from in the middle of the night.

But the office's scent was nothing compared to the *music*. As soon as Kenya heard it, she spun around to search for the speakers, as if seeing the music's source would somehow help her own it. She could not distinguish between voice and instrument. In fact, she could not say with certainty that the music was composed of either, just as it seemed to have no discernible melody, but she knew that it *was* music, meaning it was the very *definition* of music. Barely loud enough to hear, it thrilled against her ears.

Standing frozen in the waiting room, Kenya forgot why she had been angry. Or why she had come in. Or even where she was.

"That music's something, isn't it?" a man's voice said from her left.

Released from the spell, Kenya turned to see a hulking figure standing behind a half-open glass partition, wrapped inside an ill-fitting doctor's coat. He was only partially visible, the rest of him muddied behind the misted glass. She saw his enormous wiry beard, one curious brown eye, and half of his round spectacles staring out at her.

"It's . . ." Kenya searched her mind for words, avoiding not only clichés but words that were unworthy. But she wasn't really searching, because her mind was empty of words.

"Are you hungry?" the man behind the partition asked.

The question was odd, a non sequitur, a muted part of Kenya's brain realized, but her mouth nonetheless flooded with saliva. She saw the man fling something toward her at an arc, and her nose recognized long before her eyes could focus that it was a small strip of raw beef. To her own astonishment, she snapped the meat out of the air with her teeth.

"I thought your sign outside was a joke," Kenya told him later, when the music was gone and she felt more like herself. Now, sitting primly on the leather sofa in the waiting room, the woman who'd heard the music was a stranger to her. Only her satisfied stomach, and tiny bits of raw beef caught between her teeth, reminded her of who she'd been. Embarrassed, she worried at the food fragments with a peppermint-flavored toothpick the doctor had offered her.

"Sure, right. Most people think it's a gag. That's the beautiful part."

Dr. Jack, as he insisted on being called, had fixed a pot of coffee that he served himself in a mug that read, wryly, WHAT A HAIRY SIT-UATION. He offered a cup to Kenya, but she refused. Caffeine in any form, even a minuscule amount, made her crazy, she told him. Especially right after the Moon, she thought, noting that last part only to herself.

"To some people, crazy is good," Dr. Jack told her, winking. "But you're smart to keep your distance. Coffee's my vice."

Kenya tried to assess Dr. Jack the way her grandfather had taught her, looking for signs. He had a mane of intricately curled dark hair that spilled onto his face in the form of a neatly combed beard, which rode high on his cheeks and grew all the way to his mid-chest before tapering away. From what she could see of his neckline above his white smock, the hair grew freely there, too. Dr. Jack, yes, was one hairy guy.

But there was always more to it than the hair, she knew. She tried to hold his eyes, to see what she could find there, that arcane quality that had informed her grandfather's brown-eyed gaze. Dr. Jack's eyes were set back deep beyond his bearded pudgy cheeks, and they told her nothing except that he was kind. She decided, in that instant, to trust him.

"How did you know about me?" she asked

He shrugged. "The music. If you didn't have the genes, all you'd hear was Muzak. An ocarina and strings playing 'Black Dog' by Led Zeppelin."

She regarded him blankly. She didn't know the song.

"That's a joke," he said, grinning. She tried to assess his teeth, but the grin vanished too quickly. "But seriously, it's the music that gives you away. Only my very special patients hear it at all." He said this with tremendous warmth—a little too much. Kenya didn't like his eagerness; it glowed from him like the bright, giddy energy of first dates with the kind of men who typically had too many chips and dents just beneath the surface to warrant any more of her time.

"When did your condition manifest?" he asked, suddenly sounding like a doctor again.

"I don't think I want to talk about that." The awful episode right before her ninth birthday tried to goad its way to her consciousness, but she refused to open that window. Not now.

"Right. I forget, you're not a patient yet. So you do the asking, then."

"How many . . . I mean . . ."

"I have thirteen special patients, a very small part of my practice. All from the Tri-State area except for one guy from D.C. He takes the train in for group night, once a month. Last night, matter of fact. You missed it."

Thirteen! This doctor was the first person she'd met in New York who seemed to share her condition. There were *other* men, too? Kenya imagined the commuter from D.C. in a tailored suit with a briefcase in his hand, probably a lawyer, scanning the *Washington Post* or the *Times* while he rode in. Because of Lee, her days as a single woman were about to come to an end, thank goodness, but the image of the man on the train reawakened her hopeless adolescent yearnings for someone who wouldn't ask questions. She'd been so certain that no man like that would exist for her that she'd sat for hours on the back porch with her grandfather, allowing him to fill her head with nonsense and cynicism, only to escape the ache of her daydreams.

"That many? Just in New York?" she said.

"Give or take. I have to account for a few strays, pardon the expression. But you're the first new face I've seen in two years."

"You have . . ." Kenya stumbled over the word, momentarily lapsing into the desperation of a fifteen-year-old's mind, ". . . treatments?"

"Mostly cosmetic. I'm a dermatologist, understand, so I'm an expert on skin and hair."

"The hair," she said, her voice shrill and urgent. Had that really been her voice at all? "You have treatments for the hair?"

"Sure, right." He nodded, the grin floating back across his mouth. This time, unless she imagined it, she did notice a slight sharpness to his incisors. Just like her grandfather's. "That's my specialty. I'll have you smooth as a baby's bottom."

Kenya stared at him. She could feel the steadily rising pulsing of her heartbeat in her fingertips, surging with blood that warmed her face in a flare. She didn't speak. She was afraid that strange, helpless voice would fly from her mouth again.

"Yeah, I know," Dr. Jack said, as if responding to her thoughts. "Sometimes you don't even know what you're looking for until you've found it."

"Sheep don't live lives, they live *lies*," Gramp always told her. "Your mama's hell-bent on tryin' to raise you in the world of sheep. But you damn sure ain't no sheep, girl. Are you?"

There were never real answers to Gramp's questions. When Kenya was twelve and began thinking for herself, she'd tried to pose logic against him, but his questions always writhed and twisted like snakes that could change their shape and size depending on the point he wanted to make. Not that the point ever changed.

Summers with Gramp were always more fun to anticipate than they were to actually *spend*, because by the third day of her two-month visit Kenya always figured out there was no one but Gramp to talk to and even less to do. He had a seventy-year-old wood-frame house that had never heard a whisper about the invention of air-conditioning and he lived in a tiny Oregon town called Fortune, which was not big enough to be a true town. The six buildings that

made up what Kenya supposed was "downtown" Fortune were a sa-
loon, a market that served hot and cold sandwiches, a barber shop
that doubled as a post office, the two-room First Church of the Living Christ, a drugstore, and a tack and feed. The entire patch of
buildings went dark after nine, so no one driving by could even see
Fortune at night. Most people never saw Fortune at all. There, Kenya
disappeared, and so did the world outside.

Mostly, timber families lived in Fortune. There were houses dot-
ting the hilltop tree lines on large parcels of land, but the precious
few neighbors never ventured near Gramp's house, and Kenya had
never been able to identify any families with children her age.
Which left her and Gramp. Two months, each year, felt like a lifetime. She'd tried to complain to her parents that Gramp was a bad
influence on her, but either they didn't believe her or Gramp's bad
influence was exactly what they were counting on. She never knew
which.

The only nights at Gramp's she truly enjoyed, the nights that,
given her circumstances, were more incredible and long-awaited
than Christmas Day, were the Moon nights. One night each month.
And every night until the Moon, he told her, was preparation. He
told her there was only one night each month when she truly existed
at all.

"It's like any other gift. You don't pay attention to something long
enough, you forget," Gramp used to say, gazing out from his back
porch across his unkempt property where wild tiger lilies grew in
quilt patterns in the crabgrass. "And don't be afraid of that word
'monster.' That's a word invented by conventional folk either too
stupid or too scared to follow their own souls. Too scared to create
nothin' of their own."

"Monsters don't create anything," Kenya might have argued, or
something like it.

"What's wrong with you, girl? Of course they do. They create fear,
and there ain't nothing more powerful on this planet Earth." And
the snake had wiggled away from her again. Gramp gave her
headaches from so much confusion.

But the confusion vanished on Moon nights. The Moon gave her experiences that defied memory, that had no place for discussion at her parents' dinner table or among the classmates who sat in the neatly lined desks at her school: bare feet descending nearly weightless across beds of sharp twigs that could not hurt her. Wind tickling and stroking the hairs across her naked back. Foreign songs emerging from her throat, screeching across the treetops.

And twice, when she was very fast and very lucky, the opportunity to kill. Once, it had been a squirrel. Another time, a raccoon. Caught, startled, in her hands. Killed with instinctive swiftness, fur raking against her teeth.

Only on Moon nights did it make any sense at all. Only then did Kenya truly understand why Gramp lived in Fortune, secluded as a forest creature himself. And why the neighbors never once came to call.

Every year, despite the prospect of hot boredom of summer nights that made her want to scream herself to sleep, Kenya couldn't wait to go see her grandfather. When she wasn't with him, Moon nights were almost like any other. The forgetting always began right away.

Dr. Jack's office seemed much less inviting when Kenya came back for her first official appointment. The lovely incense was still in the air, so it calmed her nerves; and she could hear traces of the music, even more faint than before (it was harder to hear now, of course, because the Moon had been nearly a week ago, and her senses had faded considerably).

But she was put off when she saw his examining room. There was a framed eight-by-ten photo of Lon Chaney, Jr., in elaborate costume placed prominently on the wall, alongside a full-sized movie poster, which jarred Kenya so much in its cartoonish menace that she could taste bile in her throat. Seeing the images, she could very nearly smell her grandfather's pipe tobacco and the perfume of the pine needles of the Christmas trees that had grown wild on his property. Gramp had kept film reels of classic horror movies, and she'd watched them with him late at night for lack of anything else to do, all the while feeling slightly sick to her stomach. Now, seeing Gramp's favorite movie celebrated again, Kenya felt a prickling in her marrow that couldn't have been deeper if she'd been staring at a poster of a handkerchief-bound Mammy or a fat-lipped, watermelon-slurping pickaninny.

Why in the world had she come here? This coarse, trivial man had nothing to teach her.

But it was too late now. Already she had bared herself to her midriff, and his fingers were traveling up and down her spine, following the trail of hair.

"Geez, this isn't bad at all," he said. "Is this your typical growth?"

She trembled slightly. Was she cold? "Pretty much. I never get much facial hair, thank God. Just very fine hair on the cheeks, and it falls out after a few hours," she told Dr. Jack, yanking her eyes away from the movie poster's glare. "My back and chest are the problem."

"Let's see the chest," he said, walking around the table to face her. There, she knew, he had a perfect view of the triangle-shaped thatch of black fur between her breasts. Only a select few people had ever seen it, mostly technicians at hair-removal salons who clucked with surprise and pity at how a hormonal condition could go so badly awry. Not even her mother had seen what grew on her chest. But Gramps had, of course. Her hair had delighted him, and he promised her that if she followed the diet he taught her, she'd grow a lot more like it once she was older. Of course, she had done nothing of the sort.

"This is nothing," Dr. Jack said.

It hadn't seemed like nothing to Terrell Jordan, who'd slipped his hand beneath her blouse while they were necking in the back row of a movie theater when they were both sophomores in college. He'd been so quick she hadn't even seen it coming; and if she'd expected a maneuver like that from bookish Terrell, she'd never have necked with him at all. When his fingers met the hair, he didn't say anything or make a sound. His fingers just twitched and flew away as if he'd been burned. He pulled his lips back and stared at her, his eyeglasses reflecting the light from the movie screen. That was all she could see of his face.

No more necking after that, or movies either. But at least, as far as she knew, he never told anyone. She very nearly loved him for that.

"It doesn't feel like 'nothing' when I'm getting it pulled out, believe me," she said.

"How do you do that?"

"Well, electrolysis is a waste of time. Waxing, usually."

"Oh, for God's sake, are you kidding me?" Dr. Jack said, gazing at her with the abhorrence and concern she had come to expect from everyone who had tried to tend to her hair. He sucked his teeth. "Don't do that. Not ever again. You'll damage your skin that way, believe me. See these dark spots? That's why I'm here." From his coat pocket, he produced a white jar of unlabeled paste. He unscrewed it and showed her the texture, which was the color of peanut butter but not quite as thick. It had a sweet scent.

"This is a combination of flowers, herbs, and enzymes," he said. "Apply it to the affected area the day before the Moon, and keep applying it every six hours for the next forty-eight hours. You'll see a difference right away, if the hair grows in at all. Within a day or two, any hair you do get should wash right off. If it doesn't, we can try something else. But this works great in ninety percent of my cases, and your growth is so mild you shouldn't have a thing to worry about. I have patients who need vats of the stuff, but it works."

Con artist, Kenya thought. It couldn't be that easy.

"Money-back guarantee," Dr. Jack added. "But it ain't cheap, I'm afraid. Fifty bucks a jar. Most of the ingredients are imported."

"That's all there is to it?"

"Modern times," Dr. Jack said. "Modern solutions."

Kenya took the jar and stared at the brown paste. She wondered what Gramp would have thought of it. Or her parents, for that matter. Perhaps, armed with the paste, they might not have sent her to spend her summers with Gramp at all. What in the world had they been trying to prepare her for?

Dr. Jack pulled up a wooden chair and sat in front of Kenya with a slate. He seemed so much more conventional now than he had that first night, when he was tossing her raw meat across the room. "Since you're my patient now, how about a few questions?"

Kenya shrugged, then nodded.

"Tell me when your condition manifested."

"Uhm . . . When I was a toddler, my parents say. I had mood swings. . . ."

"On Moon nights?"

"Yes."

"And your parents?"

"No," Kenya said, momentarily despising their smooth skin and predictable temperaments the way she had as a child. "But my grandfather, yes. I got the genes from him."

"That's it? No aggravating circumstances?"

"A bite," she said softly. "More like a nip, I guess. From a wild dog." Her first and only camping trip with her parents, and it had been a disaster. Out of her parents' sight for only a few minutes, she'd offered some food to the underfed, haggard-looking animal sniffing their campsite out of a child's natural pity. The dog had bitten her instead, drawing pricks of blood. Her right hand still bore the scar, although it was so faded that only she could still see it was there.

"A dog? That's an old wives' tale," Dr. Jack said.

"Still . . . it got worse after that. I was eight. That's when the hair started coming."

"Average age of onset is about twelve, thirteen, so you were definitely accelerated," Dr. Jack said. "Certain sunblocks aggravate it. And a high-protein diet. But dog bites? Nah."

"That's what happened to me. Maybe it wasn't a dog, then."

Dr. Jack's pen paused as he considered this. His shaggy eyebrows climbed, then fell at rest. "Okay, I'll give you the benefit of the doubt on that one. What about symptoms?"

Kenya did not want to tell him about Gramp and the woods. He'd died when she was thirteen, and she'd long ago discarded those experiences as though they had never been.

"Uhm . . . irritability. I get a little jittery. A few appetite changes. Mostly, it's just the hair."

"So it's a cosmetic problem," he said.

She smiled. She wished she'd learned to think of it that way before now. "Yes," she said, at ease for the first time since her arrival. "I like that."

"You wouldn't believe how much of life is semantics." Dr. Jack put his metal slate aside. "I tell people to think of it as an allergy, if that helps."

To what? she almost said, before she realized that, of course, she knew: the Moon.

"I like that, too," Kenya said. "I'll take that over my grandfather telling me I was a freak. Oh, and that I should have pride in my freak-ishness because it makes me superior."

Dr. Jack shrugged. "I hear that too. Works for some people, doesn't for others. Listen, I offer more comprehensive services here, if that interests you. Moon-feasts. Group meetings, like I think I mentioned before."

For an instant, Kenya's spirit surged. But she drew back, compelled herself to shake her head firmly. She'd spent the past few days, and fitful nights, contemplating whether or not she would like to meet any of the others, particularly the commuter from Washington, D.C. Even thinking about the stranger made her feel disloyal to Lee, who was almost the same mysterious phantom to her because they spent so much time apart. She'd never known any others except Gramp, after all, and she'd grown comfortable with the assumption that she never would. She didn't like the part of herself that craved their fellowship. Besides, it was too late for that. She had chosen Lee, and she would make a life with him. She would be done with it.

Perhaps if she had met Dr. Jack and his peculiar circle sooner. But she hadn't.

"I have a few singles. . . ." Dr. Jack went on, trying to entice her.

"I'm engaged," Kenya said.

"Is he family?"

The word *family* confused Kenya for an instant, before she allowed herself to enjoy its reassuring quality. *Are you family, Dr. Jack?* she wanted to ask, because she really wasn't sure. Gramp would have known by a scent or something in this man's gaze, but Kenya's instincts felt dull and unreliable, so all she could rely on was his hairiness, which could be explained in so many other ways. She'd conveniently used those other explanations herself.

She thought of Lee's cherubically hairless chest, his bare back that gleamed with massage oil. They were both politically active, worked in social-service fields, liked the same books and art-house movies. He was a vegetarian, but he was a good person, and he loved her. So far, anyway. Kenya fought a sudden constriction of her throat, as if someone were strangling her.

"No, he's not family," she said. "And he doesn't know. He lives in L.A., and we only see each other every couple months. Usually I leave the hair alone until right before I see him."

"What about after you're married?"

"I'm going to tell him," she said. "Next time he comes out."

"That's brave," Dr. Jack said, staring at her with naked admiration that struck her as sad. What other choice did she have? Was she supposed to keep hiding it? Segregate herself like Gramp?

In the end, that was what gave Dr. Jack away. Not his scent or the shape of his teeth, but his envy. She wondered how much time he spent importing his ingredients, making his paste, conducting his group sessions, planning his Moon-feasts. Between that and his regular practice, she surmised, he must not have time for much else, and maybe he liked it that way, basking in the image of Lon Chaney, Jr. Exalting his own strangeness.

"Can I ask you something, Dr. Jack?" she said.

"Take your best shot."

"If your paste works so well on the hair, why don't you use it yourself?"

He didn't miss a beat before answering. "Hair doesn't bother me. Just a part of the package," he said, and in that instant she envied him, too. She wondered if he secretly scorned her the way Gramp would, and she felt a twinge of guilt for the part of her that was always fervently praying Lee would still love her after he knew who she really was.

"Good luck with your fiancé," Dr. Jack said. "That's a tough disclosure for people to swallow. At least you know we're here if you get any ugly surprises."

Ugly surprises. Nope, Kenya thought, the biggest surprise she might get from Lee would be a spontaneous hug or some profound gesture of his unswayed devotion. The ugliness was what she expected; revulsion, surliness, fear, then, if she was very lucky, gradual acceptance. If Dr. Jack's hair paste actually worked, that would make her task so much easier with Lee because he might not have to *see* it, not ever. She had to hope so, anyway.

She hoped for something much more than the way Terrell Jordan, by the end of their senior year, gave her only wistful half-waves in the hallway as evidence that he had once laughed at her jokes, or that she'd ever made his palms sweat. She'd taken those waves home with her and replayed them in her giddy imagination as if they mattered, as if they were so much more than reminders of Terrell's cowardice. When she lay very quietly on her made-up bed and closed her eyes, hugging her book bag to her chest, she could even imagine that Terrell had stroked and kissed that thick patch of hair between her budding breasts instead of pulling his hand away.

Voodoo Vincent and the Astrostoriograms

Tyehimba Jess

(2004)

The fact of the matter is that the Bronzeville statue near the intersection of Twenty-sixth and Martin Luther King, Jr. Drive is not haunted. It is only waiting and cursing and hoping and praying for a place to be safe. But in order to understand how a South Side Chicago statue can feel fear and longing and loneliness and hope, you must understand the story of Voodoo Vincent. So dig:

It was August, dog-day-deep-south-dusty-throated-damn-it's-hot August, and Voodoo Vincent, a tall straggling wisp of brown embroidered in dreadlock, pushed his cart up Fifty-third. This was the fourth trip of the day, back and forth on his Hyde Park circuit. He leaned into the rattle of his Walgreen's shopping cart, lifting his eyes to the passersby who shifted their way down the street past his patchworked form, past those who wondered how he could still be sporting that rusty old leather jacket and tall top hat over dreads in the concrete-ovened heat of Chicago.

The locals knew Vince, were familiar with the funk that flew from underneath his clothes when you got close enough to talk, had woven his comings and goings into the back of their minds. They knew that when the hawk shrieking wind came back to Chi after spring, he would disappear to wherever the smart homeless people would go—anywhere south, where the weather knew a little more about compassion for shelter seeking souls. They knew about all his little capitalist ventures, how they paid for a meal here, a flop there, and an arm-long bus ticket to wherever winter took him, and were never surprised when his new money making plan came around. Like now, for instance.

It was time for old Vince to make some cold cash money, and perhaps this new scam would provide a few more dollar bills in the pocket. This month, Vince was fully involved in his latest artistic endeavor, a collection of what he called astrostoriograms: selected magazine pictures cut and pasted into blends of black-and-white Xeroxed collages. Vince would plunder the university students' castaway books and magazines, searching for images from *Ebony*, *Newsweek*, and *Fashion Fair* pages, looking for just the right mixture of *Vibe* and *New Yorker* images to paste onto paper, in just the right way. Sometimes a word or two overlapping a smiling brown face, other times a liquor bottle or automobile falling atop the head of a well-coifed sista or brotha. The Beauty of It was in the profit margin. After all, when he spent five cents on a copy and sold it for a dollar, that was 2,000 percent nickel, dime, quarter above cost. But today, he had an even better twist: Just the other night, sleeping in a stairwell off Fifty-first and Ellis, it had come and hit him over the head like a bag of hammers.

In his dream, he saw a red coated bowler wearing brown man with a silver tipped cane sitting atop a waist high stack of 100-dollar bills, needling his teeth with a gold toothpick. It seemed he was situated on the corner of Seventy-ninth and Stony Isle, but the strange thing was that there was no traffic going through the heart of the South Side in this dream. The well dressed mack daddy tipped his hat, pushed his shoulders back, spit a grin from his lips and squint a glint from his eye. And they commenced to talkin':

"See this heah heap o' cash, brotha?"

"Uh-huh. Who is you, and why ain't the po-lice come to get you and alla that money you stole? And where the Stony Island bus at? Cuz I don't need to be around no knuckleheads getting arrested."

"Fool. This heah *my* money, boy. Every cent and more. This only my carryin' 'round cash."

"Well, Mr. Fat Pockets, seein' as how you can't even carry roun' alla that cash, either you a lyin' sonofabitch or you needs help carryin' it. So if you ain't a tall taleteller, then why not hook a brotha up wit' a lil somethin' somethin', huh?"

"The name is LegBaby, and you ain't earned nothin' yet, boy. But you could. All you needs to do is to pay attention to the signs."

"Signs? What signs? Only signs I see says keepout noloitering securitycamerasinuse novacancy violatorswillbeprosecuted nostanding nosmoking noparking creditcheckmandatory stop and yield and policelinedonotcross."

"Naw, boy. THESE signs."

And with a tap of his cane, the sky was filled with pictures floating down to the pavement. Pictures of mommas and daddies and kids and cars, and ice creams and guns and politicians and everything you could imagine floating down to the sidewalk. But as they fell, Vince could see that they was forming up with each other to make words in the sky, words like DEATH and MONEY and BIRTH and CHEAT and LOVE all floating there in the pictures falling like rain. He looked back down to the ground where LegBaby was, and there was nothing there but a voice, a raspy gnarl of a whisper that landed on his shoulder, leaned into his ear, and said, "Read the signs, boy, read the signs."

So that was how he would provide the extra sales touch to the soft touched patrons of his wares: He would make each collage different, and tell 'em something like a fortune for each collage. Yo, if Dionne Warwick can pull that 1-900-Fortune caper, if the Chinese can stuff a piece of paper into a cookie and make some money offa that racket, then why not Vince?

So this august, August day found old Vince and his cart hawking the brand new improved astrostoriograms. Hadn't found a customer for them yet. Some had bought the silver jewelry, the tiny flasks of oil that bloomed fumes entitled "Persimmon" and "Sage" and "Electric Blue" and "Sensuality Soup." Some had put out five or ten apiece for the silver twisted into amulets or sculpture to hang from their ears. Some had purchased the peddled pocket protectors, cartoon buttons, stuffed toys, cigarette lighters, flashlights, bus tokens, wool hats, umbrellas, plastic combs, and batteries. All had heard the thin, gray rasp of his voice selling the wares of a shopping carted storefront; a nomadic nest of necessities on wobbled down wheels. Vince had pitched them every time with the flashlight batteries and the fake $10 watches, but so far not a single customer wanted their future told. So he was starting to get discouraged when alla sudden he spies a happy couple, brown and browner still, young and younger still, hip to hip, arm to arm, stepping up Ellis Avenue to the movies. It was time for the romantic play:

> Yo bruthaman,
> get a astro-storigram
> to find out how you
> and your lady's future expands:
> how to make your best laid plans!

"Silly nigga, please," said the young brotha.

But his fine chocolate sista insisted on sampling the wares. "Damn, Laquann, why you always gotta act so mean? Can't you see the brotha need a little somethin' for the hunger pains? Look at the man, he 'bout to stumble into the grave any minute now. What you sellin', brotha?"

> Astrostoriograms
> the key to see the future reality.
> Pick one, sista, and I shall tell you your fate.
> Be certain of choice and make no mistake!

Vince held out a cardboard suitcase full of cut out pictures and she looked over the choice of papers, leafing through them one by one till she found one that she thought would do.

"So what do this one mean?"

Voodoo man looks at it real close-like, and he sees one thing straight off—he had never seen this picture before in his life. He turned it this way and that, up and down, side to side, and put it back in her hands, tryin' to play off his astonishment, tryin' to play the cool role. How in the hell had that thing got in his papers?

It was a large photo of a gap-toothed smilin' sista in the middle. Floating around her were various modern gods such as a new Caddy, a cell phone, a twenty-five-foot luxury yacht, and two bottles of Hennessy. Down in the corner of the page was a teeny tiny black man, wavin' up at a sun that was the gap toothed sista's head. In another corner was a suitcase, and across the top read the letters:

S-a-y-o-n-a-r-a
Fool!

Strugglin' for a comment, he was about to say somethin' nice to make the deal even sweeter, cuz he knew that people always wanna hear good about they future. But alla sudden, he knew he couldn't say nothin' other than what he saw.

So Vince turned to the brotha and said: "Brotha, soon as her promotion comes through, you is out the picture. Sista gone up and pack and move so fast that your head'll be spinnin' for a month. But it's cool, cuz you got the replacement lined up anyway, and she got wider hips than this one. Sista, watch out for them earthquakes out in Califor-ni-a."

Brotha looks at sista and says, "So *that's* why you was in L.A. last week. Visitin' your cousins, yeah, *right*!"

Sista looks at brotha and says, "What woman? He talkin' 'bout that chickenhead Laqueesha?"

And so the twisted eyebrows and hands on hips began, but I don't really need to tell you the details 'bout the yellin' and shoutin' and cussin' goin' on while Vince slowly snuck away down Fifty-third, him and his shoppin' cart, lookin' over his shoulder every so often to see them makin' a spectacle outta their own futures.

Well, that was the beginning of Vince's mystical journey into soothsayer territory, where the strangeness just got stranger every day. There was the little old widow who chose the storiogram that told her where her lost wedding ring was; the young bank teller that got told to chill with her co-worker or she would be on the next lay-off list; the down-and-out-'bout-to-quit writer that got told his next book would win awards; and there was the fine as wine sista that was told not to leave her man, he was 'bout to be right. Each and every one of 'em came back singin' the praises of the astrostoriogram, how they wanted more and more advice. Soon enough, seemed like everybody wanted to "get told" by one of Vince's mixed-up ransom note styled little pictures.

Let us fast-forward this fable. As a natural born capitalist, Vince saw opportunity and took it. The price of astrostoriograms went up and up and up, to $5, $25, $50, and then $100 each. By the end of two years, Voodoo Vincent was distributing product strictly by appointment in a three bedroom flat off Fifty-fifth and Ellis with a Jacuzzi, full bar, and leather couches, with Martin Logan wall length speakers on his Krell stereo system. No longer a denizen of the streets, our hero's shopping cart had been replaced with the first down payment on a new Jag. Cut his dreads cuz he was thinkin' 'bout how he would fit in with them Wall Street cats. Was plannin' on goin' all-out-three-piece-suit serious with his business plans. He was, like the Jeffersons, *movin' on up, baby, movin' on up*, no end in sight. A true gambler at heart, he had gained a few clients with large stock portfolios and had advanced his enterprise to money market speculation, dabbling with securities and blue chips. All this in two short years, till one day in August, on the second anniversary of his business venture, the bowler wearing brotha came once again to his dreams.

In Vince's dream, LegBaby was leaned ever so lightly on a lamp-post on the intersection of Forty-seventh and Federal, right in the midst of the Robert Taylor projects. Vince could hear the wind whistlin' between the project buildings and over LegBaby's bowler that was brandished brash as ever, leaned low on his brown forehead, casting shadow over eyes as he spoke.

"See you been eatin' good these days, huh, boy? Looks like you been spreadin' the good word and gettin' heard. How's about spreadin' some of that love back to where it come from?"

"What you mean?"

"I hooked you up, son. Now it's time to recapitulate. Reimburse. Rebuild your connection, brother. Time to ante up."

"What you want?"

"Conversation, compensation, and correlation, brotha. We need to discuss our financial arrangements and how we is all goin' to get over on this here gift."

"Look, old man, I is a *business* man, so don't haggle wit' me. What's more, you is a figment of my imagination. A undigested piece of quiche. But I will grant you audience, anyway, just for the entertainment value. Speak on, Mr. Fatpockets Figment."

"Now you look here, you Johnny-Come-Lately-Negro-Minded-Negro, you need to get some kinda wise and some humble in your eyes. You is nothin' but a ve-hicle, a mule, a horse I ride to get the message in the tide, you dig me? I chose you cuz I could see the dollar signs in your eyes, the get up 'n' go to take this gift to where it's gotta get gone to, but don't you think for one minute that your talent ain't on loan from God. And what the Lord giveth, he shall taketh a—"

"Oh, spare me, please. You must be the bad end of a butter cookie I ate last week. . . ."

"Now I'ma tell you what you need to do, boy. Half your income to the homeless."

WHAT?

"Tha's right boy. You gots the cash, so get charitable fast. Find yourself a shelter with which to share wealth."

"Oh *hell* naw. This must be some kinda nightmare I'm in. Old man, is you crazy? I don't owe them homeless, backwards, greedy moochers nothin'."

"Has you forgot where yo' dusty, homeless hide came from not more than two years ago?"

Immediately the sky is filled with shopping carts. Vince can't move because he feels the walls of every stairwell and cement floor he ever slept on slamming in his bones. Something far removed from the brand new waterbed in the condo. A minute later, the hollow boned pain stops as suddenly as it started. LegBaby talked to Vince as he would address a petulant child.

"Now look, so much for the special effects. Every time I see you seems like I gotta pull out the Hollywood stunts just to get your attention. I'm tired of all this mumbo jumbo b.s. Ain't you never heard of givin' back to your peoples?"

"Look, I made a few dimes and nickels offa what people think they wanna hear. Offa what I see printed on a bunch of paper. If they wanna believe it, then that's cool. Money in my pocket and mellow on their nerves. But this ain't got nothin to do wit' no homeless mopes. Yeah, I used to sleep on the street. Yeah, I used to not have no place to go. Yeah, I ate a few Dumpster divin' dinners. But I was a ENTREPRENEUR. Always was, always will be. Always had somethin' to vend. I gots mine fair and square and now is time to reap the benefit. Tell you what: I give a shelter a few stock options."

"Boy, you ain't got no options!"

"Yeah I do! Blue chip too! AT&T..."

"I said you got no option but to give 'em CASH, son." LegBaby was sweatin' his brow and grittin' his teeth. "You 'bout to get me MAD, boy. And I'm the last one in the world you wanna see like that."

At that point, LegBaby reminded Vince of his past with a snap of his fingers and a blast of eighty-below windchill, cold enough to freeze dry a burning match. But do you think that changed our psychic brotha's mind? That blast of shivers wasn't even warm enough to thaw Vince's cold and calculating heart, cuz he's steady thinking he'd be damned before givin' up a dime of his loot to shiftless, conniving s.o.b.s that mooched alla time. And so, while his teeth chattered, his tongue still clattered out:

"N-n-n-o way, LegBaby, I'd sooner freeze than give up
these g's.
Besides, I'm wake up any minute now in my satin sheeted
bed,
And you'll be just another bad dream memory floatin' in
my head."

At this point, LegBaby was wonderin' just how ol' boy got to be so damn Republican in so short a time, 'bout to burn his fuse down to the powder keg of his wrath. Now, I dunno if you know how mean ol' LegBaby can be, but I'ma tell you this: Once he gets hold of dislikin' you, he may not let go for a while, and you'll be in a bad way till you get your business *right*.

Some folks say LegBaby lost his cool, right then and there, and turned Vince into nothing more than the squeak you hear on a shopping cart's wobbling wheel, warblin' *please please help me* while you just keep on pushing along. Some say LegBaby was just a dream, a bit of undigested Leon's BBQ that snuck up and bit Vince in the butt. Some say that the reason you don't see Vince 'round here no more is cuz he didn't wake up that next mornin', was stone cold heart attack dead, his face all twisted up and fingers clutched around fifty thousand-dollar bills. But I heard it from my best friend's cousin's stepsister, who got it from Uncle Ras. He knows 'bout everything that goes down on the South Side, and they say he told it like this:

LegBaby turned on his heel, walked outta Vince's dream, and left him to wake up the next morning. Vince thought everything was cool. No dream was gonna put him offa his path toward millions. His only thought on the matter was: *Damn. Shouldn'a mixed Night Train with ice cream last night.*

That morning started like so many others. A glance at his appointment book after his croissant and grits. A walk down to the corner store to read the paper, cutting out one or two collages before eleven, when his first customer would roll through, and today that was Pimpin' Sam, the racetrack man, who had a penchant for horses and a love of money.

Now, Pimpin' Sam was from the West Side of Chi, where they're down home cordial till you cross the wrong nerve and find your face reupholstered with fisticuffs or bullets. Sam didn't much like these South Side Negroes no way, but he had heard that Vince was a sure bet for a winning horse pick. So he had driven his Caddy down to Hyde Park with a few of his six-five 280 pound business associates, intent on scoring some insight into who was going to place and show in the first and second races the next day at Maywood. Vince was no dummy (or so he thought) and knew that this info was primo. He demanded a first class fee for his services.

"Look, pimpdaddy, I usually don't do this low type kinda forecastin'. Horses an' all that. Kinda base, if you ask me. However, I will provide this special service as a favor to you, my brotha—at two g's per name."

Now, Sam, like I said, never did like these South Side Negroes too much. Too fast-talkin' and high toned for his taste, and Vince was provin' himself to be the epitome of both qualities at the moment. But Sam was chill. Took a long breath. Tilted back his Kangol brim and let out a sigh as he reached in his briefcase. Pulled out twelve thousand bucks, a nine millimeter pistol, and placed them both on the table, the Beretta's muzzle pointed toward Vince. Smiled as he said:

"The money is yours, and the names are mine.
But if the horses fail, you'll be doin' some dyin'.
Understand?"

"No problem, bossman. These cards ain't failed me yet. You is garron-teed."

Vince hands the cardboard suitcase to Sam, who shuffles through till he finds a ransom note lookin' card with names like Count Him In, Strong and Fancy, Totally Batty, and Devil's Details. Sam takes his names, his gun, his briefcase and business associates and heads out the door, pausing only for one last look over his shoulder before the door closes.

"If my pockets don't get fat—
best believe you'll be on your back."

Vince just smiled and waved. He knew he had the world by the tail.

Next appointment was at one, when Detective Brown from the Third District stepped in through the door. This young stud believed he was hot on the trail of the latest crack connection in the Engle-wood neighborhood, and was searching for that one piece of evi-dence that would clinch the case and move him closer to promotion. He was breathless as he explained his situation to Vince.

"I just need to know, Vince. I been humpin' for promotion for a while now, and I know if I crack this case and case this crack, I'll be wearin' lieutenant's stripes by next year. I hear you the one with the third eye, so hook me up with that knowledge, brotha, lemme know where the big deal is goin' down."

Vince sensed an earnest nature in the brotha, so he cut him a deal. Only $500 for a card. And lo and behold, when the brotha pulled out a card from the cardboard box, it had a date showin' the next day and a watch pointin' to twelve noon, all of this placed underneath a picture of a video camera and an ad for the *Strickly Bid'ness Lounge* on Michigan Avenue. Officer Brown was perplexed, but left with the card and a shake of Vince's hand.

Next appointment was at three. Vince almost called it off 'cause he figured he made enough scratch for one day, but then remembered how the woman's voice on the phone had made his hair (and other parts) stand on end, and decided to hope that she looked as good as her voice. Turns out that he was wrong. Sereeta was *twice* as delicious as her caramel covered sound—with legs as smooth as a summer's sundown makin' a strut that would cause a blind man to see, hips that would make a lame man jump fifty feet. She laid out her troubles to Vince.

"Please help me, Mr. Vincent. I need to know if my man is double-timing me. He been actin' strange, moody, and ain't been—well—tightenin' me up the way he used to do. I swear to God if this keeps going on, I'ma just burst. I don't know what to do!"

Needless to say, Vince was steady thinkin' of a few things they could be doin' right then and there to remedy her situation, but he decides to play the high road, and simply holds up a shaking hand holding the suitcase box, askin' her to dip in and get her card. "For free, this time. I suppose I could make an exception due to the dire circumstances of your lips—er—legs—er—legitimate needs."

She reached in and pulled out an astrostoriogram with the most interesting photos attached. Imagine, if you will, a collage of hard-knocked ebony gangsta features on one side of a card, while on the other side there is the most stunning picture of RuPaul, the brotha-would-be-sista him/herself, decked out in a red clinging dress, high heels, pearls, and a 'do that would make Diana Ross jealous. Between the two was an equal sign made of tiny exclamation marks, and printed around the edges was an address located in the Austin neighborhood. Sista is a little perplexed, but proceeded out the door thankin' Vince up and down, and Vince plannin' just how he'll take that thanks later on.

So much for another typical day's work in a clairvoyant's life, thought Vince as he closed shop for the day. After a run to Harold's Chicken Shack and a few drinks, he retired for the evenin' without even a trace of LegBaby stompin' through his dreamscapes. And when two days passed without even a whisper of a whine from Leg-Baby, he believed he was rewarded for his persistence.

Vince knew he had turned the corner now. Who cared about what a silly dream had to say about givin' away half his cash? To congratulate himself on his calm nerve and good sense, he went down the street to get breakfast. But lo and behold, when he got back to his bachelor pad, the front door was busted in and his once beautiful crib looked like a hurricane just swept through. Our hero was pissed, but that anger turned straight into fear when alla sudden two rhinoceros sized brothas rushed out from the kitchen (they had been pilferin' some of that $20 a pound caviar and $3 a plate Harold's wings that Vince had grown accustomed to), grabbed him up, tied his hands, and whisked him out to the fire escape. Not being very talkative, the burly gentlemen merely punctuated their requests for Vince's silence with a few well placed blows to the ribs and skull, till our protagonist was a puddle of pain perched on the perilous metal platform twenty stories above the pavement. His escorts then departed from the scene, and lo and behold, who should join our brother on the escape but Pimpin' Sam, gat cocked and eyes locked on Vince's visage. Sam threw the suitcase full of astrostoriograms at Vince's feet with disgust and sneered.

I told you not to steer me wrong—
Who the hell you tryin' to con?
My grandma could run faster than them nags
That was damn near dead befo' they could stagger
'Cross the finish line.
Punk, you was lyin'.
And not only that
But you messed with my act
And told my woman my business
Why the hell'd you give her this?

Sam's enraged, trembling hand reached in his pocket and, to Vince's horror, pulled out the card our hero gave luscious Sista Sereeta the other day, gangsta scowls and RuPaul sittin' there just as grim and happy as can be—except Vince coulda swore he saw a wink in RuPaul's eye that wasn't there before.

"Uh—I—uh—I—uh—I can explain—"

"Yeah, well explain between bullets, fool. . . ."

And just as Sam's finger tightened around the trigger, the cacophonous sounds of street shouting came from inside the apartment. Lo and behold, the ChiTown police were raidin' the room: It was the plainclothes division, but not plainclothes enough to disguise the knuckle-dragger-in-charge strut of District Commander Dirge when he walked through the door. Even Sam didn't want to bust a cap in front of the po-lice, so he chilled and puts his Beretta back underneath his belt, letting out a sigh and facing the music, which at the moment was the uptight growl of the commander steppin' out on the escape, gun drawn.

"Thank God," thought Vince. "The po-po finally doin' they job."

He was 'bout to take back all the times he'd ever surreptitiously given a police car the finger when he alla sudden notices a funny thing. Once he was out there, a sight for Vince's sore eyes, Dirge made sure the window shade was drawn, lowered his piece, and smiled at Sam, lookin' him up and down real sweet and slow-like. Vince coulda swore he saw Dirge's hand wanderin' close, *way* close, to Sam's designer jeaned rear, and grab a handful before he turned to glare at Vince.

"So this the one, huh?"

"This him."

"So how the hell did this idiot know where the deal was going down?"

"I dunno how this clueless punk knows 'bout operations, but one thing he know for sure is how to pick a loser—every last name the punk sold me came in *dead last*." Sam punctuated these last two words with kicks to Vince's legs.

Dirge turned and stood over Vince. "Lucky thing we were able to get that film back from Brown, or we'd be straight outta luck right now. Had to pull all kindsa strings to get the bastard a promotion to lieutenant. But *this* dimwit . . . this one has gotta go down, goddammit. He knows too damn much."

Vince tried to play the ignorant role. "Sir, I dunno what you talkin' 'bout, I know nothin' bout nothin' 'cept this here gang bangin' bastard busted in my house tryin' to kill—"

And Dirge's pistol whip comes so fast he doesn't see it comin', leaves him feelin' like an El train ran through his skull, and darkness placed its palm across his eyes.

Upon waking, Vince felt himself being lifted face up to heaven, his suitcase full of cards resting on his chest. He could see nothing but clouds and blue sky, and almost felt peaceful, till alla sudden he heard the rough voice of Dirge say the word "suicide" and he suddenly felt weightless, the world upside down, falling, and then the back alley pavement cement approaching at record speed. *Well, this was it,* he thought, till alla sudden, his free fall stopped when his nose was one terrifying foot above the concrete, and a familiar raspy little voice comes from midair.

"Well, well, look who done stumbled into the crossroads!"

Vince spun around while upside down, clutching his precious old suitcase full of cards, and there, dressed in purple tux and diamond studded bowler, leanin' on a silver and gold cane, was LegBaby hisself.

Vince stuttered in surprise. "Wha-wha-what the—I ain't dreamin', fool, and unless you got a way outta here, then just let a brotha die in peace.

"Look, boy, I had slowed time down for just a little bit, so we could have this here conversation, but if you don't wanna know 'bout the way outta here, then it ain't no never mind to me." LegBaby started to slowly dissolve into thin air, like a fine mist.

Suddenly, Vince had second thoughts as LegBaby continued to fade. "PLEAASE MISTA! Wait a minute, mista, wait just a minute. Anything you want."

"Anything, you say?" LegBaby stopped his fade just this side of smoke.

"Anything, brotha, anything—just don't leave me here like this."

"You did say *anything*, right?"

"Just get me outta here. Please. Just let me outta here in one piece alive."

"But I thought I was just a fig-ment of your imagination. A piece of un-di-ges-ted food. A bad dream. How could lil ol' imaginary me help a real-life fool like you?"

"Look, old man, you got me where you want me. I just want to be SAFE from these here gangstas and this here headsplittin' fall. Just tell me what you wants me to do. Tell me what you need."

LegBaby paused for a minute, and then came up close on Vince, leaned down to look him straight into his upside down eyes. "You wanna be SAFE, huh? I get you rich. I give you The Gift. I make you somebody people come to for advice instead of turnin' their noses up when they pass you on the street, give you the chance to get richer than the dreams of avarice, and then I ask you for one simple small-ish type thing, and you laugh in my face. And now you just wanna be SAFE?

"You did the worst thing you could possibly do, boy. You turned your back on what you once was. Yeah, you was a entrepreneur. A *homeless* entrepreneur. Just like alla them Mississippi/Alabama/Kentucky/Georgia born black brown refugees come up north here, lookin' for nothin' but a place to stay and a future to work on. Just like yo' great great great greats, come here in the hold of a ship.

Homeless. And you get the chance of a lifetime and you just wanna be SAFE?

"Okay, son. You gone be SAFE. And you gonna do somethin' for me. Since you didn't wanna stand for nothin' when you was livin' high and mighty, you gone stand for something right now. You gone stand for them, nigga. You gone stand for what they all is, and for what most o' them is two paychecks away from being—out on the street in a strange land, lookin' for opportunity any way they can. You gone stand tall. Nice . . . and . . . tall."

LegBaby twirled his cane in the air, and our hero felt the sky getting hard and black. The universe tipped itself ever so slightly at his feet as he was transported above the city in a black wind. He could feel the electric hum of Chicago in his heart, could sense iron slippin' through his veins, his hands slowly turnin' to steel, upraised in wind, feet finally landin' back solid, heavier than ever before on the ground, his face frozen in a northbound stare.

Ol' LegBaby stood by his word alright. Vince is completely safe. And yeah, he's standin' tall all right, about forty feet tall. If you ever go to the South Side of Chi you will see him there still, a bronzed statue facing north, standin' in the middle of Twenty-sixth and Martin Luther King Drive. His leather jacket has been turned to a bronzed patchwork of worn out leather soles from all the walkin' all the refugees done from south to north to claim a new home. His iron fist still clutches that suitcase full of future. His metal face stands solemn and waiting, hailing the future like it was a freight train headed somewhere new or, if you like, waving hello to the uncle or cousin or sister or lover he's come up north to see. And perched all around him are sixteen suitcases, one for each of the astrostoriograms from which he made his fortune, each one full of good luck, bad luck, and a huge helpin' of hope. Vince is standin' there day and night, summer and winter, remindin' us how we all are lookin' for home, how we is all homeless up in this cold and wind of ChiTown, or any other town, if we don't make ourselves a home in us. They say if you listen close sometime, when the wind is real strong, you might hear ol' Vince's voice comin' from his brown bronzed lips, askin' do you want your future told.

So that is the story of Voodoo Vincent and his astrostoriograms. I'm just tellin' you the way I heard it from my best friend's cousin's stepsister, and she got it straight from Uncle Ras. So you know it's got to be true.

THE BINARY

John Cooley

(2004)

It was fifteen minutes to five in the afternoon, and the streets were worse than I expected them to be. Even though I was driving against the heavier flow of traffic, it was a sure bet that I'd be home later than I'd said, so like the good husband I am, I called Carla and gave her the heads-up. As I walked through the front door, I could hear the dreaded sounds of her banging around in the kitchen.

My wife is a completely beautiful creature inside and out, and does all she can to promote a healthy relationship between us. Most recently she's taken up cooking at least four times a week. We've been married three good years, having no real issues to speak of, but Carla sees this as an opportunity for us to grow even closer. I won't spoil her fun, seeing that it's not malicious at all, but the only problem is . . . Carla can't cook worth a damn.

The smell spoke of baked chicken and rice, seasoned with garlic and rosemary, and was probably a recipe from one of her monthly women's magazines. Her work was so engrossing that she didn't notice me creep up behind her, which made her easy prey to my poking her right in that spot below her ribs. It went through her like a lightning bolt, and I'm sure the neighbors two streets down heard her squeal. She fell backward into me.

"Joshua you bastard! Alright, you gonna sneak up on me one day and get shot!"

"Aw baby. You don't really wanna shoot me, do ya?"

"Hell yeah! The only question is where should I aim—for your head or for your *head*." She spun away from me and punched at my crotch. Her strike missed its mark, but a threat to a man's genitalia—whether real or imagined—will cause him to bend at the knees and reach out to shield them. Now brandishing a cast-iron skillet, she wore an expression that conveyed serious business, so I surrendered.

"Okay, okay! I'm sorry!"

"Sorry for what? For making me feel completely insecure? For making me feel totally unsafe? For making me feel like anyone could just waltz their ass up in here and do God knows what to me before I even knew what hit me? What exactly are you sorry for?"

Now she was just being silly, but that skillet was giving her argument much greater weight. I had to think fast before this turned into an incident that would end up with me owing her a night out on the town, or jewelry, or, worse, a trip to see her parents.

Oh hell no, I ain't havin' that.

I went into mack mode.

"I apologize for being so insensitive to your feelings. I apologize for leaving you in this huge house alone for so long. I apologize for not being able to imbibe the sweet nectar of your love perpetually, for not being able to be warmed by the fire of your emotion eternally." I stared so deeply into her eyes as I spoke that I bypassed the physical and peered into her mind. I have to be careful of that, but I noticed her icy stance melt with my every word and knew that there'd be no visits to the in-laws anytime soon. Damn I'm good.

"'Imbibe the sweet nectar of my love'? Boy, you are so freakin' silly." She was trying to hide her smile, but I knew full well that we could chalk this one up as a win for me. Melodrama has its place, and it had just helped me trade a swing from a skillet for a long, passionate embrace. I knew then that I was the luckiest man on earth, but I also knew how quickly that luck could change, how precarious my life with Carla truly was.

My take on what happened six years ago is supplemented by too many hospital staffers to name. I can retell the story only up to the point of the accident. One evening Carla and I had just finished a fabulous meal of lobster fettuccini in cream sauce at the Southern

Carafe. We amused ourselves with conversation about the legitimacy of investigating the private lives of those who held public office. My stance was that as long as officials performed their duties effectively, I didn't need to know their dirty secrets. I mean we all had them, right?

I could see her laughing at me behind her dark brown eyes, but she somehow gathered the resolve to answer me. She felt that a person's private life would eventually affect his or her job performance, so if details of corruption or perversion did surface, it had to be considered. Something about Italian food mixed with debate always primed me for further physical indulgence, so I suggested that we continue our discourse at our hotel. As we were leaving, I found myself giddy with the knowledge that in a few minutes I'd be the main strand in a tangled web of hot, sweaty, country loud, mind altering sensuality, which sent my twenty-six-year-old maturation regressing to that of a giggling schoolboy's. Despite my rising excitement, I carefully navigated the Nashville streets. They were glistening with that fresh misty precipitation, the kind that loosens the oil in the asphalt just enough to turn it into stationary banana peels. I was being extra vigilant to ensure our safe transport, which is why I was so surprised when I awoke to find myself crouching in an open field, my shins flat against the ground as I sat atop my feet.

I had only seen this position in Japanese movies and always thought it looked far too uncomfortable to try. Strangely, I felt no discomfort at all. Wispy cirrus clouds formed brushstrokes against a pastel sky as the insects and birds soothed me with songs of their daily exploits. Trees swayed lazily in a warm summer breeze, adding accompaniment in nature's melody. I seemed to be its sole audience, and I had no idea how or why I was here. But instead of panic, there was an overwhelming sense of peace in this place, so I didn't question its plausibility. I relaxed in the all-consuming comfort of it.

"Joshua Ryan."

Who could've called my name? I hadn't seen anyone else for miles around.

"Here I am, in front of you."

Now, he definitely wasn't there earlier.

"Yes, I was. You just didn't know how to see me."

I realized that he wasn't really talking as much as conveying his thoughts to me. Speech was the communicative method to which I was accustomed, so my mind was automatically interpreting his thoughts into spoken words. Obviously my mind was opened to him, too. He mirrored my posture, and was dressed in clothes that designated him as a landowner. Don't ask me how I knew that. I simply did.

"My name is Jubei Kibegame. Do you know why you're here, Joshua?"

"Not really, but this place is so peaceful that I don't want to be anywhere else right now."

"But you are somewhere else now."

Before I could respond or question him, I *knew* rather than heard his explanation.

Apparently, the driver of the SUV fell victim to an epileptic seizure, which caused her to run the red light at the intersection we were traveling through. She hit my rented Intrepid at roughly forty-five miles per hour, flipping us over onto the car's passenger side and into a guardrail. The force of the collision was concentrated about a foot in front of the driver's-side door, crumpling the car into a crescent-shaped mess of twisted glass and metal. Carla suffered a broken left tibia and would need months of therapy to heal, but miraculously was in no threat of losing her dance career. I, on the other hand, had taken the brunt of the impact, causing so many internal injuries that there was little hope for my recovery. I thought of Carla, and the peace I'd felt only moments before disappeared.

"I asked you to come here, Joshua, to appeal to your sense of compassion and charity." Jubei's calm voice flowed from him in a slow, respectful manner. There was an air of refinement and diplomacy in it.

"What do you need from me?" The question was more for my benefit than his. I was curious about what this Japanese fella could possibly want from me in this disjointed reality.

"I need your help. I once lived in your town, and I left it with quite a bit of unfinished business. I was indeed a landowner, and in my zeal to keep it, I allowed members of my family to make decisions that will be a burden to the other townsfolk for many years to come."

"Where do I fit in all of this? It seems to me that you need a real estate lawyer, not a broker for a transportation firm. I'd like to help, but I don't see how my skills are of any use to you."

"Transportation is exactly what I need, Joshua. I know that you can feel this necessity reaching out to you in ways that cannot be understood by conventional thought."

He was right about that. I could perceive the mortal urgency of this matter without him having to tell me. I also knew that if I did turn him down, he wouldn't try to force his will upon me. It could've been his demeanor, his genteel style, or perhaps his simple, straightforward approach. Whatever it was, I felt I had no right to deny him.

When I opened my eyes, I found Carla asleep in a chair next to my bed. The memory of Jubei's calm voice in the field remained with me, but I now had a tube going down my throat forcing air into my lungs in a regulated tempo. There were two more coming out of each of my lungs emptying into rectangular containers that hung on either side of my bed. I didn't even try to count the rest of the lines connected to me either by tape or by needle. The sight of Carla brought much comfort to my mind, but it was quickly dispelled when I saw the cast on her leg. I tried to ask if she was alright, but only succeeded in trying to hack up the aforementioned intubation line.

I'd been in the intensive care unit of St. Joseph's East for ten days. Immediately upon arrival at the hospital, surgery was performed to heal the rib that almost punctured both of my lungs. The laceration across my left kidney had to be repaired, pieces of shrapnel had to be dislodged from my intestines. My left leg was broken in four places, my left arm was dislocated, the humerus snapped clean through above the elbow. I'm told my heart stopped twice while I was on the operating table.

I was alive, but the prognosis for the quality of life that I could expect was grim. It was probable that I'd suffered anoxic insult (brain damage due to a lack of oxygen during the times I flatlined), and would also have no more than fifty percent lung capacity at best, so I would need round-the-clock care in a nursing home. To the amazement of all involved, I made a full recovery, in only a few months. The best thing that came from all of this is the knowledge that Carla and I gained of life's fragility. There was no guarantee that we'd be here for each other forever, so we had to make the best of every moment we had together. We healed and grew into one another, to the point where marriage was only a formality. We were already knit in ways that no ceremony could further make legitimate.

So here I am, six years later, washing dishes from a meal that was . . . edible. She overbaked the chicken, and underboiled the rice. Still I managed to eat all that was on my plate, and acted as if I enjoyed it. I might need to take over all the cooking chores, or, better yet, make sure we tag-team better on them. Maybe that was what the woman was trying to accomplish all along. After we put away the dishes, we talked for what seemed to be about twenty minutes, but the clock told me that three hours had expired. I held Carla as she drifted off to sleep, and thanked God for my perfect wife, my perfect house, my perfect job, my perfect life.

But I wish there was a way for me to be the perfect husband. You see, I have a problem with lying to Carla. I don't see any way for me to be honest with her concerning what I was actually doing in New York. I just got back today, but she thought I was there on business, and I was—just not the kind she was expecting.

I arrived in Gotham Wednesday afternoon and actually met with a few prospective clients, for appearances. I stayed at the Towne Royale Plaza Hotel as usual, and made sure to bring back all the receipts I got while there. I like that hotel because its staff knows me pretty well and I always get a room to my liking.

Around 2 A.M. Thursday morning, I got down to the real reason I was there. I was already dressed in my workout gear (that's what I like to call it) consisting of a long-sleeved crew-neck T-shirt, neoprene gloves, BDUs, balaclava, leather and Gortex, boots all in black. I always carry my sword, Tetsuo, with me when on these types of outings. It's a 300-year-old Japanese tachi, shorter than the nodachi, longer than the katana, just right for me. I don't like to think of it as a weapon, but more of an effective tool for my extracurricular work. I may not be the perfect husband, but I am the perfect killer.

Another reason I prefer the Towne Royale over other hotels is because I know it like the back of my hand. I can get in and out of it with no one else being the wiser. I soon made my way to the roof and paused to acclimate myself to the cold northern weather. As I took slow, deep breaths of the crisp air, I could feel my transformation complete itself, and looked out at the city from a new perspective. I had to be at the Omnibus Office Building in fifteen minutes or better, and I resolved to make it in nine. I ran over to the ledge of the roof, stretched then flexed my calf muscles, and smiled as their strength catapulted my body high into the clear winter sky. I covered the twenty yards over the street to the next building with ease, then ran so fast across its roof that I ceased to feel my feet touching it. The rush I get from moving this fast is indescribable; it's the closest a human can come to flying without being a bird. Although at moments like that, I can't really call myself human. I alternated running with jumping from building to building, keeping my movement swift enough for me to appear as nothing more than a breath against the skyline. I soon arrived at my destination, and leaped fifty feet down to its roof. My descent speed reached close to forty miles per hour, but I still managed to land with nary a sound. It's a strange sight to behold. You have all this velocity that simply terminates right as you reach the landing surface. It's one of the perks of being a binary creature. Normal laws of physics cease to apply to you.

Finding a window-cleaner's scaffold, I lowered it to the thirtieth floor and let myself in. It didn't take long to zero in on the location of the people I was looking for; their collective aura showed like a beacon in the night. They had yet to detect my presence, and continued with their business oblivious to me. I crept closer, being careful not to alert them to my close proximity. Soon I was in the hallway right outside the office they were in.

There were six of them, five *oni* and one *jonin*, which makes a full war party. A jonin is a human channeler and controller of evil spirits, which the oni are. In order for them to exist in our world, they must assume control of weak-willed persons, feed from their misery, and use their bodies as vessels. Oni don't belong here on earth, and we were doing a good job of getting rid of them. Any well-trained binary can successfully fight two oni at once, while a pair of binary beings can take out a whole war party. I plan to engage them alone, which under normal circumstances would mean my doom, but we've discovered that I'm not a normal binary.

I eavesdropped on them as they talked. They were speaking aloud, and in *German*. That was a concern to me. Oni and jonin can communicate telepathically. It ensures the highest level of privacy and the most efficient means of communication between them. There had to have been someone else in that office who was neither telepathic nor Japanese, which is why I didn't notice him earlier. I reproved myself for being so sloppy.

The jonin was an overweight Japanese native. He was well groomed, dressed in an expensive suit, and had that telltale air of superiority about him. His oni were a mix of nationalities; all were fit and youthful. Let me say they appeared youthful—there was no real way to tell an oni's age without asking him. They could live for centuries in a host's body, and unless they were killed by one of their own or a binary, they could probably stay around as long as they wanted.

"Please calm yourself, Mr. Kraus. The artifact is now safely in your possession, with the museum's curators being none the wiser. You will leave for Austria in the morning, where you will deliver it to its proper owners. Everything may not be exactly as we planned, but our objectives are reached nonetheless." His words were of little comfort to the man he was speaking to.

"Dammit, Yoshi, there wasn't supposed to be any bloodletting in this venture! Too much is at stake for us to take any chances. I didn't want to attract any undue attention to this situation, but now there will surely be police sniffing around, insurance investigators will come calling, the media will get ahold of it, all because you couldn't keep your sycophants in check!"

"You are an alarmist, Mr. Kraus. There will be nothing of the sort to occur," the jonin interrupted. "My oni *are* in check, and have taken care of all loose ends in this matter. It would be best for you to bridle your emotions while around them. Your fear identifies you as prey; you don't want to be mistaken for their next meal, now do you?"

Kraus gulped and nervously walked over to his chair behind his desk and sat.

It was easy to read the oni's minds, which struck me as strange. They're usually meticulous about shielding their psyches, but for some reason, be it hubris or just a lack of discipline, they were pretty careless that night. I expanded the range of my mental sensory zone and swept up all the stray psionic details they offered.

Kraus was the representative of a German investment group interested in getting their hands on an artifact, a mask of some sort, from the Metropolitan Museum. When the museum's curators and management wouldn't play ball, the jonin and his crew were tapped to acquire it discreetly. Kraus was pissed at the oni's heavy-handedness; they ended up killing nine people for it, of whom seven were just warehouse workers.

I was intrigued by all of this, but then I realized that something was wrong. The mood in the office had changed suddenly and very drastically. Somehow, the oni were aware of my presence. I couldn't detect any slip in my actions to give away my cover, but that was neither here nor there. I withdrew farther down the hallway to a place where there was more room for action. Although I couldn't actually see into the office, I knew what was happening. The oni had allowed their human facades to give way to their true appearances.

Their eyes glowed red, their teeth became long and bestial, their mouths stretched into exaggerated grimaces, and they stank. Kraus dropped to the floor, heaving past the point of there being anything left in his stomach. No normal human could endure being around such unadulterated evil, and I could only pity Kraus as he lay writhing on the floor in utter agony.

The jonin commanded only one of his oni to deal with me. He must've thought I was a security guard or a cleaning-crew member who had the misfortune of stumbling upon their late-night meeting. The office door flew off its hinges, followed by the oni scrambling toward me, mouth agape with his tongue flapping wildly from it. I allowed some of my chi to flow into Tetsuo. It grew warm and glowed with expectation in its scabbard. I gripped my sword's handle in anticipation, waiting for just the right moment to strike. The malice in the oni's intentions was tangible; his bloodlust permeated the air between us. In a few more seconds he'd be across the hall and upon me, ripping me into pieces before devouring me. His feet left the floor as he attacked, and at the same time I drew my blade from my left side, cutting a perfect gleaming arc through the air. There was complete disbelief in the oni's eyes as he sailed past me. His body from the waist up rebounded off the wall behind me, his bottom portion slid farther down the hall. His comrades began to howl and curse, their voices joined in a most horrific cacophony of anger. I could now see Kraus wallowing in his own vomit, trying in desperation to escape the awful malevolence surrounding him. The din now created by the demons proved too overwhelming, and he collapsed on the spot. He may never recover, the poor bastard.

Over the noise I could hear the jonin speak telepathically. "He is a binary, my children. You must combine your attack and kill him swiftly. Avenge your fallen brother, then bring me the binary's eyes and liver."

It's said that you can steal your enemy's soul by taking his eyes and divine the future with his liver. I didn't plan on letting the jonin test the theory. My style of fighting is most effective when I have plenty of room to operate, so I hightailed it back to the scaffolding. I didn't have anywhere near the time it would take to draw it back up to the roof, so I grabbed one of the lines and shimmied the twenty stories to the top, where the oni were already waiting. Their minds reached out to me with the hisses and last gasps of a dying man.

"Don't fool yourself, binary."

"You will certainly die."

"But you have options."

"Will it be fast and merciful, leaving a pretty corpse?"

"Or slow and torturous, leaving only pieces behind?"

There were only four of them present, but I could "hear" five distinct voices. The jonin was near. They brandished weapons, strange, sharp, curved things that actually absorbed what little light they encountered. You would not believe what they expected to do with them. They surrounded me, constantly circling about, moving with blinding speed.

Part of the oni assault strategy is to demoralize their victim, in an attempt to defeat him mentally before attacking him physically. This makes it more pleasurable for them when their enemy succumbs to fear and dies terrified, but they would get no such reaction from me. I stood barely moving, with Tetsuo in an eccentric position, the blade held against the inside of my right arm with the tip pointing up and the sharpened edge facing out. They continued to orbit me, spouting obscenities and wishing me all sorts of ill fortune. I knew that if I ignored them, they'd grow impatient, and then sloppy, and I'd have the advantage. I never lose my cool. Losing my cool would get me killed, and we can't have that. I have a wife to go home to.

After what seemed an eternity, the jonin gave the command and his oni moved in on me. I raised Tetsuo, fending off their attack with parries and blocks. Their strategy was ingenious. They came in waves, being careful not to catch one another inadvertently in each other's blade strokes. Their swings were designed to push me directly into the path of their fellows' weapons, and I was hard pressed not to be cut into pieces. We moved with speed that would be mostly imperceivable to the naked eye, accompanied by the rings of clashing metal that underscored our deadly ballet. Had this not been such a lethal affair, one might find our complicated twists and graceful jumps beautiful to look on, but this was a most serious encounter. I soon found myself overwhelmed by the oni's offense, and if I didn't put some space between us they'd wear me down. I was smothered by them, never getting the chance to attack. It was bad and getting worse.

I crouched down, barely evading a swing from a blade that would've surely taken my head off from the nose up, then flexed my calves again and from fifteen feet in the air watched the oni's demonic expressions change from malice to disbelief. I was inverted—the soles of my feet faced the sky, my eyes stared down on them—and I saw my opening. I tucked my knees close to my chest and hurtled for the roof. Before they realized I had even moved, Tetsuo sliced completely through one of them from his nape down to his rib cage. He sank to his knees and I caught him with a side crescent kick that sent most of him barreling over the edge of the building. The next thing I knew, my back slammed into the tar-and-asphalt roofing, and through dazed eyes I saw one of the others spinning in front of me. I realized that I'd fallen victim to his leg sweep. As his two allies attacked from above, I caught a mental glimpse of what they planned: They meant to pin me to the spot and eviscerate me slowly.

Well, I planned to have nothing to do with that. I again brought my knees to my chest and kicked; the momentum I created brought me to my feet as I heard the sound of metal piercing the roof. They spat curses at me as they struggled to free their weapons. I ignored them and turned my full attention to the one who'd knocked me down. As we ran at each other with incredible speed, I could smell his hatred spilling from him. At the instant right before we would collide, I launched myself over him, spun like a top end over end with my blade extended, and heard it sizzle and pop as it cut into his upper torso repeatedly. When I landed, there lay the lifeless oni, with at least six deep sword strikes to his chest, a few stretching to the top of his head. I had no time to savor that victory as my body jerked unexpectedly and a tremendous pain ripped through my abdomen.

I'd slid about twenty feet when I concluded that I'd been kicked again, but this time I was really winded. I was abruptly stopped by a metal heating/air-conditioning vent that folded with the impact. I must be crazy for taking on five oni like that. I tried to see where the next attack would come from, but my eyes didn't seem to be working. I blinked, widened them, but still could see only darkness. From somewhere came another bone-jarring kick that lifted me into the air and bounced me hard off the roof. At that moment time stopped. I could feel eerie, sinister voices creeping in from the hazy edges of my mind.

"You're helpless now, aren't you, binary?"

"Don't fight us, or we will torture you—"

". . . teach you new kinds of suffering—"

". . . until we strip your mind—"

". . . find everything and everyone you ever loved—"

". . . and turn them into living testimonies to pain."

"Don't you love anyone? Maybe we'll track them down regardless of what you do."

"Maybe we'll kill them anyway as vengeance for our brothers you've murdered tonight!"

"Perhaps we should keep you alive long enough to witness us exact our fair share of justice for our fallen comrades."

At that moment I didn't need my eyes; hot anger snapped me out of my daze. I reached out with my mind and "saw" the two oni circling over me.

In one fluid motion I rolled forward and slashed twice, catching the closer one through both of his legs above the knees, then back through the neck. He fell down in four pieces. There was an explosion of anger and pain in my mind. The last oni was screeching and howling like a mad animal at the sight of my latest victim. He lost all sense of logic as he snarled and bayed and spat foam at me. I couldn't see him at all, but I didn't need my eyes or psionic abilities to know where he was. He lashed out at me with his blade and teeth and claws. It was a more lethal attack than when I faced four at once. His viciousness proved to be his downfall as he overextended his reach to get at me. His lunge left him off balance and vulnerable. I easily sidestepped him and brought my sword across his back, dividing him through his rib cage.

I was sweating profusely, still dizzy from the beating I'd just taken, and was struggling to breathe. I absentmindedly tugged at my balaclava only to realize that it had gotten so twisted during the fight that it covered my eyes—that was why I couldn't see. I made a mental note of it; that kind of thing could get me killed one day.

I heard footsteps from my left and smelled fear in the sweat of the jonin. Without his cadre he was at my mercy, and he probably didn't want to stay around long enough to fathom its depths. He'll never know how I got in front of him. I was moving too fast for his eyes to follow. All he knew was that his head jerked back, his body hit the gravel, and Gortex was embedded on his forehead in a backward relief. He'd be sore as hell, but he'd live. I don't kill humans.

I needed a breather and used the time to survey the carnage wrought by our battle. The last oni I killed was dissolving nicely where he fell, and by that time there was nothing left of the others except their clothing. It's an interesting characteristic about them:

Their flesh and weapons dissolve at the point of death, leaving no evidence of their presence. What's that old saying, The devil's greatest trick is to convince the world that he doesn't exist? Well, this is something along those lines.

There was no rush getting back to the office, and I was quite perturbed for having to carry the jonin's fat ass. I let him drop to the floor in a heap without being the least bit gentle about it. Although Kraus was drooling, staring off into space while mumbling something I couldn't quite make out, he did muster enough resolve to sit himself up against one of the walls. I was sure that his mind was turned into mush, and it was obvious that I wasn't going to get much information out of him. I nudged the fat guy with my foot until he sputtered and woke. He wiped at his forehead, his fingers curiously traced the "O" in Gortex that he found there. I made a mental adjustment to change the way my voice would be perceived and spoke to him.

"So, what's it going to be, jonin? Will you tell me what I want to hear, or must I persuade you?"

He coughed and spit gravel. "I have no information that would be of any use to you, binary. Even if your paltry mind was introduced to the smallest detail of our business, it would not begin to approach understanding it."

"Pompous little bastard, ain'tcha?" He looked ridiculous with that backward Gortex logo on his head.

"It doesn't matter, binary. Do what you will to me. The package will be delivered to its rightful owners eventually. You cannot stop what is to come. You can only delay it, delay the inevitable."

"And those owners would be . . . ?"

He laughed. "I will tell you nothing else, *gaijin*."

WTF? How was I the outsider?

"You are an outsider to this situation."

I didn't speak that thought aloud. I must've been careless with it for him to respond to it so quickly.

He continued. "You have stumbled into matters that have never concerned you or your kind. You should accept your role as an inferior species, and allow those who are the rightful rulers of this world to assume their position of power."

What the hell? He was talking some master race–type shit.

"You know, you're making a lot of sense. In fact, your words are so profound that I'll just go and surrender myself to your oni and allow them to kill me. Oh, wait a minute, can't do that, can I? I can't do it because I cut them into tiny moist chunks out there. I guess five of the fatherland's best weren't good enough to take out just one gaijin, hm?"

That pissed him off. "You would never have beaten them if not for that traitor inside of you. Who is it? One from the house of Tanaka? Those dogs were never able to see the wisdom in our plans, but it isn't of any concern. The sun will rise again, binary! Then not a hundred warrior spirits dwelling inside of you will be enough to make a bit of difference!"

I was finally getting somewhere.

"What the hell are you rambling about? We binary beings will always be there to hunt you and your kind down. That's why there's so few of you around now."

Hot choler burned in the jonin's eyes. He sucked in air, ready to spew forth what I was sure would be all I ever wanted to know about this sordid affair. What happened next seemed to have taken ten minutes to play out. The jonin's mouth opened to speak, but before a sound could be uttered, his head burst into pieces as a nine-millimeter bullet passed though it and struck the far wall. Kraus was still wearing that vacant stare, but he was holding the proverbial smoking gun, a P220 SIG-Sauer .45 ACP pistol. Before I could disarm him, he turned the gun on himself and ended his life. Kraus was in no condition to do that on his own. He was under the influence of another being. I could hear the thoughts of security personnel on their way to my location and determined that it was time for me to depart. Besides that, I was tired, sore, and pretty damn disgusted by what had just occurred. I also had to wind down. Operating at this level puts so much stress on the body that if you do it for too long at a time it could prove detrimental.

I fumbled around the office until I found the mask and one of Kraus's overcoats. I needed it to cover up the mess that the jonin's murder had left on me. The security guards' minds were wide open to me, so I picked a route out of the building from one of them and walked down sixty flights to the street. My encounter with the oni had lasted all of eight minutes, but I felt like I'd been worked over by a gorilla for two or three days. I was still under the influence of the change, so walking the twenty-two blocks back to my hotel wasn't all that bad. I snuck back into my room—I couldn't afford anyone knowing that I'd been out that night—destroyed my clothing, and slept for fifteen hours straight.

When I awoke, that mask was the first thing on my mind. I played with the locks on its carrying case until they popped open, revealing its contents. What I looked at was a clay Japanese Noh mask, reddish gold in color. It was shaped like a man's face, with teeth bared and red/gold eyes, which indicated that it represented a warrior's spirit. On the inside was a name inscribed in Japanese characters: Ayakashi, which held no particular significance to me.

For a few seconds I toyed with the idea of placing it up to my face as if I were trying it on for size, but I thought better of it. Who knew where this thing had been? I'd make sure to share all I knew of it with Jubei. He had access to more sources of information than I did, so maybe he'd know why Kraus and company went to so much trouble to get it. I thought I'd hold on to it for a while, maybe keep a few more warehouse workers safe if it was in my care.

I got to JFK two hours before my flight was scheduled to leave and spent the time putting down wrong answers in my crossword puzzle book and engaging in polite conversation with a motherly old woman who was headed to Texas. I had turned my attention to the TV suspended above the waiting area when a news story about an apparent murder-suicide began to air. They played footage of two covered bodies being moved from the front of the Omnibus Building to coroners' vans, and co-workers of who I now knew as Helmutt L. Kraus III sharing their disbelief and sorrow at this tragedy. I began to sink down into my seat, knowing good and well that no one there had any idea that I was involved with what had occurred last night, but I felt like every passing glance my way was an indictment of my character.

Sometimes the grim reality of what I do gets to me, and I wonder what makes me any different from mass murderers like the ones who are dominating the newscasts lately. I decided to take my mind off that before I sank into a depressing rut that might prove difficult to climb out of. The old woman had been offering me a homemade cookie the whole time, so I took her up on it. It was fresh and gooey and I could taste the vanilla, butter, and chocolate in my whole face. Just like she promised, it was like getting a hug from the inside out.

My flight to Hartsford was uneventful, thank God. If I jumped on 285 east it would only take fifteen minutes to get to my house, but I needed to talk to Jubei, and I knew I wouldn't get the chance once I got home.

I sat in my car, relaxed, and closed my eyes. When I opened them, I was in the field, listening to the birds and cicadas sing, and Jubei was crouched before me, mirroring the way I sat.

"I don't have the slightest idea what the jonin meant by 'the sun will rise,' Joshua. I've conferred with my brethren, but all we could determine was that there is a great desire for that artifact to be obtained by the group from Austria. It's strange that there is no information about it from any of the networks that we deal with. It's as if the mask never existed. I think keeping it is the best thing to do, until we can discern its significance. We should take solace in the fact that we disrupted their plans by intercepting it."

Jubei's suggestion was sound. "I agree," I answered, "but what's really eating me is what happened to Kraus. His brain was *toast*. He didn't have the mental capacity to wet himself on purpose, let alone fire a gun."

"You're right. There was another force at work. It animated Kraus's body and assassinated the jonin before he could tell us anything of value. That other spirit is like nothing else I've ever encountered before. It was so dark; I felt my resolve weakening even to recognize its presence."

Now that was scary. Jubei represented the purest entity I'd ever encountered. He was strong, patient, and full of optimism. For something to affect him in such a way left me uneasy about my chances if I ever ran into it.

"Do not fear, Joshua. We are binary. We share the same body; our spirits join together to empower each other in our struggles. We have more than enough resources to defeat our foes, but doubt must never be allowed to become part of the equation. The only foe that can conquer us is our own insecurity. We must never lose focus on our goal for victory. We defend this realm from those who would destroy it, from those who would use this world's inhabitants for food and sport. We are all that stand between them and the murderous oni. We mustn't fail. We will not fail."

I awoke, wiped my eyes, and started for home. My mind went back to the day of the accident, how Jubei first came to me, how I had no idea what he was talking about when he asked for my help. I thought about how his spirit joining with mine gave me the ability to heal from my fatal wounds, about how when I allowed his spirit to rise to the surface I gained supernatural abilities, about how I could never let Carla know about this part of my life. I also considered how angry I became when the oni threatened to find her. God, I can't bear even to think about that possibility—it's my worst nightmare.

So there I lay with my wife napping noisily beside me, having just put away an imperfect meal. Those kinds of moments are dear to me, so I can never allow my two lives to intersect. I don't want my marital bliss to be destroyed by my outside activities. I took a deep breath and decided I'd had enough of thinking about it. That was an issue better left pondered another night. I looked down at my wife, nuzzled up to her short curly hair, and considered the angel's face she wore as she slept. I have to enjoy all the peaceful moments I get, because I know that with each new day comes a new challenge, and more oni to fight. It's the life I've chosen. We are binary.

BLACKout

Jill Robinson

(2004)

I love Alana, I just wish she didn't live in Harlem. My Brooklyn ass is tired of making the hour trip uptown just to get some. If it wasn't for her, I would have been in Flatbush when the news broke instead of standing here on this train platform feeling for the first time like an outsider amongst my own kind.

"Reparations, brother!" someone shouted, patting me on the back. They were all shouting, frantically congratulating each other, celebrating the passing of S9821—the reparations bill that promises to compensate American citizens of African descent for years of unpaid slave labor.

I have no reason to celebrate because I have been deemed ineligible.

"Hello?" I said, walking closer to the train exit to get better cell phone reception.

"Nigel? It's Alana."

I didn't answer. I was still fuming from our argument this morning.

"Nigel, can you hear me?" I heard her sigh but I still didn't answer. "I'm sorry. I didn't mean to be so . . ."

"Insensitive," I said, coming to her rescue. "What you said was insensitive, beyond insensitive. You think just because my parents are from Jamaica that I don't deserve reparations? Huh?"

Now she was quiet. I leaned against a poster of an enlarged subway map and waited for her to speak. Two trains had come and gone. I was already late for work.

"You said it. Be a woman and stand behind it," I said, egging her on.

She sighed. "I meant . . . Look, I have slave ancestors on one side of my family, so I'm gonna get at least half of the forty million. That's enough for both you and me to do what we want to do. . . ."

"No thanks," I said to both Alana and the man passing out free T-shirts with a mule on the front and the words 40 ACRES on the back.

"Come on, Nigel, you can borrow some to finance your film—"

Borrow? I immediately cut her off. "Which half of you is going to submit the claim? The white half or the black half? Or are you still hanging on to 'other'?"

She hung up. I knew that would end the conversation.

I don't even feel like going to work now. The whole white office will be talking or trying not to talk about the bill. Ever since it was introduced, my co-workers and I tiptoe together, making small talk about current events but always careful not to mention what its opponents call the Guilt Bill.

I choose going home over work. My block is 95 percent West Indian, so I know there will be someone to empathize with me. I brace myself for the massive crowd awaiting me on the next train. I don't care how hard I have to push to get on, I can't stand being surrounded by all these liberated cotton slave blacks any longer. Sugar cane enslaved, too.

The conductor doesn't have to announce the stops for me to know that I'm getting closer to home. As the train makes its way downtown and into Brooklyn, the emotional energy in my car drops from elation (Harlem, which is now 90 percent American blacks) to surprise (privileged Upper West Side whites) to guilt (downtown SoHo's white liberals) to overwhelming disappointment and anger.

"Flatbush Avenue!" announces the conductor.

"Welcome home," I say aloud.

It's as if the Harlem celebration happened in a foreign country. This train platform is devoid of happy shouts and dancing people. No

one's passing out free T-shirts or embracing strangers with congratu-
latory hugs.

I make my way up the stairs and out onto the street. I'm hit with
the warm smell of just-baked plantain tarts and the angry blares of
megaphones and chants. The street is saturated with homemade
picketlike signs, country flags hanging from store and car windows,
and multicolored flyers telling you to get mad and take action.

I maneuver through the chaos and take a shortcut home. As soon
as I spot the new Jamaican soccer jersey and the glow-in-the-dark
material of the latest sneakers, I know I've found Lennox and Akiel.

"What does reparations mean?" asks Lennox, whose fifteen-year-
old ass should be in school. He's the soccer fan.

"It means we gettin' paid, son!" says Akiel, jumping up and down
to show off his new kicks. "We gettin' paaaiiidd!"

Lennox runs to greet me. "Give me some love, Nigel," he says,
giggling so much he can barely give me the hug he requested.

"I'ma get me one of dem BMW bikes, the ones they got in the
new James Bond movie," Akiel announces, giving me a w'sup nod.

"Yeah, those shits is hot," Lennox says, getting caught up in
Akiel's dreams.

"*And*, I'ma buy my moms a place of her own," Akiel adds as he
puts his long thick locks in a ponytail. It's that hair and his coolie
looks that make the young girls on our block fight over him.

I interrupt their conversation and run down what I know to be the
truth.

"Akiel, you Trini, right?" He nods yes, proud to claim his Trinida-
dian roots. Even if you didn't know it, his singsongy voice would give
him away. "Then you're not eligible." He starts to ask why, but I cut
him off. "It's because you're Trini—this country don't think us West
Indians are good enough for they likkle lott'ry." It feels good to have
someone to share my misery with.

"Naw, man," he says, shaking his head. "I'm an American citizen.
I was born here." His six-one lean frame stands up straight, ready to
challenge me. Lennox shirks back and lets his boy speak for both of
them.

"That doesn't matter. You're not American *enough*. To get the money, your parents and grandparents have to be American-born too."

Akiel screws up his face in disbelief, so I drag them to the corner store to prove it. I point to the eligibility requirements listed on the front page of the three major newspapers. We stand there for about fifteen minutes as Akiel reads silently and Lennox mutters a few words aloud.

"Yo, how you jus' gonna walk up on niggas and casually drop some shit like that?" Akiel yells. He chucks the newspaper on the curb and slams his bottle of carrot juice on the brick-faced apartment building behind us. Lennox just continues to stare at the papers and says nothing.

"See, that's why your asses need to leave the block. There's a protest up on Flatbush that's bigger than the one we had when the police killed Boogey," I said. I wanted to break it all down to them. Tell them how guilty I felt because I was one of those who helped the great-grandson of the late, well-known black activist Aaron Harpton in his efforts to get every single black citizen to support the Guilt Bill. It was largely due to my neighborhood's grassroots campaign and the fact that I worked at a major cable network that Harpton landed appearances on numerous TV and radio shows, begging black people to rally behind our new female president and Reformist congressmen. If I had known my American citizenship would be cast aside, I never would've volunteered to put my TV contacts up for sale.

"It will help strengthen and revitalize the black community!" Harpton urged. "Renew our sense of pride! Finally legitimize our plight," he proclaimed. Liar. The bill has done nothing but deteriorate our community.

It's been six months and four days since the reparations bill was enacted into law. Since that time, I've come to hate any Black American as defined by the language in the Guilt Bill: American-born descendants of Black African slaves purchased and owned for use in the United States of America. Up in Harlem, they hate us sugar-canin' West Indians and down here in Brooklyn, we hate them cotton-pickin' niggas.

There's always been a lack of understanding between the two, but the Guilt Bill has brought it to a head. God forbid you choose to fly your country flag instead of the stars and stripes or don't refer to yourself as an African American—Black Americans are all over you. They have this notion that nationality is a race.

That's why I refuse to go anywhere near Harlem, not even to see Alana. Somehow and for some reason, we're still together. Although I don't see how, because she's become more intolerable ever since she discovered that she, too, is ineligible to receive compensation. That $40 million she was so willing to share with me, lend to me, it was whisked away from her because she's not a full three-quarters black. When I found out, all I could do was laugh because she had already made an appointment with a plastic surgeon to have her fat cells regulated to her hair follicles. Instead of her body gaining weight, her hair would grow and thicken.

The only thing we seem to agree on these days is that the entire bill is one big catch-22. I've been familiarizing myself with the provisions of the appropriations process. I want to be thoroughly informed for the upcoming Senate hearings (they just want to see us dance and sing for our supper), which are being held in response to what the White Supremacy groups have coined the BLACKout. Africans, West Indians, mulattos, octoroons, Native Americans (what? you think they're not part of us?), Spanish-speaking people of color, and all others conveniently excluded from America's so-called apology, are refusing to work.

My job sent me a notarized letter yesterday telling me that I had until the end of the month to return to work or I would be terminated. If I had gotten that money, I'd be making my dream happen—producing meaningful, socially conscious movies—not forced to take part in an employment boycott.

It took some time, but I finally convinced my family to join me. My brother quit his cab gig, my mom put her nanny "mother for hire" job on hold, and my bus-driving father pulled over to the side of the road and told the passengers to have a nice day. People like my family have thrown the entire country off. They started taking that "one nation under God, indivisible" shit literally, and now transit systems, cab service, and trash collection have come to a halt in cities nation-wide.

I'm glad. Maybe White America will take the Senate hearings seriously now that the BLACKout's stripped it of their migrant work-ers, housekeepers, secretaries, airport crews, and janitors. I'm one of the lead cameramen at the news station, so I'm sure I too am missed, but more difficult to replace. I'm trying to explain the significance of all this to Alana, but her non-white, non-black ass can't seem to understand.

"You think the BLACKout's a good thing? People need those jobs. They gotta eat and pay rent. Besides, how long do you think it's gonna take for the government to fill those positions with white workers or some no-job-havin' people who desperately need work?"

"It's not that easy," I said, annoyed that the thought had crossed my mind, too.

"Why isn't it?" She was on a roll now. "Those jobs don't pay much. They have to be done. White America's not going to play nice but for so long. Check the history books and see how it's been han-dled before."

"Do you ever actually listen or do you just wait for the pause in conversation? It's a modern-day slave revolt! We been serving them for years. Serve, serve, serve. Then they say we'll do you a favor and free you. But most of us are still stuck serving them in some way and now they realize that the people who built this country are the same ones responsible for its day-to-day maintenance."

"You are so naive. We can't even come together for the little things and you think we can mobilize ourselves to make this boycott work?"

"We? Who's we . . . you?" I stood up and started pacing because I was getting excited. I couldn't just sit still and look at her barely-there black face anymore. Damn, her mom must have had some white genes to pass on, too.

"Just because my father's white doesn't mean the black in me is any less."

"You don't understand because you win either way."

"No, I don't!"

"Your mom is eligible. And you know she'll make sure her spoiled daughter gets enough to pursue her little modeling dream."

"She can only get compensation like free college tuition or money for a down payment on a home because my dad's job puts the household income over $300,000."

"That's what she gets for marrying a white man."

"Are you into that religion . . . that people-of-Israel rhetoric again?"

"Israelites, baby."

She started to speak but I shushed her and turned up the volume on the television so we could hear President Charlene Duffy try to kiss and make up. The more she talked, the more she rationalized the provisions for eligibility, the more I realized that America never meant truly to repay us for its sins.

I began comparing what President Duffy said to the Senate hearing notes I had taken during the live broadcast. Ineligible: any persons with ancestors who were free at any time before the enactment of the Emancipation Proclamation; any persons whose parents or grandparents were not born in the United States of America; any person who has or whose parents have been engaged in anti-government activities or activities that threaten the national security of the U.S. (e.g., members of the Nation of Islam, Black Panthers, draft dodging); any persons who have lived outside of the U.S. for a period of time exceeding two years for reasons other than military duty or employment assignments.

We continue watching but get sidetracked by gunshot and horn-blowing noises. I turn off my living room lights so I can peek out the window undetected. I can't see much, but I can tell there is a protest about to turn riot going on.

Alana looks over at me and rolls her eyes. "You're not going out there, are you?" She answers my yes with an I-don't-care shrug, but I can tell she's worried. Her nervous twitch is kicking in, causing her to braid and unbraid her wavy dirty-blond ponytail. I ignore her and go outside anyway.

There's no riot, just organized protesters of all ages. They seem to be headed toward the park, so I follow. What I see is not what I expected. Harpton is standing up on a large stage platform alongside newly appointed head of the Nation of Islam minister Kwali Mohammed and president of the NAACP, Margaret Washington.

"Black people. My beautiful people, despite what they may say, you are all my people. Thank you for coming out tonight." That's Mohammed. "We have a problem"—he turns to his companions— "and Brother Harpton and Sister Washington have come to help us work it out."

Harpton's presence at the podium illicits boos and fiery words. Minister Mohammed raises his hand in the air and the crowd stills immediately.

"Thank you for inviting me, Minister Mohammed,"says Harpton. "Sisters and brothers, tonight I will discuss the Reformist Party's push to move negotiations along. Yes, it is true that anyone wishing to claim the full reparations benefit package must be able to prove slave lineage both paternally and maternally. And that forty million dollars will be granted per parent provided the person submitting the claim did not violate any provisions outlined in subsection twenty-nine-A. But we recognize the fundamental—"

"An American citizen is an American citizen!" a group of men shout. "Give us our due!"

"*Pfft.* Look at him lying. Harpton don't mean us no good. He workin' for dem, you know," someone said.

People had stopped listening. Harpton wasn't there to negotiate; he was there to get us to go back to work. Get us to serve.

"You're not hurting anyone but yourselves. Let go of the riot-in-our-neighborhoods mentality. Your minds are bound in mental slavery! There are other ways of making statements. Demonstrate your economic power. . . ." Immediately the crowd started mumbling.

I started thinking of all the awful things I had seen this country do to make sure black stayed black and never got too close to white. I had accepted that I would always have to prove my manhood. I couldn't be accepted as a man just because I was an adult male the way my white co-workers were. I had to prove it because I'm black. But now they want me to prove that I'm black? And then prove that I'm the right kind of black?

"President Duffy has assured me that she will only be open to negotiations for twenty-four more hours," Harpton continued. "Once the final hour has passed, your jobs are for the taking."

That's a load of crap. Even during Senate hearings they admitted that they didn't have enough resources to fill the jobs, especially the low- and middle-wage positions.

Minister Mohammed takes the microphone and speaks in a controlled whisper. "Perhaps Brother Harpton speaks the truth. My people, beautiful black people, we have another option. We shall patronize only those businesses owned by our own kind and our brothers and sisters of color. Let the white man pay you, but don't put his money back into his pocket."

The crowd hushes. It's not a profoundly original idea, but it does have more of a chance of surviving than our employment boycott.

"The Nation will work with local ministries to run church buses along city bus routes. Instead of the subway, you can opt for gypsy cabs and vans, which will be used as commuter vehicles into Manhattan. We have also called on our community of black farmers to provide us with organic fruits and vegetables. Black people, my beautiful people, we will work to ensure that the suffering of our ancestors and our toil in this country do not go in vain."

I keep listening, but the fact that we are shifting from one boycott to another frustrates me. I feel defeated. I know those before me had gone through much worse, but I hadn't, nor has anything this monumental happened in my lifetime.

I could just pick up and live with my grandmother in Jamaica, but that's not really my home either. I come up with a better idea and run all the way from the park to my apartment and then up four flights of stairs to tell Alana my decision.

"That's it! I'm out!" I yelled, trying to catch my breath.

"What? Why are you yelling?" Alana asked, annoyed that I had woken her up.

"Nothing will change," I said, still trying to catch my breath. "I don't belong here. I don't belong in Jamaica. I have no true home, so I'm going to make a new one. You coming?"

"Where?" she asked as she chewed on her bottom lip, her way of holding in tears.

"I don't know yet." I hadn't thought that far ahead. "I guess I could transfer to one of the station's international offices." I shrugged.

"Why?" This time her voice cracked.

"Because if I'm going to be treated like a non-citizen or an outsider, then I might as well be one."

Now the tears were flowing. She forced herself to calm down so that she could speak clearly. "You're really leaving?"

I walked over to her and kneeled down. "Yes, baby. I'm leaving." I tried to get her to look at me, at least glance at me, so I could read her eyes.

"I'm staying, Nigel," she finally said.

At first I didn't understand her decision. I just couldn't understand why someone would want to stay in a country where Black Americans can't be compensated for the unjust society they've lived in all their lives simply because they have a fusion of ancestry, of cultures.

But for Alana there was no fusion. American culture was the only one she had ever known, felt, fought against, and formed her identity in. For the first time, my contempt for her switched to pity.

I dangled what I thought were tempting offers for her to leave, but there she is, still in the States, and here I am.

"Next."

I answer the call, step up to the immigration officer, and answer a series of questions.

"Race?"

"Black."

"Nationality?"

"None."

"None?" he said, looking at me to see if I was serious.

I nodded yes.

The look on his face made it clear that he didn't know what to do.

He was black too, so I tried to give him a hook-a-brotha-up smile. Sometimes that works and sometimes it backfires.

Finally he shrugged and stamped my passport.

"Thanks, man," I said, tucking it away with the round-trip ticket I knew I would never use.

"We all black people, right?" he said, winking at me.

"Right," I said, staring at the green, peacock-like rays fanned across the coat of arms I would now call my own.

SWEET DREAMS

Charles Johnson

(2004)

Please, come in. Sit down," he says. "I'm sorry I had to keep you waiting."

You cautiously enter the Auditor's tiny office, holding in your right hand the certified letter you received yesterday, the one that says *Department of Dream Revenue* in the upper left-hand corner and, below that, the alarming words *Official Business*. The letter knocked you to your knees. It has been burning in your hand and giving you a headache and upsetting your stomach all day long. So it's almost a relief finally to be here, on the twentieth floor of a gray government building on First Avenue—almost as if you have been a fugitive from the law, running and hiding, and looking nervously over your shoulder. In fact, the letter said you *would* face prosecution if you didn't travel to downtown Seattle and take care of this business immediately. But now the anxiety is over.

You are there to pay your dream tax.

As administrative offices go, this one is hardly more than a cubicle. The furniture is identical to every other bureaucratic compartment in the building so that no government worker feels that he or she has been issued more or less than his or her co-workers. There is a cluttered desk, a wastebasket on top of which sits a cross-cut paper shredder, a small table containing a Muratec fax machine and a Xerox copier. At the rear of the room a four-drawer filing cabinet is pushed against the wall. Resting on this is a small Dream Meter just like the one the government attached to your bed and *everyone's* bed three years ago—a little black box roughly the size of a cell phone, with an LCD that digitally reads out the number of dreams you have on any given night, their duration, category, and the fee assigned for each one. Not being a very technical person, you're not sure exactly how the Dream Meter works, but you *do* know there is a hefty fine for tampering with it—greater than for tampering with a smoke detector in an airplane's toilet—and somehow the Dream Meter works in conjunction with the microscopic implant your doctor inserted in your neck through a hypodermic needle, using the same process by which stray dogs are given their own bar code for identification at the city's animal shelter. To the left of the cabinet, on which sits the Dream Meter, is a calendar turned to today's date. It is October first, the year of our Lord 2008.

"Can I get you anything?" the Auditor asks. "Coffee? Tea?" When you tell him no, you're fine, he sits back in his chair, which creaks a little. He is a pale young man; his color is that of plaster, perhaps because he sits all day in this windowless cubicle. You place his age at thirty. Thirty-five. He has blond hair, perfect teeth, and wears a pinstriped shirt with his sleeves rolled up to the elbow. All in all, he seems anonymous, like the five hundred other bureaucrats in cubicles just like this one—like functionaries in Terry Gilliam's movie *Brazil*—but your Auditor has tried his best to personalize and give a bit of panache to both his office and himself. He wears a brightly colored Jerry Garcia tie. On his desk, where your dream file wings open, he has a banker's lamp with a green glass shade on a solid brass base. And he wears a ring-watch on his right index finger. A bit of ostentatious style, you think. Something that speaks to his having a smidgen of imagination, maybe even an adventurous, eccentric spirit beneath the way the State has swallowed his individuality. Right then you decide your Auditor is someone like you, a person who is just trying to do his job and, who knows, maybe he really understands your problem and wants to help you.

"Is this your first audit?" he asks.

You tell him yes, it is.

"Well, don't worry," he says. "I'll try to make this as painless as possible for you. Have you been read your rights as a taxpayer?"

You nod your head yes. His assistant in the outer office did that.

"And," he asks, "did she inform you that if you fail to make a full payment today—or make arrangements to pay in installments—that we can take your paycheck, your bank account, your car, or your house? Did she explain that?"

For a moment your heart tightens in your chest. You feel the sudden desire to stand and run screaming out of this airless room, but instead you bite down on your lower lip and bob your head up and down.

The Auditor says, "Good. Don't be nervous. You're doing fine. And I assure you everything we say here is confidential." He peers down at the paperwork on his desk. Slowly, his smile begins to fade. "Our records show a discrepancy in the amount of dream tax that you paid in 2007. You declared on Form Ten-sixty that you enjoyed the experience of 365 dreams during the year 2006. But your Dream Meter recorded 575 dreams for that same period. Dreams, I regret to say, for which you did not pay. Do you have an explanation?"

Now the room has begun to blur and shimmer like something seen through a haze of heat. You feel perspiration starting at your temples, and you tug on your shirt collar, knowing the Auditor is right. You tell him you *love* to dream. One of your greatest pleasures is the faint afterglow of a good dream once it's over, the lingering, mysterious images as wispy and ethereal as smoke, which you try to hang on to for the rest of the day, tasting them like the memory of a delicious meal, or a secret you can't share with anyone else. You tell him you enjoy taking a nap in late afternoon, a siesta like they do in Spain, and that's why your Dream Meter reading is so high. You thought only dreams at bedtime counted. You didn't know naps in the daytime counted too.

"They do—and so do daydreams," he says. "You neglected to declare 180 dreams experienced during naps. This is a *serious* offense. Ignorance is no excuse for breaking the law. By my computation, you owe the Department of Dream Revenue $91,645. 14."

That much? you say.

"Yes, I'm afraid so," he says. "The amount of your dreams places you in a thirty-three-percent tax bracket." From his desk he lifts a sheet of paper that details your dream underpayments and a long column of dates. "Do you see this?" he says. "Your actual underpayment comes to $50,000. But we charged you a penalty because, according to our records, you did not estimate the dreams you intended to have and pay the correct amount of tax due. You did not file for an extension. Furthermore, that payment is now two years late. So we had to charge you interest. I must say that a few of your dreams were very lavish and long-running. They were in Technicolor. Some of them were better than the movies at Blockbuster. You *do* have a vivid imagination. And you should be thankful for that. Did you know that in a few Native American cultures dreams are seen as an extension of waking consciousness, that a dreamer considers his visions when he's sleeping to be as much a part of his history as the things he experiences when he's awake?"

No, you say. You weren't aware of that.

"You know," he says, "I especially enjoyed that dream of yours where you find yourself shipwrecked on an island in the South Pacific, with no one there but you and a whole tribe of beautiful women who play a game of tossing a golden ball back and forth to each other. I've been thinking about that. Do you suppose the ship that goes down, the one you escaped from, symbolizes your job? But I can't figure out—in terms of Freud, Reich, or Maslow—what that damned golden ball means."

You tell him you don't know what it means either. But the night you had that dream, just before you went to bed, you were reading Homer's *Odyssey*, the part where Odysseus meets Nausicaa and sojourns among the Phaeacians.

"Oh, *that* explains it then." With his fingers, the Auditor makes a steeple as he leans forward, nodding. "That one dream cost you $25. You should be more careful about what you read at bedtime. Well, let's get back to business. We have all your dreams recorded. I've reviewed each one, of course. Recurrent dreams—like the one where you marry your high school's homecoming queen—*those* must be taxed at twice the rate of regular dreams. Nightmares, like the one where your mother-in-law comes to live with you and your wife for-ever, or the one where you are giving a presentation to your com-pany's board of directors and discover you are naked, are taxed three times higher. And it shows here that you had sixty-seven undeclared wet dreams, which—as you know—place you in a higher tax bracket. Does all this make sense to you? Do you wish to contest anything I've said?"

No, you say, you won't argue. You *did* do all that dreaming. But you tell him you can't afford to pay that amount. That it will devas-tate your savings, maybe drive you into the poor house. You will have to borrow money from friends. Take out a second mortgage on your home . . .

The eyes of your Auditor soften for a second when he hears that. He sits back in his chair again, folding his hands, and sighs. "I know, I know. Those who dream more always pay more. I wish to God I could help. All I can do, in my official capacity, is explain the situa-tion to you."

Please, you say. How did all this come about?

He says, "Oh, that's easy to answer. The Dream Tax started back in 1999. In Seattle, voters were presented with Initiative I-695, a bal-lot measure that would cut vehicle-license fees to $30 and require public votes on all state and local tax and fee increases. The initia-tive failed that November, but passed four years later. And not just in Seattle. It passed all over the country and caused such a revenue crisis that the government had to find another way to fund highway projects, public-health programs, and day-care inspections. As they say, necessity is the mother of invention. The Dream Tax, and all the technology to support it, was rushed into place by 2005." The Audi-tor pauses to reach into his desk drawer and remove a receipt book. "Now, will you be paying by check or cash?"

A check, you say, wearily. In fact, you already have it written, and you hand it over to the Auditor, asking him if he can perhaps work with you a little on the payment by waiting a day or two before the Department of Dream Revenue cashes it.

"Yes." He smiles. "That's the least we can do. After all, we are here to be helpful."

Just then the room seems to tilt, leaning to the left like a ship on tempestuous waves. You squeeze the bridge of your nose with two fingers to steady yourself until this spell of dizziness passes. Then you turn to leave, but stop suddenly in the doorway because there is one final question you need to ask.

Does he, the Auditor, *dream*?

"Me?" he says, touching his chest with two fingers. "Dream? Oh, no, I can't afford it." He looks at your check, smiles again, and slips it into the top drawer in his desk. "Everything seems to be in order, at least for now. You have a good day, sir. Thank you. And sweet dreams . . ."

BUYING PRIMO TIME
Wanda Coleman
(1988)

The Life Security Assurance Council has reviewed your application thoroughly, Miss Niobe. I'm afraid we can't help you. Loans of this nature—well, I'm sure you understand."

The man was a beet-red Benjamin Franklin clone in twenty-first-century garb. Della understood all too well. She felt that mid-gut gnawing again. The statuesque cocoa-skinned woman struggled to contain her feelings. Control meant the difference between life and death—a lesson she was continually relearning.

"Secretary Decius, my potential as a painter merits this loan. I've so much to give mankind, I assure you." Her smile was suggestive. Women are always reduced to using their bodily charms with these kinds of men. Della Niobe figured she might as well shoot her best shot. There was everything to lose.

"The amount of this loan is far from staggering, but—" He eyed her openly, lightly drumming his fingers against the fiberglass desktop. He could find no reason to equivocate. She had nice, if bowed, legs.

"When you balance that against what it would cost the government to raise my four children, I'm sure you can see the state would be ahead in the game," she appealed. "The upper class profits by keeping me alive." A woman had to use every means available. Della had banked on it with her first pregnancy out of wedlock.

"Your argument is reasonable." Decius wondered when the feds would finally get hip to the ploys afester in the subculture.

"And look at it this way, you'll have four additional citizens, well-raised, who'll also be of great social merit and creative genetic coding." That expensive course in rhetorical logic had more than paid for itself.

"I find it impossible to agree with you. All of this is beyond my area of expertise."

She had him.

"Consider this: Would you prefer my children as artists giving to society or as criminals taking from it?"

"Artists, of course!"

He visualized himself being mugged. Rather than decrease under the Population Control Amendment, crime had tripled. To every reasonable man this was deplorable.

"Then you must concede there's something to be said for the artist in society."

"That has always gone without saying!"

"Secretary Decius, history doesn't support the assertion."

His eyes fluttered briefly. Decius reached for the elegant gold cigarette case Della extended to him across the desk. He sniffed the aromatic fag, fired it, and inhaled.

"Hemp?"

"Quite. Black market." She lit one for herself.

"Hmmm. Far superior than anything legitimate."

Della was grateful, at such moments, that marijuana had finally been legalized. Unfortunately, federal regulations resulted in low resin and poor plant quality, and taxes kept even that out of the reach of most poor folk. Underground production remained a viable enterprise. She returned the case to her purse.

"Secretary Decius, I want the council to reconsider my loan application." Della managed to maintain her stony, unconcerned expression. Her stomach churned.

"I must admit, purchasing one's life one year, one month, one day at a time is extremely difficult. But it's the supreme sacrifice we all make for our better world."

"Not all. Just those of us unlucky enough to be born in the lower classes and who haven't yet achieved upper-class status."

"How many days do you have left?"

"Two months, give or take a day."

"There are many miserably more qualified than you, Miss Niobe. Some down to a matter of hours and they can't raise the money. It's a dastardly situation, isn't it?" What a shame, he thought, all that delicious Black cunt going to waste. She knew full well the closer the deadline the more impossible obtaining funds became. One was labeled a loser. It was an insidiously delicious snare.

"Well, I'm sure all who voted for the Population Control Amendment are enjoying their liberty. Since they don't have to pay for it. And I bet you did, didn't you?" Della delivered her bitterness with a salacious smile.

"Vote for it? I authored the amendment, Miss Niobe, so don't expect sympathy from me. The upper classes have never had it so good. And they control legislation. Besides, we all benefit in the long run. Each individual must do their maximum best to stay alive. By the end of this twenty-second century, we'll be a world of geniuses. A perfect domain in perfect balance."

Decius thoughtfully dropped his ash into the Mexican onyx ashtray. Della crossed her legs, uncrossed and crossed them again, then stubbed out her smoke impatiently. "Look, will you at least examine this additional case material?" She went into her attaché case and took out the sheaf of papers. "I made four photocopies as per your original specifications." She handed them to him. He took the one on top and flipped through it.

"Hmmm. Very nicely assembled." He looked at her legs again. He tamped out his cigarette and reached into his slacks and began to finger his cock.

"I process a hundred and fifty words per minute—if you're looking for an information engineer." She noted his degree of intense arousal. She went into her purse for the condom. He took it from her and watched as she lifted her flex-paper skirt and carefully slipped out of black true-lace panties. Real fabrics, including cotton, had gone the way of the dinosaur. Everything was chemical-based synthetics.

He gasped. "Where did you get those? I've only seen them in rare twentieth-century fashion catalogs."

"The bra is a match." She unbuttoned her blouse and showed him. "C-cup. A great-aunt, bless her soul, willed her wardrobe to me." She twirled the panties on a forefinger, then laid them neatly on the fiberglass.

"How many years would you take for the set?"

"They're not for sale. For sentimental reasons."

He stared at her blankly.

"Well, if I can personally be of help. You understand, I only make recommendations to the American Eugenics Council. Although I'm pleased to note, they carry considerable weight. Indeed, I'll do my best. Though a loan from us, should we grant it, would provide you with only half the amount needed. You'd still require a second loan."

She sauntered around the desk and teasingly assisted him in positioning the condom. It was French ribbed and lubricated.

"No matter. I've worked as many as four jobs—when the situation demanded. And I always pay off my loans."

"Amazing. You're a superwoman. No wonder you've managed to last as long as you have." He meant it.

"What a lovely compliment." She meant it.

He stood ready. She balanced her butt solidly on his desk, raised her legs and circled her hips. He entered her, rooting in rhythmically, kneading her healthy brown rear with broad, soft, blushing hands. It took a full twenty minutes. He gasped and fell into her, hugging her for a few seconds' recovery. She reached for the tissue box on the desk. He withdrew slowly, quickly tossed the condom into the wastebasket and, likewise, tidied up with a fistful of tissues, then turned to her with a smugly officious smile.

"Frankly, Miss Niobe, your civilized manner has convinced me you deserve help. A mature colored—ah—African-American person of your decorum and ability is rare, indeed." He seldom encountered Blacks in her age bracket doing so well. It was a sad thing so many of them continued to remain at the bottom of the official economic pyramid.

"You're too generous!" She deftly slid the antique panties back into place.

"Not generous enough. Let me do you a favor. There's a man I'm acquainted with—Jake Zeno. He's very powerful. Here's his card. Go to him and tell him Mr. D. sent you—D for Decius." He laughed at his own jerkoffishness. "You know, I love those—what do you call them?"

"Monikers."

"Yes. Tell Jake Zeno I said you're a good risk. He'll call me if he needs confirmation. In the meantime, I'll bring this addition to your loan application before the council on appeal. I'll do my best. In any event, this gentleman'll prove helpful."

"Thank you, Secretary Decius. I'm eternally grateful."

"Good day, Della Niobe. Good luck."

"So like what's Mr. D. say your chances are for the council to change their decision?" Jake Zeno believed in dark colors and expensive things. He was particularly turned on by Della's large, shapely rear. He knew Decius was an old fuck and had to have scored a taste.

"Excellent. But I don't want to take any chances. So he sent me to you. For insurance." Della couldn't keep her hands off the mahogany desk. He smiled, amused, as she ran admiring hands over the cool surface of the dark wood, thrilling to the elemental beauty. Rare woods—not much of anything was made of genuine wood anymore. She sighed.

"You wouldn't believe how much this desk set me back. A person could buy themselves a decade of primo time. Now what can I do for you, Miss Niobe?"

"I need money." She had heard of Jake Zeno, a good-looking man of outlaw status. She had heard he was into whips and chains on the serious side. She had no love of pain, the mental, spiritual, or physical. But business was business.

"Everyone needs money. Especially you poor."

"I'm an artist. I'm also working-class poor. We're a determined class, and we'd all be dead if it weren't for the underground economy."

"And gentlemen like myself."

"Yes, gentlemen like you, Mister Zeno."

"Then do you consider me a gentleman?"

"I'd rather consider you a lifesaver."

"Business it is!" He liked her looks and her independent air. He had a thing for reducing strong women to submissive states and then hard-dicking them senseless.

"The government is charging me an additional five hundred a month because of my A-5 rating."

"A-5? That's a new snag." She was A-1 in the exotic erotica department, he thought.

"Artist, fifth rank. I do have a few one-woman shows scheduled in the latter part of the year that are guaranteed to pull me up to an A-4 rank and reduce my monthly Breathing Permit Charge to half, if I live long enough. Should the worst scenario play, my children will receive any posthumous monies."

"Hmmm. You're not doing too badly." The thought of her pleading to be freed from his frantic clutch gave him a buzz. He'd love to put the handcuffs on her.

"That's the idea, Mr. Z. I'm not just 'some people.' "

She radiated a sultry beauty. He felt a wetness in his jock.

"I'm taking on a third job—again, Mr. Zeno. Just in case my appeal to the court fails. Mr. Decius will do his best, but . . ."

"Better to be safe than short of breath, as we say."

"You sound like a supporter of Population Control."

" 'deed I am. I'm in a very lucrative profession because of it. Time brokerage is as sure as death and taxes. Usury's never been better. It's the sweetest setup. You charge low-ranking people between twenty-five and sixty for the right to live. Give 'em a head start—enough time to finish college, get established, marry and start a family. Then you've got 'em. Fear of having their children raised in a government youth camp keeps them hustling, and society benefits. They *want* to live. Short of accidents and disease, to live is to pay nominal fees to the state and astronomical interest rates. And if you can't earn enough legitimately, that means taking risks—going into crime, going to the council, or alternative freebooters like me. To fail to support yourself means execution by the state. Believe me, Miss Niobe, I'll kill you a lot more humanely than the feds. With me you keep your dignity."

"I'll bear that in mind."

"How much do you need?"

"Five M. Cash or credit will do."

"Credit, then. There's a ten percent surcharge plus handling, payable in advance." He smiled and went into his desk for the voucher. He signed it, slipped it into an envelope, and slid it to her across the mahogany surface. She glanced at it then tucked it into her purse. She took out a condom.

"Forget it. I like authenticity. Why don't we step into my inner sanctum?" He rose to escort her through the door, which opened into a virtual museum of sado-maso paraphernalia.

"What do you have in there?"

"A bed of nails." He gripped her harshly and pushed.

She stumbled across the threshold. *Well*, she observed philosophically, *another dollar, another day*. She laughed softly.

"What's so funny?" Jake Zeno asked as he locked and bolted the door behind them.

"That," said Della, smiling, "is a private joke."

CORONA

Samuel R. Delany

(1967)

Pa ran off to Mars Colony before Buddy was born. Momma drank. At sixteen Buddy used to help out in a 'copter repair shop outside St. Gable below Baton Rouge. Once he decided it would be fun to take a 'copter, some bootleg, a girl named Dolores-jo, and sixty-three dollars and eighty-five cents to New Orleans. Nothing taken had ever, by any interpretation, been his. He was caught before they raised from the garage roof. He lied about his age at court to avoid the indignity of reform school.

Momma, when they found her, wasn't too sure ("Buddy? Now, let me see, that's Laford. And James Robert Warren—I named him after my third husband who was not living with me at the time—now little James, he came along in . . . two thousand and thirty-*two*, I do believe. Or thirty-*four*—you sure now, it's Buddy?") when he was born. The constable was inclined to judge him younger than he was, but let him go to grown-up prison anyway. Some terrible things happened there. When Buddy came out three years later he was a gentler person than before; still, when frightened, he became violent. Shortly he knocked up a waitress six years his senior.

Chagrined, he applied for emigration to one of Uranus's moons. In twenty years, though, the colonial economy had stabilized. They were a lot more stringent with applicants than in his Pa's day: colonies had become almost respectable. They'd started barring people with jail records and things like that. So he went to New York instead and eventually got a job as an assistant servicer at the Kennedy spaceport.

There was a nine-year-old girl in a hospital in New York at that time who could read minds and wanted to die. Her name was Lee.

Also there was a singer named Bryan Faust.

Slow, violent, blond Buddy had been at Kennedy over a year when Faust's music came. The songs covered the city, sounded on every radio, filled the title selections on every jukebox and Scopitone. They shouted and whispered and growled from the wall speaker in the spacehangar. Buddy ambled over the catwalk while the cross-rhythms, sudden silences, and moments of pure voice were picked up by jangling organ, whining oboe, bass and cymbals. Buddy's thoughts were small and slow. His hands, gloved in canvas, his feet in rubber boots, were big and quick.

Below him the spaceliner filled the hangar like a tuber an eighth of a mile long. The service crew swarmed the floor, moving over the cement like scattered ball bearings. And the music—

"Hey, kid."

Buddy turned.

Bim swaggered toward him, beating his thigh to the rhythms in the falls of sound. "I was just looking for you, kid." Buddy was twenty-four, but people would call him "kid" after he was thirty. He blinked a lot.

"You want to get over and help them haul down that solvent from upstairs? The damn lift's busted again. I swear, they're going to have a strike if they don't keep the equipment working right. Ain't safe. Say, what did you think of the crowd outside this morning?"

"Crowd?" Buddy's drawl snagged on a slight speech defect. "Yeah, there was a lot of people, huh. I been down in the maintenance shop since six o'clock, so I guess I must've missed most of it. What was they here for?"

Bim got a lot of what-are-you-kidding-me on his face. Then it turned to a tolerant smile. "For Faust." He nodded toward the speaker: the music halted, lurched, then Bryan Faust's voice roared out for love and the violent display that would prove it real.

"Faust came in this morning, kid. You didn't know? He's been making it down from moon to moon through the outer planets. I hear he broke 'em up in the asteroids. He's been to Mars and the last thing I heard they love him on Luna as much as anywhere else. He arrived on Earth this morning, and he'll be up and down the Americas for twelve days." He thumbed toward the pit and shook his head. "That's his liner." Bim whistled. "And did we have a hell of a time! All them kids, thousands of 'em, I bet. And people old enough to know better, too. You should have seen the police! When we were trying to get the liner in here, a couple of hundred kids got through the police block. They wanted to pull his ship apart and take home the pieces. You like his music?"

Buddy squinted toward the speaker. The sounds jammed into his ears, pried around his mind, loosening things. Most were good things, touched on by a resolved cadence, a syncopation caught up again, feelings sounded on too quickly for him to hold, but good feelings. Still, a few of them . . .

Buddy shrugged, blinked. "I like it." And the beat of his heart, his lungs, and the music coincided. "Yeah. I like that." The music went faster; heart and breathing fell behind; Buddy felt a surge of disorder. "But it's . . . strange." Embarrassed, he smiled over his broken tooth.

"Yeah. I guess a lot of other people think so too. Well, get over with those solvent cans."

"Okay." Buddy turned off toward the spiral staircase. He was on the landing, about to go up, when someone yelled down, "Watch it—!"

A ten-gallon drum slammed the walkway five feet from him. He whirled to see the casing split—(Faust's sonar drums slammed.)—and solvent, oxidizing in the air, splattered.

Buddy screamed and clutched his eye. He had been working with the metal rasp that morning, and his gloves were impregnated with steel flakes and oil. He ground his canvas palm against his face.

(Faust's electric bass ground against a suspended dissonance.)

As he staggered down the walk, hot solvent rained on his back. Then something inside went wild and he began to swing his arms.

(The last chorus swung toward the close. And the announcer's voice, not waiting for the end, cut over, "All *right* all you little people *out* there in music land . . .")

"What in the—"

"Jesus, what's wrong with—"

"What happened? I told you the damn lift was broken!"

"Call the infirmary! Quick! Call the—"

Voices came from the level above, the level below. And footsteps. Buddy turned on the ramp and screamed and swung.

"Watch it! What's with that guy—"

"Here, help me hold . . . Owww!"

"He's gone berserk! Get the doc up from the infirm—"

(". . . *that* was Bryan Faust's mind-*twisting*, brain-*blowing*, brand-new release, *Corona*! And you know it will be a *hit*! . . .")

Somebody tried to grab him, and Buddy hit out. Blind, rolling from the hips, he tried to apprehend the agony with flailing hands. And couldn't. A flash bulb had been jammed into his eye socket and detonated. He knocked somebody else against the rail, and staggered, and shrieked.

(". . . And he's come down to Earth at *last*, all you baby-mommas and baby-poppas! The little man from Ganymede who's been putting *the* music of *the* spheres through so many changes this past year arrived *in* New York this morning. And all *I* want to say, Bryan . . .")

Rage, pain, and music.

(". . . is, how do you *dig* our Earth!")

Buddy didn't even feel the pressure hypo on his shoulder. He collapsed as the cymbals died.

Lee turned and turned the volume knob till it clicked.

In the trapezoid of sunlight over the desk from the high, small window, open now for August, lay her radio, a piece of graph paper with an incomplete integration for the area within the curve $X4 + Y4 = k4$, and her brown fist. Smiling, she tried to release the tension the music had built.

Her shoulders lowered, her nostrils narrowed, and her fist fell over on its back. Still, her knuckles moved to *Corona's* remembered rhythm.

The inside of her forearm was webbed with raw pink. There were a few marks on her right arm too. But those were three years old; from when she had been six.

Corona!

She closed her eyes and pictured the rim of the sun. Centered in the flame, with the green eyes of his German father and the high cheekbones of his Arawak mother, was the impudent and insouciant, sensual and curious face of Bryan Faust. The brassy, four-color magazine with its endless hyperbolic prose was open on her bed behind her.

Lee closed her eyes tighter. If she could reach out, and perhaps touch—no, not him; that would be too much—but someone standing, sitting, walking near him, see what seeing him close was like, hear what hearing his voice was like, through air and light: she reached out her mind, reached for the music. And heard—

—your daughter getting along?

They keep telling me better and better every week when I go to visit her. But, oh, I swear, I just don't know. You have no idea how we hated to send her back to that place.

Of course I know! She's your own daughter. And she's such a cute little thing. And so smart. Did they want to run some more tests?

She tried to kill herself. Again.

Oh, *no!*

She's got scars on her wrist halfway to her elbow. What am I doing wrong? The doctors can't tell me. She's not even ten. I can't keep her here with me. Her father's tried; he's about had it with the whole business. I know because of a divorce a child may have emotional problems, but that a little girl, as intelligent as Lee, can be so—confused! She had to go back, I know she had to go back. But what is it I'm doing wrong? I hate myself for it, and sometimes, just because she can't tell me, I hate her—

Lee's eyes opened; she smashed the table with her small, brown fists, tautening the muscles of her face to hold the tears. All musical beauty was gone. She breathed once more. For a while she looked up at the window, its glass door swung wide. The bottom sill was seven feet from the floor. Then she pressed the button for Dr. Gross, and went to the bookshelf. She ran her fingers over the spines: *Charlotte's Web, The Secret in the Ivory Charm, The Decline of the West, The Wind in the Wil—*

She turned at the sound of the door unbolting. "You buzzed for me, Lee?"

"It happened. Again. Just about a minute ago."

"I noted the time as you rang."

"Duration, about forty-five seconds. It was my mother, and her friend who lives downstairs. Very ordinary. Nothing worth noting down."

"And how do you feel?"

She didn't say anything, but looked at the shelves.

Dr. Gross walked into the room and sat down on her desk. "Would you like to tell me what you were doing just before it happened?"

"Nothing. I'd just finished listening to the new record. On the radio."

"Which record?"

"The new Faust song, *Corona.*"

"Haven't heard that one." He glanced down at the graph paper and raised an eyebrow. "This yours, or is it from one of your books?"

"You told me to ring you every time I . . . got an attack, didn't you?"

"Yes—"

"I'm doing what you want."

"Of course, Lee. I didn't mean to imply you hadn't been keeping your word. Want to tell me something about the record? What did you think of it?"

"The rhythm is very interesting. Five against seven when it's there. But a lot of the beats are left out, so you have to listen hard to get it."

"Was there anything, perhaps in the words, that may have set off the mind reading?"

"His colonial Ganymede accent is so thick that I missed most of the lyrics, even though it's basically English."

Dr. Gross smiled. "I've noticed the colonial expressions are slipping into a lot of young people's speech since Faust has become so popular. You hear them all the time."

"I don't." She glanced up at the doctor quickly, then back to the books.

Dr. Gross coughed; then he said, "Lee, we feel it's best to keep you away from the other children at the hospital. You tune in most frequently on the minds of people you know, or those who've had similar experiences and reactions to yours. All the children in the hospital are emotionally disturbed. If you were to suddenly pick up all their minds at once, you might be seriously hurt."

"I wouldn't!" she whispered.

"You remember you told us about what happened when you were four, in kindergarten, and you tuned into your whole class for six hours? Do you remember how upset you were?"

"I went home and tried to drink the iodine." She flung him a brutal glance. "I remember. But I hear Mommy when she's all the way across the city. I hear strangers too, lots of times! I hear Mrs. Lowery, when she's teaching down in the classroom! I hear her! I've heard people on other planets!"

"About the song, Lee—"

"You want to keep me away from the other children because I'm smarter than they are! I know. I've heard you think too—"

"Lee, I want you to tell me more about how you felt about this new song—"

"You think I'll upset them because I'm so smart. You won't let me have any friends!"

"What did you *feel* about the song, Lee?"

She caught her breath, holding it in, her lids batting, the muscle in the back of her jaw leaping.

"What did you *feel* about the song; did you like it, or did you dislike it?"

She let the air hiss through her lips. "There are three melodic motifs," she began at last. "They appear in descending order of rhythmic intensity. There are more silences in the last melodic line. His music is composed of silence as much as sound."

"Again, what did you feel? I'm trying to get at your emotional re-action, don't you see?"

She looked at the window. She looked at Dr. Gross. Then she turned toward the shelves. "There's a book here, a part in a book, that says it, I guess, better than I can." She began working a volume from the half-shelf of Nietzsche.

"What book?"

"Come here." She began to turn the pages. "I'll show you."

Dr. Gross got up from the desk. She met him beneath the window. Dr. Gross took it and, frowning, read the title heading: "*The Birth of Tragedy from the Spirit of Music . . . death lies only in these dissonant tones—*'"

Lee's head struck the book from his hand. She had leapt on him as though he were a piece of furniture and she a small beast. When her hand was not clutching his belt, shirt front, lapel, shoulder, it was straining upward. He managed to grab her just as she grabbed the window ledge.

Outside was a nine-story drop.

He held her by the ankle as she reeled in the sunlit frame. He yanked, and she fell into his arms, shrieking, "Let me die! Oh, please! Let me die!"

They went down on the floor together, he shouting, "No!" and the little girl crying. Dr. Gross stood up, now panting.

She lay on the green vinyl, curling around the sound of her own sobs, pulling her hands over the floor to press her stomach.

"Lee, isn't there *any* way you can understand this? Yes, you've been exposed to more than any nine-year-old's mind should be able to bear. But you've got to come to terms with it, somehow! That isn't the answer, Lee. I wish I could back it up with something. If you let me help, perhaps I can—"

She shouted, with her cheek pressed to the floor, "But you can't help! Your thoughts, they're just as clumsy and imprecise as the others! How can you—*you*—you help people who're afraid and confused because their own minds have formed the wrong associations! How! I don't want to have to stumble around in all your insecurities and fears as well! I'm not a child! I've lived more years and places than any ten of you! Just go away and let me alone—"

Rage, pain, and music.

"Lee—"

"Go away! Please!"

Dr. Gross, upset, swung the window closed, locked it, left the room, locked the door.

Rage, pain . . . below the chaos she was conscious of the infectious melody of *Corona*. Somebody—not her—somebody else was being carried into the hospital, drifting in the painful dark, dreaming over the same sounds. Exhausted, still crying, she let it come.

The man's thoughts, she realized through her exhaustion, to escape the pain had taken refuge in the harmonies and cadences of *Corona*. She tried to hide her own mind there. And twisted violently away. There was something terrible there. She tried to pull back, but her mind followed the music down. The terrible thing was that someone had once told him not to put his knee on the floor.

Fighting, she tried to push it aside to see if what was underneath was less terrible. ("Buddy, stop that whining and let your momma alone. I don't feel good. Just get out of here and leave me *alone*!" The bottle shattered on the door jamb by his ear, and he fled.)

She winced. There couldn't be anything that bad about putting your knee on the floor. And so she gave up and let it swim toward her—

—suds wound on the dirty water. The water was all around him. Buddy leaned forward and scrubbed the wire brush across the wet stone. His canvas shoes were already soaked.

"Put your blessed knee on the floor, and I'll get you! Come on, move your . . ." Somebody, not Buddy, got kicked. "And don't let your knee touch that floor! Don't, I say." And got kicked again.

They waddled across the prison lobby, scrubbing. There was a sign over the elevator: Louisiana State Penal Correction Institute, but it was hard to make out because Buddy didn't read very well.

"Keep up with 'em, kid. Don't you let 'em get ahead'n you!" Bigfoot yelled. "Just 'cause you little, don't think you got no special privileges." Bigfoot slopped across the stone.

"When they gonna get an automatic scrubber in here?" somebody complained. "They got one in the county jail."

"This Institute"—Bigfoot lumbered up the line—"was built in nineteen hundred and *forty*-seven! We ain't had no escape in ninety-four years. We run it the same today as when it was builded back in nineteen hundred and *forty*-seven. The first time it don't do its job right of keepin' you all inside—then we'll think about running it different. Get on back to work. *Watch* that knee!"

Buddy's thighs were sore, his insteps cramped. The balls of his feet burned and his pants cuffs were sopping.

Bigfoot had taken off his slippers. As he patrolled the scrubbers, he slapped the soles together, first in front of his belly, then behind his heavy buttocks. *Slap* and *slap*. With each *slap*, one foot hit the soapy stone. "Don't bother looking up at me. You look at them stones! But don't let your knee touch the floor."

Once, in the yard latrine, someone had whispered, "Bigfoot? You watch him, kid! Was a preacher, with a revival meeting back in the swamp. Went down to the Emigration Office in town back when they was taking everyone they could get and demanded they make him Pope or something over the colony on Europa they was just setting up. They laughed him out of the office. Sunday, when everyone came to meeting, they found he'd sneaked into town, busted the man at the Emigration Office over the head, dragged him out to the swamp, and nailed him up to a cross under the meeting tent. He tried to make everybody pray him down. After they prayed for about an hour, and nothing happened, they brought Bigfoot here. He's a trustee now."

Buddy rubbed harder with his wire brush.

"Let's see you rub a little of the devil out'n them stones. And don't let me see your knee touch the—"

Buddy straightened his shoulders. And slipped. He went over on his backside, grabbed the pail; water splashed over him, sluiced beneath. Soap stung his eyes. He lay there a moment.

Bare feet slapped toward him. "Come on, kid. Up you go, and back to work."

With eyes tight, Buddy pushed himself up.

"You sure are one clums—"

Buddy rolled to his knees.

"I *told* you not to let your knee touch the floor!"

Wet canvas whammed his ear and cheek.

"Didn't I?"

A foot fell in the small of his back and struck him flat. His chin hit the floor and he bit his tongue, hard. Holding him down with his foot, Bigfoot whopped Buddy's head back and forth, first with one shoe, then the other. Buddy, blinded, mouth filled with blood, swam on the wet stone, tried to duck away.

"Now don't let your knees touch the floor *again*. Come on, back to work, all of you." The feet slapped away.

Against the sting, Buddy opened his eyes. The brush lay just in front of his face. Beyond the wire bristles he saw a pink heel strike in suds.

His action took a long time to form. *Slap* and *slap*. On the third *slap* he gathered his feet, leapt. He landed on Bigfoot's back, pounding with the brush. He hit three times, then he tried to scrub off the side of Bigfoot's face.

The guards finally pulled him off. They took him into a room where there was an iron bed with no mattress and strapped him, ankles, wrist, neck, and stomach, to the frame. He yelled for them to let him up. They said they couldn't because he was still violent. "How'm I gonna eat!" he demanded. "You gonna let me up to eat?"

"Calm down a little. We'll send someone in to feed you."

A few minutes after the dinner bell rang that evening, Bigfoot looked into the room. Ear, cheek, neck, and left shoulder were bandaged. Blood had seeped through at the tip of his clavicle to the size of a quarter. In one hand Bigfoot held a tin plate of rice and fatback, in the other an iron spoon. He came over, sat on the edge of Buddy's bed, and kicked off one canvas shoe. "They told me I should come in and feed you, kid." He kicked off the other one. "You real hungry?"

When they unstrapped Buddy four days later, he couldn't talk. One tooth was badly broken, several others chipped. The roof of his mouth was raw; the prison doctor had to take five stitches in his tongue.

Lee gagged on the taste of iron.

Somewhere in the hospital, Buddy lay in the dark, terrified, his eyes stinging, his head filled with the beating rhythms of *Corona*.

Her shoulders bunched; she worked her jaw and tongue against the pain that Buddy remembered.

She wanted to die.

Stop it! she whispered, and tried to wrench herself from the inarticulate terror that Buddy, cast back by pain and the rhythm of a song to a time when he was only twice her age, remembered. Oh, stop it! But no one could hear her, the way she could hear Buddy, her mother, Mrs. Lowery in the schoolroom.

She had to stop the fear.

Perhaps it was the music. Perhaps it was because she had exhausted every other way. Perhaps it was because the only place left to look for a way out was back inside Buddy's mind—

—when he wanted to sneak out of the cell at night to join a card game down in the digs where they played for cigarettes, he would take a piece of chewing gum and the bottle cap from a Dr Pepper and stick it over the bolt in the top of the door. When they closed the doors after free-time, it still fitted into place, but the bolt couldn't slide in—

Lee looked at the locked door of her room. She could get the chewing gum in the afternoon period when they let her walk around her own floor. But the soft-drink machine by the elevator only dispensed in cups. Suddenly she sat up and looked at the bottom of her shoe. On the toe and heel were the metal taps that her mother had made the shoemaker put there so they wouldn't wear so fast. She had to stop the fear. If they wouldn't let her do it by killing herself, she'd do it another way. She went to the cot, and began to work the tap loose on the frame.

Buddy lay on his back, afraid. After they had drugged him, they had brought him into the city. He didn't know where he was. He couldn't see, and he was afraid. Something fingered his face. He rocked his head to get away from the spoon—

"Shhh! It's all right. . . ."

Light struck one eye. There was still something wrong with the other. He blinked.

"You're all right," she—it was a *she* voice, though he still couldn't make out a face—told him again. "You're not in jail. You're not in the . . . joint any more. You're in New York. In a hospital. Something's happened to your eye. That's all."

"My eye . . . ?"

"Don't be afraid any more. Please. Because I can't stand it."

It was a kid's voice. He blinked again, reached up to rub his vision clear.

"Watch out," she said. "You'll get—"

His eye itched and he wanted to scratch it. So he shoved at the voice.

"Hey!"

Something stung him, and he clutched at his thumb with his other hand.

"I'm sorry," she said. "I didn't mean to bite your finger. But you'll hurt the bandage. I've pulled the one away from your right eye. There's nothing wrong with that. Just a moment." Something cool swabbed his blurred vision.

It came away.

The cutest little colored girl was kneeling on the edge of the bed with a piece of wet cotton in her hand. The light was nowhere near as bright as it had seemed: just a nightlight glowed over the mirror above the basin. "You've *got* to stop being so frightened," she whispered. "You've got to."

Buddy had spent a good deal of his life doing what people told him, when he wasn't doing the opposite on purpose.

The girl sat back on her heels. "That's better."

He pushed himself up in the bed. There were no straps. Sheets hissed over his knees. He looked at his chest. Blue pajamas: the buttons were in the wrong holes by one. He reached down to fix them, and his fingers closed on air.

"You've only got one eye working so there's no parallax for depth perception."

"Huh?" He looked up again.

She wore shorts and a red and white polo shirt.

He frowned. "Who are you?"

"Dianne Lee Morris," she said. "And you're—" Then she frowned too. She scrambled from the bed, took the mirror from over the basin and brought it back to the bed. "Look. Now who are you?"

He reached up to touch with grease-crusted nails the bandage that sloped over his left eye. Short, yellow hair lapped the gauze. His forefinger went on to the familiar scar through the tow hedge of his right eyebrow.

"Who are you?"

"Buddy Magowan."

"Where do you live?"

"St. Gab—" He stopped. "A hun' ni'tee' stree' 'tween Se'on and Thir' A'nue."

"Say it again."

"A hundred an' nineteenth street between Second an' Third Avenue." The consonants his night-school teacher at P.S. 125 had laboriously inserted into his speech this past year returned.

"Good. And you work . . . ?"

"Out at Kennedy. Service assistant."

"And there's nothing to be afraid of."

He shook his head. "Naw," and grinned. His broken tooth reflected in the mirror. "Naw. I was just having a bad . . . dream."

She put the mirror back. As she turned, suddenly she closed her eyes and sighed.

"What'sa matter?"

She opened them again. "It's stopped. I can't hear inside your head anymore. It's been going on all day."

"Huh? What do you mean?"

"Maybe you read about me in the magazine. There was a big article about me in *New Times*, a couple of years ago. I'm in the hospital too. Over on the other side, in the psychiatric division. Did you read the article?"

"Didn't do much magazine reading back then. Don't do too much now either. What'd they write about?"

"I can hear and see what other people are thinking. I'm one of the three they're studying. I do it best of all of them. But it only comes in spurts. The other one, Eddy, is an idiot. I met him when we were getting all the tests. He's older than you and even dumber. Then there's Mrs. Lowery. She doesn't hear. She just sees. And sometimes she can make other people hear her. She works in the school here at the hospital. She can come and go as she pleases. But I have to stay locked up."

Buddy squinted. "You can hear what's in my head?"

"Not now. But I could. And it was . . ." Her lip began to quiver; her brown eyes brightened. ". . . I mean when that man tried to . . . with the . . ." And overflowed. She put her fingers on her chin and twisted. ". . . when he . . . cutting in your . . ."

Buddy saw her tears, wondered at them. "Aw,—" he said, reached to take her shoulder—

Her face struck his chest and she clutched his pajama jacket. "It hurt so much!"

Her grief at his agony shook her.

"I had to stop you from hurting! Yours was just a dream, so I could sneak out of my room, get down here, and wake you up. But the others, the girl in the fire, or the man in the flooded mine . . . those weren't dreams! I couldn't do anything about them. I couldn't stop the hurting there. I couldn't stop it at all, Buddy! I wanted to. But one was in Australia and the other in Costa Rica!" She sobbed against his chest. "And one was on Mars! And I couldn't get to Mars. I couldn't!"

"It's all right," he whispered, uncomprehending, and rubbed her rough hair. Then, as she shook in his arms, understanding swelled. "You came . . . down here to wake me up?" he asked.

She nodded against his pajama jacket.

"Why?"

She shrugged against his belly. "I . . . I don't . . . maybe the music."

After a moment he asked, "Is this the first time you ever done something about what you heard?"

"It's not the first time I ever tried. But it's the first time it ever . . . worked."

"Then why did you try again?"

"Because . . ." She was stiller now. ". . . I hoped maybe it would hurt less if I could get—through." He felt her jaw moving as she spoke. "It does." Something in her face began to quiver. "It does hurt less." He put his hand on her hand, and she took his thumb.

"You knew I was . . . was awful scared?"

She nodded. "I knew, so I was scared just the same."

Buddy remembered the dream. The back of his neck grew cold, and the flesh under his thighs began to tingle. He remembered the reality behind the dream—and held her more tightly and pressed his cheek to her hair. "Thank you." He couldn't say it any other way, but it didn't seem enough. So he said it again more slowly. "*Thank* you."

A little later she pushed away, and he watched her sniffling face with depthless vision.

"Do you like the song?"

He blinked. And realized the insistent music still worked through his head. "You can—hear what I'm thinking again?"

"No. But you were thinking about it before. I just wanted to find out."

Buddy thought awhile. "Yeah." He cocked his head. "Yeah. I like it a lot. It makes me feel . . . good."

She hesitated, then let out: "Me *too!* I think it's beautiful. I think Faust's music is so," and she whispered the next word as though it might offend, "*alive!* But with life the way it should be. Not without pain, but with pain contained, ordered, given form and meaning, so that it's almost all right again. Don't you feel that way?"

"I . . . don't know. I *like* it. . . ."

"I suppose," Lee said a little sadly, "people like things for different reasons."

"You like it a lot." He looked down and tried to understand how she liked it. And failed. Tears had darkened his pajamas. Not wanting her to cry again, he grinned when he looked up. "You know, I almost saw him this morning."

"Faust? You mean you saw Bryan Faust?"

He nodded. "Almost. I'm on the service crew out at Kennedy. We were working on his liner when . . ." He pointed to his eye.

"*His* ship? *You* were?" The wonder in her voice was perfectly child-ish, and enchanting.

"I'll probably see him when he leaves," Buddy boasted. "I can get in where they won't let anybody else go. Except people who work at the port."

"I'd give"—she remembered to take a breath—"anything to see him. Just anything in the world!"

"There was a hell of a crowd out there this morning. They almost broke through the police. But I could've just walked up and stood at the bottom of the ramp when he came down. If I'd thought about it."

Her hands made little fists on the edge of the bed as she gazed at him.

"Course I'll probably see him when he goes." This time he found his buttons and began to put them into the proper holes.

"I wish I could see him too!"

"I suppose Bim—he's foreman of the service crew—he'd let us through the gate, if I said you were my sister." He looked back up at her brown face. "Well, my cousin."

"Would you take me? Would you really take me?"

"Sure." Buddy reached out to tweak her nose, missed. "You did something for me. I don't see why not, if they'd let you leave—"

"Mrs. Lowery!" Lee whispered and stepped back from the bed.

"—the hospital. Huh?"

"They know I'm gone! Mrs. Lowery is calling for me. She says she's seen me, and Dr. Gross is on his way. They want to take me back to my room!" She ran to the door.

"Lee, there you are! Are you all right?" In the doorway Dr. Gross grabbed her arm as she tried to twist away.

"Let me *go!*"

"Hey!" bellowed Buddy. "What are you doin' with that little girl!" He bounded up in the middle of the bed, shedding sheets.

Dr. Gross's eyes widened. "I'm taking her back to her room. She's a patient in the hospital. She should be in another wing."

"She wanna go?" Buddy demanded, swaying over the blankets.

"She's very disturbed!" Dr. Gross countered at Buddy, towering on the bed. "We're trying to help her, don't you understand? I don't know who you are, but we're trying to keep her alive. She has to go back!"

Lee shook her head against the doctor's hip. "Oh, Buddy . . ."

He leapt over the foot of the bed, swinging. Or at any rate, he swung once. He missed wildly because of the parallax. Also because he pulled the punch in, half completed, to make it seem a floundering gesture. He was not in the Louisiana State Penal Correction Institute: the realization had come the way one only realized the tune playing in the back of the mind when it stops.

"Wait!" Buddy said.

Outside the door the doctor was saying, "Mrs. Lowery, take Lee back up to her room. The night nurse knows the medication she should have."

"Yes, Doctor."

"Wait!" Buddy called. "Please!"

"Excuse me," Dr. Gross said, stepping back through the door. Without Lee. "But we have to get her upstairs and under a sedative, immediately. Believe me, I'm sorry for this inconvenience."

Buddy sat down on the bed and twisted his face. "What's . . . the matter with her?"

Dr. Gross was silent a moment. "I suppose I do have to give you an explanation. That's difficult, because I don't know exactly. Of the three proven telepaths that have been discovered since a concerted effort has been made to study them, Lee is the most powerful. She's a brilliant, incredibly creative child. But her mind has suffered so much trauma—from all the lives telepathy exposes her to—she's become hopelessly suicidal. We're trying to help her. But if she's left alone for any length of time, sometimes weeks, sometimes hours, she'll try to kill herself."

"Then when's she gonna be better?"

Dr. Gross put his hands in his pockets and looked at his sandals. "I'm afraid to cure someone of a mental disturbance, the first thing you have to do is isolate them from the trauma. With Lee that's impossible. We don't even know which part of the brain controls the telepathy, so we couldn't even try lobotomy. We haven't found a drug that affects it yet." He shrugged. "I wish we could help her. But when

I'm being objective, I can't see her ever getting better. She'll be like this the rest of her life. The quicker you can forget about her, the less likely you are to hurt her. Good night. Again, I'm very sorry this had to happen."

"G'night." Buddy sat in his bed a little while. Finally he turned off the light and lay down. He had to masturbate three times before he finally fell asleep. In the morning, though, he still had not forgotten the little black girl who had come to him and awakened—so much in him.

The doctors were very upset about the bandage and talked of sympathetic ophthalmia. They searched his left cornea for any last bits of metal dust. They kept him in the hospital three more days, adjusting the pressure between his vitreous and aqueous humors to prevent his till now undiscovered tendency toward glaucoma. They told him that the thing that had occasionally blurred the vision in his left eye was a vitreous floater and not to worry about it. Stay home at least two weeks, they said. And wear your eye patch until two days before you go back to work. They gave him a hassle with his workmen's compensation papers too. But he got it straightened out—he'd filled in a date wrong.

He never saw the little girl again.

And the radios and jukeboxes and Scopitones in New York and Buenos Aires, Paris and Istanbul, in Melbourne and Bangkok, played the music of Bryan Faust.

The day Bryan Faust was supposed to leave Earth for Venus, Buddy went back to the spaceport. It was three days before he was supposed to report to work, and he still wore the flesh-colored eye patch.

"Jesus," he said to Bim as they leaned at the railing of the observation deck on the roof of the hangar, "just look at all them people."

Bim spat down at the hot macadam. The liner stood on the take-off pad under the August sun.

"He's going to sing before he goes," Bim said. "I hope they don't have a riot."

"Sing?"

"See that wooden platform out there and all them loudspeakers? With all those kids, I sure hope they don't have a riot?"

"Bim, can I get down onto the field, up near the platform?"

"What for?"

"So I can see him up real close."

"You were the one talking about all the people."

Buddy, holding the rail, worked his thumb on the brass. The muscles in his forearm rolled beneath the tattoo: *To Mars I Would Go for Dolores-jo*, inscribed on Saturn's rings. "But I *got* to!"

"I don't see why the hell—"

"There's this little nigger girl, Bim—"

"Huh?"

"*Bim!*"

"Okay. Okay. Get into a coverall and go down with the clocker crew. You'll be right up with the reporters. But don't tell anybody I sent you. You know how many people want to get up there? Why you want to get so close for anyway?"

"For a . . ." He turned in the doorway. "For a friend."

He ran down the stairs to the lockers.

Bryan Faust walked across the platform to the microphones. Comets soared over his shoulders and disappeared under his arms. Suns novaed on his chest. Meteors flashed around his elbows. Shirts of polarized cloth with incandescent, shifting designs were now being called Fausts. Others flashed in the crowd. He pushed back his hair, grinned, and behind the police block hundreds of children screamed. He laughed into the microphone; they quieted. Behind him a bank of electronic instruments glittered. The controls were in the many jeweled rings hanging bright and heavy on his fingers. He raised his hands, flicked his thumbs across the gems, and the instruments, programmed to respond, began the cascading introduction to *Corona*. Bryan Faust sang. Across Kennedy, thousands—Buddy among them—heard.

And on her cot, Lee listened. "Thank you, Buddy," she whispered. "Thank you." And felt a little less like dying.

MAGGIES

Nisi Shawl

(2004)

Tata's skin was golden. Sometimes she let me help her feed and brush it. She showed me how my first worlday on New Bahama.

I was way off schedule. After a couple of hours I couldn't stand to stay in my room, let alone in bed, pretending to sleep. I had masturbated all I wanted. My desk was on, but empty. No matter what my father said, I had to get up, run the small circuit of the station's corridors.

Some were smoothly familiar, plasteen walls like any ship or tube. Others, where the station's prefab had burrowed into New Bahama's unpolished bedrock, seemed sullen in their unreflectiveness.

I wasn't going to think about things, about my mother, whether my father really wanted me to come here and live with him, would she ever get better, if I could have done anything to help. I just wanted to walk. One flight down, generators, locks, stores, vats. Big, smelly objects I'd already been warned to keep away from. The opposite flight of steps back up, kitchen lab, private rooms, all with curtains closed.

On my third go-round, though, Tata's curtain hung to one side, offering a glimpse of her tiny living space. Her skin gleamed in its frame. She stood behind it, fussing with one of the securing ties. When she saw me, she signed a welcome. I hesitated, and she signed again. I was pretty sure she was the same one who'd helped me with my luggage, so I went in.

She showed me the port where the nutrient bulb fitted into the skin, and the way to squeeze it—slowly, steadily.

Her skin's thick, retracted facemask repulsed me—maybe because I'd seen pictures of how the things flattened and brutalized their wearer's features. And of course I knew not to touch the skin's underside. Even though I hadn't been taught all the history of its abuse, I understood that I could hurt Tata there. I didn't want to do that.

But I fell in love with the alveolocks, her skin's fur. They rippled so softly beneath my brush. Later, I learned that these rhythmic contractions aided a skin's oxy uptake and diffusion. That night, and for a long time after, all I cared about was their beauty.

I had a heavy hand with the protective oil. When you're young, you don't realize how precious things are; you think there will always be plenty, at no cost. And that's how it should be—when you're young.

So Tata never corrected me when I oiled her skin so lavishly that clear droplets splashed down upon the metal frame where it was strung. She only guided my hand gently, so that my overenthusiastic brushing wouldn't pull the golden fur out by its roots. I felt proud of my handiwork.

Tata didn't really need my help, though. Her skin had plenty of time to reoxygenate without the brush's added stimulation; she didn't wear it much.

She was supposed to go out into the Nassea every Day, supervising my father's other maggies as they planted coral buds on the submerged mountaintops of New Bahama.

But the others didn't need her watching them, telling them what to do. Terraforming work is simple, though hard; repetitive, dangerous, but nothing that requires any initiative. They were used to it; it's the sort of thing they had been engineered to do in the first place, before the rebellion.

My father plotted the maps, which the hull window displayed. The maggies had no trouble reading them. They filled their quotas, mostly. Dad's team was a little ways behind all but two of the other stations. I don't know if there would have been fewer problems if

Tata had gone out there as often as her contract said she was supposed to. Dad didn't think so.

Tata wore her skin once a worlday, swimming in it through the Nassea to Quarters. I went with her, once, fifteen Days after I arrived. That is, I followed her in Dad's scooter. Squirming to keep from slipping down its couch's gentle curves, I wondered what sort of passenger its designers had had in mind. Not me; I was so short I could barely keep my face in the navigation display's headsup field. But not Dad either. I have great spatial-relational skills for a girl, and I could see he'd have a hard time fitting in here. Which was probably why he never used the thing.

Not that that would keep him from punishing me for borrowing it.

I struggled back to the headsup. Tata's skin lost its golden color in the infrared, but it gained a luminescent trail, a filigree of warmth flowing from her skin's alveolets as they dissipated her waste gases. Fizzing like a juice-tab in the murky silence of the Nassea, my father's chief maggie dropped down toward Quarters.

Or so I assumed. All I saw in the headsup were a few patches of heat, hardly more than a supercolony of microbes could produce.

I settled into the sediment and switched on the visibles. The headsup compensated quickly, and I saw an opening in the silver egg-shape of Quarters, cycling shut on shadows. The scooter's lights shone steadily into the diminishing hatch. Tata had to know I was out here now, if she hadn't sensed me earlier. I'd been hanging back, more shy than afraid of being shooed back home.

So what exactly did I expect to happen, now that I'd gotten this far?

Quarters were detachable modules, little self-contained living units sent out from the maggies' huge Habs. Maybe the rules against us entering their protected areas were relaxed here. Or maybe they'd make an exception for a child . . . But that hatch was obviously too small for the scooter. I knew there was an inflatable suit somewhere under the cushions. After I put it on, though, I'd have to flood the scooter to get outside, and I was probably in enough trouble already. The headsup's clock warped and disappeared as I slid lower and lower, disappointed with the limits of my success.

I jerked up like an electrified water-flea. The phone! I let it ring a few more times before cutting it on with one wavering hand.

"Kayley?" It was Tata, voice only. Among themselves, especially, maggies mostly signed. But of course since the rebellion, they'd maintained a strict embargo on visual broadcasts from their Habs. And from Quarters, too, it seemed. "Your father knows that you're here?" she asked.

"Well, not really." He might, if he'd noticed that I was gone.

"Your presence equals a desire for what?"

I had no answer to that but an honest one. "I want—to—I want to way with you."

Tata had adopted that bit of solar slang almost as soon as she heard it from me. Using one word to denote a deliberate inter-dependency of time and space and attention was apparently a very maggie concept. But a short silence followed my statement, as if she hadn't understood me. "Here? This would not be in alignment with the highest good of all involved."

In other words, no.

"Okay." I didn't know what else to say. I reached out to close down the connection. Maybe I could get home before Dad noticed the scooter missing.

"Wait."

My hand hovered. My arm began aching.

"My task here is to be rapidly accomplished. Then I can return with you. Would this carry adequate compensation?"

I wasn't exactly sure what she meant. Compensation for what? For being unable to enter a space forbidden to non-engineered humans for the last one hundred and fifty Years?

"Not complete compensation, of course, I understand. But an adequate amount?"

"Okay," I repeated. "Yeah. All right."

Waying with Tata through the Nassea was much more than all right. The background itself was boring, dead, a waste of water pop-ulated only by muddy motes. But Tata's presence charmed the empty scene to life. And the facemask gave her a faintly silly sadness, in-stead of the menacing air I'd expected.

I wished I was able to hear her singing, the sonar she used to navigate. I couldn't hear the music, but I watched her, and I saw the dance.

Switching between infrared and a cone of visible, I followed her homeward, entranced by the strength and delicacy of her movements. For a while I tried to get the scooter to imitate them, swooping and halting clumsily. But sliding back and forth on the cushions interfered with my view.

Even though I knew practically nothing of the language at that point, I understood some of what she signed: big, small, honor of your trust, straight to the heart. These things sound so abstract, but they seemed extremely solid when she showed them to me. Her long limbs stretched, swept, gathered softly together.

I wish now I'd saved a recording of at least part of her performance. Maggies have wonderfully expressive faces, but the fine muscles of the alveolocks are, we're told, even more minutely controlled. Within their skins, maggies are able to communicate multiple messages simultaneously, with ironic, historical, and critical commentaries layered in over several levels. So the scholars say.

I couldn't swear to the truth of that. There was only one other time Tata wore her skin while speaking to me.

Because of course my father knew I'd taken his scooter. No more trips out into the Nassea for Kayley. Not for at least a Year. I wasn't even allowed to poke around in my lousy little inflatable.

I told my father this was an overly repressive reaction typical of reformed criminals. He smiled. "Good. I wouldn't want to do anything abnormal. Think of the psychic scars you'd have to bear."

Tata's infrequent trips to Quarters continued after this, naturally. I begrudged them; I didn't see why she couldn't just stay and way with me. Didn't she know how much I missed her, how the loneliness curdled up in my throat as she swam out of sight, out of the misty particulate light shining such a short way into the water?

I think she did.

Tata always made it a point, on her return, to give me some treasure found on her excursions. Something interesting, something different, with a story behind it. This must have been hard for her. Far

off, over invisible horizons, maggies spread corals around other stations as ours did here. Aside from this the Nassea was empty of life,
void of history. There were the sludges, various excretory masses of
bacteria that accumulated in the presence of certain chemicals.
There were fossilized sludges, and other mineral formations. That
was it.

I let the third sulphur sword she gave me fall to the floor. It shattered on the napless carpet, dull yellow shards of petulant guilt. It
had been a pretty good sword, maybe half a meter long. But I had two
almost as good in my room; the first from a hundred and fifty-five
Days ago.

I tried to lie. "I'm sorry," I told Tata. "It slipped." I looked up,
ready to elaborate, and saw it wouldn't work. It never did, with her.

"That's all right, Kayley," she said aloud. "I don't have to bring you
presents. You don't have to like them." Her soft, round face looked
embarrassed for us both.

"I'm sorry," I said again, using my hands the way Tata had taught
me. And this time I meant it. She nodded, then walked down the
tunnel to her room.

I didn't know what to do with the sword's pieces. I picked them
up and took them to my Dad. He was in the kitchen lab, putting a
coral bud in the micro-slicer. "Tata's back?" he asked. "Poor specimen
you've got there."

"It's broke," I explained. "I don't want it."

"Maybe your mom will be able to use it somehow." Penny was
planning the cities that were going to be built on the land masses
the coral was going to produce. Mostly she used cad, but sometimes
she liked to work directly on models, making physical changes before she molded them into the program. Touching stuff with her real
hands gave her different ideas on how to use things, she said.

I walked past Tata's room on the way to Penny's. Tata was singing.
Her curtain was on one side of the doorway; that's how I could hear
her. Through the arched rock I caught a glimpse of her skin, half-
stretched upon its frame. I decided I would help her on my way back.

Penny was Dad's latest wife. She wasn't really my mom, though
sometimes I called her that to make her feel good. She had the

biggest room, a natural cave. The ceiling and some parts of the walls had been left exposed: raw basalt, rough and black. White, blue, and green spots hung suspended from the roof.

On the floor a display rose: a pink nest of concentric rings, like the crests of ripples spreading out, higher and higher. The highest came to my waist.

I walked to the center, where Penny crouched down like she was the stone that had made the splash-of-pink city. "Hi, Mom."

"Hi. Gardens in here," she said without looking up. "Protected from storms and high seas."

"Clean. So then these low rings are where people live?"

"That's right. And the next out are trade and culture, then storage, processing . . ." She looked up, pulling down her smock's sleeves and putting her hands on her hips. "Trouble is this coral foundation we're building on is so sickin fragile. Can't let it get exposed, but what else are people going to walk on?"

"Dirt?"

"That's what I'm thinkin', Kayley, but I hate to have to make it from scratch. Sludges from the bottom," she said, as if I had suggested it. "That's a possibility, but . . ." She continued the conversation without me, silently. I left the sword shards on her workbench and walked out.

Tata's curtain was now in place. Its reddish tresses still stirred, settling themselves in their optimal array, fluffing up over their insulating air pockets. Not long since she'd shut herself in, then.

Dad was gone from the kitchen. I figured he was probably in his room, behind his curtain, too. I had learned on the ship coming out here to join him that in cramped off-Earth accommodation the right to privacy deserved and got the utmost respect. In other words, I could have gone to him. He would have interrupted whatever he was doing. But then he'd want to know what was wrong. It would turn out to be a very big deal. I didn't like very big deals.

I punched myself a pbj on white and went off to my room to do some school. I was way ahead for the semester. Only another worlday's worth of program left. Maybe Tata could do something about that.

After I finished a section on Latter Day Lacanians, ortho and heretic, I switched to a book I'd pirated from Penny. It was about strong-limbed athletes, a man and a woman. The woman wanted to squeeze the man. The man wanted to be squeezed, but he didn't like the *way* he wanted it. He spent a lot of time trying to determine if the problem was with him, or the woman, or if it was the result of well-meaning interference from his coach. In between his bouts of reflection there was some pretty hot sex. I stayed up reading and masturbating till midnight.

Usually, Tata got me up. But not this Morning. I woke up because I was hungry. The swimming clock-faces on my desk's default read nine-thirty-three. I had to hurry if I wanted breakfast.

The kitchen program was pretty strict. The idea was to keep the scattered reef-builders on the same planet-wide circadians, disregarding New Bahama's five-Day rotation. Less mental isolation. More likelihood of a healthy global culture developing later on. So meals were on a schedule. Snacks I could always have, but I really didn't feel like another pbj. And I hated gorp, which was the only other thing there would be till lunch if I didn't make it in time.

I showered quickly, with only the most cursory of examinations. Still no pubic hair, breast development, enlarged or parted labia. Any year now, they'd be showing up.

I made it to the kitchen before ten and was rewarded with a choice of grits and kippers or yogurt and granola (gorp without even the saving grace of chocolate). "Who programmed this thing?" I muttered, punching for the gruel and fish-bacon as the lesser of two evils. I made the grits into a sort of white, starchy pudding by entering Dad's sugar codes along with my own. He wouldn't mind; he never used up his share anyway. I forced down the kippers by closing my eyes and visualizing the charts from med class: In North American historical studies, early onset of puberty correlated directly with increased protein consumption. I chewed as quickly as I could, and swallowed, determined not to hold back my sexual maturity by one unnecessary moment.

I dumped my dishes in the tub for Tata to deal with. It was empty, nothing from Penny or Dad, so she had to be up. I wondered where. I wondered if she was still mad at me. Why else hadn't she got me up?

She was in her room, curtain back. She smiled as I came in. No, she wasn't mad. But she wasn't happy either. She sat half-fetal on her bed, black, hairless curves rich with captive light. Delicate indentations, the wells for her skin's funiculi, formed swirling, tattoolike patterns, subtly shining with deeply embedded drops of protective fluids. Her smooth head rested sideways on one knee.

On their Habs and in Quarters, maggies supposedly went naked, or maybe they wore jewelry or a hat. The extra layer of fat made them uncomfortable in clothes. Their nudity made us equally uncomfortable. In our place, Tata wore a sort of super-loincloth, which came up over the front of her long breasts and was held in place by a knotted strip of elastic. This one was red.

I signed. Signs are better than words for expressing all sorts of concepts, and I'd gotten pretty good by this time. I told her something like "Tata's sadness equals/creates the sadness of Kayley. Is Tata's sadness also equivalent to/the result of Kayley's imbalanced behavior? This would lead to even further loss of Kayley's balance and cool, but knowledge is the first step toward the retrieval of alignment." Only it didn't take that long or sound that pompous and detached.

She raised her head and pointed at me with her chin (the only polite way to point at some*one*, as opposed to some*thing*), then twisted it to show that I should sit next to her, on the bed.

I only knew how to make words with my hands. Tata signed with her whole, huge, wonderful body. She spoke like water, flowing from one phrase to the next by the path of least resistance. She uncurled, and that meant her sadness was not so heavy she couldn't leave it behind to be fully present with a friend. Her right hand swept aside the chopping, stabbing motion of her left—the sword. She barely bent to notice the imaginary sword fall to the floor, then casually rubbed it out with one eloquent toe. It was not worth the bother of classifying it as unworthy.

"What's wrong?" I asked her, slowly. Sometimes I felt too awkward to use anything except maggie "phonemes," laboriously spelling out English words. "What can I do to help?" She sat still and silent for so long I tried again. "Can Kayley aid Tata in any way to receive the gifts of her highest heavenly head?"

"Stay close," signed Tata. "Don't leave me. Don't leave me alone with—anyone else." She pulled me closer to her, and I nestled against the soft, warm folds of flesh exposed by her loincloth.

We were like that when my Dad came in. He spoke. He had never learned to sign. He said, "We have to talk." He looked at me. "About my plan for the next worldday."

"Yes," said Tata.

"In my office."

"Okay. Come on, Kayley." She stood, still holding me close to her side.

"Kayley can stay here."

"No. She needs to be with me."

Silence. Even Dad must have heard the lie. "I see," he said. "All right." He turned and left the room. We followed.

Dad grew up on an old tube, in orbit around Saturn. He was always shouldering his way through imaginary crowds, eyes and ears open for the first signs of a fight or a panic. Even in middle age, even flight years from anyone else's turf, he walked like a bangboy on patrol. He stopped in front of his door and automatically looked both ways down the dim corridor. The glow from the glamp showed his short, blond hair swinging around his head, his round, blue eyes narrowing to sweep the air for trouble spots. Then he pulled the curtain, which parted for him, and we went in.

Dad's room wasn't quite as big as Penny's. It could have been twice the size and still it would have seemed too small, because of all the stuff. Three walls full of holoscreens, with crates of 2-D transparencies ready for the hull display stacked alongside them. His glass kiln against the outer wall. And the rows and rows of shelves filled with bottles, bowls, balls, and figurines. In the midst of this maze of fragility was his desk. Somewhere, too, he had a bed, though I think he almost always slept with Penny.

He took Tata to one wall and showed her the latest maps, which looked nothing like the Nassea I saw outside the port. These were bright, abstract topos, with clouds of yellow, golden-orange, and crimson to show where different varieties of coral buds had been sown. Projected plantings for Dad's station were turquoise, green, and aquamarine. All these colors dappled the highest peaks, warm ones at the center, cooling as they reached the upper edges of the display. Tata placed one black finger in a valley near the map's bottom. "Quarters."

Dad nodded.

"It will be far to the new sites. Too far for skins."

My father shook his head impatiently. "That's not what my figures say. You're capable of two Days' work and travel in a skin."

"Oh, no. I don't think so . . . or, perhaps. But capable means only that it can be done. Not that it should. We are capable of many things which nevertheless it is better to refrain from doing."

"Fine. You look at the topos. Come up with a more efficient array and I'll use it, Tata. Over here." Dad led her off through the shelves to his desktop. She invited me along with her eyes, but I stayed near the wall, sure I would be bored by the rest of the discussion. Why would she need me to stay *that* close?

A familiar configuration caught the corner of my eye. It was a face—mine. I moved toward it. Not all the holos were maps, charts, graphs, and grids. There I was, in all my preadolescent splendor. And there were images of Mom, my real mom. She looked pretty, not crazy at all. The way she used to be. Next to her were pictures of other women. Probably more former wives. Nobody I knew.

Then something very interesting: interior shots of a maggie Hab. I was as familiar as anyone with their exteriors. The twisted, droop-ing silver loops were a design cliché. I had a pair of earrings shaped like that. But here were walkways, rising unevenly out of training pools, past racks of skins, golden, brown, auburn, and black. Here was a mat full of necklaces: light, titanium beads strung with bone frag-ments and flat, rough-textured air-vine seeds. Smooth black fingers were frozen in the act of lifting a strand for the viewer to examine. I wondered if I could pirate the book these stills came from. Or maybe I could even just ask for it.

There were several more. One, which showed a small maggie, a toddler of perhaps two or three Years, had a caption in alpha below the image. I struggled to decipher it. Something about the skin growing on his scalp and neck, still attached, and how carefully it needed to be groomed to prevent painful overstimulation. No mention, as far as I could see, of anyone doing so on purpose.

That made me wonder how old the book was. It had to have been written pretty soon after the rebellion, before the maggies decided to exclude us from their Habs. Or maybe it predated that. The whole thing might be in alpha. That'd be a challenge to read. Anyway, it'd keep me busy till I got some more school.

I decided to find Dad and tell him it would be a truly enlarging experience for me to get a copy of this maggie book. I tried to home in on him by listening for voices, but there were none. The ventilators sighed. The glass glittered silently as I passed up and down the shining paths.

"I can't." That was my father, very quiet, very close. They must be just on the other side of this set of shelves, to my left. "I can't," he said again. I'd never heard him like this. He sounded small and helpless. "I can't."

"I know." Tata's voice. "I'll go tomorrow, as soon as my skin is ready. And I'll ask about this imbalance, about our paths, just to be sure, but—"

"I love you," he said, interrupting her, and he sounded more familiar now: bitter, and tired. "And I can feel it, I can tell what's going to happen next, and I mustn't do that with you, I *mustn't* hurt you the way I want to hurt you, *but I can't*—"

I realized that I was eavesdropping and jerked back, bumping two bowls together on the shelf. They chimed, a high, perfect hum that hung on the air after my father's voice choked to a stop.

"Kayley?" Tata called softly under the ringing glass.

"Coming." I turned a corner and there they were, facing each other and looking anywhere but in each other's faces. "Dad, can I borrow—"

"Why the hell not?" he said. "Sure." He brushed past me and I started to follow him.

"No," said Tata. She didn't sign. "This way. Where were you? I thought you were going to stay with me." She headed in the opposite direction, which turned out to be a shortcut to the door.

She took me to her room and pulled the curtain closed. I sat on her bed, waiting for her to ask me what I'd heard. But instead she turned to her skin, not brushing it but checking the ties that held it in place, loosening them to accommodate its growing fullness.

In dormancy, the skin's sluggish circulatory system accumulated an ever-swelling supply of hyperoxygenated blood. Its nerve sheaths, worn by long contact, regenerated themselves. Tata held the back of one hand close to the skin's underside. I was too far from her to see it happen, but she had shown me before how the thin white funiculi erected themselves, anticipating connection with her wells. Like the curtains, they responded to pheromonal cues.

I couldn't tell from Tata's reaction if the response was satisfactory. Her face was smooth, her black body blank. When she spoke to me, she kept using words. "Kayley, in the Morning I will need to return to Quarters. For the balance of my highest head."

I tried not to sulk. She'd just gotten back, and she was going out again. "Why?"

"I must . . . consult."

"Oh." I felt stupid. Of course the work crews had to decide what to do about the new, more distant sites. That was what I'd over-heard—wasn't it? I asked Tata if it was really bad to be out in a skin for Days. She looked at me blankly for a moment, then averted her eyes and answered.

"The elders say that it becomes a strain. We get 'tipsy'; our heads unbalance easily, going so long without enough oxygen, and we drop things. A tingling which grows painful, or numbness . . . There is some compensation: danger pay, and the contract will be shortened if we take that path." When the contract ended Tata would leave. Unless my dad or Penny purchased a permanent agreement.

"So is that what's going to happen?"

"Probably not. It would be cooler to move Quarters nearer to where the work is being done." This sounded depressingly likely. It was, after all, their module, at their command. It would take a couple of Days to shift and re-anchor, but they'd still save time in the long run.

I sighed and let my chin sink down into one cupped hand.

"Kayley?" said Tata.

"What?" I didn't bother to look up.

"Your sorrow equals?"

"You'll be gone so much, traveling back and forth. . . ."

"Kayley, must you always try to reach so far in front of your arms? These troubles are unborn. Each path has many branchings." She came over to me and put her hands on my hunched-up shoulders.

"I'm here," Tata continued. "I don't have any work right now, and I'd really like to way with you. So ask your head to tell you what it's best for us to do."

My head was empty of suggestions. We wound up hacking my father's book codes. Despite what she'd said, Tata was not wholly there, and it took longer than it should have. We succeeded about supper time, fed her skin, then hurried to join Penny and Dad in the kitchen.

I watched them all carefully. Penny and Dad were already at the counter, sawing away at grilled swordfish steaks. "Something's wrong, Tata," he joked as we entered. "You forgot to program me the sword I need to cut this thing."

Penny winced. "Your wit, dear. Use your *wit*."

"I am. Maybe yours is a little sharper. Mind if I borrow it a moment?" He reached over and started rummaging through her wild curls. "Looks like what you've got here is mostly hair."

All very jolly and fine, all throughout the meal. Except once I caught what Penny's book would have called a long, burning look. Dad to Tata. Tata to Dad. Then both of them were studying their empty plates.

Afterward, Penny asked Dad to come cad with her. I stayed behind, pretending to help Tata clean up, wondering whether or not I was jealous. At last I decided I just wanted to know what was going on.

"You love him, don't you, Tata?"

Her hands stayed busily silent, smoothing creases from our crumpled paper napkins.

"Tata—"

"Yes. It hardly matters, but yes, I love your father very much." She tossed the napkins into the paper cycler and turned away to face the sink.

"What do you mean?" I asked. "It doesn't matter why?"

"Because." For a moment I thought that was all she was going to say. Then the words came flooding out.

"Because it is unlikely that this love will advance either of us on our path of light and destiny. Because your father knows this as well as I do, though we both wish we didn't. Because your father is strong for me, and I am weak for him. Because, because, because . . ." Tata stopped talking and turned on the water, flushing food scraps from the sink. "There are many, many reasons. Good ones."

"All right," I said. I kept quiet while she unloaded the washer and stacked our clean, dry plates in their hopper. When she was done, I followed her out into the corridor. "Do you still want to way with me?" I asked. "I could stay in your room tonight, if . . . if you'd like?"

She stood still, considering. "I might."

Tata's desk had such a tiny screen. "Or you could come spend the night with me." That way we could read.

"Perhaps that would be most cool." But when we came to her doorway, she stopped. "There are a few things it would be better for me to do tonight, before I leave for Quarters." I could see she was still trying not to sign, though her soft, dark shoulders curved in some awkward emotion: shame, embarrassment? I didn't know.

"Anything I can do, Tata?" I asked her.

"Wait. I'll come when I'm through." The glamp-light glimmered on her curtain's fur as it closed behind her.

I went on to my room. Leaving the curtain open, I activated my desk and took a look at this afternoon's discovery.

The book was called *Space-Apes in Eden: The Anti-Domestication of a New Racial Archetype*. It was a load of filth.

I was eleven Years old, up to my fortieth semester of school. I had heard of the antiquated notion that humanity is divided into races, special variations due to local inbreeding. But no one had ever discussed the inferences once commonly drawn based on this theory: that members of these racial subsets possessed differing abilities, qualitatively and quantitatively. That certain of these abilities made their possessors more fit to survive and reproduce than those possessed of other, and therefore inferior, abilities. That the inbreeding that had produced these races was a highly desirable occurrence, one to be cultivated and encouraged—"by any means consonant with the rapid colonization of space."

I struggled to comprehend these repulsive assumptions as they were presented to me. The murky mysteries of the written word forced me to formulate this nastiness within my own mind. There were a few useful pieces of information; the origin of the word "maggies," for instance. It had nothing to do with the works of Dylan, the twentieth-century Welsh songwriter. "Maggie's Farm" may have been an anthem of the rebellion, but the name came first. It derived from magnesium, the only element the rebels couldn't mine or synthesize. With no access to planetary bases, it became their sole trade-link with Earth.

I also learned the names of the team that designed humanity's first (and only?) self-replicating artificial mutation. It *was* a team, though Harding gets the credit, for the maggies, the curtains, and all the other spin-offs.

The rest—I couldn't tell what was true, what contained a grain of truth, and what was pure, poisonous nonsense. The author implied, rather than stated, that maggies were animals, or anyway, less than human. Because they were made for us, to work for us. The more I read, the more I felt like I was agreeing with things I absolutely knew were wrong. At one point I stared so long at the screen, too stupefied to scroll any farther, that my default clicked on. The swimming clocks showed two sharp. Late. My circadians would be way off.

Where was Tata? She'd have to help me deal with this. I didn't care what she was doing. I needed her. I went down the tunnel to her room.

Her curtain was closed. I slapped it in frustration, and it opened slightly. Maybe it hadn't been drawn completely shut. Or if she had sensitized it to my touch, she did so without telling me. I swear I didn't know that it would open, that I would see them there like that.

Actually, I heard them first. A sound too soft to be a groan, followed by a low, desperate sobbing. I was in the room, then, and I saw.

Tata lay on her bed, on her side, eyes closed. She was naked—no, without clothes, but not naked. Her long, beautiful breasts and her belly and thighs blazed black between the edges of her partially closed skin. With one gold-clad arm she lifted her leg, with the other she braced herself to thrust against him. Him. Dad.

Dad was behind her. I only saw his hairy knees, and his hands on her shoulders. But I recognized his voice.

"Tata, Tata, won't forget me Tata, won't forget who loves you, Tata—" Tension tore his words apart then, left ragged gasps fluttering in the air.

I should have gone away.

But I stayed.

It lasted a long while without changing, then slowed a little. Tata opened her eyes. I know she saw me.

It was my dad who spoke, though. "Sweet, sickin *God*, Tata, this will never be enough." And quite deliberately his hands sought out the edges of her open skin, touching her there, underneath.

She screamed. It was nothing like Penny's books. I wanted to die, I wanted to come, I wanted to run away and hide.

I was moving toward her, somehow, to help her. Spasming with pain, she signed me to stop.

My father's hands continued their torture, brushing and plucking at the skin's exposed funiculi. Tata's scream had subsided to a hoarse grunting, nearly drowned out by my father's moans. I hesitated, and she signed again: Go. Her imbalance was extreme. I could not aid her. Go.

I went.

At the door I turned, still unsure. The hands went suddenly limp. Tata lay still beneath them. Then she showed me one more sign, simple, yet nuanced. Swimming through a virtual Nassea, she slipped into the contracting lock of Quarters, into the arms of healers, elders that would assist her in retrieving her coolness and alignment. She rested there, with them, depending on their love. And the memory of mine.

She was telling me good-bye.

I shut the curtain.

In the morning, Tata was gone, and next Day another maggie came to take her place. His name was Lebba. Dad didn't care how often he left the station, and he never tried to stop me from going out with him, either. I thought sometimes I'd ask him to tell Tata I was well, I was fine, I was growing, developing quite normally. I thought I'd ask him to convey to her my wishes that she continue to receive the blessings of her highest heavenly head. But I haven't done anything like that yet, and I still don't know if I'm going to.

It's been over six Years. With the last of the seeding done, my father has left New Bahama. I surprised him when I told him I wanted to stay here, with Penny, in what he called "this Surge-abandoned mud-hole." But I'm eighteen now, no longer in need of a guardian.

I have settled down here, sinking into the darkness and silence of the Nassea. Penny provides me with an easy, unassuming companionship, and I help her with her work. Which is about to move into construction. For soon, according to our maps, the carefully nurtured coral will break the surface of the Nassea.

When that happens, the maggies will be moving on, to another waterworld, or something rare, a world of ice or dust. Tata, too.

Does she realize how much I miss her, how the loneliness is always there, still curdled up inside?

I think she does.

Excerpt from *Mindscape*

Andrea Hairston
(2004)

**Prologue: Tombouctou Observatory and Galactic Library
on the Outskirts of Sagan City, Paradigma**

Old age ain't for sissies.

Celestina couldn't remember who used to say that, all the time.

I'm telling you, it's stand-up tragedy, so don't laugh. You'll see.

But they were both laughing. Why couldn't she remember? Didn't she remember several lifetimes? A very old woman, Celestina remembered before the Barrier even, before the world had been chopped up into petty little Zones. Humanity covered the planet, lush and vibrant, coming and going as they pleased, wreaking havoc in global style, racing out to the stars. . . .

How could she remember before the Barrier—hadn't she been just a baby? Not even born. It was Femi who'd lived in the other time, before the Barrier swallowed the sky and people were locked out of their world. "Swallowed the sky," was an imprecise image, but Celestina let it pass. Femi would have said that instead of "extradimensional spacetime interference" or other scientific jargon. And nobody understood the Barrier better than Femi—which is to say, nobody understood it much at all, and hadn't he coined the term "Barrier"? Now Femi's stories were her stories, his medicine bag of tricks and truth, hers. Indeed, his lifetime of wisdom was hers to pass on.

Femi had gone on to dance with the ancestors, leaving Celestina to sort out this Interzonal Treaty fiasco with no clear vision. Certainly, if it were Femi's Treaty about to be ratified, he wouldn't hide from the festivities like Celestina in an empty planetarium watching ancient Entertainment all night. He wouldn't cringe at random adulation, run from power trips, or miss a second of pomp and ceremony. And Femi would never have said *Old age ain't for sissies.* That line had to come from her other life. Yes, Robin said it to Thandiwe and maybe Vera said it to Robin. *Stand-up tragedy.*

A gaggle of voices in her head screamed at her like achy joints every time she tried to make a move. Femi Xa Olunde, lover, mentor, enemy, *Geistesvater*—spirit father—was loudest of all, shouting fury at her. *Sell-out, traitor, assassin!* Who was she to chart the course of the future? Celestina stuffed popcorn in her mouth and focused on the planetarium's giant Electrosoft screen.

"Old age ain't for sissies," the over-the-hill hero warned his grandson again. Nothing like old-time movies to distract you from personal crises or global insanity. Even an orthodox shaman like Femi would concede that. Celestina refused to fight herself over *Do the Right Thing, The Shawshank Redemption, Mississippi Masala, A Beautiful Mind,* or Chaplin's *The Great Dictator.* . . . Not a single archive film was twisted enough to contaminate *her* soul. Celestina would take old Hollywood over her own nightmares any day. But sooner or later the credits rolled, they called your name, bellowed praisesongs, and reality smacked you in the face.

"We apologize for the delay, ladies and gentlemen." A rogue transmission ghosted across the planetarium screen, interrupting *The Fugitive* upload.

"*Schade.*" Celestina cursed in old German as a priority broadcast overrode the planetarium's local system. She scanned the vast auditorium for invaders. Not much longer to hide; they'd be coming for her soon.

Blurry images came into focus: Ray Valero, Entertainment superstar, tall, dark, and handsome devil, beloved by all. What a coup for the Treaty Commission to have him master the ceremonies, smooth out the wrinkles. "The architect of the Interzonal Peace Accord, Celestina Xa Irawo, will be the final delegate today to sign the Treaty into law. Rumor buster: the great Lady ditched the party scene last night to meditate, conjure a few spirits, check in with eternity. In deep trance, shamans get fuzzy on time."

"Time's not my problem," Celestina shouted at Ray. She stumbled out of her back-row seat, feet in one body, pounding heart in another, and lurched into darkened fiberplastic windows.

"Over a century since the Barrier burst on the scene and kicked our behinds, and humanity's staging a comeback!" Ray continued in close-up. Perfect teeth flashed. Dark hair framed sculpted features. Celestina could see a direct line from Cary Grant and Denzel Washington to Ray Valero, and he had the voice of James Earl Jones! "We're a reunited world, about to inaugurate peace. Can't rush this gig. History in the making." Applause and cheers; the crowd was in his hip pocket. "Before signing, Madame Xa Irawo will follow New Ouagadougou custom and pour libation to the brave souls who died to make today a reality. Give us reformed thugs a little style."

Celestina laughed out of both sides of her mouth. Ray provided impeccable cover, but could she trust him or any of them with the future? The Barrier raged outside the window, amplifying the voices in her head to hysteria. Celestina swallowed her laughter and squinted at the spacetime contortion blazing just a breath or two away. Beautiful and lethal, a potent mystery that dictated the geography of their lives, however by what authority no one could say.

"Too much mystery for one mind," Celestina muttered.

The Barrier looked as it had once when she was a child: a storm of diamond dust, a wall of crystal confetti stretching across the horizon, blotting out half the sky. Barrier wisps caught fading sunlight and turned it silver, occasionally twisting out a rainbow sign. The Barrier hadn't put on this particular show in eighty, ninety years. Was it in honor of the Treaty?

"Why do you think the Barrier cares what we do?" She covered her mouth. Talking to herself was a bad sign. No psychic snap allowed, not yet. How had she come to this? In none of her incarnations had Celestina ever wanted an ordinary life. Meet a hunk, drop some babies, fight over pennies, struggle to raise the kids up right, weep when they dashed off into *their* future, rock on the porch in sunset smog, tell big fat lies, serve sausage and Kuchen to the grandkids, and flirt with the young things who happened by. Celestina shuddered. Truth be told, she'd always had contempt for normal life. She'd always wanted to do something grand and glorious! From childhood, when she realized the Barrier broke humanity apart, exiled them to separate Zones, and executed transgressors, she dreamed of reuniting the world, hubris in every fiber of her being.

"Madame Xa Irawo will sign away a hundred years of war," Ray proclaimed. "No more Death Percent marched into the Barrier or Extras dying in snuff takes. No more corridor coups in the name of democracy. No more famine and plague, or organ markets devastating the generations for profit. This is a glorious day." What did Ray know about it?

Today was the worst day of Celestina's hundred-plus adventure years. Worse than Femi slashing her skull, driving her to insanity; worse than betraying and poisoning herself; worse than holy war, hunting down innocence to save the race. Today was even worse than driving away all her daughters—Elleni, Sidi, and Mahalia. Not blood daughters of her body, but *Geistestöchter*, children of her spirit who, when she passed on, were to sing her song, carry her story into forever. Without them she was a spirit with no future. A personal tragedy, but the Interzonal Peace Accord was the future of the world. Like so many treaties, it would definitely fall short of expectations and could as easily bring about catastrophe as peace and prosperity.

Footsteps echoed in the hallways around the planetarium. A stampede. They'd found her hiding place. She sank down in the comfort chair. Twenty doors into the planetarium rattled and shook, but did not open. Reprieve.

The week of celebration leading up to the Treaty signing had been a horror show. She couldn't stand the naïve, trusting looks, feigned or sincere, from politicos and Zone glitterati who had committed almost as many crimes against humanity as she had. Seven days and nights at the mercy of hollow, fawning strangers. None of her daughters had deigned to come. Could she blame them for abandoning her?

Last night, in desperation, Celestina begged a cameraman for sanctuary—Aaron Dunklebrot, a former Extra rising up, expert with the newfangled bio-corders, what the Treaty was all about.

"Don't sweat this bullshit," he said and stashed her in the planetarium with his ancient Entertainment stockpile. "A million and a half hours of escape," he bragged, honored to accommodate her. "I feel you."

How could this Aaron "feel" her, know what she'd done, know who she really was? Nobody knew, not her spirit daughters, not even Femi, the all wise. Aaron, Ray, and everybody gathered at Tombouctou for history-in-the-making expected her to glide like an angel through thunderous applause, to pass through hypocrisy like a *Vermittler*, a go-between sculpting a corridor through the Barrier unscathed. She was their hero, personal savior, God's next of kin. Her smile was a benediction, her words sacred texts; Saint Celestina, she'd put an end to war.

Not one of them suspected her of betrayal or genocide.

Lights flooded the planetarium and before she could scurry behind a pillar, Aaron Dunklebrot stuck his dimpled cheeks, chiseled chin, and blue-green-algae eyes in the emergency exit. He had the same shadow of beard from yesterday on baby-face, flawless skin. Gene art, high end, looked like a full body makeover. He'd obviously worked with a real pro, a renegade scientist. Playing around with virus and genetic code for killer looks.

How can you betray us and make a treaty with these people?

Femi had asked that, dying in her arms.

"You ready?" Aaron shook her shoulder and interrupted the memory. "Gotta move." His flat, tense English marked him as a Los Santos native—a reformed gangster barely clinging to civilization. He must have betrayed somebody to survive; plenty of somebodies to go from death-row Extra to wonder-boy cinematographer. Nothing else was possible in cutthroat Los Santos. *A treaty with these people?*

"Of course I'm not ready." Celestina grabbed her medicine bag, heavy with several lifetimes of wisdom.

"Shall I carry that for you?" Aaron asked with old-movie charm.

"No!" she snapped and clutched it to her chest. "My burden."

Aaron slipped an arm around her waist and guided her out the emergency exit, through the backstage labyrinth, and to the Great Hall of Images, where humanity had once communed with the stars. Those glory days were long gone, only ashes in her memory. She froze in the entranceway.

"Breathe," he commanded.

"I have a story for you." She sucked a breath. "When you become a director."

"A director?" Aaron laughed. "In your dreams."

"Nobody's been able to tell my story yet."

"Outlaw Entertainment? Maybe after tonight, after the Treaty, they won't be banning stories and I could shoot whatever Entertainment I—"

"Don't count on it." She gripped his arm down to the bone. "I can't go out there."

"Look, the grandstanding and signing is a piece of cake. Bringing all the Zones together, that was the hard part. Now enjoy the ride."

"Promise me to tell the whole story."

Aaron nodded and thrust Celestina into the Hall. She forced a smile for the ring of bio-corders that transmitted her quicksilver eyes and craggy brown cheekbones to viewers in every Zone of the inhabited world. The synth-marble floor sent shivers from her bare toes to her teeth. Ants in her pockets stung her thighs, spreading itchy heat.

"Ladies and Gentlemen," Ray shouted. "The First Lady of Peace!" He dropped to one knee and kissed her hand.

Celestina had no time to chastise Ray's silliness. VIPs from Los Santos, Paradigma, and New Ouagadougou roared in her ears, crying, laughing, and singing her name. They surged forward, crushing the guards against the stage, stretching out hands stained with blood and tears. In deference to Ray's improvisation, she pulled a flask from her medicine bag and poured libation. The wine stained her robes and feet and pooled like blood on the nonporous surface.

"To Femi Xa Olunde," she said.

"To Femi!" the crowd repeated.

Did she mourn his passing or rejoice in his death?

"To all who died for this peace," she said, not wanting to think too much. "Bless them, bless us."

"Bless you!" someone shouted from the back.

Ten feet in front of Celestina on a transparent fiberplastic table, a paper document generated especially for the ceremony curled in the

moist air. Delegates from every Zone had signed in ink as well as elec-
trons. An aide thrust a fountain pen and a glass stylus into Celestina's
twitching fingers. Her feet cramped, her hands knotted up. She
couldn't move. The glass stylus slipped from her fingers and rolled
across the stage.

Elleni Xa Celest, her *Geistestöchter*—spirit daughter—snatched
the device before it crashed into the monitors. Her braids and skin
glistened in the shadows. "Almost home," she murmured and pressed
the stylus into Celestina's gnarled hands. They had not spoken to
each other in six years.

"You came," Celestina whispered, tears blurring her vision.

"Last night," Elleni said.

She clutched her daughter. "You came." One of Elleni's braids
snaked around Celestina's wrist, spitting yellow discharge. Elleni's
tears. "I'm so sorry," Celestina said, and buried her face in her daughter's hissing hair.

Sidi Xa Aiyé stood beside them, pressing palms together in a gesture of respect.

"You too?" Celestina kissed Sidi's feathery fingers.

"How could we miss your day of days?" Sidi said, a delicious smile
on her full lips.

Of her daughters only Mahalia Selasie was absent.

"Will you hold this?" Celestina offered them her medicine bag.

Elleni and Sidi exchanged electric glances. Celestina felt her soul
wilt.

"While you sign?" Elleni spoke first. "I'd be honored." She clasped
the bag to her heart.

Perhaps Celestina wasn't a spirit without a future after all.

"Are we ready yet?" Aaron beckoned to them from behind a bio-
corder.

Celestina allowed Elleni and Sidi to walk her out of the shadows
and up to the Treaty table. She glanced at the paper beneath her
hands. In a few thousand words, they had written down their best
selves. Her story was coming to an end. Why worry about factions
and splinter groups who boycotted the signing? The hard work of the
Treaty would be done by Elleni, Sidi, Aaron, Ray, and committed

people in every Zone, maybe even Mahalia Selasie. Her absent daughter was a rogue scientist, but she wasn't against the Treaty.

An ancient West African prayer dropped from her lips before she could catch herself. New Ouagadougou delegates would be pleased. "*Aboru, Aboye, Aboşişe*. May what we offer carry, be accepted, may what we offer bring about change." The old Yoruba words relaxed her knotted hands. Celestina leaned forward and with sweeping gestures, signed the Treaty. "Our time is no worse or no better than other times. We are not inevitable. We didn't have to happen this way. There are many threads, many Earths." She waved the Treaty up to the stars then down to the ground. "We live just one of the stories, one fine line in a universe of possibilities. It is up to us to make our story beautiful."

The live audience exploded with applause, which Celestina tasted more than heard, spicy, ginger-beer applause, spraying her sinuses clear and sweet, bubbling down her throat, boiling in her belly, hot and potent. "Thank you, I am nothing. . . ." The blight on her soul faded in her daughters' burning eyes and the crowd's stomping feet. She felt like another self—the one they imagined her to be. "You are the future. I see tomorrow in your faces."

She recognized his torn face before she spotted the weapon— someone she'd healed, an Extra she'd brought back from the edge of death. Piotr Osama, disfigured by torture, hidden in a crowd of believers, passing as born-again Sioux. His skin was silver and he wore the white robes and moss headdress of the Ghost Dancer cult. This didn't fool Celestina. Born-again Sioux were treaty-shy. They refused to sign away their sovereignty and had boycotted the convention. Piotr aimed a sham bio-corder at Entertainment royalty or perhaps Paradigma's Prime Minister. Or maybe the gestapo Security. Any one of them could be sweet revenge.

Celestina closed her eyes, wishing to see no more, eager to die herself—*Ebo Eje*, a blood sacrifice for peace, redemption. She was, however, not eager for more killing, but with less than a second, how to warn people against that? Still clutching the Treaty, she walked into the line of fire.

"Aşe . . ." So be it . . .

302 DARK MATTER: READING THE BONES

Piotr's spray of bullets ripped through the paper and slammed into Celestina's chest. Her blood gushed onto the Treaty before she could think of what else to say.

1: Archive Transmission/Personal

From: Lawanda Kitt on diplomatic mission to Angel City, Los Santos

To: Herself, waitin' at the Barrier outsida Sagan City, Paradigma, goin' nowhere fast

I do not believe this.

The Treaty convoy s'posed to be goin' down a corridor thru the Barrier hours ago. Why we still hangin' 'round some ole dusty wasteland, fartin' funky exhaust? Bad air, bad dirt, and everywhere you look shit done shriveled up and croaked. My butt's way too big for this tight ass enviro-suit. Miracle fibers ain't wickin' nothin' away. Sweat poolin' at the crotch like I peed my pants. One big itch. I can't take much more.

What's up with Miss Freaky Thang Elleni Xa Celest? She a Vermittler ain't she? A go-between, Barrier griot, mutant witch, Celestina's anointed one, WHATEVER—all her big talk 'bout not waitin' for no seasonal corridor to travel from Paradigma to Los Santos or Los Santos to New Ouagadougou. Yeah she goin' make a eight-lane super highway for the whole diplomatic convoy! She out there in the dust, nose in the Barrier and her evil funky hair crawlin' and spittin' like snakes in heat, so why don't she just hoodoo the damn thang open and get it over with?

All us so-called diplomats lookin' ready to riot. Nobody's Zen enuf to be patient no more. Well, I ain't Zen enuf, that's for damn sure.

How come I say yes? Me, Vice Ambassador to Los Santos? Celestina must be squirmin' in her grave. Lawanda Kitt, ethnic throwback, in the executive suite, steada just workin' the crew? I don't mind buildin' some houses or throwin' down a few roads. I'd do farm labor too and beat back the desert or hospital duty, or even school work, save a mind. I'm down for Celestina's people-to-people diplomacy, gettin' these Los Santos folk back on they feet. What I know how to do. But VICE AMBASSADOR, scopin' Treaty implementation and infractions? Yeah, like just bump me up to the big house and won't nobody notice you fuckin' up the Treaty.

The Major play me like an ad-opera jingle.

So at six A.M., ain't nobody been asleep all night, the whole convoy's hot to trot. Sun's comin' up over the wasteland, a picture perfect day for the bio-corder crews. They goin' get some trippy Elleni footage. My vehicle be first in line cuz I don't wanna miss the show and Vermittler don't make me no way nervous. Elleni and me been around the block a coupla times. She my girl. I just wish she'd fix herself up. Who let her out the house with that nasty hair runnin' wild on her head?

At five after six, the Major slide by my transport, like he doin' a publicity run. Secret Services ace checkin' on us regulars not just the big shots, but really he wanna see me, his main squeeze. I'm thinkin' that's too sweet and gettin' all mushy inside. Ain't me and the Major fight for Celestina's Treaty together in Paradigma? Didn't I rescue his cocky ass when he was 'bout to be "expendable personnel"? Ain't I the woman who show him his heart? Now we 'bout to turn the mess all the way 'round and he dump this shit on me.

"I'm not going," the Major say.

"You not goin' where?" I ask. Clueless.

"Armando Jenassi has been appointed Ambassador in my place," the Major say, sotto voce like he really don't want me to hear.

"You lyin'." I sound like plantains fryin' in hot oil. "You gotta be lyin'. Jenassi can't ambassador diddly in your place. What about our plan?"

"We're promoting you to Vice Ambassador." He up in my face tryin' to smile but can't get his mouth to do it.

"Vice Ambassador? What the hell is that?"

"The Prime Minister's idea, but we can make it work."

"I got your back, not her." I sound jealous, but it's more than a catfight. "Prime Minister Jocelyn ain't part of our plan."

"Unforeseen circumstances . . ." The Major be usin' his voice of authority now.

"How far ahead you gotta see for straight-up truth?" I can't look at him no more. "Vice Ambassador? Y'all just make that up."

"It's good PR."

"Prime Minister Jocelyn and her posse be tryin' to kill the Treaty and you—"

"Listen to me." He always interrupt me when he be bullshittin'. "The situation here at home is critical. Several rogue scientists have defected—"

I interrupt him. "Mahalia Selasie leadin' more nerds astray? Naw. Snatchin' you offa our team ain't about diva scientists goin' AWOL. They been runnin' outta here since forever." I wanna run too, but ain't no where to go 'cept up against a transport wall. I lean my head into the viewscreen and close my eyes. Why I gotta be in love with this sucker?

"I'm needed at home. The Prime Minister is worried about security. She can't afford to loan me to the diplomatic corps. A genetic conspiracy could be brewing."

"And what is that exactly?"

"Bio-terrorists. Classified."

"Bullshit." I suck my teeth, almost too disgusted for words. "Can't you see, they playin' you?"

"Where's your proof?" He walk in close to me; his hot breath be all down my neck.

"They ain't stupid enuf to drop proof when they play a guy like you."

"So it's just speculation." He got his hands on my waist, tuggin' at me. "Intuition."

"What? You don't speculate?" I start squirmin'. I don't want him touchin' me.

"Stop it, Lawanda." He turn me 'round and squeeze me close. I feel his heart poundin'. Then he get hisself under control and I don't feel nothin'. "Calm down," he say, like a threat. "Stay frosty."

"Why? So you can sweet-talk me outta my mind? Who am I? What can I do in Los Santos?"

"You can adjust your attitude and appreciate the historic opportunity that's falling in your lap! Don't let anybody play you out of being all you can be."

"You almost have a point, 'cept sendin' me 'cross the Barrier to gangsta heaven with Armando Jenassi ain't historic, it's messed up. Man, this ain't nothin'!"

"Ahh"—his voice be like a caress, hot hands on my back make me shiver—"but you're just the person to make something out of nothing. I know from personal experience. We need you in Los Santos, especially if they're playing us. We can't just leave the Treaty mission up to Jenassi, can we?" I feel his heart again, a different beat tho'.

"Well, no, but . . ." My heart's beatin' just like his.

"You've got to make sure we don't let Celestina down, let the world down."

"I ain't lettin' Celestina down."

"We knew turning the tides of history wasn't going to be easy. I need you in Los Santos."

"So I gotta hold up the sky by myself. . . ."

"Make Celestina proud of you."

Celestina go off like fireworks in my heart, in everybody's heart. She a saint, walkin' on water, boxin' with God, dyin' for our sins, and shit like that. We fall all over ourselves tryin' to . . . I don't even know what. Live up to a legend? How can I say no to that? Then the Major fill my mouth up with his chocolate kisses, talkin' 'bout he believe in me. And ain't that just what I wanna hear? So I'm moanin' and groanin' 'steada thinkin' straight or tellin' him he's full of shit.

Weak in the knees, pussy-brain pathetic.

The bio-terrorist BS is a smoke screen. Prime Minister Jocelyn be tryin' to kill the Treaty, I know it. Without somebody fierce like the Major headin' this Treaty convoy, them gangstas in Los Santos just goin' laugh at us heart-on-our-sleeves-diplomats. I oughta call the shit on the world screen, speak truth to power with all the bio-corders runnin'! The Major think my attitude was set on stun before, wait! Course, who'd believe me? Everybody would just think I was whinin' to cover my own incompetence.

Maybe the Major really be offerin' me a historic opportunity, maybe not, but I let him make love to me then walk outta here like he ain't just worked me over. Any way I turn, feel like somebody else callin' the shots and when it get nasty, tellin' me to chill.

Chill out yourself, motherfucker, that's all I got to say.

Elleni and her booty ugly Vermittler self need to open up the Barrier and get this show on the road.

2: Barrier Wasteland Outside of Sagan City, Paradigma

The universe is permeable, continuous beyond comprehension. All Barriers are the magic of Mind.
    —Vera Xa Lalafia, *Healer Cosmology: The Final Lessons*

Elleni Xa Celest doubled up and vomited blood. She crouched at the Barrier, head bowed, eyes squeezed shut, thighs clenched—trying to sculpt-sing a corridor from Sagan City, Paradigma, to Angel City, Los Santos, for the eager diplomatic vehicles thrumming at her back. A high-profile Treaty mission, and the Barrier refused Elleni's melody without explanation for the first time in memory. She squinted up at the frustrating enigma, seeking any sort of sign. The Barrier didn't look like much at midday: no roiling fireworks display, no jewel mountains reaching to the sun, just geysers of smoke and shadows, milky undulations stretching across the horizon and up beyond the sky. A traveler from the twenty-first century might have mistaken it for a harmless fogbank, rolling in from the northwest.

Elleni knew better. She was no ordinary Healer shaman, but a *Vermittler*, a go-between, who didn't need seasonal corridors to travel from Zone to Zone. She communed with the Barrier in what Healers called the sound beyond sound. Her fingers had carved hundreds of passageways through the Barrier's lethal energy fields. She was furious. How could the Barrier treat her as *Murahachibu*, as an outcast, an alien nobody, and with everybody watching?

Behind Elleni in the wasteland, cordoned off by Paradigma's security forces, a mob of physicists, tech grunts, biologists, Los Santos Entertainment crews, politicians, and unaffiliated gawkers sucked in a collective breath and shuffled a thousand skeptical feet. Eddies of gray dust swirled across the featureless landscape. Ordinary Paradigmites didn't believe she could open a corridor with her bare hands. They'd come to watch Elleni make a fool of herself on the world screen. Sagan City scientists, however, were desperate for hard data on *Vermittler*, desperate to unmask the mechanism of her "magic." Entertainment crews from Los Santos just hoped for a good show. Gelatinous bio-corders whirred furiously, yet these organic smart-machines weren't able to capture Elleni, who was a visual, acoustic blur as she sang impossibly high arpeggios and clawed at the Barrier. Suspecting sabotage, Sagan Institute technicians and the Mifune Enterprises crew snarled at each other, a Zone war brewing.

Yellow tears dribbled down hissing hair. The Barrier left her sitting on a powder keg, but Elleni disappointed herself. She wasn't furious with the Barrier because of the threat it posed to the Treaty, to Celestina's vision of a "new world." She didn't cry for plague victims in Paradigma or tortured Extras in Los Santos. She didn't rage against the persistence of the old regime. Her throat and heart were tight with personal humiliation. She felt as if betrayed by a lover whose faithfulness she had taken for granted, whose passion 'til now had been unconditional and without limit. No matter what a disaster she was to everyone else, no matter what worms crawled in her belly, no matter how freaky she seemed, the Barrier had welcomed her song, had opened itself to her touch, had danced her from one world to another. From adolescence, when humans shunned her body, brushed her love aside, showered her with insult and contempt, she didn't holler at the wind or ache alone in the night. She slipped into the arms of a secret lover whose touch meant disfigurement or death for others, but for her, sweet visions and magical journeys. The Barrier was her sacred sanctuary. Her skin shimmered with a flash of spirit from beyond the Earth.

Elleni was a mortal beloved by gods, Celestina's only real heir, yet this morning, as she was about to flaunt her power on the world screen, the divine connection snapped, and emotions she'd kept secret even from herself raged. The Barrier sucked the song from her throat three times, but made no reply, offered no passageway. Elleni imagined looking down from space, from halfway to the moon. Her "secret lover" was a monster that sliced through the sky and the oceans, a conquering invader that had ripped up continents, reconfiguring the world into the inhabited Zones—Los Santos, Paradigma, New Ouagadougou—and a vast uninhabited Wilderness. Before the Treaty, while the Zones waged war on each other, Elleni had welcomed the Barrier's unfathomable power into her body and allowed it to paint her mindscape with delicious images. She still savored these otherworldly experiences, but perhaps the monster had tired of their dalliance. Perhaps the monster was angered by the chutzpa of a puny whore who would make a world spectacle of their intimacy.

Sidi Xa Aiyé, her *Geistesschwester*, spirit sister, had said as much to the Healers Council, the wisest men and women in New Ouagadougou. They had survived the Final Lessons, carried the richest medicine bags, and guided their Zone through good times and bad. Sidi declared Elleni a Barrier traitor, spiritually unfit to center this auspicious group.

"Nobody despises fire and wraps it up in a cloth."

Elleni tried to force herself calm. Despite Sidi's objection, the Healers Council had given her a vote of confidence. Elleni sucked in great quantities of hot, dry air and slowed her heart's drumbeat. She unclenched aching muscles and stacked her weight on carefully aligned bones. Sidi had no love for Celestina's Treaty or the Barrier and she did not understand Elleni. Elleni didn't understand herself. What transpired between a *Vermittler* and the Barrier was a formidable mystery. Elleni was neither a good scientist nor a practiced shaman. Celestina, her *Geistesmutter*, had been killed before they completed the Final Lessons. Would Celestina have preferred Sidi to accept her medicine bag? She looked disappointed when Elleni agreed to carry it. Dead four years, Celestina would answer no more questions. On her own now, Elleni communed with the Barrier like a honeybee who danced to magnetism with no inkling of Maxwell's Equations or quantum theory. Her understanding lay beyond consciousness. She didn't have a clue why the Barrier refused her song this morning.

Seasonal corridors would not open for several weeks. Paradigma's Treaty convoy hoped to reach Los Santos and shore up fragile Interzonal alliances before tourists, spies, mercenaries, and Entertainment crews muddied the waters. Or that was the lie Paradigma's Prime Minister told. Elleni hadn't challenged her. She seized the opportunity to show off on the world screen and promised safe passage through a corridor of her own making. Now was the time to stand and deliver.

Since she could think of nothing else to do, Elleni swallowed her shame, chased every thought from her mind, and began a new corridor. She pulled a bass note from her pelvic floor, slid up her range, vibrating bones and organs until ultrasounds resonated her nasal passages and shot out her skull. Her fingers danced in and out of the Barrier's domain. As she hit her highest notes, an archway crystallized just beyond her fingertips. She was so stunned she almost lost the song. Struggling back onto the melody, she shaped a wider opening. Relief flooded her and she would have rushed into the gateway except someone was already there. The song rattled around in her throat, then faded, but the archway was stable enough to linger a millisecond.

Femi Xa Olunde, his lean form hidden by bulky mud cloth robes, his dark hands and feet dusted with ashes, blocked Elleni from moving into the corridor. The cloud of white hair framing his face glowed.

"*Vermittler* traitor, drunk on power, Barrier whore!" Femi accused Elleni, his beard and bushy eyebrows flecked with the cinders that burst from his mouth as he spoke. "Playing on the enemy battlefield, you are the enemy!"

But the old shaman was dead. Gunned down by an assassin.

Celestina Xa Irawo was also dead, yet she fussed and fumed at Femi, iridescent starfish clinging to her hennaed braids. "Who are our enemies but our other selves?"

Femi flicked bony fingers at Celestina, dismissing her question, and the corridor around the ghost shamans started to break up.

"Wait," Elleni shouted and reached for them.

"No time. The world has been thrown off its course." Femi evoked an old Yoruba metaphor, but still spoke English. His mud cloth robes danced in a hot breeze. "And who are you but the enemy?" he asked. "Who are you?" His words caught fire.

"Who indeed?" Celestina nudged Femi aside. Opalescent eels circled her belly. She pressed a clay funeral pot against her cheek, then hurled the pot toward Elleni's feet.

"Fire and water, mingle the ashes." As the clay shattered, the archway dissolved.

The Barrier was once again a foggy veil. *Drunk on power, Barrier whore!* Panic set Elleni's hair crawling across the damp skin of her exposed back. The dead shouldn't be coming down the Barrier to invade her mindscape and dissolve corridors. Not even legendary Healer shamans like Celestina and Femi could do that. Barrier corridors connected one Earth Zone to another, perhaps tunneled through spacetime to other star systems or universes, but corridors couldn't connect the living to some mythical afterlife. The phantoms blocking her entry with old West African proverbs must be interference, amplified distractions from her own mindscape, or a message from the Barrier to be decoded. Nothing more.

She tried to sing again, but after ten milliseconds of desperate wailing, her throat was on fire and she vomited black blood. Exchange with the Barrier required a phase shift from one sensibility to another, like switching from visible light to magnetism or modulating spacetime. Phaseshifting was murder on her stomach. Behind her in the wasteland the crowd was turning ugly. Elleni felt a bone snap. She adjusted her perception of spacetime, slowing down to register the jittery scene.

Techies from Paradigma and grips from Los Santos exchanged blows over incompetent bio-corders. Two men were bleeding from their ears and broken noses. A minor interzonal skirmish that could escalate. This mob had been standing in the wasteland since dawn. They had a touch of Barrier fever. Elleni felt a knife pierce dangerously close to a heaving lung. Paradigma's security whisked away the culprits before blood touched the ground, but a whiff of pain lingered behind. Elleni was appalled. Not just corridors collapsing; nothing was going as she'd imagined it. Her great moment on the world screen was about to blow up in her face. No wonder Femi *and* Celestina were haunting her. Elleni was a disgrace to the memory of her spirit mother. She pushed a frantic braid out of her eyes and, as swallowing hurt too much, spit bloody saliva on the ground.

She wouldn't be able to sing another note for days.

"What's wrong?" Ray Valero's voice was molasses in her ears.

Elleni shifted all the way to human standard time, careful not to skid down to tree or mountain time, and leaned into him. Her Entertainment Hero. His Barrier dawn eyes sparkled, and he smelled like a storm brewing.

"Talk to me, babe," he said and ran his fingers through the tangle of bangs, beads, and dreads that fussed on her forehead. She felt a shiver of desire, but her hair settled down under his touch. "You milking this for high drama or what?" He smiled a camera-ready, Entertainment grin.

What could she tell him?

"I can't do a corridor," Elleni whispered and ran burnt fingers across Ray's cheeks, then waved at a shadowy Barrier. The diplomatic vehicles had inched closer, their motors whining at her. "The Barrier's not responding and I'm a wreck."

Ray registered the extremity of her distress, but didn't break. A consummate actor, tall, muscular, Los Santos handsome, he'd played most of his life on the world screen for a fickle public, and after almost twenty top screen years, they still loved him. As he stroked her sallow skin and nuzzled wormy hair, Elleni wondered, just like his fans, what on earth did he see in her? She blinked lizard eyes. Was it forbidden fruit, jungle fever, or what?

"You're pretty beat up," he murmured and slid his hand around her waist, like he was playing a love scene. "What happened?"

"I can't sing. My throat's a disaster," she muttered and spit more blood in the dust.

"You were fine an hour ago."

"Sorry about this, but it's easier to talk if the whole world can't listen in." Drawing on Barrier energy, she modulated spacetime for both of them.

"Whoa," Ray groaned at the still life of angry diplomats, biocorder techies, and scowling spectators behind them. "This hyper slow motion is rough on my brain." He squinted at staccato bursts of light snagged in the Barrier's murky tendrils. "I really hate you mucking around with my perception and—"

She put her fingers on his lips, interrupting his litany of discomfort. "I don't know about you going to Los Santos today. I don't know about anybody going through. If I can't sculpt-sing, we might have to wait for seasonal corridors. . . ." English consonant clusters hurt her throat. She wished Ray spoke Spanish or Yoruba. English made everything sound blunt and pathetic. But those languages were dead to him.

"Performance anxiety." Ray flashed her a thousand-watt grin. He played the audience even in private, which irritated her today more than usual. "You can do it," he said and nibbled her burnt fingers. "It's just nerves."

"Worse than that." She winced and pulled her wounded hands away from him.

"Don't let a hostile audience throw you. You got the juice."

"I don't need an actor's pep talk." She turned her back to him.

"What do you want, a kick in the butt?" Ray said, trying to laugh. Elleni bit her lip. Several of her braids snaked around his neck. "Oh, you want to strangle me."

"I can't explain this to you."

"Am I too much gangster to understand Healer subtlety? Don't patronize me. I know what's going on with you and the Barrier."

"What do you know?" Elleni's hair stiffened around his throat.

"You're not the enemy. You're opening the Barrier for peace." He stroked her shoulder. She turned to face him, pulling her dreads from around his neck. "They're dead wrong about you," he insisted.

Elleni filled her lungs with his emotion. His breath was sweet with anger, but he didn't know her secret. "Who's so wrong about me that your breath burns?" she asked, moving close to his face, sucking him into her.

Ray hesitated, obviously uncertain as to what to say. Elleni could wait. In their Barrier bubble, time was practically at a standstill. She watched him with unblinking eyes. He drank in a breath of her and spoke. "The Healers Council sent a public message."

"It was Sidi, wasn't it? *Geistesschwester* watching out for my soul."

"Who else?" Ray shook his head. "Some sister."

"But transmitting across the Barrier? Impossible." Elleni was puzzled. "Healers would wait for seasonal corridors, which don't open for several weeks."

"Not a transmission, but a state 'gift' you brought from Sidi and her consort, Duma, for Prime Minister Jocelyn Williams. Sidi doesn't think you should special-order Barrier corridors."

"Show me," she said softly.

"Later."

"Now."

Ray sighed and thrust his Electro mini-pad at her. Elleni steeled herself for Sidi Xa Aiyé's midnight eyes, velvet skin, ochre braids, and plum lips, for her elegant infallibility. Didn't she get tired of always being right? But instead of directly chastising her, Sidi's message was illuminated calligraphy, text that morphed into music and images and then back to words.

The Earth broke from its orbit and smashed through the asteroid belt, dragging the Moon in its wake. A bloody Elleni, carrying ancient weapons, staggered through crumbling forests and fallen cities to an ocean on fire. As the Earth raced past Saturn, the Moon collided with the ringed giant. Shock waves ripped apart the fabric of spacetime. Elleni was dragged into a black tornado that sucked up the Sun.

Elleni,

Barrier junkie, drunk on power, while the world has been thrown off its course.

Playing on the enemy battlefield, you are the enemy!
Sidi Xa Aiyé and Duma Xa Babalawo for the Healers Council Majority

"You can't let Sidi or Duma shake you," Ray said, "you know what's what."

Elleni felt the ground fall from under her feet. It couldn't be coincidence that Sidi and the ghost shamans in the Barrier used the same words to attack her. The blood rushing into her head roared in her ears. Ray shouted something at her but she didn't hear him. Her heart was a Tama drum, beating so fast she could barely breathe. The Barrier, like Celestina, favored Sidi, was on the side of her enemies. Elleni let the Electro screen slip from her fingers. Ray caught the mini-pad before it smashed on the ground. He effortlessly attached it to his belt. Perhaps he held her up, too, like a good hero. But what did that matter? Mission impossible. Elleni was *Murahachibu*, outcast from the Barrier. She wouldn't be opening a corridor anytime soon.

TRANCE

Kalamu ya Salaam

(2004)

Juno listened intently, his lean body hunched forward and tightly coiled as though he was preparing to leap into the screen. Bashe paced back and forth across the back wall of the control center, her head down but obviously attentive; she would pause every time a salient point was made. The debate was winding down and it was almost time for the vote of the extraordinary session. We all knew the decision could go either way.

"Don't be so stupid as to think that only tomorrow counts," Juno snapped as one anti-project elder spoke, citing the meagerness of our resources and a need for more defense development. "What better defense than completely knowing our history?"

A decision to discontinue the time-travel, history-recovery project had never been this close before, but then again, we had never before been so besieged. Most people on the planet had either been overwhelmed by or had voluntarily accepted merger into the One-Planet scheme, and only a few pockets of Diversity proponents were still active.

For me it was simple, no matter how mixed my history: I wanted Blackness always to exist. Everybody turning beige just didn't appeal to me. But then, Juno always said, the only color that counts in One-Planet is the color of money. Social values and a way of life is where the real difference is, and that's what we are fighting to preserve and develop.

I couldn't take it anymore. I got up and started to walk back to quarters. Sometimes I just get so frustrated. Why couldn't we just be left alone? We were already reduced to tiny outposts, strategically located across the southern zones of the Americas, Africa, and the Pacific Isles. We were barely twenty million strong. We just wanted to be ourselves, we—

"Sheba, don't leave." Bashe didn't even look up as she said that while continuing her slow strides. Her intonation told me her injunction wasn't a request.

"This is so stupid," I muttered to no one in particular as I sat back down.

Just then Muta entered control. "Have they voted yet?" he asked, flopping down into the console seat next to me.

"I think they will as soon as this asshole—"

"Sheba." Bashe got on my case again.

"Sorry, but this is getting on my last nerve. And all we can do is sit here and wait while these guys decide our fate. And you know half of them are—"

"Quiet. They are about to vote." I looked over at Juno, who held up his left hand, palm out, as he gave his full attention to the screen. Muta and I moved over to Juno's console to look over his shoulder.

The tally was almost instantaneous: 19 green, 10 red, 1 yellow. "Oh, shit. What do they do now? How do you count a yellow?" I asked, turning around to stare at Bashe. We needed at least 20 votes.

She looked up unsmiling. "If it's a vote to maintain an existing policy, yellow is counted as a green and if it's a vote to initiate a new policy, yellow is counted as a red."

I looked around; neither Juno nor Muta seemed pleased. "So why is everybody looking so glum?"

"Because the yellow vote came from my father," Bashe said as she moved to the center of our module.

I knew his enthusiasm had cooled on our project after we lost Celine on that last jump, but I thought Bashe would be able to persuade him to continue his support.

"Listen up." All eyes fastened on Bashe as she started running down the game plan. "We just got a reprieve, but it's only temporary.

My father is going to vote to cancel our program in the next session if we don't retrieve Celine."

"That means we're through."

"Juno, don't say that. We've got two more months before the next council session, and"—Juno never even looked up as I babbled on, trying to paint the most positive picture I could—"once the new scanner is calibrated, we should be able to find her."

"Sheba, I'm not so sure of that. It takes two of us to safely operate the scanner and the transport system." As much as I would be glad when the project was over, I didn't want it to end unsuccessfully. As Bashe spoke, my mind started to drift. "And the council won't authorize us to accept any more jumpers this cycle. Which means we have, at the most, a total of three more jump opps."

"Bashe, technically I could do two more jump operations." I finally spoke up, but not very loudly and not very confidently.

Muta shook his head and delivered the bad news in a slow monotone as though he had no emotional investment, even though we all knew how much he wanted to retrieve Celine. "The real problem is if we go searching for Celine we won't be able to gather critical history to complete this phase of the project and—"

"If we don't find Celine, there won't be support to continue our project."

"You're exactly right, Sheba. But—and you know I want to find Celine—we do have a chance to finish the project without finding Celine. If we go searching for Celine, we won't have enough jumps left to finish the project, especially if we lose another jumper."

Muta's assessment hung heavily in the artificial air of the module. When we started almost ten moons ago we were a team of twelve, plus Bashe as commander. We were now down to four.

"I'm not feeling searching for Celine." Juno looked over at Muta, then slowly swiveled his head to take in each one of us. "Look, realistically, the technicalities don't matter. We only have two jump opps left and what's been our return ratio? The average is only one of every three jumpers makes it back. Celine had the best record out of all of us. We've got jumpers out there who never made it back from their first jump."

It got awfully quiet. Finally, Bashe attempted to bring closure. "Okay, okay. If Juno's assessment is correct, then it's either finish the project or try to find Celine—we don't have the resources to do both."

"I vote we finish the project," Muta spoke up.

I could tell Muta wasn't speaking his heart but instead was just saying what he thought a good trooper was supposed to say. "Well, I vote we search for Celine."

"Who the hell said this was a democracy," Juno hissed as though Muta and I had no right to speak. "We knew this was a goddamn suicide mission when we signed up. But we all thought salvaging our history was worth all the risks. Besides, what's so special about Celine? We've got eight other jumpers out there. I don't hear anybody talking about searching for them." Juno stood up slowly. "The fact of the matter is, we've got two jumps left, maybe three. . . ."

"What do you mean, maybe three? You just said—"

Juno cut me off before I could finish. "I know what I said. Two jumps to finish the mission and one jump to find Celine. Bashe, you've got to stay. Sheba and Muta, in that order, should jump to complete the mission, and after the mission is complete, I'll take the third jump to try and find Celine."

I looked over at Bashe to see what her reactions were. As the team leader she was going to have the last word.

"Juno, we can't afford to lose you. You're the only one of us left who really understands the technology."

"Yeah, but I wouldn't jump until the project was complete and then . . . well, if I didn't make it back, we still would have a completed project."

"That's true, but there are other considerations. Eventually . . ." Bashe looked up at the module ceiling. We knew everything we did was recorded. "Look, there is some classified info I can't say, but Juno, you're going to be needed. I'll take the last jump."

"Permission to enter space." At the sound of Elder Hodari's voice code, all of us except Juno, jumped to switch our console screens on.

"Screen on," Bashe gave an immediate command.

Elder Hodari's handsome image flickered and quickly stabilized into a sparkling picture. He looked stressed. "I assume you all saw the vote."

Bashe answered for all of us. "We did."

"Commander Bashe, I'm sorry. I know how much this project means to you, but it's basically over. I was able to negotiate a stall period, but there are other pressing priorities." He let that hang for a moment. We looked at each other but said nothing. "Bashe, did you mention the FutureBlack project to your crew?"

"No. It's classified and not everyone here is cleared for that level."

Muta stood up and moved away from the line of vision of his console screen, looked over at me, and silently mouthed, "What's FutureBlack?" I hunched my shoulders in response and looked over at Juno. Juno just shook his head no. Meanwhile, Elder Hodari continued talking. "Bashe, hit me back on a secure line."

"Forty." Our screens blanked out as Bashe started pushing code. The lights dimmed. We were switching power and frequencies. "Everybody go to helmets," Bashe ordered, and we each plugged into the black box console. We had direct contact with each other in the module and encrypted, relay-delayed contact with the outside.

"Standby." Bashe punched in some more code. An old identity shot of Elder Hodari filled the patches on our goggles as he came online. I hated these things. Every time someone talked they just showed an image of who was talking, an old ID shot. "Elder, the team is on-line."

"I'll make this brief. FutureBlack is a classified project. The official clearances will come down shortly, but Commander Bashe, your whole crew is going to be switched off the history project and on to FutureBlack. The Creoles knocked out another module early this morning. We have had to make the decision to accelerate our escape program. Our immediate future depends on finding a future. Some of us are betting on you guys to find that future for us."

Nobody said anything. We were trained to listen when a ranking officer was speaking. Whatever questions we had would be discussed later.

"We're bringing you guys in. The gang over at R-D have constructed working, time-forward transports and we have to do some quick forward probes to find a suitable space where we can build a community. We have no idea how far future we will have to go, nor do we have any idea of what we will find. They've been sending out box probes but . . ." He hesitated.

Juno spoke up. "They come back empty."

"How did you know that, Officer Juno?"

"The same thing happened when we first started our jumps. I thought those guys in R-D would understand that by now. Time warps can't transport unprocessed matter. That's why the jumps are so hard. When we get there, all we can bring back is what we remember . . . if we can get back at all."

"The R-D guys told us they could design a transport to jump as many as twenty people at a time."

"Yes, Elder. We can transport any number of people, we just can't guarantee retrieval, nor can we bring anything concrete back. Plus, there's the problem of pinpointing where we send people. Our calibrations are just not that good. About ten minutes is max before we lose reference signals. What you need are jumpers to act as scouts. The problem is that ten minutes is not enough time to reconnoiter whether a spot is safe. But then again, I imagine the new scanner might give us a bit more time."

"Between twenty-four and thirty hours, Officer Juno."

Juno let out a long, low whistle. "How did they do that?"

"I really don't understand all the technical stuff like you do, Officer Juno. Anyway, Commander Bashe, your crew has the most experience with time jumps and we have had to accelerate our escape plan. The new scanner calibration will be complete on this end within a couple of hours. It works exactly like the previous model except it has a finer calibration. The council has decided that the FutureBlack project is critical to our survival and for the time being we will put on hold all history-retrieval probes except for one more ju—"

"You want us to find Celine?"

"Officer Juno, I want you to test the new scanner. Now if you happen to find Celine during the test run, then so be it. After the test run, we will start immediately on the FutureBlack project. Copy?"

We all answered "forty" near simultaneously.

"Commander Bashe, download your new assignment. Oh, and one more thing. You're running silent from here on in. There will be no further direct contact until you file a mission report. Good luck, brothers and sisters. Commander Bashe?"

"Yes."

"Daughter, I love you."

"Love Black back at 'cha."

"A luta continua."

We all answered the salute and then the screen went blank. As I pulled off my helmet, I saw a faint smile on Muta's face. Maybe he and Celine would be reunited after all.

Jump center is eerie—we've got nine bodies laid out on slabs, surrounded by translucent tubes. Each of them looks like they are sleeping—or dead—and they are neither. They are suspended. Their minds are gone. No, not their minds. Juno always tells me it's not the mind we send out but the spirit, the life force. Their minds are still functioning—er, functional. If they had the life force they could get up and move and think and respond. I don't understand all of it, no matter how often Juno tries to explain.

Muta is, of course, looking at Celine, I mean, looking at Celine's body.

"Muta, I've got a good feeling that Juno is going to find Celine."

Muta doesn't respond to me. He touches the Pyrex shell with the tips of his fingers on his right hand. "Sheba, I appreciate your gesture, but—"

"No buts, Muta." I move past Ishmael's tube, stand beside Muta, and place my palm next to his hand. "If any of us can make it back, Celine will. She was . . . is our best jumper. She knows what she's doing. And Juno . . . you know Juno can work that scanner. He's going to find her and they'll make it back."

"We couldn't retrieve any of the others." He steps away from me and slowly looks around at our comatose comrades. I look directly in front of me to the unnerving sight of Harriett with her huge, unblinking, dark brown eyes popped wide open like she's playing a game of holding her breath, except her body metabolism is slowed so much she is technically alive but practically a vegetable.

Unfortunately, Muta was right. It really didn't look too good for Celine. Even though we had gotten pretty good at retrieval and we had had four successful jumps before we lost Celine—and it couldn't have come at a worse time. We lost her one day before yesterday's council meeting. Buzzard luck.

"Muta, I know how you feel."

"No, you don't. You know how *you* feel. You only *think* you know how I feel." An undercurrent of bitterness thickened the quiet wisp of Muta's normally massive voice. He stares at me and then looks away. After a short moment that seems like an eternity, Muta returns to his post at the head of Celine's pod.

This was why command was always discouraging intimate relations among team members, but here we were. Living in close quarters with each other for over a year at a time in this spherical module that was only about 4,500 meters in diameter, no human contact except among ourselves. Buried deep into the side of a mountain in what used to be Suriname. What else were we going to do but grow closer or get on each other's last little nerve, or both?

Muta leaned over and kissed the shield right above Celine's face. And then he embraced the tube like he was going to lift it physically, but instead he laid the side of his face on the coolness of the covering. I went to him and bent to hug him. I couldn't think of anything to say, so I didn't say anything, I just hummed an improvised song, hoping the vibrations would make Muta feel better, and, more than that, would make me feel better.

The intercom crackled with the unmistakable double whistle calling us to the control center.

I reluctantly peeled myself from Muta and started slowly out of the jump center. While the computer read my palm print before disengaging the automatic lock on the door, I turned to look at Muta, who was still looking at Celine. Even though my eyes had grown accustomed to the blue dimness of the jump center, at the distance of only ten meters or so, the whole scene was like I was in the audience watching a science fiction movie. It was hard to believe that nine comrades in suspension and one comrade nearly immobilized by grief was real.

"We've got a problem, y'all?" Juno was talking into his fist, which he was bouncing back and forth against his lips.

"The scanner's not ready?"

"No, Sheba, it's up and running fine. All systems go."

"So what's the problem?" I asked as I looked back and forth between Bashe and Juno. I could tell they had been talking before Muta and I arrived. Bashe had her arms folded and was peering at me like she was trying to look through me. I knew she didn't like me, and I knew why she didn't like me. I turned away from the nearly palpable distaste of her unblinking gaze. I flopped down to my console and as I looked around at the twelve empty consoles, I suddenly felt very, very weary. When I looked up, Bashe was still staring at me. I glanced briefly at Muta, who appeared to be deep in thought, then I peeped at Juno, who had his head down—as though the answer to whatever the shitty problem was lay between his boots—and then I closed my eyes.

"The new scanner only goes forward."

My head snapped up as I processed in shocked disbelief the meaning of what Juno had just calmly uttered. Juno avoided my eyes and turned toward Bashe. I followed his lead and clearly saw her nod an almost imperceptible but unmistakable signal to Juno. It was like everything had already been decided and nobody had told me or Muta any goddamn thing.

"So, we're just going to abandon Celine?" I blurted out louder and with more of an accusatory edge to my voice than I actually meant.

"So, so what's the problem?" Muta folded his arms across his chest and locked stares with Juno. For almost a full minute nobody said anything.

"Fuck! Why doesn't somebody say something?"

"Take it easy, Sheba."

Before I could spit my disagreement at Juno for even suggesting that I should be cool about *the problem*, Bashe interrupted our exchange, just like she had interrupted us when I was in Juno's pad.

Bashe gave me that same damn look, that same timbre in her voice. "Oh" was all she had said. Just "oh." As if one little silly syllable could explain everything. Could explain what I was doing sitting on Juno's bunk, and explain what she was doing visiting Juno's pad when her quarters were on the other side of the module. Oh!

"That's not the *real* problem."

I glared at her. What wasn't the real problem? The scanner? The fact that both of us were trying to get next to Juno? What?

"Not being able to go back and search for Celine seems like a *real* problem to me," I icily responded.

Juno got up and walked toward me. "We've got a solution for that, Sheba. The problem is the new scanner only goes forward and network central is only going to bring us topside for one more launch before they retool our module."

I knew we had to be on the surface to make a jump, and being exposed to satellite surveillance was a big risk that our position might be discovered or our security compromised, but Juno seemed to be suggesting something else. "So, I don't understand."

Bashe cut in quietly, "If we're going to search for Celine we have to do it on this next jump."

"But I thought he said the damn thing only went forward." I waved my hand with my thumb extended in Juno's direction without taking my eyes of off Bashe. "We can't find Celine by going forward."

"We're going to do a double jump."

"A what?" I blurted out incredulously.

"A double jump, Sheba," Juno said quietly, as though he was talking about running a routine module check.

"The problem is I don't know how to use the scanner. I mean, theoretically I know, but I don't have any experience at it and neither do you." Bashe actually gave me warm body language as she spoke. First she pointed to herself and then, as she said "neither do you," she placed her hand lightly on my shoulder.

It took me a minute to figure out what was going on. "Wait a minute, if we do a double jump and we use the old scanner and the new scanner, we're going to need an operator at each one—who's going to operate the transports?"

"I can handle the transport but I . . ." Muta stopped and we all silently filled in the rest, each of us remembering the day before yesterday when Muta had fumbled with the codes on what was supposed to be a routine jump. I was working the transport. Juno had been standing next to Muta assuring him that he could handle the scanner, when something went terribly wrong and within the short space of a few seconds we lost contact with Celine and by the time Juno took corrective measures her signal was fading fast.

Bashe walked over to Muta and stood directly in front of him. "Trooper Muta, you and Officer Juno will operate the scanners *and* the transports while Officer Sheba and I make the jumps. You *can* do this. You *have* to do this."

Muta visibly flinched as Bashe issued her instructions.

"But the old scanner. Is. In a different area. From the new. Scanner." The words leaked out of Muta's mouth in awkward clumps. "Suppose. Something. Goes wrong?"

"Nothing is going to go wrong." Bashe firmly grasped Muta by the shoulders. "And if something does go wrong, you will just have to deal with it. We will all have to deal with it." Starting with Juno, Bashe slowly surveyed our tiny crew.

"Muta is going to operate the old scanner and Juno is going to operate the new scanner." Bashe paused as the full impact of her words penetrated each of us. She turned to face me. "I will inject you and then I will inject myself. We will preset the transports and hope for the best."

"But you know that sometimes you have to adjust the levels on the transport. The risk is—"

Bashe cut off Muta's objections. "We have one shot, and one shot only, at retrieving Celine. We have lost nine other jumpers. We can't afford to lose Celine."

"I don't understand." Everybody looked at me like I was suggesting a mutiny or something. "You know I want to find Celine, but I don't understand taking the risk that we will lose Commander Bashe—I mean I'm not even worried about me." I hesitated to say what I was really thinking because I didn't want Muta to think I was being callous, but like Juno had said, what was so special about Celine other than that she had made eight successful jumps before we lost her? Of course, that was amazing, considering that nobody else had done more than three successful jumps.

"I don't believe we lost the other eight."

"Juno, what did you say?" This was tripping me out. Juno slumped farther down in his console.

"I said I don't believe we lost the other eight. I believe something happened. I don't know what, but I know it wasn't pilot error. . . ."

"So you're saying I lost Celine but all those other eight people just disappeared?" Muta took a few steps in Juno's direction. I could see that Muta was really roiled. "You were at the controls for six of those other eight. What happened if it wasn't pilot error?"

"I don't know what happened, trooper, but I do know it wasn't pilot error." Juno had such a fierce expression on his face when he looked up at Muta that Muta actually backed up two steps.

"Muta, we reviewed the logs. I personally inspected each entry, looked at the video of the procedures, pored over all the printouts. There was no indication of pilot error and—"

"Except for when I lost Celine."

"Except for when *we* lost Celine." Bashe moved next to Juno. "We lost Celine on Juno's watch, Muta. I have never held you responsible. Besides, the question now is how to carry out our mission."

"That's simple," I replied. "We do a forward jump. Gather the required information, file it with control central, and that's all she wrote as far as fulfilling our mission."

Bashe shook her head from side to side. "Officer Sheba, we have multiple missions. One is to do a forward jump and the other is to retrieve Trooper Celine. And I intend for us to accomplish both. Understood?"

Bashe took turns silently assessing each of us. No one moved or said anything. Finally, I broke the silence. "So, when is jump time?"

"07:00 hours."

I checked my console. It was 22:48 hours. "Well, I guess I ought to go get some sleep. Or is there another problem we need to solve before jump time?"

"You and I just have to decide who's jumping forward and who's jumping backward," Bashe said just as I was about to shove off.

"Tell you what. Why don't you just surprise me in the morning," I said sarcastically and started walking toward quarters.

Bashe reached out and touched me gently, not to stop me but to share her feelings physically. "Sheba, you know me. You know I hate surprises and bes—"

"Oh," I interrupted Bashe's comments. "Well, surprises don't bother me. I'm a jumper. I've been there and back three times before. Since this will be your first time"—I looked Bashe dead in the eyes and as I brushed past her, I cavalierly tossed my decision over my shoulder without breaking stride—"you make the call. Make it easy on yourself."

I kept expecting Bashe to order me to stop, but the only sound I heard was the slap of my sandals thudding against the double-thick synthetic hard rubber flooring.

I don't handle rejection well and that's why I'm careful about what I ask for. I don't even know why I am sitting here. I know Juno doesn't have any deep feelings for me and—

"Unless I'm really misreading the situation, you're going to have to search for Celine and Muta is going to have to be your operator. He's not comfortable enough at the scanner controls to work the new scanner and the old scanner doesn't go forward, and . . ."

He just stopped talking. I looked up at him as I leaned back against the wall. All of the compartments were the same tiny size: a six-foot bunk, a small desk with a hutch, a cabinet, and that was it. Everything looked just like my compartment. Juno was staring at me. He sat down on the bunk on the opposite end from where I was hunched into the corner.

"What?" I gathered myself for whatever Juno was about to say.

"Sheba, I know you didn't come over here to talk about the jump tomorrow."

I hate it when people want to make you beg for what you want. One part of me was pissed. Pissed that I was here. Pissed that I even thought about coming here. And another part of me was so damn needy. I knew tomorrow I could be dead, or worse—who knows what happens to your spirit when you get lost out there? Your body vegetates here in jump control and your spirit . . . fuck it. I start to get up but don't. When I look up, Juno is not even looking at me.

"Why do you think I came?"

"Sheba, I'm not going to play that game."

"I'm not playing."

He looked away, silently took a deep breath, and then looked at me. Without sounding like I was some kind of freak, how could I explain to him that I didn't want to die horny? Sacrifice is one thing, but if liberation doesn't include lovemaking then how liberated are we? Was it my fault that there were only four of us left? Muta is thinking about Celine. And Bashe is our leader.

The intercom buzzed, interrupting my scheming on how to make a move on Juno without looking like I was just throwing myself at him. I knew it was Bashe; maybe I had conjured her up by thinking about her at that moment.

Juno responded, "Yes."

"Juno, can we talk?" It was like she knew I was there and was choosing her words carefully.

"Affirmative. I'll be over in five."

"Okay."

Juno looked at me as he stood up. "This shouldn't take long."

"Does that mean you want me to wait here for you to come back?"

Juno hesitated. "Sheba . . ."

"Tell you what. I'll be in my compartment if you want to stop by when you finish talking with Bashe."

"No, Sheba, let's not play those games. I'm not going to stop by and I—"

"And you don't want me to wait here."

Juno didn't say anything. I put my head down on my knees. When I looked up he was still standing in the doorway. "Sheba, I'll see you tomorrow morning, 06:30."

I got up and started toward the doorway, squeezing between the desk and the bunk. Juno stepped into the corridor. He grabbed my arm as I brushed past him. "It would be worse if I let you stay."

I looked him full in the eyes. He let go of my arm and then turned away. "Don't forget to secure your quarters," I said. Juno kept walking away, not even acknowledging what I had just said. Then I heard his door automatically slide shut and lock. I headed in the opposite direction back to my compartment.

After I rounded the first corner I stopped and sat down on the floor. I didn't want to go back to my little lonely space. I didn't want to be alone. I know it sounded so undisciplined not to be able to face the severity of our situation. But sometimes you get tired of being strong, alone. Sometimes it would be nice to be held by someone before you made a leap into the unknown.

Suddenly all I heard was the hum of our module, all the equipment and computers, the air supply, the power generators. I put my hand down on the floor and could feel vibrations. I knew I was just going stir crazy. Except for the jumps, I had not been topside in the natural world for almost a year. And the last time I had made love was with Harriett and that was over six months ago. And . . . I threw my head back and intentionally bumped it on the wall. Two, three, four times. I never saw people get horny in none of the space movies. There might be a romance, but . . . I jumped up. I must have been sitting there feeling pitiful for at least ten minutes. Although I tried not to think about it, I knew I was going to do what I usually did when I felt this way: masturbate, fall asleep, and forget about it.

When I turned the last corner and saw Bashe, her bald head bowed, eyes closed, sitting in a lotus position, meditating beside my compartment door, I was shocked. I thought she and Juno would be going at it by now. I stopped, but she must have sensed my presence because she calmly looked up at me and smiled. I saluted her as she stood up. She returned the salute and then opened her arms to embrace me. I just stood still. Bashe stepped forward and hugged the rigidity of my body to her.

"Sheba, I'm not your enemy. In about seven or so hours we are going to face a very tough situation." Bashe relaxed her arms and stepped back. "I came here to talk with you because . . . well, because I need, no, because I *want* our team to be a team. We are down to four people and after tomorrow . . . well, who knows. This situation has been very tough on all of us. I admire the way you have held up. I wish I had your spunk."

Bashe was trying to use textbook psych on me. I looked her in the eyes briefly. What I saw there frightened me. She was totally in control of herself. I was shaking inside. I turned to face my door.

"Sheba, I am thirty-seven years old. Juno is thirty-four. You are twenty-six. I know—"

"Don't forget about Muta."

"Muta is not part of this triangle."

I refused to look at her. I started to say What triangle, but I knew I wasn't prepared for whatever might be Bashe's response.

"I have prepared myself for years to be able to do whatever needed to be done and to control my emotions. I believe I can face anything. Right now, I have questions. Make no mistake, I am going to go forward with our mission, but at the same time I am questioning. Questioning everything."

"I don't understand."

"There is something happening out there and we don't know what it is. We don't know what happened to our crew. There is a great unknown, but I am prepared to face it and I think you are, too. But the unknowns outside are not my major concern at this moment. What concerns me is our inability to face the problems we know about."

She paused. I looked over at her briefly. Bashe's unblinking stare was fixed on me. "I don't understand," I pretended.

"You want to be with Juno and I want to be with Juno. Neither one of us is going to get our wish. We don't need to carry this baggage with us when we do our jumps tomorrow. Juno is committed to celibacy during the course of this mission. I know because we've talked about it. And because he practices . . ." Bashe paused. She was still staring at me. She was still not blinking. "It is my responsibility to monitor everything that happens on this unit."

I cannot return Bashe's unblinking focus so instead I look at a spot in the middle of her forehead just above her eyes, the place where the mystics say the third eye is located, the place where Hindu women wear a red dot. I hate it when I lose a battle of wills, but Bashe is by far the most intense person I have ever encountered. I have never been able to stare her down. Never. At the same time I am trying not to succumb to her hypnotic force, I reactively wonder, How much was "everything"? Did she really mean everything—bathroom, bed? Did she mean there is never a time when someone isn't watching us?

Bashe firmly but softly repeated herself, "Everything."

"That's a lot." Did they lie to us about not having cameras in our compartments, about allowing us that small bit of privacy? Had Bashe watched me touching myself?

"Sheba, I came here to thank you for not attacking me and to let you know that I do not stand between you and Juno." Then she reached out and embraced me again.

I actually shuddered. I couldn't help myself. Bashe scared the shit out of me.

"Good luck on your jump tomorrow."

I mumbled something in reply, but I don't know what. Probably, Yeah, and good luck to you, too. Her hug was both a shelter and a trap. As she stepped back after holding me, all I could think to do was snap off a salute.

"Comrade Sister Sheba, every little thing is going to be all right." Bashe didn't return my salute; instead she kissed my right cheek, smiled at me, turned slowly, and seemed to float down the corridor back toward her quarters. I found out just how much I was shaking when I pressed my trembling palm to the cool screen to I-D open my door.

There is no time. Time is an illusion. Everything is now. The past. The future. It's all now. All going on at the same time. And no matter how random or chaotic, it's always the same. Changing but the same. And I have no fear because I don't need to be me. In order to exist. I could ride the wind as a leaf, hug the earth as a tree.

Juno is so clever. He tried to explain to me that every death is a birth because to die is to be born on another plane since we can neither add to nor subtract from existence, only transform in terms of what plane we exist on.

I guess if I could have children I might feel differently. I jump so well because it really doesn't matter if I come back. I have no fear. No anxiety.

I am trying to describe the color I see when I close my eyes. To myself. I'm trying to explain me to me. Inhale nostrils. Exhale mouth. Suppose I am not coming back but going to. Suppose. Suppose. Suppose.

I tried to talk to Celine about jumping. But her experience was so different from mine. I think she wanted to be conscious. I just let myself be. And become. We searched by vibrations. I was confident that people who struggled gave off a certain vibe and tried to tune in to that vibe of struggle, and let my own self-awareness merge into my host. In a sense, I guess, I became one with my host.

I remember, once, when I was in this guy who was living in the swamps, I don't know. It was so comfortable. He was so sure of himself. All alone out there. It wasn't even a thought process. It was a certainty of spirit. He was going to die out there rather than return. And I had to struggle with myself not to stay with him. Maybe that's what happened to the other jumpers. Maybe once we got inside a host who was really committed to our people, maybe we decided to stay. Just add our spirits to them. Make them that much stronger.

Something like Bashe. Maybe she has a jumper from some other place inside her. Juno says that a lot of the traditional ceremonies with the potions that people drank, and all the dancing and drumming, was just another way of time-traveling and that people actually plugged into other times and other places and other people when they went into those trances.

I don't know. All I know is that we don't really know as much as we think we know. Who really knows what life is and how life works? Our job was to find the ones who didn't give up, regardless of what odds they faced. Find them. And learn their stories. Because those were the ones who were lost to us. And at the same time, those were the ones who made it possible for us to be us.

I found myself thinking about being in that brother in the swamp and the time he slipped back to the plantation one night to be with this woman. She didn't hardly know him. But she knew what he was. She gave him some food. And she gave him herself. And I was with him when he lay down with her. And when he came I came. Damn. What an orgasm that was.

Did she get pregnant? Is any of this passed on in the DNA? Juno says that there is never just one explanation for anything. Everything has a multiplicity of factors and for sure, every new birth is a result of the mating of at least two separate forces. I'm not a thinker. Juno likes to deal with these kinds of questions, but I know how to make stuff happen. That's why I'm jumping right now.

Bashe was who I last saw. She had injected me. And was leaning over me. And squeezed my hand gently. And I felt loved.

Now it's that pulsing dark, that warm brown that you get when you hold your face toward the sun with your eyes tightly closed.

I always go to sleep, just totally relax and drift. Usually I think about colors. Yellow-cream. The feel of warm water. The sound of my own breath: in through my nostrils, out through my mouth, in, out, nostrils, mouth. Butter. I've only tasted it once. It was soft, soft. Had been lying in a shallow dish on a counter all morning. Soft to the touch. I tasted it on my fingertip. Looked over the ridge and there was the soft sun rising, yellow. Yellow as the butter.

I have the feeling that I have been someone else before and am becoming someone else now. I lock in on the vibrations. I feel like I am getting close to Celine but I'm not there yet, and yet, somehow, I'm getting these vibes that feel good, feel right, feel Black like the Black we're trying to save. I will go with this and see where it leads. . . .

This is strange. Because I know this neighborhood. I know these sidewalks. The houses. What goes on behind closed doors. The people. I recognize almost everyone I see. Foots is standing on the corner. I lower the driver's-side window and stick my fist up in the air.

"Hey, Kalamu."

"Give thanks, Foots. How you be?" He crosses the street toward me, I ease my foot down on the clutch and ease the shift into first but keep the clutch to the floor.

"Man, I'm just getting ready for Jazzfest. I got some designs to lay on them."

Foots, sibling of Billy Paul, he's got some heavy new jewelry to sell. He pushes his hand into my open window and shakes. The car is rocking, I have Incognito turned up so loud. I like to ride with the windows up and the music up higher than the windows, which are all the way up. Foots smiles at me, bopping his head to that beat. I ease up on the clutch and swing on 'round the corner.

I'm fifty-four years old and sometimes I feel weary, but then I get a spurt of energy. I don't know where from. Actually, I believe all my extra energy comes from either one, or maybe both, of the major life forces other than the one I was born with. They are: one, the here and now; two, the been here and gone; and three, the soon come to be. The been here and the soon come offer a reason to keep going, 'cause if it were left to me in the present, I could just check out at this point. My work is relatively complete. I have done my do. Fought the good fight. Reared—actually, to be honest and correct about it, *helped* to rear—some slamming young people, those biologically from me as well as a number of others whom I have touched. And, well, what else is left but a little bit more of the same?

I think about my parents. My mother dead of cancer at fifty-seven, and my father dying suddenly some years later. There are days when I dream about one or the other of them, usually my father—and when they were both alive, I always thought I was closer to my mother, but life is its own reality, not what we think, or wish, or hope for, but what it is, and the truth, the real, is sometimes something other than we are ready to admit.

There is something in me that will not let me stop, and yet, I don't believe in god. I don't disbelieve. I just have no opinion on that issue. Once I left the church as a teenager, no organized form of religion has ever appealed to me. Spirituality, well, I studied stuff, but anything organized around a specific system was just, well, was beyond where I was willing to go, or maybe not as far out as where I am. So when I say I believe in the ancestors and the unborn, I don't mean it in any concrete way except to say that there is something inside me I can't explain. Except I know it's there.

It's almost noon and I have not eaten anything at all yet today. But the music has me feeling *upful*. After unfolding myself from the driver's seat, I stand beside the car a moment. The weather is warm. Sun in March.

When I get inside I call Lynn and we talk about workshop next week. I will be out of town and she will lead workshop and choose the study piece. Immediately I jump on-line and spend the next couple of hours doing e-mail. Fortunately, I don't have to teach school today and then, as is always happening in Treme, I hear a brass band in the distance, sounding like it is coming this way. I jump up.

Sometimes I ignore the bands, but other times I go see what's going on. As I step down to the sidewalk, the procession is rounding the corner and there is this little girl, maybe six or seven years old, prancing beside the lead trumpet. At times she looks up at the horn player, at other times she is dancing so intently her eyes get that faraway stare like you see when people catch the spirit. Her little limbs jerk lithely, but not like a puppet on a string, rather like there is something inside her bucking to get out. Her knobby little knees wobble from side to side. She can't weigh no more than a matchstick but she's flowing like a willow tree rocking in the breeze. I am transfixed by her; there is something about the way she dances that is older than she is. Something familiar. But I don't know her, have not seen her in the neighborhood before. I feel like I should know her. She has that Dionne Warwick kind of face, triangular with almond-shaped eyes that sit at a slight upward angle on her dark face. She is not smiling. She is so serious about this dancing. I just look at her. When she jumps, turns around, squats, hands on knees and backs it up, I fall out. A whole procession of people passes, but all I see is this young girl. Dancing. Dancing. Dancing down the street.

"We're locked on. We got her!"

At first I didn't know what Muta was talking about. I'm leaning against the transport table for support. I always feel weak after a jump, like I want to sleep.

I look around the launch area for something yellow. There is nothing. Why am I looking for something yellow? And then I look up and directly above me is a yellow light on the ceiling connected to the transport control. I smile. I knew I wasn't crazy. . . .

"Sheba, did you hear me? Power up Celine's transport. We got her."

Celine? Transport? Power up . . . ?

"Sheba, hurry. We're going to lose her if the transport is not functioning."

I try to move quickly, but I stumble. I don't know what's wrong with me. It takes so much effort to take one step. What am I doing? I have that lost feeling, as if someone woke me in the middle of a deep sleep and asked me to solve calculus problems.

"Fifty-eight ticks and counting."

Celine looks so perfect. It's funny, she could be dead. . . . Damn, what am I saying. She is dead. For all practical purposes. She is dead. But she doesn't really look dead, or is it that I don't want her to be dead, or to look dead? Her skin is healthy looking; there is blood circulating through her, although at a very, very slow rate, sort of intermittent rather than continuous.

I remember us playing around once. Wrestling. She had me around the waist trying to flip me, and I was holding her neck for leverage; she couldn't flip me without me falling on top of her. And our heads were close together. I remember the wonderful sweetness of her breath. Not an artificial sweetness, but real sweetness. Deep inside of her she is sweet. And I know she shits like everybody else does, but her intestines, or at least her stomach, has got to be the healthiest in the world. Soft and cool. That was the thing. We were wrestling but her breath was still coming out soft and cool. And sweet. But her body was tough. I mean mostly muscle and bone, no fat, no padding. She must have had muscles all up in her breasts. Her neck was like a steel cord. And I could feel her fingers gripping me in a dead man's grip. . . .

"SHEBA! Code Black. Fourteen clicks and counting. Set the switches, Sheba."

Eight-zero-niner. Enter. The switches run through the colors. Starting at red, burn through to amber. And then one by one. Green. Green. Green. Power up.

I look over at Muta. "Power up."

Muta is lost in the gyrations of multitasking. Keeping the beat, easying back on the transport accelerator. Tapping in code with his right hand. Holding the frequency attenuator with his left hand and bumping it up at appropriate moments. His left foot tapping a beat for the vibration resonator. And his right foot dropping harmonics— Juno always said the harmonics is the key to making everything work. Watching Muta from the rear he looks just like a jazz drummer playing keyboards and drums at the same time.

This was Juno's innovation. Instead of using a gyroscope to set and lock the rhythm, the operator had to establish the flow. Juno said flow allowed for maximum variation. The jumper could go wherever, experience whatever, change, flip in and out of time zones, in and out of hosts and it was no problem, except if the operator couldn't keep up. The old way with the fixed rhythm never yielded great results because we would so seldom find somebody functioning at whatever vibrational frequency we were locked on, but this way we could change to fit the conditions.

"Celine!" Muta pushed me aside like I was a fly buzzing his face. He was lifting the cover on Celine's transport before I fully understood what was happening.

I looked down at Celine's body. It wasn't moving. But the gauges on the transport control panel indicated that she was alive. She was back.

"Celine." Muta was almost crying. Celine was not moving. He started checking for her pulse, and then he shook her gently. "Come on, baby. Wake up. Wake up."

There was no sense in telling him to stop. He felt for her pulse by the big vein in the side of the neck. And he smiled his huge smile, the one that made him so attractive.

"Her heart is beating."

I leaned over to put my ear next to her nose and I smelled her breath. "She's back," I whispered. "Celine is back."

Muta broke down at that point. Sort of made a choking sound and let his head keel over onto Celine's chest. He was crying, softly at first, then loudly enough that I knew he was not embarrassed about it and was just letting it go. Happy crying. He was hugging her, his face buried into her bosom. Hugging her and crying. And calling her name, between sobs. Over and over.

Then Celine's hand rose up; the gesture was so slow and so graceful it looked like something you see in a dream. Her hand moved. Up and then out like she was reaching for something, and then her fingers spread apart, wide apart. And just as slowly she brought her hand to rest on Muta's head and stroked his head over and over, like what I imagine a mother does to a baby suckling her breast.

Now I had to turn away. This was too intimate for me to witness. Muta was still crying when I heard Celine's voice drawl like she had been drugged: "Muuuu-taaaaa. Whyyyy. Youuuuu. Cryinnnng?"

None of our palm prints would open the module. We had not been coded in, but we could see through the glass. Juno was thrashing away, his fingers flying, rocking back and forth, his knees pumping furiously—I had never seen him so animated at the controls. Something must have gone wrong.

"Dag, I didn't know we had two scanners," Celine says out loud, although not directly to either Muta or me.

"It's brand new. This is the first time—" I said.

"Whose jumping—not Bashe?"

Muta answered quietly. "There's no one else left to jump."

"How far back are they going?"

"Celine"—I reach out and touch her elbow—"it's a future jump."

"A future jump?" Her eyes grow wide as though she dared not believe me. "When did all this happen?"

"You've been gone a long time."

"Sheba, I thought you said it was only three days, some hours."

"Yeah, well, three days is a long, long time around here."

"Damn, something is wrong." We both turned and stared at Muta as he quietly sized up the situation and confirmed my suspicion.

"How can you tell?" I asked.

"Because look at the rhythm he's using with his left foot and see how rapidly he's stopping and going with his right foot. That's not normal, that's an extremely high level of activity. Plus he keeps swinging the attenuator to extremes in both directions. Damn."

"What?"

"It's beautiful. Beautiful the way he's working those scanner controls. How can he move that fast and not lose it, but look, he hasn't dropped a beat." Muta had his hands up beside his face like he was cutting off glare, or like a kid staring into a movie-scope. "But I still think something is wrong."

Now all three of us had our faces pressed to the transparent wall separating us from the control module.

"This is weird. I feel like we should be in there."

"Doing what, Celine?"

"Muta, you know there is always something we can do. Didn't you just say it looks like something is wrong?"

I suck my teeth. "If they wanted us in there, they would have included our palm prints in the access codes."

"Maybe they didn't think about it. But on the other hand, even if they don't want us, maybe they *need* us."

"Celine, you're always so positive."

"Thanks, Sheba."

"That wasn't a compliment," I half joke.

"No, you were just telling the truth, and it's good to know that I am appreciated." Celine chuckled. It was good to hear her laughter again.

For a couple of long minutes no one says anything. Juno has been working like a man possessed. Suddenly I notice that Juno is wearing a helmet—Muta only wore earphones. "Muta, why is Juno on helmet?"

" 'Cause he's flying blind."

"Flying blind? What does that mean?"

"It means he's blocking out everything around him and only seeing the scanner codes and getting aural feedback through the ear phones," Celine answered me matter-of-factly.

"Yeah, but the helmet does funny things to your hand-and-foot coordination; you can't hear yourself operating the controls and there's almost no tactile feedback."

"Yeah, you get more control of the input but you get less feedback in terms of what you're doing. Juno tried to show me how to use the helmet but I preferred the earphones."

I glanced over at Celine; not only was she our best jumper, she also was pretty good at operating the scanner controls.

"Look, you see how fast he's doing code with his right hand and how smooth he's maneuvering with his left hand at the same time? I believe he's bringing Bashe back now."

I couldn't see any difference in what Juno was doing.

"Damn, when I grow up, I want to be able to control a scanner like Juno," Muta muttered softly, shaking his head in admiration.

"If you put the time in, you can do it. But even if you don't get any better, you can transport me anytime," Celine said, and then those two fools smiled at each other like they were both the first and the last people on earth to fall in love.

"Oh, no. Bashe!" Muta pounded on the window trying to get Juno's attention. Bashe was back alright, but her body was thrashing from the waist down, her head spastically jumping like she was convulsing. Juno finally looked up, tore off his helmet, and tossed it aside in one quick motion while bounding over to Bashe, who was still strapped in the transport, her arms flailing frantically.

Juno threw himself atop Bashe's body and locked restraints on her wrists and then he gripped her head with both hands.

Celine figured it out immediately. "She's epileptic. That jump could have killed her. Secure her tongue, Juno, so she doesn't choke on it. Give her an injection and then hope she pulls through okay."

Juno moved as though he heard everything Celine said, right down to the injection. That went too smoothly. It was like Juno was prepared for the seizure to happen. And then it hit me. "I bet you that's why they locked us out; they knew."

"No," Celine said, "it's not that simple. They know I've got the most medical training; they would want me in there."

"Yeah, but you just got back, and nobody knew where you were or if you wanted to come back," I joked, even though it wasn't funny.

"I hear that, Sheba. But damn, Juno looked like he was prepared—"

"Celine, that's just what I was thinking."

Bashe was completely still now. Juno finally stopped to look around and noticed us standing there. He went to the console and opened the door.

We rushed in, nobody saying anything, everybody looking at Bashe. Juno eventually came over and hugged Celine. "Welcome home, Trooper Celine." And then Juno dapped up Muta. "Good job, Trooper Muta."

We all smiled briefly.

"Celine, please run a check on Commander Bashe. Officer Sheba, have you done a full debriefing yet?"

"No. We came straight over here to see if you all needed some help."

"Trooper Muta, do a full debriefing with Officer Sheba. After you and Officer Sheba have recorded the debrief, return to this module. Celine and I will see to Commander Bashe."

Both Muta and I snapped off salutes. Juno was not hesitating in taking charge. He was clear and direct in his orders and unhesitating about what had to be done, but I could see the concern swimming in his eyes, which were glazed over with moisture that I assume was tears or stress, or both.

As we were leaving, I heard Juno say something about Bashe predicting this might happen. How do you get up the nerve to volunteer for a jump if you know you're an epileptic?

After everything was over, we all received promotions except for Bashe, who was already a commander. The ceremony, as such, was scheduled to take place within another two weeks when our small crew was to be brought topside. Meanwhile, here we were receiving final orders from Bashe.

Bashe looked at each one of us before saying a word, and then she looked down before finally raising her head proudly.

"Please stop me if I go too fast. I'm going to skip the official rigmarole. The deal is a truce has been declared and we are all being disbanded. Of course it is not going to be announced like that, but the end result will be, the war is over."

"Bashe, wait—you said, disbanded?"

"Yes, Muta. Disbanded. CC is being absorbed into—"

"I don't want to hear it," I blurted out my immediate reaction. "The jumps, the units . . ."

"Sheba, we were the only unit to survive. All the others either failed to complete their assignments or they were captured or destroyed. The elders decided the cost was too high and—"

"What about 'no surrender, no compromise'?" I asked.

"Sheba, the truth is I don't know." There was a long silence while we waited for Bashe to continue. "I don't think any of us know. This movement has been our lives. I grew up this way. My father was in this movement before I was born." Bashe fell silent. Her head was angled slightly upward and to the side. If you watched her eyes you saw them shifting back and forth like she was reading something.

"This can't be it. Not like this!"

"Sheba, calm down."

"Not with a bang, but with a whimper."

I looked over at Juno. Leave it to him suddenly to quote poetry at a moment like this. "Who said that?"

Bashe didn't even look in my direction when she answered my question. "T.S. Eliot."

"Damn, Juno, at least you could quote a Black poet," I retorted quietly.

"Is there some kind of amnesty program or something? You know some of us . . ."

"I know, Muta. Some of us are wanted. From what I understand there is some kind of table of responsibilities and consequences, and depending on what you're wanted for, they've worked out . . . Look, all of you are cool. Any of you who wants to go back can do so without prejudice. I've checked on your cases."

"Bashe, what are the options? I mean suppose we don't want to go back. Where else can we go?"

"Celine, as far as I know there is no other place to go. OnePlanet is everywhere."

"Well, I'm not going back. I'll stay here, if I have to." I looked at Bashe, who was listening to me and sending out support-vibes.

"When I said, no surrender, no compromise, I meant it. I meant every word of it."

Juno spoke up suddenly. "Bashe, what about you? Can you go back?"

"No."

"No, you can't or no, you won't?"

"Sheba, I can't and I won't."

"So, what are you going to do?"

"I don't know."

"Well, I tell you what, wherever you decide to go, count me in, 'cause I don't want to go back."

"I'm with Juno on that," I said.

Before Bashe could respond, Celine spoke up. "Muta and I really, really have to talk this over. You know . . ." Celine paused. "My first inclination is to stay here with Bashe. . . ."

"Y'all, there is no here to stay at. Don't you understand? This is the last module and tomorrow it will be turned over—"

"I mean, Bashe, I understand. But what I was saying is that my first inclination is to go wherever you go and—"

"I thank all of you for your support and for the confidence you have in me, but right now you are being confronted with a reality you probably never imagined. You don't need to make any rash decisions. You need to think about your future. You understand? Think about what it is you want for the rest of your life. Sheba, you are still very young. You could literally start over. Celine and Muta, you two have each other. Go start a family. If you register, you can have a child." Bashe looked deep into my eyes and then deep into Celine's eyes and Muta's eyes. Her look was saying much more than her words.

"What about Juno?" I asked, even though I knew the answer already, or at least I thought I knew the answer. Juno wasn't going back.

"What about Juno?" Bashe never even glanced his way, but instead bore into me with those searching eyes.

"No, I was just saying, you gave advice to me and to Muta and Celine, but you didn't say anything to Juno."

Bashe smiled. "Are you asking me if Juno and I are getting together?"

It got quiet. Real quiet. I looked away. It was still quiet. I peeked over at Juno. He never even looked up.

"Well, Sheba, is that what you want to know?"

"Ah, I was just, ah, I mean Juno did say he was going to go wherever you go."

"I repeat, are you asking me if Juno and I are getting together?"

"What the fuck, it doesn't make any difference, does it? Just like that, it's over. The Community Council has cut some kind of deal and some people will get taken care of and the majority of us will become some little cog in some urban center. And shit. Who cares, fuck it. I guess it was nice while it lasted but the fun is over and it's back to the goddamn real world."

"Sheba, you're hurt and confused at the moment. Don't say any more . . . but then again, maybe you should. Maybe you should get all of that out of your system." Bashe walked over to me and put a hand on my shoulder. "The truth is CC negotiated a deal for the whole community. Most of you will be acquired as normal citizens, and all of us, rank commander and above, will be sent to a restricted zone for an indefinite time."

Her touch felt so light and yet so strong.

"Sheba, do you want to be exiled on a restricted zone with me?" Of course I did not answer her. I could not lie and say I was ready for a life that was closer to death. Those zones were everything we were fighting against.

"I didn't think so. I don't think any of you wants to go through that. Right?" Bashe looked at each of us in turn. None of us spoke up to say we wanted to join her in such a harsh and pitiful place. "CC offered us the option of remaining underground, but we would probably never get back to the world again. I wouldn't even bring that up to you all; confused as you are right now, we might have elected to do something irreversible that we would surely come to regret."

Bashe was right. I really couldn't see myself living the rest of my life on this module. I could easily see myself dying in battle, but living like this, I just never foresaw anything like this as being our future.

"Our movement ebbs and flows. There are no guarantees except that we must struggle. Sometimes we will have to withdraw and lie dormant, other times we must throw ourselves against impossible odds. Muta, Celine, Sheba, Juno, I love each of you. Fiercely. I do. I know your hearts are strong. I know your minds are clear. Your beliefs are with our people. I know this like my blood knows my body."

Bashe looked at me last. I didn't realize I was crying until Bashe stepped to me and wiped a tear off my cheek with her bare hand. Bashe hugged me and then drew back.

"You know how in our studies we found out that different groups of our ancestors had different ways of dealing with slavery? Some of us adapted and some of us committed suicide. Some of us resisted and most of us just kind of did whatever we had to do to survive."

At first nobody answered Bashe. We all just waited for her to continue. And then Juno spoke up. "Bashe, we know the story. You're going to walk into the sea, aren't you?"

"Yes."

Bashe stepped away from me and continued talking to all of us. "I guess I just don't have it. I don't have that something inside that enables a person to put up with bullshit. You know, I used to wonder what our ancestors did when a slave revolt failed. The ones who were still alive but who had been part of the rebellion. What did they do? Well, we're about to find out, aren't we?"

"Bashe, you are the bravest person I know." Celine was speaking very, very softly. "You took that jump knowing that it could have killed you . . . and you did it so that there would be a chance, just a chance, that I could be brought back. I owe you my life; I know that."

"Celine, you know what you owe me?" Bashe walked over to Celine and embraced her and then embraced Muta. "You owe me the two of y'all having a child together. I chose not to have a child. Maybe if I . . ." Bashe didn't finish her thought.

"I tell you what, crew, this is a lot to think about. Let's reassemble in the morning. Why don't we all just sleep on what we want to do. Juno, Sheba, Celine, and Muta, each of you has the option of going anywhere in the world you want to go. You will receive full global citizenship, a grade-omega passport, and a choice of service or research jobs. The details of the deal are being finalized as we . . . I'm terrible at giving speeches. Meet back here 09:00. That's all. Dismissed. Oh, there is one more thing: CC is bringing us topside in the morning. Tonight will be our last night aboard this module. That's all. Dismissed."

We started to snap off a salute, but the words wouldn't come. "We can't even say 'a luta continua' anymore," I said to no one in particular.

"Sheba, we can still say it." Bashe looks at me with a tenderness I hadn't recognized before. "It's just that the struggle will now have to take a different form."

The jerk of the module docking topside woke me up early, a little after six. Our compartments are soundproof. Someone could have been shouting outside our door and we would not be able to hear him, but we could feel the motion of the module, which was always moving this way and that through a maze of tunnels. To evade detection, our module was never still for more than five or six hours except when we docked topside for a jump, and that usually took no longer than two hours.

Before I even realized what I was doing, I had finished packing and placed the bundle on my bunk. When I got tired of standing up and looking down at my gear, I flopped on the bed and kicked at the backpack. The kick felt so good I let go with a second and stronger kick. The pack thudded against the wall at the foot of my bunk. I kicked it again. And then another kick.

All my possessions were in that pack and I doubt if it weighed fifty pounds. None of us really owned anything much. We didn't need much, not even clothes, in this controlled environment.

I wondered what Juno was doing, what Bashe was doing, whether they were doing whatever they were doing together. I looked over at the computer screen. It was just a little after seven. I couldn't just sit anymore.

Out in the hall, I just started walking. I didn't have any particular destination. I was avoiding Juno's compartment. That's one place I wasn't going.

Where was I going to go?

I decided to go say goodbye to all the jumpers who never made it back. When I got to the jump room, the room was completely dark; not even the usual night lights were on. And the door was open. We never left this door open. Even before I keyed up the lights, I knew something was wrong, but I had no idea how wrong. An involuntary gasp jumped out of my mouth when I saw that the room was empty. For almost a minute, I couldn't believe it. All the pods were empty. Empty!

Things were moving too fast. How could all this have happened so quickly? I had no choice. I had to go see Bashe.

The door was open. Her compartment was empty. I ran to the control center. Sprinted. No one was there. Everybody couldn't have left me. At control center I turned on the security monitors and started searching for Bashe, Juno, Muta, and Celine. Anybody. Everybo—and there was Juno operating the new scanner. But who was jumping? I ran down the hall.

When I got to the new scanner room, Juno was standing in the open doorway, just like he was waiting for me. He started talking without looking up at me. "She's gone. Jumped somewhere into the future, and she's not coming back."

I looked into the room and there was Bashe's body, laid out, perfectly still and unplugged. I glanced over at the scanner, it was off. None of the transport lights were on.

I kept trying to get a grip on my mind, but I couldn't think a straight thought.

She'd left us. I looked over at Juno and when he finally looked up at me, I was stunned. His eyes were troubled, reddish. He wearily rubbed the heels of his hands into his eye sockets.

"Bashe woke me up early this morning and asked me to send her on a jump and to disconnect her after she was out there."

"You could have said no."

Juno just sadly shook his head in response. "If you had asked me I wouldn't have told you no. Why should I tell Bashe no?"

I didn't know what to say. This was all too much for me to process. I just sort of shut down, turned away from Juno and looked at Bashe's body.

"I used to believe in karma," Juno said, "at the same time I believed in evolution. I mean, all the scientific evidence supports some form of evolution. But then I could never get with white people ruling the world, being the dominant branch of the species. Dominance and karma just don't go together. In fact, dominance seems to be what evolution is about and . . . well, there are so many people who didn't survive, who are now extinct. That was evolution, but was there any justice in that?"

I only half heard what Juno said. It was like he was babbling, talking to himself more than talking to me.

"Juno, I don't understand. Everything is breaking down and you're talking about karma and evolution, and . . . and, well, this doesn't make sense. None of this, I mean all of this . . . it's like chaos, just plain chaos."

"Exactly. Like I said, I used to believe in karma and evolution."

"And so what do you believe now?"

"Sheba, I believe shit happens. It just happens. Some of it be sweet, some of it be bitter. We endure the bitter and enjoy the sweet. I mean some of us. Some of us endure, some of us enjoy. But there's no rhyme, no reason."

I must have been looking at him like he was crazy, because he laughed, a hard and almost cynical laugh.

"You think I've lost it, don't you?"

"I don't know. I don't know anything. What do I know?"

I turned to look at Bashe for the last time. Her face was calm. Her eyes were closed. At least she was at peace with her decision. Impulsively I bent over and kissed her. Her lips were already cool.

"Sheba?"

"What?"

"I said, do you want to jump too? If you do, we have to do it now. We're almost out of time."

"What . . . ?" I was totally disoriented. "Juno, I don't know. What are you going to do?"

"I'm going to be one of the ones who stay on the shore."

"What? Juno, what are you talking about?"

"I'm talking about how some of us walked into the sea and most of us stayed on the shore."

"Oh."

A chill went through me. I knew I was going to stay on the shore too, even though I had made four back-jumps; right now I just wanted to . . . to what? What did I really want? Before I realized what was happening, words were tumbling out of my mouth: "Juno, can we . . . I mean since I don't know and you don't know, can we kind of don't know together?"

Juno smiled a half smile.

"Can I take that smile as a yes?"

"Yes, you can take it as a yes, but that's not why I was smiling."

"Oh."

"Come on." Juno grabbed my hand. "I was smiling because the last thing Bashe said was if you stay, stay together. Don't try to face down OnePlanet by yourself."

Suddenly the main lights went out. The module automatically switched to backup power. Juno hardly reacted except to murmur, "They're here." He was still holding my hand.

The Second Law of Thermodynamics

Transcription of a Panel at the 1997 Black Speculative Fiction Writers Conference Held at Clark Atlanta University

Jewelle Gomez

(2004)

When I first circulated my novel The Gilda Stories, the New York publishing establishment shook with a weird mixture of laughter and distaste. The rejection in their letters to me was framed differently in each, but essentially I was told that my main character was unsellable because she was a woman of color, a lesbian, and a vampire. The sting I felt was as much a personal wound as a dismissal of my novel because certainly two out of the three charges applied to me.

Years later, when Professors Mary A. Twining and N'Diaye invited me to participate in the 28th annual writers' conference at Clarke Atlanta University, I felt like I finally got the last laugh. Entitled "The African American Fantastic Imagination," it was the first time such an event had ever been convened and I was certain it would not be the last. Over the two and a half days, students, hopeful writers, and fans had the opportunity to listen to and talk in depth with the most significant names in the field of speculative fiction.

The six of us gathered at Atlanta's Auburn Avenue Research Library in African American Culture for a final panel and discussion with the au-

dience, which was more freewheeling than perhaps the organizers had in mind. The conversation was far ranging and frequently punctuated with sly humor and loud laughter. It was an engaging and enlightening experience for each of us in that auditorium. Speculative fiction is a field that has, until recently, all but excluded people of color and women. For me, to sit at a table with five other people of color who are committed to the genre and working practitioners was like a dream come true. But one of the most significant aspects of the event for me was a realization that is also at the heart of so much science fiction writing—as people of color writing speculative fictions: We are not alone.

—Jewelle Gomez

Octavia E. Butler is the author of twelve books, including the groundbreaking novels *Kindred* and *Parable of the Sower*. Award-winning science fiction novelist Samuel R. Delany has authored numerous books, many of which have become classics, including *Dhalgren*. Steven Barnes, the author of *Lion's Blood*, has had a long career as a writer for television as well as a novelist. Tananarive Due is the author of the award-winning novels *My Soul to Keep* and *The Living Blood*, as well as two other bestselling novels and a memoir she coauthored with her mother. William Hudson is an Atlanta-based documentary filmmaker who is developing a film entitled *Witchcatcher* for PBS. Jewelle Gomez is the author of seven books, including the award-winning novel, *The Gilda Stories*.

    Samuel R. Delany opened by asking each of us about how we got started on the path of speculative fiction writing.

WILLIAM HUDSON: I used to jot everything down and come up with the stories. Then I'd bring everybody together in the house. And I'd go through the whole story and I play everybody, with all the voices. We'd be on another planet or something like that and I'd have to rescue someone with my cohorts. And that happened for four or five years, then I realized I was looking like a real geek. So I started keeping it to myself and writing it down. But I was going to be a doctor. I figured you can't make any money writing but all the while I kept writing things down.

If you're a writer the only thing that can stop you from writing is the lack of oxygen going into your lungs. So I kept writing all through pre-med. Then a filmmaker friend of mine came over to borrow a dish drainer; he said he was making a movie upstairs. I followed him out of curiosity and asked if I could watch. He said yes, if I'd help out. That was at three in the afternoon and I didn't get back downstairs to my apartment until the next day. I changed my major the next month and have been a filmmaker ever since.

TANANARIVE DUE: I've always been a reader. My house was full of books. I made a quick association between reading and writing. I remember writing what I called a book when I was four years old, and stories all throughout my childhood. I didn't act them out like William, but I remember the TV show *Emergency* and I wrote little plots about those firefighters. Then they started getting kidnapped by satanic cultists. I thought my plots were much more interesting than the ones that were on television. I then wrote stories about my friends and gained some popularity. Some of them were semipornographic, actually, which made me very popular in junior high. From then on I've been hooked.

I'd always had a love of the supernatural. My mother raised us on *Creature Features*, *The Mummy*, *The Fly*, and other classic horror movies. And I read a lot of Stephen King, so later that all translated into writing.

STEVEN BARNES: As far back as I can remember I wrote stories, and before I could write them I told stories out loud. Before I could tell them orally I just told elaborate lies. I used to tell kids in my elementary school that I was a vampire. A little girl in my class once came up to my mom and asked: "Mrs. Barnes, is Steven really a vampire?" And when my mother asked me if I'd really told the little girl that, I just said: "How could I tell her something like that? Vampires only come out at night!"

My dad was a backup singer for Nat King Cole, and there was something about watching my dad make records that convinced me that it was possible to make a living in the arts. It was possible to do something that you loved. As to why I was specifically attracted to sci fi and fantasy, I think the real answer is that it chooses you. You don't choose it.

But the more cynical, not so serious answer I've given is that since I didn't see any black people in movies at all, at least watching horror movies, I got the pleasure of seeing white people die horribly. My mother would find what I wrote and tear it up into little pieces, probably thinking she was saving my immortal soul. I'd stay awake at night taping it all back together. Not having any athletic prowess, my answer to school bullies was what I considered the Scherherazade technique. I'd find the biggest baddest dudes in school and I'd tell them stories, but I'd only tell them about half the stories at lunchtime. So after school if the bullies came after me after school the football players would say: "Leave the little brother alone. I want to hear the rest of the story." So writing equals less pain. You can program a white rat to understand that. So I started writing plays for the stage. By the time I got into college I tried to stop writing. I figured let me do something sane for a change. Anything—Amway, you know! But one day they had an essay contest and I wrote a short story and I stood in front of the assembly and I was looking at their faces as I read and the bottom fell out of my heart. I suddenly realized that this is all that I wanted to do. All I wanted was to tell stories. There was no place else in the world for me. There was nothing else that was going to heal my heart. It was this or nothing. If I didn't do this it didn't matter to me if I collected garbage or slept in the street. I had to do this.

I just dropped out right then. I left college and went to work at CBS so I could be around as many people as I could who were writing and making images. I read as many books and scripts as I could. It really did choose me. I think it might have been Thoreau or one of those guys who said something like: The secret to life is to find the river through which the substance of your life runs and to live as close to the banks of that river as possible. That's your biggest chance for success. That's your biggest chance for happiness. If I could have made another choice I would have, but I didn't have any option.

JEWELLE GOMEZ: Like a lot of us, my early images came from television and film. I was a *Star Trek* fan, *Twilight Zone*, *The Outer Limits*. And the one horror film that did star a black man, who died first, of course, *Night of the Living Dead*. I used to watch that film repeatedly just to see Duane Jones, who I met later when I worked in theater in New York. It was one of his great regrets, because he did go on to become a respected theater actor, but that film was the one thing he was always known for. But the visual medium really led me into writing fantasy fiction.

The other element most important was growing up with my great-grandmother. That meant living with someone who was literally spanning time. She'd been born on Indian land in Iowa in 1883, then migrated to Massachusetts. When I would sit with her and watch things on TV or just look out of our windows, I was experiencing fantasy fiction with a woman who'd seen the world change so drastically over time that it would be Orwellian. And the fact that she was a good storyteller, as was her daughter and my father. So I always had this urge to tell our stories as they told me theirs.

One of the first stories my great-grandmother told me, one I always remembered, is, I think, why I started writing. It was about the woman in the picture on the cover of my first novel—Effie, my great-grandmother's half-sister. She'd been sitting at the piano playing when she heard Effie call her name as clear as day. My great-grandmother kept playing until she heard it a second time, but she knew that Effie lived many miles away. The third time she heard it she got up and went to a neighbor's house and called a neighbor near her sister who had a phone. She was then told that her sister had just died.

A lot of us have those stories. My great-grandmother told me that one as casually and with such conviction that it actually happened that I realized that we are not all living in the same place or in the same time. That there are things that we don't know but perhaps could know, and that there was nothing really especially bizarre about anything that happens in our lives. Bizarreness is in the perception. African Americans were bizarre and inhuman to white people when we arrived. At once I understood that there were all different planes of reality and that storytelling was important to our culture and to our living. The writing just grew from there.

SAMUEL R. DELANY: As the grandfather here, I guess I started writing science fiction before there was a *Star Trek*. It wasn't even a glimmer in Gene Roddenberry's eye when I started writing. I had a great deal of trouble reading and writing in school. My writing was strictly from hunger. And it turned out that I was severely dyslexic. But as a result, a kind of bug bit me to make up for it. All you had to do was tell me that a book was too hard for me to understand and I'd be on that book in an instant.

In the high school, which was connected to my elementary school, a teacher gave students "The Wasteland" to read and they were all twisted out of shape. They didn't understand it. So I read it and I didn't understand it either. So I read it again and again and again. Then I discovered there were books on it, so I started reading those. So all you had to do was say something was beyond me and I was fascinated.

I also fell in love with a word. I was reading along in some article and I came across this word: wolverine. Wolverine! I thought that was the most beautiful word in the world. I went around saying wolverine for days. I must have been about eight or nine years old and I just kept saying wolverine. Then I began making up stories about wolverine. I didn't know what a wolverine was exactly, but I knew it was a wonderful word.

About that time I was fortunate enough to encounter two story-tellers. One was from Ireland, the grandfather of another student, Seamus McManus. He came to our school to tell stories. When he told the stories there was a great deal of verbal play. They were always about Jack who'd set out on a journey that was always twice as far as I could tell you and three times as far as you could tell me and four times as long as anyone else could tell the two of us. And they seemed to have a lot to do with the word wolverine!

The other storyteller was a very bright kid at summer camp, Sheldon Novick. One day he started telling us a story and it was called "Who Goes There," which is actually a novel by John W. Campbell and is the basis of the movie *The Thing*, recently remade by John Carpenter. Anyway, as Sheldon was telling the story, of course he had his own version. The names of the characters had nothing to do with the characters in the novel. The story was the same, there was a lot of "they walked through the ice, they slogged through the ice, they waded through the ice," which again seemed to have something to do with saying wolverine!

Or at least the notion was that there was a certain amount of poetry involved in the language of storytelling. I think that poetry is an aspect of narrative. I think you can take it away and make something that is just a poem, where what we think of as the narrative elements don't weigh heavily. But fundamentally in any kind of narrative there is always a poetics to it. The combination of the two is what I got interested in.

And the next thing you know I was trying to write a novel. In the beginning my way of writing was to put all my English papers together as chapters, my science papers as well. My first novel has a chapter that is a report on viruses. I put them all together and had seventy-seven pages, and that was my first novel when I was about thirteen.

OCTAVIA E. BUTLER: A lot of people have been told that we aren't supposed to be doing this. I was told by an aunt flat out at thirteen that Negroes don't write. My answer, out of ignorance, was, Yes they do. I think my aunt was trying to save me from a life of poverty and destitution and borrowing money from her when she said this. She was absolutely certain that I couldn't possibly make a living writing and that I should get a nice civil service job and write in my spare time. I had one teacher who pushed me. I couldn't have not written, but it's possible I wouldn't have become a writer making a living.

People still find that difficult. When I tell people I'm a writer they sometimes say: that's nice, maybe one day you'll sell something. When we tell them we're writers they think we're telling them about our hobby. My teacher, not an English teacher but oddly enough a gym teacher, did something for me that really got me going on the theory that I can't expect people to help me because even when they help me they do me an injury. She was probably the toughest teacher in the high school. She was the type who'd scream curses at kids who would go home and tell their parents and she'd get in trouble. She'd see kids not doing their best and she couldn't stand it. She decided this poor, awkward huge kid (I grew very tall very quickly) *was* doing her best. I was trying to learn to climb a rope. I'd decided in gymnastics that that was what I was going to learn to do. So I'd pulled myself up a couple of feet the first time. And the next day I got a little farther and I gradually made my way up that rope. And anyone who's ever tried climbing a rope in gym shorts knows that this was not a comfortable exercise.

I finally got to the point where I was only about six inches from the pan you hit at the top of the rope and I thought, well, tomorrow I'll get there. It didn't bother me that tomorrow I'd get there because I'd been working for a long time. But for some reason this huge person climbing the rope had caught everyone's attention. Here I was climbing and the whole gym had gone silent and everyone was watching me, which was really the wrong thing to do at that time. I really couldn't get those last inches but I knew I'd do it the next day. But they were shouting encouragement, and when I came back down they all said "Ahhh" sadly. And the next day when I started out the teacher said, "You tried so hard, I'm going to give you the grade for climbing it anyway."

I never climbed that rope to the top. However, I hiked my way down to the bottom of the Grand Canyon. On my way back up it was raining sideways and I thought I was going to die from falling off the edge or from weariness or thirst. I got to the top. No one was going to have to come and get me.

When I hurt my knee hiking in Peru—I don't know why I make these decisions to climb things! Here was this mountain, it wasn't so difficult; other folks had climbed it. But I was going up, and all the way up I kept thinking: I've gone high enough—I can quit now. This teacher living in my head kept saying, Yeah you poor thing. I climbed all the way to the top and through a cave that wasn't much bigger than I was, wondering how many tons of rock are over me. I think without that teacher living in my head I wouldn't have done that.

And that was learning no one was going to help me even though they may mean to. Like my aunt who was trying to help me by telling me get a nice civil service job, give it up you poor thing you don't understand the limitations of your race. Or of your sex or you don't understand you're not very bright so give it up now and go and do something easier. Those two people helped me more getting going in my writing than anything else.

SD: One of the things that encouraged me but might make science fiction a little difficult for people is that it really does have something to do with science, as opposed to fantasy which is about magic, et cetera. And one of the things we tend to forget is that basically the scientific view of the universe is a pessimistic view. Basically the view of sci fi is built on the second law of thermodynamics. And the second law of thermodynamics is that nothing lasts forever; everything runs down and eventually it stops. The notion of world without end that runs through so many religions is one that grows when the world is no larger than what is under the particular arc of sky that you can see. Because then you can see things lasting forever. But as soon as the world is seen as this ball that's finite, rotating around the sun on its axis, eventually it's all going to run down. The sun's going to grow large and eat up the world and we're not going to be here anymore. That's a hard thing to take.

Hal Clement the sci fi writer says from time to time, "The universe is contriving to do me in. I'm fighting against it as hard as I can. But eventually it's going to win." I think that is what's behind the science fiction worldview. It makes you very isolated and feel very alone and scared. The awe toward the universe that we have when we look out at the stars—a lot of it is wonder but a lot of it is terror.

JG: To a great extent vampire mythology, which is more fantasy than sci fi, is also growing out of that second law of thermodynamics. Vampire mythology, which has a home in every culture in history, not just Victorian England with Dracula, comes out of people's fear of dying. Fear that the time is just going to run out. Some people have created the idea of heaven and hell; writers, well not just writers, but people themselves through folklore, created the mythology of vampires. Ancient African, Greek, Roman, Norse, all of that mythology has a character who can beat the clock. And of course that has to come through something terrible, which is the destruction of other human beings. It would be interesting to do this as a Ph.D. thesis for some of you later, to see how that law of thermodynamics follows through in speculative fiction.

That was the big challenge for me, trying to create a vampire who would break from that mold of having to kill repeatedly. It meant creating another kind of ethic, an opposing ethic with vampires who would take their place in the natural order of things, acting as supernatural but still part of the natural order.

The idea of speculative fiction, which I use as a phrase to put everything together, is that speculative implies possibilities. A lot of times people think of fantasy fiction or specifically science fiction as apocalyptic, a kind of doomsday, end-of-the-world narrative. For me spec fi always implied possibilities. Meaning we can imagine the world to be a very very different place. As African Americans, this seems to be at the core of our getting from day to day. Speculating that there are other possibilities other than doom. Somehow this came to me as we're talking about the law of thermodynamics!

SB: As we're talking about how people deal with their fears of the end, there's a great line in Randy Newman's opera *Faust* where Satan is talking to God and says: You and I are alive, inventions of an animal that knows it's going to die. There's a part of me that believes the law of thermodynamics, that there's an enormous amount of ego in most human behavior, and one of the most interesting to me is the belief that the mind that perceives the thing is large enough to contain the thing. To me the inherent limitations of perception imply that no matter what we think we know, there is always something beyond that. What lies beyond the horizon of our perceptions? Anytime people start to say, Well, now we understand, I laugh to myself and say let's go another generation down the road and see what we think we understand. If a thousand years from now people don't look back and think that we're the Stone Age, I'll be very surprised. I probably won't be around to be surprised, but that's the envelope of my own existence.

A lot of philosophy, a lot of mythmaking and storytelling, has to do with what was the shape of your face before your parents were born. What lies beyond the edge of your existence? And when your mind starts going beyond the question of your little trivial life and death and you start asking yourself what is it you want to leave afterward. What is it that formed you that came before? Do you look at yourself as an interference pattern between genetics, nutrition and conditioning, environment, and a bunch of other things that sort of temporarily created this little bit of protoplasm that is walking around right now? That yes we're children in adult bodies. In another sense, both children and adults are part of a continuum of action that manifests itself partially in childhood when we're children and partially when we're adults. We're animals that have a particular ability to be aware of the fact that we're going to die, that have the ability to learn and to modify our behavior.

In another sense we're just these things that are. It's just existence. It's not a matter of we're alive or dead, just that we exist, I'm alone by myself. If I wake up in the middle of the night I don't think about myself as being Black, I don't think about myself as being male, I don't think about myself particularly being human. I think in those moments that there is just this thing that has an awareness of its existence and I marvel to myself. To me science is one of the tools by which we explore the universe, and it has given us many gifts. And religion, spirituality, mythology, and philosophy, which manifest differently in different cultures, are other sets of tools that give us another perspective on who and what it is we are. Each of these things tells the truth about which we are. Fantasy, horror, which deals with the dark aspect of fantasy, often the issue of death; sci fi, which deals with the intellectual constructs we use to lay over reality. Each of these different ways we have of looking at who we are all equally valid to the degree that the storyteller, the poet, the scientist, the dancer, was telling the truth as they receive it at the moment and sharing it as they feel it at the moment of creation.

My most important task as an artist is to simply try to share my view of the world, my experiences of the world. There are times when you'll need a logical structure like science. You look at science and other times you need a metaphor, and a fantasy gives you that or a poem does that. To try at every moment to choose the most appropriate medium for what is being communicated, to do the most honest job I can. Then to sit back and see what the person on the other side got. To just sit back and enjoy that communication that happens between people, that happens between people and animals. Those of us who garden have been able to see what happens between humans and plants and see the way they respond. And the writing of this thing called science fiction is one aspect of that communication that attempts to see if there's somebody out there, that "alienness" outside ourselves to stave off that unavoidable sense of darkness. I don't know, if I lived forever maybe I wouldn't have as much of an urge to communicate. Or maybe I'd have even more of an urge just to fill the void of boredom of infinite existence. But again, not having that option, I don't know.

TD: When I was in college I was haunted by John Keats because of that poem of his "when I have fears that I will cease to be before my pen has gleaned my teaming brain." The brother just did not want to go before his time, before he had everything said. He wanted it desperately, yet he died at twenty-five. So as a twenty-year-old in college I thought, Wow, you just have five years left. It was kind of a mind game. Like a lot of people who write fantasy, there is a preoccupation with death. Just the scenario, in which you're driving in your car, listening to the football game on the radio, your children are arguing in the backseat, your wife is sitting beside you. You hear a noise, you turn away for a half-second, then the next instant you're dead. This is a reality. That's the last moment of your existence. It's not any particular moment of revelation. So is it any wonder that we can create monsters? Here's the joy of monsters.

People ask me, Why do you like being scared? Well I don't really like being scared on some levels. I don't like being scared by a strange noise outside of my window, for example. I don't like to be scared by a shadow moving in my home. I do like artificial stimulation. I do like experience, because experience to me makes life so sweet. Through experience I can watch something I know is not real and feel a genuine emotion, which is what I value almost above all else. I am an emotional person. Emotion is what makes me feel most alive, even when I'm unhappy. I'd much rather be unhappy than feel nothing at all. There are some people who are good at feeling nothing, but I'd choose unhappiness over feeling nothing. I'd choose joy over unhappiness, but sometimes we don't have that choice. So you make the most of whatever emotion it is. Horror is—I wish I could remember who said it: Horror is not a genre as much as it is an emotion, a sensation.

In creating something that's not real and having the ability to walk away from it, as in the case of *The Between*, to try to tame it and understand it . . . [my character's] life could have ended pretty quickly in the book. It could have been over in five pages. You create all kinds of scenarios that seem very horrifying to us—you think, Man this poor guy, he's having a terrible time—but an end comes to everyone, and an end is always a horrible thing as far as I'm concerned. So this is a way to make it seem less terrible than what I think it is when you take away all the bells and whistles.

My Soul to Keep, which is my second book, is another launch at the same subject, which is that we all crave immortality but would that really be such a wonderful thing? That's the question I'd like to answer in that book: What if immortality was literal? Not in the form of a vampire but you're just immortal; you don't die. And fear of life, since for those of you who don't share my fear of death, there's sometimes a fear of life. A fear of what happens tomorrow, which we can't know or can't expect. So I grapple with these things and my books always cheer me up. I don't know that they cheer up my readers. But deep down what I'm really trying to do is perform a public service.

WH: I was really struck by a book that dealt with this topic, the fear of death, Joanna Russ's novel, *We Who Are About To* . . . The premise of the book is "We who are about to die." It's about a situation in which a group of people is forced to deal with their impending death. It's about to happen. It's basically a bunch of people who are stupid and end up on a planet. Because they're stupid they have no way of getting off. So they're faced with the fact that they're about to croak.

And when I say they're stupid, I mean they're stupid in the way that we all are. You know how we always do stupid things. A friend of mine did something that was the epitome of dumb things. I think he and his family were together for the Fourth of July, and they were all having a great time. And suddenly he just had this burst of energy and he had a baseball in his hand and he just threw it. And of course it went right through the window of a car. And then he's grabbing his head. Everybody is thinking how could he be so dumb? But that's really the stupidity of life. Something just kind of comes up on you and you realize you haven't been paying attention and you've done something dumb. So *We Who Are About To* . . . is about a group of people who've all come together in a place like that. I know you're all wondering where is this going! But that's the most important thing to me. How do we get out of these stupid moments we get into, like now? All of our characters end up in situations in which things are put on them whether or not they're people who have ability or they're learning. No matter where they come from, the question is, When things come at you out of left field that want to turn your life into a cesspool, what do you do next?

That's where the challenge happens. And I know when I write something that you like—that's what you want to give people, something that makes them feel better. The feeling that I want to convey to people in my work is a sense that they can get out of these stupid moments, those horrible moments. That you can get beyond them with the tools that you have at your disposal. That's always enough, no matter where you think you are, no matter how hopeless you think it is. Yeah, even though the universe may be falling apart according to the second law of thermodynamics, there's nothing you can do about that. But you can use what you have right now because we do make up God and the devil, so we have plenty of tools at our disposal.

TD: I'd like to add one thing: Hopefulness is also an issue for me, because I think writing brings so much hopefulness. I don't remember the name of the poem by Audre Lorde. She was dying of cancer when she wrote it, but it actually cheers me up. The last line of the poem is ". . . but not today." Imagine that a dying woman can write a poem and it was not that day. As the reader you know it was not that day. And it lifts my spirit. It softens the edges. And I think that's also what we try to do.

SD: All the narratives that tell the varied aspects as Steve said are valid, however, not all the stories are deeply efficient. I think efficiency has been the response to the second law. Once you have the realization that everything is going to run down, you have the imperative to make use of your time.

OB: I want to say something about that second law of thermodynamics. Yes, everything is running down, but what it's doing within our awareness—and I'm not talking about within our lifetimes, because that's very brief—but within our awareness it's creating new things. A perfect example of that is the Hawaiian Islands. Even as the volcanoes are building them, they're also being, in some way, destroyed by the volcanoes. So I don't see it as entirely a pessimistic or a negative thing, because of what we do with it. Here the earth is losing some of its heat as it spews out lava, but it is creating these islands that are beautiful that people want to live on. And that's what we're doing. As we live we're creating things, and when we die we leave them behind for other people. I see this inevitable change as not a terrible thing, which is good since it's inevitable.

Q: Someone talked earlier about the differences between fantasy, sci fi, and horror, and as I study physics we see that the higher you go, the more things blend together, so I can't see value in differentiation.

OB: Before everything crunches back together it spends a long time flying apart.

SD: Also it's important to remember that information is difference, it's distinction. What we need to learn is what are useful and efficient distinctions and what are inefficient and useless. What we know is that on some absolute and transcendental level the distinctions of race are meaningless. They don't do anybody any good. That's on an absolute transcendental level. Now if we want to talk about culture, it's a very useful distinction. We have to find the level on which the distinction is made.

SB: We know that on some level everything is just energy, that there's no difference, but it is useful to have a distinction between ground glass and cabbage on some level.

SD: Or a difference between air and rock.

Q: Engineering majors and science majors don't want anything to do with each other, but don't they each need the other?

SB: Develop a set of skills that you're pretty sure you can sell, then in your spare time figure out how to be any kind of artist you want. First figure out how to pay your rent.

Q: What are the implications of sci fi? Is it defining the function of the writer as things get more and more specialized?

JG: You're experiencing the educational system, and things are becoming more specialized. As capitalism becomes more evolved, things have to become more specialized because of the profit motive. On the other hand, all of us are products of that educational system. Human nature will always carry those with multiple interests into those fields where multiple interests will be found. So I don't think we can necessarily worry about if the writing we're going to do is going to be embraced by the educational system. It's your interests that will carry you. I remember my graduation from the largest private university at that time in the country, and they were giving out degrees to 30,000 people in the Boston Garden. As I sat there at this endless thing to get this degree for my major in sociology and minor in theater, I was reading a book on bees. Why? I don't know why I was interested in it and that's what I was doing. At any moment we're perceiving so many different things. That will always persist— that intellectual curiosity, that complexity. That's what leads to the writing.

SB: There's always an enormous amount of cross-pollination in the fields of writing.

Q: Do you think about the mass consciousness of the people who are reading your work and the seeds you're planting?

OB: When writing—no. I have to assume that the things that interest me will interest other people. As a responsible person I should at least try to tell the truth as I see it or as I hope that it is. There are things that I've been very careful not to say in my work simply because I recognize that the potential for misinterpretation would be enormous. That's the only kind of self-censorship that I exercise, but when actually writing the story that's the important thing. If you're sitting there imagining your audience, you're scattering your forces to such a degree you don't write much of a story.

SD: Another sad bit of news about the way this world works is that in this country, with a population of about 240 million people, there are fewer than 5 million people who buy one book a year. Within that population are those who buy three or four books a year. Then you have these funny people—and I expect they're like everyone on this panel—they buy one or two books a week. Well for better or for worse, one of the things that's happened in commercial writing is the assumption that the kinds of techniques that are used on a mass audience can be used on a mass audience of readers. There is no mass audience of readers. The number of people who see a televised show or a movie is so much greater than the number of people who ever read a book. You're just dealing with two different ballparks. PBS ran a series of Shakespeare's plays and announced that they'd doubled the number of people, who'd ever, in all history, seen Shakespeare, just by running them once on PBS. Who watches PBS? So you've got

to keep a perspective on what you're doing. Whether you want to acknowledge it or not, to write is an elite activity. Like Octavia, I'm not
concerned about my audience per se. I assume that somewhere in
that 5 million there are a mere 100,000 who are more or less interested in the same things that I am. One of the things that's terribly
pernicious is that some publishers would like to believe that there is
something that somehow you can do in writing the book that will
make people passing by on the street suddenly run right to it. It
doesn't work that way. People have to choose to read your book.
There's nothing you can put between the covers that will make them
open it up. They have to have at least heard something or see something on the cover. So I think you just have to write the best you can
about what you're passionate about and hope for the best.

JG: I don't agree with either of those positions totally. I think because
of the way I came to literature in the first place, through the Civil
Rights Movement and the Black Arts Movement, going to hear
poets like Sonia Sanchez for the first time and feeling my life completely change, because I was hearing a voice I didn't know existed—
that is, my own. I think that's a big part of me, even though I do try
not to picture the audience, because I think you can start to censor
yourself. But I do think I believe that I'm able to change the world.
There is a part of me that feels if I can invent in my story the thing
that I believe in the most passionately around social change, around
self-improvement and improving the world, that I have contributed
in some way to the changing of the world. It may only be for the
25,000 people who've bought my book, but it's good. What's so powerful for me, especially at this kind of event, is when people come up
to me and say, "I read your book and I'll never feel the same again
about"—fill in the blank. And whether it's about African Americans, or about women, or about the potential for sisterhood and
brotherhood, or the humanity of the lesbians in our lives, or the
youth of our future, or about family, all of which I'm writing about,
people come up and say that. And even if it's only one person, I feel
like I have changed the world in some small way.

SD: I find it interesting that Jewelle disagrees with me but I quite agree with everything she says.

JG: I actually think we are in agreement, but then there are the added parts we each consider!

SB: I've had both positive and negative experiences with the question of social responsibility. I had a young man who was dying of Hodgkin's disease who told me that something he read in *Gorgon Child* helped him deal with mortality. And that was very sobering and made me feel that writing was a positive thing. But then there was also the experience where a man who I know had read my work was accused of murder and tried for it. And if I looked at the scenario of the murder he'd been accused of, it looked so much like something that happened in one of my books and it just made me sick. I hoped to God he didn't do it, and if he did it, what do I think about this?

And the conclusion that I came to was asking myself the question: Was the scene in my book a valid scene? Was I aware that there were problems in that scene when I wrote it? The answer is yes. I felt very uncomfortable about that scene. But given the way the situation was set up, it just felt like that was going to happen in the story. I'll always wonder about this. And I'll always wonder about myself. I can't have a clue what will be in someone else's mind. I can hope that it'll have a positive impact, but if you write about nothing but a positive universe, it'll have no flavor. The light is defined by the darkness.

TD: That's an experience I hope I never have. I know when I was writing *The Between* there were scenes that stayed with me when I tried to go to sleep, because they dealt with issues that were very close to me. But I know there were many readers who skipped right past them and they had no resonance in their minds whatsoever. I know we've each had readers come up to us and they've had an entirely personal interpretation of something we've written that's entirely valid but that has nothing to do with what we were trying to say. And that's given us food for thought. I had one reader almost convince me that [my character] Hilton was insane. And that had never crossed my mind. And she explained it to me and almost proved her point!

Books really are living entities unto themselves. That's what makes them so incredibly powerful—the ability to dive into a world and live there. Yes, we think about the audience to a degree. There was a reverend here, and we talked about this. He said that he'd always wanted to write about a vampire preacher, but we all have met vampire preachers! But the issue for him was that as an African American preacher himself, what kind of statement would he be making. So he's never attempted to write it. Those are questions that all writers deal with. And there are no easy answers.

WH: I like what Chip Delany wrote in *Dhalgren*. One of his characters says of the place they exist: "When everybody comes here they become more of what they are." I think that's what life does to you. In the process of reading your work, that's really all that you can give them. It does get back to what was said earlier. When writing the scene you think about the truth of it. Do I like that scene? You may ask is it too much on the edge or not enough on the edge? But ultimately you did what you intended to do and you live with that. And people who make a decision based on what they pull from the work; they should live with that. Yes, you have to live with what you say. But they have to live with what they do. I think that's the nature of communication.

HER PEN COULD FLY: REMEMBERING VIRGINIA HAMILTON

Nnedi Okorafor-Mbachu

(2004)

> The past moves me and with me, although I remove myself
> from it. Its light often shines on this night traveler: and when
> it does, I scribble it down. Whatever pleasure is in it I need pass
> on. That's happiness. That is who I am.
> —Virginia Hamilton, 1936–2002

Myths, tales, and magical times. Her stories were those of a different kind. And what wonderful things they did to a child's mind. Including mine. Hamilton's stories came at a time when there were very, very few stories featuring African American characters that were fantastical. None that I knew of. When I discovered Hamilton's books it was as if my eyes were opened. Though I knew that there could be fantastical books that centered on African folklore with black main characters, there's something about actually seeing one of these creations that makes the idea more real.

Virginia Hamilton was one of America's greatest children's authors. Within her books were mermaids, witches, ghosts, tricksters, talking animals, haunted houses, vampires, and people who could fly. Hamilton came from a background where magic was always in the air. She was born and raised close to the earth on a small farm in rural Ohio and she was highly influenced by her parents, both of whom were storytellers.

"I grew up around storytelling," she told me during an interview three years ago. "I also had a lot of extended family around and everyone was very talkative." Hamilton said she'd been writing since she was in grade school. On February 19, 2002, Virginia Hamilton passed away after a ten-year battle with breast cancer.

Hamilton was a writer of history, herstory, myth, stories, and fantasy. She made the world magical and mythical and taught a lesson somewhere between the words. Hamilton's stories were like a blast of fairy dust to African American literature. As a writer of both adult and children's speculative fiction, I inhaled Hamilton's fairy dust of a darker shade like clean fresh air. And for this reason, Hamilton will always hold a special place in my heart. She showed me that it was okay when monsters, spirits, mermaids, and talking animals mixed with or highlighted issues of race and culture in my work. Her magnetic storyteller's voice is part of the chorus of voices in my head that speak to me as I write.

I didn't start writing stories until I was twenty years old. But from the day that I learned to read, I ate books like chocolate. I spent half of my summers in the empty weed-filled lots catching grasshoppers and frogs, and the other half in the library. I naturally migrated toward books with witchcraft, magic, spirits, creatures, and beasts. I savored books like *Miranty and the Alchemist*, *The Five Chinese Brothers*, *Rebecca's World*, and *The Lion, the Witch, and the Wardrobe*.

I grew up in a predominantly white neighborhood and was forced to be very aware of my race (this forcing ranged from being called a "nigger" to teachers making fun of my nappy hair and to peers making fun of my funny name and so on). I noticed that there were few fantastical books with main characters of African descent, let alone fantastical books written by people of African descent.

I think because of this I began to read books where the main characters were animals or nonhumans. My favorite children's book series was the *Moomin* series by Finnish author Tove Jansson. The Moomins were bipedal, extremely polite, white hippolike "people" who lived in a magical world. They weren't black people but they had a kind of otherness that I could identify with.

When I discovered Hamilton's books, it was a pleasant shock. My library only had two of her books, *The People Could Fly: American Black Folktales* (1985) and *Zeely* (1967), but those were enough. When I found these books, something clicked into place. But at a young age I wasn't fully aware of the effect they had on me. Children are rarely conscious of such moments. All I knew at the time was that the books made me feel warm and fuzzy.

It was when I started writing my own stories that Hamilton's influence really came out. The story that affected me the most when I was young was *The People Could Fly*. This was one of Hamilton's most well-known books. It consists of twenty-four retold African American folktales. But the one that stuck to me most was the folktale it was titled after.

> They say the people could fly. Say that long ago in Africa, some of the people knew magic. And they would walk up on the air like climbin up a gate. And they flew like blackbirds over the fields. Black, shiny wings flappin against the blue up there.
>
> —*The People Could Fly*

The story is about enslaved Africans remembering their ability to fly and thus choosing to fly away from their imprisoned lives, heading back home to Africa. It's a haunting story about power, memory, and myth. After the story, Hamilton mentions how there were numerous accounts of flying Africans. She said that a plausible explanation might be that "Come fly away" was a code for running away.

Me, I like to believe the literal: that long ago people could fly. The idea has always tickled me. About three years ago, *The People Could Fly* popped into my head and I took it a little further. Mixing the retold story with my fascination with birds, freedom, and travel, I wrote a myth that I quickly grew obsessed with. I called it the Windseeker Myth. Set in what is now called Nigeria, long ago, there were people who could fly called Windseekers. As time passed and horrendous things happened, the people of Nigeria began to forget. Thousands of Windseekers were lost to the sea when they broke from their slaveship shackles and flew away. Even more were born into families that did not acknowledge who they were. These Windseekers either died of confusion or were executed for witchcraft. Today few have even heard of Windseekers. And those who have associate them with evil.

Since then I've written several Windseeker stories. My first young adult novel, *Zahrah the Windseeker* (Houghton Mifflin, scheduled for release in early 2004), sprouted from this series of connected stories.

It's about a thirteen-year-old girl who, born a Windseeker, goes on an unthinkable quest. It's set in a place called Ginen where technology and nature have achieved a happy marriage. I have Hamilton to thank for introducing me to the old legend of flying people.

And somewhere on a subconscious level, I think her first book, *Zeely*, affected me too. My favorite Windseeker character, Arrö-yo, is an Efik Nigerian woman who stands over six feet tall, with skin black as the night sky, and a lot of attitude.

In *Zeely*, a young girl named Geeder is enchanted by a six-and-a-half-foot tall dark-skinned regal woman who lives near Geeder's uncle's farm. This coming of age novel creates Zeely as a mysterious sort of living legend. Geeder dreams up stories about Zeely, whom she believes is an African queen. For me, this book was the first book I ever read that seemed to celebrate "African-ness" in black women. Hamilton's first book broadcasted that black was beautiful, something I don't think black women and girls are told often enough.

I discovered Hamilton's other books as an adult, and they each helped to reinforce my drive to write what I call African fantasy (fantasy based in African myths and culture). Hamilton went on to write over thirty children's books, all very different from each other and all possessing the magic that was Hamilton's vision.

Her Stories: African-American Folktales, Fairy Tales, and True Tales (1995) is a book of folktales featuring female characters from fantasy to legend to real women in history. *The Dark Way Stories of the Spirit World* (1990) is a collection of really scary stories from around the world. It'll take one right into the spirit world with its tales of horned women, witches, banshees, and shape-shifters. *The Planet of Junior Brown* (1971) is about two black eighth-grade boys trying to get by in a troubled world. One is a 300-pound musical prodigy named Junior Brown. The other is his friend Buddy Clark, who is homeless. *Willie Bea and the Time the Martians Landed* (1989) is an old-fashioned novel whose plot revolves around the October night in 1938 when Orson Welles's infamous radio broadcast of a Martian invasion of Earth scared the daylights out of the entire nation.

The Magical Adventures of Pretty Pearl (1986) is a mythical tale about a god-child who decides to leave the African mountaintops where she dwells with other gods to live among human beings. When she discovers the slave trade, she knows she must do something about it. *Jaguarundi* (1995) takes place in the rain forest. When human beings threaten the rain forest, Jaguarundi the wildcat plans to flee and search for the "promised land." Only a coati (a raccoonlike creature) agrees to go with him; the other animals decide to stay and "adapt." In the end, neither the wildcat nor coati finds the "promised land," and they too must adapt. "The story parallels humans who escape their homelands in search of better, safer lives," Hamilton said in a speech at the Tenth Annual Virginia Hamilton Conference.

The House of Dies Drear (1968) and its sequel, *The Mystery of Drear House* (1988), are mysteries that feature haunted houses, hidden treasure, and ghosts. *The Girl Who Spun Gold* (2000) is the African version of Rumpelstiltskin. Hamilton also wrote biographies on W. E. B. Du Bois and Paul Robeson. For a list of all her books, go to her Web site at www.virginiahamilton.com.

Hamilton's writing career spanned over thirty years and, not surprisingly, her list of awards is long. To name a few, she was the first African American to win the John Newbery Medal for "the most distinguished contribution to literature for children," for M. C. *Higgins, the Great* (1974). And in 1995, she became the first and only children's literature author, and one of the first speculative fiction authors, along with Octavia E. Butler, to win the MacArthur Genius Award.

She's won the Hans Christian Andersen Medal, the Coretta Scott King Award three times, the Edgar Allan Poe Award, and the 27th NAACP Image Award. *The People Could Fly* was also a *New York Times* Outstanding Children's Book of the Year and a *New York Times* Best Illustrated Book.

Hamilton herself said that her work was part of a bigger literary movement. "African Americans are buying and reading more children's books," Hamilton said. "First and foremost, I encourage people to read. But it's also important to be able to read about one's self and those that are not like one's self. Through our reading, we learn more about ourselves and people not like ourselves."

Virginia Hamilton, master storyteller/writer, was a warm soul and she will be painfully missed. Nevertheless, her spirit will live on in her books . . . and other places, of course. Her books are the children of her mind, and they're running around all over the world causing mischief and joy and spreading plenty of black fairy dust.

Celebrating the Alien: The Politics of Race and Species in the Juveniles of Andre Norton

Carol Cooper

(2004)

I began reading science fiction as a fourth-grader at Chancellor Avenue school in Newark, New Jersey. It was the mid-1960s, and I just happened to be the type to prefer the school library to the school yard during recess. I had already finished off Andrew Lang's Red, Pink, Green, and Grey Fairy Book section, plowed through the three-foot shelf of Greek and Roman myths, tackled Homer's two epics, and taken a hopeful stab at two somehow unsatisfying collections of American Indian and African folktales. I remember being both surprised and enlightened by how honest myths tended to be about the adult realities of sex and violence. Even fairy tales suggested that the world was a strange, often cruel, and dangerous place—information that my contextual reality (which included an often bloody Civil Rights struggle, frequent Cold War bomb scares, and high-profile political assassinations) merely confirmed. Then I discovered SF. Our school library was better than average: chocka-block full of what was called "young adult" fiction, which included the juvenile SF of Robert Heinlein, Isaac Asimov, and Andre Norton.

Of all the books I read before entering high school, the only ones to convince me of the utter malleability of the future were science fiction. Even *dystopian* SF stories were thought experiments based on trying to imagine a future untainted by our congenitally troubled present and past. I *got* that. I understood the veiled critiques of present-day human behavior couched in the best of these books, which were steeped in sardonic disdain for human hypocrisy. And I quickly recognized that Heinlein and Norton were both better at these kinds of critiques than Asimov. But what Norton did better than Heinlein, in my preadolescent opinion, was place women and non-white characters in central roles.

It's also important to note that for the thousands of kids who encountered Andre Norton in the 1960s like I did, there was no question that "Andre" was male. Back then, as far as the publishing world was concerned, the most authoritative voice in the kinds of genre fiction Norton liked to write was a male voice. So many female authors used initials or took male pseudonyms to appropriate that authority for their own work. Alice Mary Norton began publishing as Andre Norton in 1934, and that same year legally changed her name to Andre Alice Norton. For impressionable youngsters taken in by this standard marketing tactic, it really mattered that this *male writer*, this *white male writer*, Andre Norton, demonstrated a soft spot for women, telepathic animals, oppressed racial minorities, and "half-breed" combinations of all three in the form of witchy, shape-shifting aliens. It also mattered that this putatively white male writer saw technology and magic as two sides of the same coin, and was smart enough to explore and exalt the science in magic as well as the magic in science.

Alice Mary Norton was born in the relatively liberal city of Cleveland, Ohio, in 1912. The late-born second daughter of a local rug merchant, hers was a fairly enlightened, middle-class upbringing where weekly trips to the library and a supportive, intellectually inclined mother opened Norton's mind to the broad range of ideas and possibilities later explored in her novels.

The first Norton book I discovered was *The Beast Master*, originally published in 1959. Despite several subsequent film and series-television rip-offs of this classic work, no one but the creator of the literary franchise was brave enough to make her titular protagonist non-white.

Hosteen Storm, the protagonist of *The Beast Master* and its 1962 sequel *Lord of Thunder*, was not only created as a full-blood Navajo, but he was also envisioned by Norton as the holder of traditional shamanic powers and one of a handful of native Terrans still alive after the destruction of earth in a disastrous interstellar war. At the height of xenophobic Cold War paranoia and postcolonial struggles all over the globe in which non-white peoples struggled to free themselves from both white racism and exploitative European domination, Andre Norton imagined a future where one of the few terrestrial humans left alive was from a non-white racial group once on a fast track to extinction courtesy of invading whites back in the 1800s.

Boy, was I impressed! First of all, I'd hitherto encountered little or nothing in the way of adventure stories about heroic, supernaturally endowed Indians functioning as central characters in a "modern" multicultural world. Not even in Westerns. Secondly, unlike adventure writers like Edgar Rice Burroughs and H. Rider Haggard—whom Norton cites as early influences—Andre clearly admires non-white cultures. Hosteen Storm possesses many different skill sets, but in the end those skills that come from his Navajo background are shown to be more important and useful than anything derived exclusively from the white world. With the *Beast Master* tales Norton did her homework, and incorporated translated excerpts of "The Night Chant," one of the most beautiful ritual poems in American Indian literature, which introduced a generation of American children to the sophisticated concepts behind Navajo healing ceremonies.

Was I disappointed as a black American girl that Norton chose to work with Indian characters rather than black ones? Actually no. Back then, black issues were constantly in the news. Moreover, the publishing world had begun to release a flood of autobiographical books by hyphenated Americans, with particular attention paid to color politics within the black and Latino communities. Yet there was no equivalent high-profile coverage of America's Indian populations, hidden and largely forgotten on their reservations, consigned to a kind of mythic history, like the unicorn. In my opinion, Norton was fighting a single-handed civil-rights struggle for the American

Indian, using her imagination and sense of historical fair play to guarantee them a future.

The protagonist of "The Sioux Spaceman" (1960) and the Apache time travelers and astronauts of books like *The Defiant Agents* (1962) and *Key Out of Time* (1963) were very easy for me to identify with. Norton gave them unequivocally dark skin color, and deliberately chose representatives of those tribes who offered the fiercest physical and/or cultural resistance to white domination. What's not to like about all that? Had Andre Norton used black American characters to make the same points, she might have fallen grievously afoul of the racial sensitivities of the time and not gotten her books published at all. Those of us willing and able to read between the lines (so to speak) could recognize in Norton's Amerindian characters the archetypal Defiant Non-White Hero, just as able to mirror some young Vietnamese or tribal South African child as a black American kid.

Norton telegraphed her xenophilia early on. In the demi-Gothic adventure *Ralestone Luck*, a first novel written while Norton was still in high school (but published as her *second* book about a decade later), the central premise is the search for a 700-year-old family heirloom brought back from the Crusades by a British ancestor to preserve magically the good fortune of all his descendants. Norton is quite specific as to the heirloom's provenance; it is a "lucky" sword, forged out of two older Middle Eastern weapons and crafted according to the specific advice of an Arab alchemist/astrologer. Far from imagining medieval Arab culture and esoteric knowledge as evil, barbaric, and in thrall to unwholesome Powers—as ur-fantasist H. P. Lovecraft did with his widely influential Cthulu myths—Norton chose to acknowledge the frequently superior knowledge and abilities of the non-white, non-Western Other.

Further, this lifelong history buff chose to set her first novel in New Orleans, where Norton could indulge her fascination with historical intersections among Cajun, Creole, white, black, rich, and poor folk in their various, ever-shifting class and caste configurations. Although the blacks in *Ralestone Luck* (published in 1938) speak the local patois and function largely as paid servants and tenant farmers, they are never deprived of ambition, honesty, self-esteem, or intelligence. Nor does Norton choose to disrespect the "poor white swamptrash" character Jeems, who speaks French as well as the English patois of the blacks and turns out to be a lost relative of the fallen Ralestone nobles as well. Throughout this book the young Norton's class analysis is surprisingly acute and unromantic. Her European nobles rose to power via war, murder, strategic piracy, and pillage; "good" family trees frequently produced bad seeds; and neither wealth nor social standing becomes any definitive measure of either talent or virtue. These points of view were doubtlessly influenced by Norton's own changing fortunes during the Depression, which forced her to quit college in 1931 after only one year and to write on the side while working full time in the Cleveland library system.

In many of her earliest books, Norton wrote historical fiction and adventure fantasy as a way of time-traveling to places in history she thought particularly intriguing or underexplored in young adult fiction. By the 1940s and 1950s the notion of time travel became one of her favorite points of entry into hard SF. By combining key elements from six thousand or so years of human seafaring lore with the notion of time travel, Norton began developing an approach to space opera that incorporated both the mercantile impetus of the ancient Phoenician fleets and the imperialistic flavor of the Portuguese "voyages of discovery." But she wasn't above playfully inverting the conventional iconography of space and time travel in a relative universe for the amusement of her brighter young fans. Within her popular *Witch World* fantasy series (launched in 1964), calculating women replaced brawny men as key protagonists, fragile interdimensional portals replaced heroic interstellar voyages as modes of transport, and phallic spaceships gave way to vaginal wormholes as the means by which humans traveled to alien worlds.

In her space novels, whether aimed at the adult pulp market or children's libraries, it was a given that mankind would go into space, and that they would meet other intelligent life and be offered the chance not to make all the same mistakes they had made when sailing ships encountered new terrestrial populations.

In books like *Star Born* (1957) and *Star Gate* (1958) the related ideas of human mutation and human hybridization are tackled with a candor and calm acceptance America *still* struggles to apply to the relative commonplace of interracial marriage. Freed of the need to conform to her external reality, Norton writes about humans not being afraid to change and expand the very definition of "humanity." Note the following excerpt from *Star Born*:

[P]erhaps the change in temperament and nature had occurred in the minds and bodies of that determined handful of refugees as they rested in the frozen cold sleep while their ship bore them through the wide uncharted reaches of deep space for centuries of Terran time. How long that sleep had lasted the survivors had never known. But those who awakened on Astra were different. And their sons and daughters, and the sons and daughters of two more generations, were warmed by a new sun, nourished by food grown in alien soil, taught the mind contact by the amphibian mermen with whom the space voyagers had made an early friendship—each succeeding child more attuned to the new home, less tied to the far off world he had never seen or would see. The colonists were not the same breed as their fathers, their grandfathers, or great-grandfathers. So, with other gifts, they had also a vast, time-consuming patience, which could be a weapon or a tool, as they pleased, not forgetting the instantaneous call to action which was their older heritage.

In *Star Gate*, published the following year, a mutated race of brown-skinned, golden-haired Terrans finally land on a habitable yet *already* inhabited planet, then find themselves struggling not to "play God" with rustic native humanoids. Although advanced technologically and nearly immortal, the Terrans find it difficult to reproduce themselves. Many begin to mate with the locals, which results in a small but significant number of half-breed children. Norton portrays these half-breeds as caught in a kind of social limbo much as the American mulatto once was, since they are made to suffer in the subsequent power play between two races. And yet it is Norton's half-breed hero who helps reconcile all three sides. All this action incidentally takes place against the mind-boggling solution of a form of "parallel world" time travel, which allows Norton's protagonists to escape into innumerable alternate histories for the same planet.

The near-future dystopia of *The Stars Are Ours!* (1954) postulates such an alternative history for Earth during the Cold War. Scientists are demonized and enslaved in this world as being the untrustworthy tools for global domination. As Norton explains:

> Scientific training became valued only for the aid it could render in helping to arm and fit a nation for war. For some time scientists and techneers [sic] of all classes here were kept in a form of peonage by "security" regulations. But a unification of scientists fostered in a secret underground movement resulted in the formation of "Free Scientist" teams, groups of experts and specialists who sold their services to both private industry and governments as research workers. Since they gave no attention to the racial, political or religious antecedents of their members, they became truly international and planet- instead of nation-minded, a situation both hated and feared by their employers.

As subversive projections go, the one above is particularly provocative, and Norton takes it even further by having a small coalition of nationalist mercenaries frame the nonsectarian Free Scientist network for an orbital weapons takeover that accidentally incinerates large portions of the industrialized world. In the subsequent panic and devastation, a Luddite leader comes to global power, who is then assassinated and usurped by a cabal of even more radical technophobes to form the worldwide dictatorship Pax:

> Renzi's assassination, an act committed by a man arbitrarily identified as an outlawed Free Scientist, touched off the terrible purge which lasted three days. At the end of which time the few scientists and techneers left alive had been driven into hiding. . . . With the stranglehold of Pax firmly

established on Terra, old prejudices against different racial and religious origins again developed.

In this scenario the only escape from endless cycles of human prejudice is intergalactic travel, which is where most of Norton's most profound meditations on interracial and interspecies cooperation take place. This is the same conclusion the black American SF author Octavia Butler would posit four decades later in her *Parable* series, written *after* desegregation, the fall of Apartheid, Nixon's trip to "open" China, and Russia abandoning communism. Like Butler, Norton also writes strong, interesting female characters. But because Butler has never blended magic and fantasy into her work the way Norton did, there is a cool, overtly seductive sensuality to Norton's female *and alien!* protagonists that is missing from Butler's. There is always more than a whiff of the Turkish seraglio in Norton's *Witch World* tales, and even the *Free Trader* quartet, beginning with *Moon of Three Rings* (1966), offers a female sorceress whose compassion, beauty, and passion are like something out of a Shakesperean fairy tale.

It is almost as if because she was ostensibly writing for children, she could restore a charm and an innocence to sex, and to the body itself, which becomes more difficult when dealing with the more jaded and rigidly conditioned adult mind. Women in some of her stories are allowed to be casually, unabashedly nude at the height of their power and self-realization. This happens to the black-skinned heroine Simsa when she discovers she is the last living heir of the immensely ancient and powerful *Forerunner* race. In *Toys of Tamisan*, the dreamweaver/courtesan Tamisan becomes nude not only to ensorcel her clients, but also as a kind of ritual celebration of her strength, talent, and beauty. Hosteen Storm strips down to his most minimal Indian desert wear when he channels the power of his ancestors. Body consciousness and its implied sexual boundaries are such a big part of racial politics that it would be odd if a writer as sophisticated as Norton didn't deal with them, so she does . . . in a typically oblique—yet thoroughly effective—way.

In *Moon of Three Rings*, two alien humanoids, one human, and several animals fall into a situation that results in the "souls" or consciousness of these discrete entities having to spend time in bodies not their own. Norton deals brilliantly with the traumas and taboos that must accompany such a change, and makes readers think deeply about how much of their identities are invested in their flesh, and how pitiful, in the end, such a shallow identity must be. How many other children's books of that time simultaneously tried to convey what it might feel like to be a man in a woman's body, a human in the body of an animal deprived of speech, or a member of a despised underclass suddenly given the fleshy exterior of his planet's all-powerful elite? When one of these transmigrating souls ultimately finds out he can never return to his true body, it is an astonishing moment of shock and epiphany for the reader. I remember it allowed me as a child to recognize a place of great loss and great freedom that was always near me but that I otherwise would never have found. It is a place I still return to from time to time when I need solutions to trivial worldly problems that require a completely "out of the box" perspective. Andre Norton was one of the first writers to knock me completely out of the temporal world in which I could never be more than a second-class citizen, and let me know I never needed to live there again. We need science fiction to get out of this sort of world. Especially when we are children.

Contributors

IHSAN BRACY, artist, author, and educator, is a graduate of Bennington College in Vermont and the author of two plays, *Against the Sun, the Southampton Slave Revolt of 1831* and *N'toto*, a spirit play, as well as two volumes of poetry, *cadre* and *the ubangi files*. Twice a CAPS finalist in poetry, he is a former member of the New York State Council on the Arts and a member of the New Renaissance Writers Guild. He is currently working on a novel.

KEVIN S. BROCKENBROUGH, aka "Brock," is a writer of the stories you'd find "if you did Vulcan Mind Meld with Stephen King and Spike Lee." He gives thanks to Gil Scott-Heron for inspiring him to write and to New York's Frederick Douglass Creative Arts Center for helping him polish his skills. A graduate of Clark Atlanta University's MBA program, Brock works for a large Black ad agency, helping deprogram Fortune 500 executives who think all African Americans are poor and drink malt liquor. He is also a member of the Organization of Black Screenwriters, and is currently shopping two screenplays "full of black folks, black magic, and black humor." He lives in Newark, New Jersey, and can be reached at *brockstories@aol.com*.

WANDA COLEMAN, a National Book Award finalist, is the author of *Mercurochrome*, the novel *Mambo Hips and Make Believe*, the collections *Heavy Daughter Blues: Poems and Stories 1968–1986*, *African*

Sleeping Sickness: Stories and Poems, Bathwater Wine, A War of Eyes and Other Stories, Hand Dance, and *Imagoes.* Her honors include fellowships in poetry from the National Endowment for the Arts and the Guggenheim Foundation. Her fiction received a fellowship from the California Arts Council and the 1990 Harriette Simpson Arnow Prize (*The American Voice*). Widely anthologized, her work appears in *Breaking Ice: An Anthology of Contemporary African-American Fiction, The Best American Poetry* (1988 and 1996), *Trouble the Water: 250 Years of African-American Poetry, The Norton Anthology of African American Literature,* and *The Norton Anthology of Postmodern American Poetry,* among many others.

JOHN COOLEY is an illustrator and comic book author based in Memphis. His work has appeared in *Black Issues Book Review* and *African Voices.* "The Binary" is his first short fiction publication.

CAROL COOPER is a Manhattan-born, Harlem-based freelance journalist who has cranked out more than twenty years' worth of articles for various publications, including *Elle, Essence,* the *Black American, Billboard, Latin N.Y., Rolling Stone, Film Comment, New York Newsday,* the *New York Times,* and the *Village Voice.* She earned a B.A. in English and a master's degree in Liberal Studies from Wesleyan University. While Ms. Cooper was there, Professor Cynthia Smith was instrumental in awarding the summer scholarship that sent Ms. Cooper to the Clarion Writer's Workshop for Fantasy and Science Fiction in 1974. The experience prompted Ms. Cooper's successful submission of a near-future science fiction novel for her master's thesis. After temporarily abandoning fiction to review world-beat, funk, and post-punk concerts for the entertainment press, she spent half of the 1980s and early nineties scouting talent as a corporate A&R director during highly profitable (and educational!) stints with A&M Records, Columbia Records, and RMM Records in New York.

SAMUEL R. DELANY is the author of such classic science fiction novels as *The Einstein Intersection, Babel-17, Nova,* and *Dhalgren,* as well as the *Return to Nevèrÿon* fantasy series. Most recently, Delany has produced the novels *They Fly at Çiron* and *The Mad Man*, the collections *Aye, and Gomorrah* and *Atlantis: Three Tales*, and the nonfiction books *Silent Interviews: On Language, Race, Sex, Science Fiction, and Some Comics; Times Square Red, Times Square Blue; Shorter Views: Queer Thoughts & The Politics of the Paraliterary*; and *1984*, fifty-six letters and documents written in the mid-1980s to various friends, relatives, and colleagues. He also wrote the graphic novel *Bread & Wine: An Erotic Tale of New York*. Delany has won the Nebula Award, the Hugo Award, and the James Tiptree, Jr., Award for his work in SF, as well as the William Whitehead Memorial Award for a lifetime's contribution to gay and lesbian literature. He is currently a professor of comparative literature at Temple University.

W. E. B. DU BOIS (1868–1963) was an American historian, essayist, novelist, biographer, poet, autobiographer, editor, and activist. He was the first black Ph.D. from Harvard, one of the founders of American sociology, the founder of both the Niagara Movement and the NAACP, and he edited its journal, *The Crisis*, which published some of the trailblazers of the Harlem Renaissance. As a major force in helping to define black social and political causes in the United States, he is perhaps best known for his 1903 volume *The Souls of Black Folk*, in which he introduced the concept of "double consciousness" and explored the role of blacks in American society. He is also well known for his historiography and pioneering role in studying black history (in 1909 he conceived of the *Encyclopedia Africana*, the first comprehensive history of the African diaspora), as well as his activism, prompting Herbert Aptheker to call him one of the eminent "history makers" of the twentieth century.

TANANARIVE DUE is the author of five novels, including *The Good House* and *The Living Blood*, which won a 2002 American Book Award. She is also the author of *The Between, My Soul to Keep*, and a historical novel written in conjunction with the Alex Haley Estate, *The Black Rose*. Her science fiction short story "Patient Zero" appeared in two Best SF of the Year anthologies in 2001. With her mother, civil rights activist Patricia Stephens Due, Tananarive co-authored *Freedom in the Family: A Mother-Daughter Memoir of the Fight for Civil Rights*. She lives in Longview, Washington, with her husband, science fiction novelist Steven Barnes.

HENRY DUMAS (1934–1968) was a poet, short fiction writer, and mythopoetic folklorist. Born in Sweet Home, Arkansas, Dumas spent his early years "saturated" with religious and folk traditions of the South. The poetry of these roots can be seen in his first collection of short stories, *Ark of Bones and Other Stories* (1974), edited by his friend and colleague, poet Eugene Redmond. Dumas's promising career was cut short when he was "mistakenly" shot down by a New York City Transit policeman on May 23, 1968. Due to Redmond's dedication to keeping Dumas's literary legacy alive, readers were able to later discover the posthumously published collections *Goodbye, Sweetwater* (1988) and *Knees of a Natural Man: The Selected Poetry of Henry Dumas* (1989, Random House). His poetry also appeared in *Play Ebony, Play Ivory* (1974). Dumas's work was inspired by folk roots and by African American music, particularly blues and jazz. Dumas studied with Sun Ra and developed a craft that was distinctly his own vision.

DAVID FINDLAY is a graduate of the Clarion Science Fiction and Fantasy Writers' Workshop 2000. He lives in Toronto, Ontario, Canada, and does a different day job every month. He daydreamed through his few childhood visits to Sunday school.

JEWELLE GOMEZ is an activist and writer whose work has appeared in innumerable journals and anthologies. They include *Children of the Night, Home Girls, Daughters of Africa*, and *Afrekete*. She is the author of five books, including the award-winning *The Gilda Stories*, the first black vampire novel published in the United States; more Gilda stories can be found in *Dark Matter: A Century of Speculative Fiction from the African Diaspora* and two recent anthologies from Firebrand Books, *To Be Continued One* and *Two*. Her stage adaptation of the novel was commissioned by the Urban Bush Women Company in the 1996 season. Gomez also coedited, with Eric Garber, a collection of fantasy fiction entitled *Swords of the Rainbow*. She has written reviews and articles for the *New York Times*, the *San Francisco Chronicle*, the *Village Voice*, *Ms.* magazine, and *Essence*. In 1968 she was on the original staff of *Say Brother*, one of the first weekly black television programs, produced in Boston, and later was on the staff of *Black News* and *The Electric Company*, both produced in New York City. She was featured, along with Steven Barnes, Octavia E. Butler, Samuel R. Delany, and Tananarive Due, in the first conference of black speculative fiction writers of the United States, held at Clark Atlanta University in 1998. Born in Boston, she lives and teaches in the Bay Area. Visit her Web site at *www.jewellegomez.com*.

ANDREA HAIRSTON is a professor of theater at Smith College, where she directs and teaches playwriting and African, African American, and Caribbean theater literature. A playwright, director, actor, and musician, she is the Artistic Director of Chrysalis Theatre and has produced original theater with music, dance, and masks for over twenty-five years. Her plays have been produced at Yale Rep, Rites and Reason, the Kennedy Center, StageWest, and on public radio and public television. She has also translated plays by Michael Ende and Kaca Celan from German to English. Ms. Hairston has received many playwriting and directing awards, including a National Endowment for the Arts Grant to Playwrights, a Rockefeller/NEA Grant for New Works, an NEA grant to work as dramaturge/director with playwright Pearl Cleage, a Ford Foundation Grant to collaborate with Senegalese master drummer Massamba Diop, and a Shubert Fellowship for Playwriting. Much of Ms. Hairston's work has been about imagining the impossible and rehearsing the future in the face of adversity. *Mindscape* is her first speculative fiction novel. Transforming from a playwright/poet speaking through a chorus of theater artists to a live audience into a novelist was indeed a magical feat.

NALO HOPKINSON was born in Jamaica and grew up in Jamaica, Guyana, Trinidad, and Canada, where she has lived since age sixteen. The daughter of a poet/playwright and a library technician, she has written the acclaimed novels *Brown Girl in the Ring*, *Midnight Robber*, and *The Salt Roads*, and her short fiction has appeared in a number of science fiction and literary anthologies and magazines. Her short story collection, *Skin Folk*, won the 2002 World Fantasy Award and she has edited two anthologies, *Whispers from the Cotton Tree Root: Caribbean Fabulist Fiction* and *Mojo: Conjure Stories*.

TYEHIMBA JESS is a member of the Cave Canem Poetry collective. He won the 2001 Gwendolyn Brooks Open Mic Poetry Award and was a 2001–2002 Ragdale Fellow. He was also awarded an Illinois Arts Council Artist Fellowship in Poetry for 2000–2001. Jess's writing has appeared in *Beyond the Frontier: African American Poetry for the Twenty-First Century*, *Role Call: A Generational Anthology of Social and Political Black Literature and Art*, *Bum Rush the Page: A Def Poetry Jam*, *Power Lines: Ten Years of Poetry from Chicago's Guild Complex*, *Slam: The Art of Performance Poetry*, *Ploughshares*, *Black Issues Book Review*, the *Oyez Review*, *Blu Magazine*, *580 Split*, *Obsidian III: Literature in the African Diaspora*, *Warpland: A Journal of Black Literature and Ideas*, *African Voices*, *Mosaic*, *e-poets.net*, and the *Source*.

CHARLES JOHNSON, writer, philosopher, educator, and illustrator, is the winner of the 1998 MacArthur Fellowship and has published five novels, including the widely celebrated *Middle Passage* (1990), which won the National Book Award for fiction, and *Dreamer* (1998). Born in Evanston, Illinois, Johnson's first love was drawing. He worked as an editorial cartoonist while attending Southern Illinois University. In the early 1970s, he published two collections of drawings. In 1974, he wrote his first novel, *Faith and the Good Thing*, a book heavily influenced by John Gardner, Ralph Ellison, and Buddhist thought. After writing several screenplays, including *Booker* (1984), which appeared on PBS, Johnson became a teacher of creative writing at the University of Washington, where he is currently the distinguished S. Wilson and Grace M. Pollock Professor of English. Johnson's recent works include *Soulcatcher and Other Stories* (2001), twelve original short stories written as a companion volume to the 1998 PBS series; *Africans in America: America's Journey Through Slavery*, which he coauthored with Patricia Smith; and *King: The Photo Biography of Martin Luther King, Jr.* (2000), coauthored with Bob Adelman.

DOUGLAS KEARNEY is a Cave Canem Fellow and a firm believer in feeding crows. He likes swords and might be carrying one to the supermarket right now. He lives in Altadena, California, with his wife, Nicole, and bookshelves full of folklore.

WALTER MOSLEY is the *New York Times* best-selling author of *Futureland: Nine Stories of An Imminent World*, *Bluelight*, and the Easy Rawlins novels *Bad Boy Brawley Brown* and *Fearless Jones*. His books have been translated into twenty languages and his short story collection, *Always Outnumbered, Always Outgunned*, received the Anisfeld-Wolf Book Award. Born in Los Angeles, he has been a potter, a computer programmer, and a poet. Walter Mosley lives in New York.

PAM NOLES works as a journalist in Southern California. A graduate of the Clarion Writers Workshop, her prose shorts have appeared in *Andrew Vachss' Underground* and *Pulphouse* magazine, and she is collaborating with artist Mia Wolff (*Bread & Wine: An Erotic Tale of New York*) on a graphic novel. *Whipping Boy* is her first novel. She can be reached at *shakaz@earthlink.net*.

NNEDI OKORAFOR-MBACHU is a journalist for *Africana.com*, and a technology columnist for the *Chicago Sun-Time*'s sister paper, the *Star* (the column is called "Nnedi on the Net"). She is a gradaute of the Clarion Science Fiction and Fantasy Writers Workshop (MSU) and is currently working on her Ph.D. in English at the University of Illinois, Chicago. She won third place in the Hurston/Wright Awards for her story "Amphibious Green." She also received honorable mention in *The Year's Best Fantasy and Horror: Fourteenth Annual Collection*. Okorafor-Mbachu's short story "Windseekers" was a finalist in the L. Ron Hubbard Writers of the Future Contest. She also was chosen to present her master's thesis paper, "Virtual Women: Female Characters in Video Games," at the Association for Education in Journalism and Mass Communication 2001 convention. Her short stories appeared in the following literary journals: the *Women's International Network* magazine, *Margin: Exploring Modern Magical Realism*, *Moondance* magazine, *Shag*, *Umoja*, *Strange Horizons*, and *The Thirteenth Floor*. In 2001, "Crossroads," a short story, was published in *The Witching Hour Anthology* by Silver Lake Publishing, and in 2003, "Asuquo" appeared in *Mojo: Conjure Stories*. Her first young adult novel, *Zahrah and the Windseekers*, will be published by Houghton Mifflin in early 2004.

JILL ROBINSON is a marketing specialist for a multinational financial institution who writes articles and fiction for adult and teen audiences. Her work has appeared in *shine.com*, *GenerationNeXt*, *Anansi: Fiction of the African Diaspora*, and *Role Call: A Generational Anthology of Social and Political Black Literature and Art*. The Cinnaminson, New Jersey, native currently resides in Brooklyn, New York, and can be reached at *bluvoices@yahoo.com*.

KALAMU YA SALAAM, a prolific New Orleans writer, is founder of the Nommo Literary Society, a black writers' workshop; cofounder with Kysha Brown of Runagate multimedia; leader of the WordBand, a poetry performance ensemble; and moderator of e-Drum, a listserv of over 1,600 black writers and diverse supporters of literature. His background includes thirteen years as editor of the *Black Collegian* magazine and five years with the Free Southern Theatre. His latest books include the anthology of Nommo writers *Speak the Truth to the People*, edited with Kysha Brown; *The Magic of Juju: An Appreciation of the Black Arts Movement*; and the anthology *360° A Revolution of Black Poets*. Salaam's latest spoken word CD is *My Story, My Song*. He can be reached at *e-drum@topica.com* or *Kalamu@aol.com*.

KIINI IBURA SALAAM is a writer, painter, and traveler from New Orleans, Louisiana. Her first short story, "How Far Have We Come?", was published in the *Black Collegian* magazine in 1991. Her second story, "Rebellious Energy," was published in the *African American Review* in 1993. After graduating from Spelman College in 1994, Kiini traveled to five countries as a Thomas J. Watson Fellow and published "Of Wings, Nectar, & Ancestors" in the *Fertile Ground* literary journal. In 1997, her short story "MalKai's Last Seduction" (which was included in *Dark Eros*, a collection of erotica) received mention in a *Publishers Weekly* review. Also in 1997, her essays "Brothers Are" and "A New Understanding" were included in *Men We Cherish* and *Father Songs*, respectively. The March 2000 issue of *Essence* magazine featured her article "Navigating to No," causing a flurry of radio and television interviews. Most recently, her short story "At Life's Limits" was included in *Dark Matter: A Century of Speculative Fiction from the African Diaspora*. In 2001, Kiini was one of ten authors who contributed to the collaborative novel *When Butterflies Kiss*, and her essay "No," was included in *Ms.* magazine's June/July 2001 issue. Kiini regularly leaves the country to devote time to her writing. She is currently crafting *Big Boned*, her first novel, and *Lust Heals*, a collection of erotic short stories. She is the author of the *KIS.list*, a weekly e-report on life as a writer. Kiini Ibura Salaam intends to be one of the most important authors of the twenty-first century. She lives in Brooklyn.

CHARLES R. SAUNDERS, a native of Pennsylvania, has lived for the last three decades in Canada, where, in the intervals between teaching the social sciences, "the odd creative writing seminar," and publishing nonfiction, he has been writing African-based fantasies since 1971. His short fiction has appeared in *The Best Fantasy Stories of the Year*, in the anthologies *Amazons I*, *Hecate's Cauldron*, and *Dark Matter: A Century of Speculative Fiction from the African Diaspora*, and he published three novels for DAW: *Imaro*, based on his popular short story series; *Imaro II: Quest for Cush*, and *Imaro III: The Trail of Bohu*. He recently completed a non-Imaro African fantasy and is currently working on a novel based on his character Doussouye.

NISI SHAWL'S short fiction has appeared in *Asimov's Science Fiction* magazine, *Daughters of Nyx*, *Semiotext(e) Science Fiction*, and *Dark Matter: A Century of Speculative Fiction from the African Diaspora*. *Gnosis* magazine and the *Stranger*, Seattle's notorious newsweekly, have printed her articles and reviews. Nisi moved to Seattle from

Ann Arbor, Michigan, as directed by her ancestors. She is a volunteer and board member for the Clarion West Writers Workshop. In her spare time, she works forty hours a week at Borders Books and Music, unpacking shipments and running writing and critique groups.

CHERENE SHERRARD, a native of Los Angeles, has lived in New York and Atlanta, but now resides in Madison, Wisconsin, where she is an assistant professor in the English department at the University of Wisconsin. In addition to teaching nineteenth-century African American literature, she is currently working on her first novel, *Yard Girl*, and a book of poetry. A Cave Canem and Hurston Wright Fellow, her poetry and short stories have been published in several journals and anthologies.

SHEREE R. THOMAS is the editor of *Dark Matter: A Century of Speculative Fiction from the African Diaspora*, winner of the World Fantasy Award and the Gold Pen Award. She is also the founding editor of *Anansi: Fiction of the African Diaspora*. Her fiction and poetry have appeared in the anthologies *Mojo: Conjure Stories, Role Call: A Generational Anthology of Social and Political Black Literature & Art, Bum Rush the Page: A Def Poetry Jam,* and *2001: A Science Fiction Poetry Anthology,* as well as the journals *Black Renaissance/Renaissance Noire, Meridians: Feminism Race Transnationalism, Drumvoices Revue, Obsidian III, Voices: The Wisconsin Review of African Literatures, African Voices,* and *Ishmael Reed's KONCH.* In 2003 she received the Ledig House/LEF Foundation Prize for Fiction, the New York Foundation for the Arts Fellowship in Poetry, and was nominated for the 2003 Rhysling Award. She also received honorable mention in *The Year's Best Fantasy & Horror: 16th Annual Collection.* A Clarion West alum and a Cave Canem Fellow, Thomas, originally from Memphis, teaches fiction at the Frederick Douglass Creative Arts Center and lives in New York City with her family.

IBI AANU ZOBOI is a writer and researcher of the science, myth, and oral tradition of the Diaspora. She draws from the revolutionary history of her native Haiti and African cosmology to create inspirational tales of triumph and resurrection. Ibi is a graduate of the 2001 Clarion West Science Fiction and Fantasy Writers Workshop and a winner of the Women Writers of Haitian Descent (WWOHD) Fiction Award for her short story "At the Shores of Dawn," published in *One Respe!* literary journal and the *Boston Haitian Reporter*. She lives in Brooklyn with her husband and is currently working on her first novel.

Copyrights and Permissions

ACKNOWLEDGMENTS

Many thanks and praise are due to my family, friends, colleagues, and all the gifted writers who helped make editing this second volume, *Dark Matter: Reading the Bones*, such a wonderful experience. Much love and affection for Marie Dutton Brown, the Frederick Douglass Creative Arts Center and the talented, beautiful artists there, Arthur Flowers and New Renaissance, Angeli R. Rasbury, Ronda Racha Penrice, and the Beyond Dusa Women's Collective (Ama, Pan, Andrea, and Liz!), Tony Medina, thank you for your friendship, laughter, and generosity of spirit, Jacqueline Joan Johnson and Patricia Spears Jones, thank you for your poetry and grace, Nikki and Jose (congrats to you!), Robert Fleming and Donna Hill of the Langston Hughes Library, Carolyn Micklem and the Cave Canem Family, D'anetta Jimenez of Olmec Arts, go on wit yo bad self!, my friends at the Franklin H. White Caribbean Cultural Center, thank you for hosting the "*Dark Matter* Revival: Tent of Miracles!," thank you Paul D. Miller a.k.a. DJ Spooky and the Sun Ra Arkestra for the great kick-off at the Knitting Factory, Lawrence Wayne and Wintrell Pitman of the Memphis Black Writers Conference, Carolyn Butts and Layding Kaliba, celebrating ten years of *African Voices*, Cornelia and Julius Bailey for your storytelling, good food, and kind hospitality, Kalamu ya Salaam and the evergrowing E-Drum family, the Afrofuturism.net list and Gardner Dozois for hosting the chat on SCIFI.COM, Troy Johnson of www.aalbc.com, Ron Kavanaugh and

Mosaic, Marcia Mayne, Tia Shabazz, tireless literary cultural workers, Reginald Harris and the Enoch Pratt Library, thank you for the terrific reading with Chip Delany (in the Edgar Allan Poe room, no less!), Cassandra and Faye of Sisterspace Books in D.C., Jennifer Brissett of Indigo Café and Books, Dr. Brenda Greene and the Nkiru Center for Education and Culture, The Schomburg Center for Research on Black Culture and The Harlem Book Fair, New York Is Book Country, Readercon and Wiscon: The World's Only Feminist Science Fiction Convention!, the Go On Girl Book Club, Linda Addison, Gerard Houarner, and Elizabeth Hemingway, Rhony Dostaly and family, Tracey deMorsella and the SciFiNoir Literature list, the Carl Brandon Society (www.carlbrandon.org), journey onward!, Smith College, Molloy College, Binghamton University, Norfolk State University, The Franklin Institute, the Hudson River Museum, Darrell Stover and the Hayti Heritage Center, much gratitude to Dr. Robert Farris Thompson, thanks for your time, and the late Tom Feelings, *adupe!*, Barbara Krasnoff and Jim Freund of WBAI's "Hour of the Wolf," the *New York Review of Science Fiction* Reading Series at Dixon Place, Daniel Minter for your beautiful art. And special thanks to Jaime Levine, Devi Pillai, Bob Castillo, Linda Duggins, and the Warner family.

Printed in the USA
CPSIA information can be obtained
at www.ICGtesting.com
LVHW032017271223
767555LV00001B/34

9 780446 693776